Gift of the Black Goddess

by
John Mack Howells

Tangible press

Gift
of the
Black Goddess

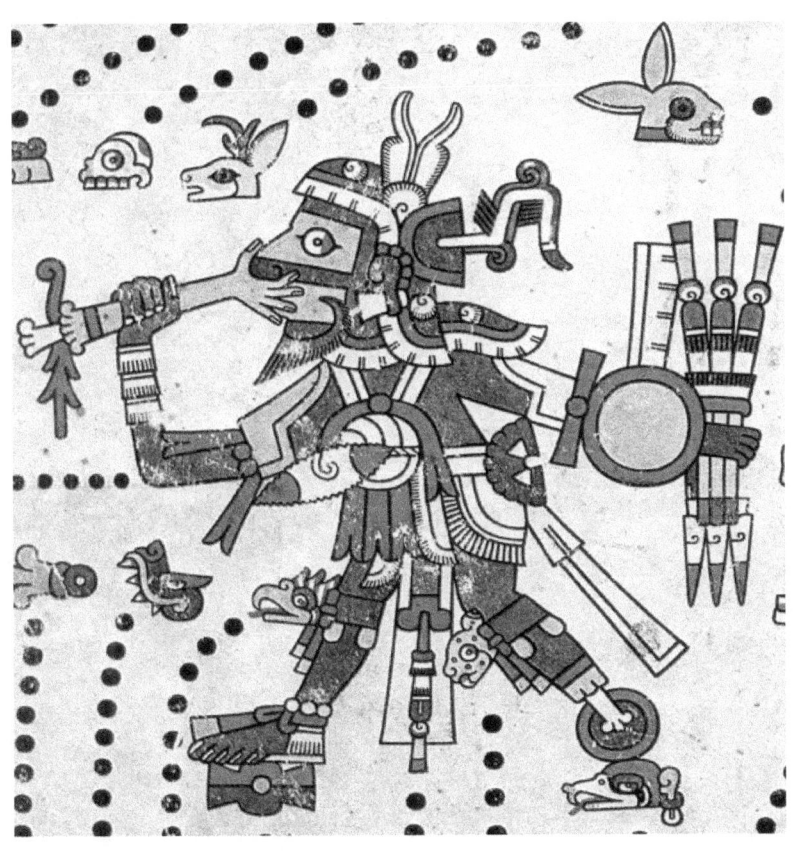

This is a work of fiction by the late John Mack Howells, my father, who had written many books on travel and retirement but had never published fiction. This was his first novel, and Tangible Press is pleased to present *Gift of the Black Goddess* for the first time.

John Howells, Jr
Publisher, Tangible Press

Chapter One

Tezcatlipocas, August 19, 1980

Cold mists descended upon the village just before dusk. Erratic winds gusted down the mountain's slope, driving needles of rain into already-soaked thatched roofs. A week of intermittent rain had turned the cobblestone trail into a slick treachery. Blue smoke wisps from cooking fires blended with the smell of moss, wet clay and mildew.

Despite the chill, villagers stood outside to witness an unusual trespass against their solitude. Some huddled in front of their huts of mud-caulked lava rock. Others stood near the village's decaying, roofless church.

Curious women, men, with brown faces with wide eyes, peered through openings in frayed serapes or rebozos. Some men wore broad sombreros to keep rain from their faces. Others draped green plastic bags over their heads. A few, already soaked beyond hope, wiped rivulets from their faces without taking their eyes from the passing parade.

The intrusion was a mud-splattered parade of autos and trucks jolting over the cobblestones, laying a trail of evil-smelling exhaust. Something serious must have happened down on the highway. Presumably an accident or a landslide. Traffic would not travel through the village of Tezcatlipocas voluntarily, not without exceptional cause. It had been over a year since the last detour. Villagers whispered questions back and forth, but no one had answers. The procession lumbered past, one behind one another, bouncing over uneven cobblestones and swaying drunkenly.

Suddenly, a mud-stained Rolls Royce swerved out of line. It braked to an angry, sliding stop in front of the abandoned church. The villagers' eyes widened with puzzled surprise. Automobiles just did not stop in Tezcatlipocas!

Except for Gustavo Sanchez, no one in the village had ever before seen a Rolls Royce. Gustavo once worked as an illegal bracero in California; he knew expensive cars when he saw them. This Rolls was a brand-new Silver Cloud. Yet, it didn't look new. Streaks of red-brown mud dulled its finish. The car had been in a wreck, perhaps a series of mishaps. The front fender displayed an accordion-like surface. The chrome bumper almost rubbed against the front tire. The left rear door suffered a deep scar of raw metal.

"*Jijole, manito*," Gustavo exclaimed as he nudged his friend in the ribs, "Would you just look at that auto? Worth a mountain of money! I saw some of them when I worked in *Califa*. Everyone is rich there. And look, you see that little plate on the bumper? That signifies the car's owner lives with the richest of the rich. Yes, I know these things, because I used to work in that place as a gardener." Gustavo nodded proudly, basking in the glow of his compadre's proud attention.

The plate read: *Del Monte Properties, Pebble Beach, California.*

A film of steamy moisture fogged the windows, but observers could see the figure of a woman inside. She was shaking a clinched fist at a sullen figure hunched over the steering wheel. On the rear seat a small boy stood, thumb in mouth, staring solemnly out the window as bitter words flew about the inside of the Rolls Royce. The boy seemed bored, as if he had been through scenes like this many times before.

Suddenly the door flew open. The woman climbed out into the rain. She shouted at the driver, her voice harsh with anger. He snarled something angry in return. She kicked the door closed and turned her back to the automobile, hugging her arms to her side.

When the man gunned the motor, as if threatening to leave, she turned and snatched open the rear door. With a single movement she scooped the little boy into her arms. After another angry outburst of English words, which of course the villagers couldn't understand, the woman set the boy on the muddy ground and reached for a leather suitcase which stood on the floor of the luxurious automobile.

The boy's lips curled in revulsion as he stared at the muck oozing around his polished shoes. He appeared to be about four years old but was dressed like a little man. He wore a tailored jacket, a striped necktie and expensive-looking slacks which were pressed to a knife-edge.

The woman traded insults with the driver as she tugged an expensive-looking piece of luggage from the car. The leather suitcase teetered for a moment, then fell to the ground, splattering mud on the boy's pressed pants.

The boy shook his head in dismay. He gave the woman a look of indignant disgust.

Before she could slam the door shut a final time, the Rolls Royce spun its wheels, slinging a rooster tail of mud and water. The opulent car forced its way back into the stream of traffic, its rear door swinging back and forth lazily.

Diana Cranston glared hatefully at the Rolls as it rounded the curve by the ruins of the abandoned church. It disappeared from sight.

Then she wheeled around to stare belligerently at the Indians who watched the drama with open curiosity. She whipped a black scarf from her pocket and draped it over her head in a futile attempt to keep the mist from ruining her coiffure. Actually, the rain had almost ceased at this point.

Micaela Montalvo watched the drama closely. She pulled her rough wool serape closer to her body and shivered. Eyes wide with interest, she stared at the woman and the boy. Especially the boy. Something strange stirred in her stomach. Like a moth, fluttering, looking for an escape. Inexplicably, the strange woman seemed vaguely familiar. Micaela sensed that others felt the same way, for they began whispering in astonished tones. Micaela stepped closer to hear what her neighbors were saying.

"She looks like the Madonna!" The whispers carried husky undertones of awe and wonder. "Yes, just like the Madonna in the movie!"

Standing there in the mist, the lady actually did look like the white man's version of the Virgin Mary. Her skin was pink-white and her hair straw-yellow, just like the Madonna in the Protestant bibles that a troop of evangelists once brought to the village. But of course, she was not like the true Virgin, the Indian's Virgin of *Guadalupe-Tonantzín*.

Lithographs of Guadalupe-Tonantzín adorned every wall in the village. Her dark *indio* skin and black hair emphasized her mystery. Sometimes She was actually depicted with black skin as well.

No question, this blonde woman resembled the Madonna in the motion picture that a traveling cine entrepreneur had shown a few months ago, when he set up his projector and charged ten pesos apiece to watch his movie as it flickered against a whitewashed wall inside the roofless church.

Suddenly, to everyone's surprise, a freakish crack in the cloud cover permitted a weak shaft of dying afternoon sunlight to break through the gloom. The sunbeam glowed for a moment on the lady's head, as though heaven were pointing out an angel on earth. Some villagers crossed themselves. This was the most beautiful woman they had ever seen.

Gustavo Sanchez wasn't particularly impressed—for he hadn't spent the ten pesos to see the movie. Truthfully, Gustavo wouldn't give a pinch of shit to see anything religious. Churches and religion are for old women and men on deathbeds. But Gustavo had to admit that this lady truly did have a great figure, with a nice pair of *chichis*. Just the right size.

Gustavo had to admit that.

Despite the sickly-looking pink skin and painted lips, the stranger did indeed resemble a Protestant saint. As they drew closer, they inspected the boy.

Unlike his mother, the boy's hair was black and healthy looking. His skin, deeply tanned by the tropical Acapulco sun, made him almost as dark as some Tezcatlipocas villagers. But it was the boy's eyes that drew murmurs of astonishment. Instead of obsidian irises floating on café con leche background—like normal eyes, like the eyes of the villagers—these eyes were a startling, impossible, gray color. The orbs were pure white. The irises silver gray—with a touch of blue. Later they would learn that his eyes glistened with a hint of gold when the light struck just right, like flecks of mica in a stream bed.

At this moment, these peculiar eyes were as cold as frost. The child stared haughtily at the curious circle of faces. Instead of withdrawing shyly as would most Mexican-Indian boys his age, this one returned the strangers' gaze with an unwavering glare. He sent a clear message of contempt and disdain.

Clearly, this was a little boy, but something about his demeanor suggested an adult. Even at four years of age, Rickey Barron had that confidence, that sureness about himself, a duplicate copy of his father, Richard Alexander Barron II.

As the villagers moved closer, the woman looked less and less like a Protestant Madonna. For one thing, she was drunk. She swayed unsteadily as she stared in the direction of the vanished Rolls Royce, as if trying to make it return through sheer will power.

The woman was neither as young, nor as beautiful as she appeared from a distance. Much of her beauty came from skillful application of cosmetics. Even when fuzzy with vodka, Diana Cranston-Barron knew her business when it came to makeup. Still, there was something about her that awed the villagers. No one could explain precisely why. They suspected it had something to do with the movie they had seen in the abandoned church. But what could be the connection?

Diana noticed the tightening semicircle of brown faces. She frowned and pulled Rickey to her side. When she sensed the staring faces were curious rather than threatening, the frown dissolved into resigned disapproval. Diana Cranston was used to curiosity seekers and autograph pests, although they hadn't bothered her for a time—not since her career went down the toilet. Yet she found it difficult to believe anyone in this tiny village would recognize her. Few movie fans in Mexico pay attention to Hollywood stars, and her last picture was released over four years ago, just before Rickey was born. It bombed horribly, hardly any distribution. Besides, there couldn't be a movie house in this little village.

She shrugged her shoulders and wished she had a drink, something to wash the bad taste of the argument from her mouth.

First in English, then in very poor Spanish, she asked, "Where can I get a taxi for Mexico City? A bus?"

Gustavo Sanchez, who knew a handful of English words, tried to explain to the lady that buses didn't stop in Tezcatlipocas. Furthermore, once the highway was clear, no traffic of any sort would be passing through the village. No buses, no cars. *Nada*.

"What about a telephone?"

The villagers recognized the word telefono, and they smiled at the thought.

After much repetition and hand-signaling, Guatavo got the message across. "*Nada de eso.*"

Indeed, traffic began thinning dramatically now. The bulldozer working below must have cleared the main highway. The detour was over.

"Then, I'll pay someone to drive me to the next town." She gestured as if she were turning a steering wheel. "*Comprende?* Drive me to next town? Automobile?"

Gustavo spread his hands helplessly. "*No hay ningún auto*

aquí." She looked puzzled, so he tried in English, "No autos. Maybe mañana or next day, Culio Lázaro, he come here. Have truck. Maybe next week, *Quién sabe?"*

"Next week?" Diana puffed her breath in annoyance and asked, "Then, is there a hotel here? Understand? Hotel? A room? Some place to stay the night?"

For a reply she received only astonished looks. The thought of a hotel in Tezcatlipocas was ludicrous! Villagers politely suppressed smiles. And clearly, no one wanted to suffer the humiliation of offering this elegant lady and her adult-son the extreme embarrassment of a squalid village hut. Most families slept, cooked, ate, made love, and repaired harness in the same room. Most homes were of one room, two at most, of black lava stone laid without mortar which permitted cold air to breeze through the cracks—as chickens, and occasionally pigs, wandered freely about the packed dirt floors. As for making love, well, since most people in town were older than old, few sounds of lovemaking disturbed the village nights these days. The young ones had long ago fled to *la Capitál* in search of jobs.

For a long, embarrassed moment, no one replied.

Then, with her face dark with shame, Micaela Montalvo stepped forward. She clutched her rebozo gathered around her neck. Although Micaela was barely nineteen years old, her demeanor was that of a much older woman. Her shoulders slumped, as if from years of hard work. Her head bowed forward in an expression of humility.

All Diana could see were the young woman's eyes. They had a strange, glazed look. They seemed to focus on the boy— yet the words were clearly intended for Diana.

In soft Spanish, she said, "In my house, señora, I have one extra bed. But it is a poor house. Very humble."

She spoke slowly, distinctly, as if that would help the saintly-looking woman understand. As she spoke, her eyes remained fixed on the boy with an intense yearning that told the villagers a great deal.

Some shivered with vague, unspeakable fear, uncertain of what might be going on in Micaela's troubled mind, a mind that wavered between vacant passivity and murderous violence. All feared the girl. All felt uneasy at the way she stared at the youngster.

Diana didn't actually understand the words, but the offer of a place to stay seemed obvious. She looked once more down the deserted road and frowned. Worry replaced her anger. The Rolls Royce obviously was not about to return. She shrugged in resignation and nodded acceptance of Micaela's offer.

Micaela eagerly grabbed the suitcase and took the boy's hand in hers. Dianna followed, stepping carefully over the slick cobblestones like a tipsy tightwire walker in high-heeled shoes. Once she nearly fell. The villagers suppressed snickers with their hands or covered faces with rebozos.

Of course, everyone in the village knew Micaela Montalvo didn't have an extra bed. Ridiculous. She had a separate bedroom, true. And her house was larger than most, for it also contained a small room in front which served as a store where her husband used to sell soft drinks, cigarettes, matches, and during the religious holidays, sugar cane rum. But the villagers had precious little to squander on soft drinks and cigarettes these days—and rum—well, forget it. Since Micaela's husband fled for his life a few months ago, business had all but ceased.

The villagers knew Micaela would set up a cot in the store front and give her bedroom to the elegant lady and the strangely dressed little boy. The villagers wondered what might happen next. Again, some shivered. When the Gods took Micaela's only child, four months ago, evil spirits took possession of her soul. A cruel, black energy floated in and out of her body, dangerous, unpredictable and evil.

Villagers gave Micaela plenty of space, particularly after she tried to kill her husband with a hatchet. Tried twice, actually. Small wonder he abandoned her. And such a fine man he was—

kind, soft spoken, devoted to Micaela, and he adored Micaela's son as if it were his own offspring.

Since her husband left, Micaela seldom spoke. More often than not she wouldn't even reply when spoken to. She would sit and stare at a picture of the Virgin Guadalupe-Tonantzín for hours on end, stirring only when someone came around to purchase a box of matches or a paper cone of ground chili.

What a shame, they all agreed. Micaela was the youngest person in the village, only nineteen years old. The youngest by at least thirty years. She was pretty, too. Delicately formed features that twinkled when accompanied by a sparkling smile. But smiles stopped the day her son died.

From the first day she set foot in the village, Micaela scandalized the village. Pregnant, less than fifteen years old, she wore rags and her hair hung across her face in tangles that reminded one of dirty snakes. But the storekeeper—recently widowed—took her in, as a "clerk." He cleaned her up, fattened her cheeks with meat and pozole, even dressed her in pretty clothes.

She married the storekeeper one month later, even though he was more than three times her age. That scandalized the villagers almost as much as when the baby came one month to the day after their civil vows in Orizaba. The villagers were horrified that an older man should marry such a child. Scandalized the baby should be born to a fifteen-year-old. Yet in time, scandal transformed to joy at the thought of a child in the village. They realized this might be the last baby ever born here, the last ever, for the few remaining villagers were too old for that sort of thing.

Yet, for some inexplicable reason, the Black Goddess Tonantzín took the baby away, when he was not yet four years old!

As Micaela led the way to her house, villagers followed at a discrete distance. Some considered warning the Gringa about Micaela's mental condition, but none knew how to begin, clearly not in English. Well, they tacitly agreed, whatever happens is God's Will.

When the procession reached Micaela's house, Diana Cranston's mouth dropped open in surprise. Somehow, she had expected a small hotel, guest house, something like that, but this... A giggle stirred in her chest as she thought of the fun she would have relating this adventure to her friends when she returned to Alex's winter home in Acapulco.

Micaela Montalvo's house, built of black stone, differed from other village hovels in that it boasted a galvanized iron roof instead of rotting thatch or shingles of mossy pine. A Coca-Cola sign and several plastic advertisements for Delecado cigarettes brightened the structure's facade. Wisps of blue smoke seeped through seams in the metal roof, carrying odors of pine pitch and old charcoal.

"Thank God it won't be any longer than tonight," Diana told herself. "I'll figure out something tomorrow." Her mouth felt brown and sticky, varnished. She needed a drink.

She waited while the dark figure fumbled with a padlock on the battered wooden shutters that closed off the front of the house. Inside, once her eyes adjusted to the darkness, she realized that she was in a small store. A musty odor of mildew and rancid grease sent a slight shudder of revulsion through her body.

Suddenly, a comforting sight caught her eye. On a high shelf, like happy old friends, stood a row of dusty liquor bottles, pocket-sized, each full of pale rum. In the corner of the room, cases of empty soft drink bottles reached almost to the ceiling. Diana's eyes devoured the sight of the rum bottles, nothing else.

She caught the woman's sleeve and pointed to the liquor. "For sale? Can I buy one? Just one?"

The woman understood immediately. Soon Diana was holding a jar with rum and cola, cooled by a splinter of ice that Micaela chopped from the inside of a kerosene refrigerator unit.

Diana sipped luxuriously. The warmth in her stomach

canceled the clammy chill of the village. The odor of damp clay floor and burrowing rodents was another item, but she knew that one more drink should render these invisible to the senses. She drank slowly as she stared out the door in the direction of the pass. She fantasized that the next sight she would see would be Lance Rexford returning with the Rolls Royce.

For the moment, Diana didn't give a damn if she ever saw the phony bastard again. From the other room came the sound of Micaela chattering happily and incomprehensibly to Rickey. The smell of rain mixed with village cooking fragrances created a delicious feeling of well-being. But then, a sudden gust of cold wind blew the door shut with a nerve-jarring thud. Diana's head whirled dizzily at the sound and she almost spilled her drink.

"God*damn* that phony Lance Rexford," she said beneath her breath fiercely. "It was all his fault. *He* started me drinking again. *He* wrecked Alex's Rolls. *He* started the fighting."

She drained the last of the sweet rum and cola and felt the warmth in her stomach reassuring. The pain behind her forehead eased as the magic of alcohol soothed her brain. A kerosene lamp cast an orange light through the room, making the shadows stygian black.

The dark-skinned woman opened a bottle of Coca-Cola and took it to Rickey. Diana watched through the open door as Rickey shrugged and accepted the gift haughtily. When the woman tried to kiss Rickey's forehead, he pulled away.

"Get away from me! You stink!"

Diana continued her internal monologue: "Oh Goddamn, God*damn*! Is Alex ever going to be pissed off! After all my promises to behave, to stay off the booze. But how was I to know that jackass Lance Rexford would do this to me? I hope Alex punches the bastard good when he sees what happened to his new Rolls! And, about my drinking... Alex's going to freak out over that!"

She brushed a lock of hair away from her face. It felt damp

and stringy. Dirty, just like her conscience.

Suddenly she remembered what she and Lance had done last night—right in the hotel room—with little Rickey sleeping in the next bed! She pressed her hands together and gave a small prayer that the boy had been sleeping.

"He's not even four years old, would he know what we were doing? Did we turn out the lights? Oh, *shit*! And I was doing so well, too. No booze for almost three months!" She tried to recreate the scene in the hotel room, but the only thing she could remember clearly was her climax, probably screaming and moaning as she often did. "Oh, God, please make it so the boy was asleep!"

Although Rickey Barron was her son, she unconsciously categorized him as "the boy" rather than "my son." They'd never truly bonded as mother and offspring. And she couldn't deny that it was largely her fault. She refused to see him at the hospital on that horribly painful, frustrating evening of his birth. Angry that pregnancy had interfered with her career, full of hate for the boy's father, and resentful of the fickle world of Hollywood producers and agents, Diana relinquished all claims on the boy in return for complete freedom to pursue her career. Unfortunately, her career went nowhere without Alex Barron to guide it. Another in a series of life's mistakes.

But now, with a professional association between Alex and herself in the wind, she had felt an urgent need to establish a bond with the boy. She needed to atone for years of separation. The possibility of a role in Alex's new production—her first important screen part since before Rickey was born—hinged on a successful reconciliation. She repeated her prayer, "Please, God, make it be that Rickey was asleep last night!"

Diana's bed turned out to be a large sack stuffed with thatch and pine needles. It sagged in the middle. Diana considered it dubiously as Micaela gently tucked Rickey in, pulling a cover of heavy quilts up to his chin. The dark woman kissed him on his cheek and said something soft in Spanish before she tiptoed out of the room. Rickey scrubbed his cheek with the back of his hand, obviously disgusted at the thought of the woman kissing him. Then he rolled over and tried to sleep.

Diana closed the door after Micaela left and sipped at her fourth drink. She paced about the room, worrying what Alex was going to say about this episode. She stumbled against the bed and shook Rickey awake.

He sat up and lazily wiped sleep from his eyes.

"Where are we, Diana? Why can't we go home to my dad?"

"Rickey dear, why can't you call me *Mommy* instead of Diana? I *am* your mother, you know. I don't see why..." She cut herself short. This wasn't the time for an argument.

"I want to go home! I don't like it here! This place is filthy! It stinks! Why can't we go home? Dad's gonna be pissed off."

"In the morning, dear, we'll go home. I'll find a car or a taxi and we'll be in Acapulco before you know it. And we'll just explain things to your father. You can help me, Rickey. Help make him understand that this was not my fault."

She pulled the covers up around his chin with one hand, almost spilling the drink in the process. "Now kiss me good night and go to sleep."

He turned away to avoid the kiss. "I hate it here. It's dirty. It smells. And I don't like that Mexican woman. She's weird. She keeps touching me."

"We won't be here long, sweet."

"Why can't we go home now, Diana?"

She stamped her foot angrily and leaned over him, her face just inches away from his. Hatred flared in her eyes.

"It's *Mother*! You little bastard! Can't you say *Mother*?"

Rickey returned her hostility with quiet contempt. He rolled over on his side and looked away.

She glared for a moment, then drained her glass. This isn't working at all, she realized. Somehow, I need to get close to the boy. If he would only respond in a respectful way, I'm sure we could develop a love between us. But sometimes, he's a goddamned, insufferable brat. She considered this for a moment, and concluded: No, not sometimes. Always a rotten, spoiled, little brat!

She frowned at him for a moment, then drained her glass. She felt miserable. She reached down and tousled his hair and said, "Rickey, your mommy loves you. Try to understand that. The reason I haven't spent much time with you is... Well, I just had so much to do, and your father and I haven't been friends for a long while. Believe me Rickey, things'll be different. Your father and I may be working together again. If so, I'll try to see you every day. I promise. We'll have time to get to know and love each other, and..."

Suddenly, she realized that he was sleeping. Either that, or he was pretending to be asleep. A red flash of anger clenched her fist. She caught herself just in time. She felt her heart beating thickly in her throat.

What's wrong with me? I was going to hit him! That's all I need — Alex accusing me of child abuse as well as drunkenness. Definitely kiss my career goodbye. She went for a refill and poured the last of the rum into the glass jar.

When the jar was empty, she crawled into bed without removing anything but her coat and her shoes. Before she went to sleep, she resolved, "Starting tomorrow, I am going to make my son love me. I will never, ever shout at him. Never make a fool of myself in front of him again. Oh, *God*, I hope he didn't know what we were doing last night!"

Chapter Two

Micaela could not sleep. She set up the stretched burlap cot in the store front, just as the villagers suspected she would. She lay there, envious, while the strange woman and the beautiful boy slept in her bed. She shivered from the chill. Her only turkey-feather comforter lay over her guests. A loud snore echoed from the bedroom, no doubt coming from the woman. Micaela imagined that she could smell the woman's thick cosmetics and sour alcohol breath with each throaty rumble.

Micaela tossed and turned, unable to keep her mind off the boy in the next room. She knew his name was *Riki*; something like that, because the mother kept using that word when she talked to him. *Riki*. A beautiful name! A beautiful child! Tears welled up in her eyes as she remembered her own infant, the agony of watching him moan with pain, suffer and waste away, until the final moment he stopped breathing forever. She tried clearing her mind, making it ready for sleep.

Then, just as she started to drift away, an obscene picture began playing in her brain like a flickering movie shown against the church wall, an episode over which she had no control, a horror which she had to watch to completion. Over and over again. She knew she couldn't prevent the scene from playing itself out.

First comes the frightened whimper her son always makes when it starts. Micaela sees herself crawling from her cot and stumbling toward the door. She presses her shoulder against the heavy wood, knowing the iron bolt on the bedroom side will hold the door tight. She cannot get into the room to protect her son.

Her little boy's whimper changes to a groan of pain. She pounds on the door with both fists. "Carlos! Stop! Not again! Please! Not again!"

But she knows it will not stop. The boy's cries of pain increase in rhythmic crescendo. The moans finally end with mewing whimpers.

Next comes the sound of the heavy bolt slipping back. The door creaks open. The grinning, bearded face of her husband appears.

"Finished with the boy, Mica. Now it's your turn," he says softly.

His eyes are rimmed with red lust. She knows his breath will smell of alcohol and rotting teeth. She knows it will be useless to struggle; it only makes things worse. When she pretends to enjoy it, he always finishes sooner. He carefully closes the door and –

But this time, to Micaela's relief, she succeeds in breaking away from the nightmare. It stopped when it reached the part where the bearded man's filthy hands reached down to force her thighs open.

Suddenly her mind shifted from revulsion and horror to a soothing picture of the boy in the next room, *Riki*. A tranquil smile replaced the feeling of resigned despair that always accompanies the nightmare. Over and over she enjoyed the scene of Riki laying in bed, the covers up to his chin, smiling up at her. Almost smiling.

As she lay in bed, staring at darkness, Micaela began to feel a new awareness. The rape memories mercifully dissolved into one of those fuzzy dreams that dissipate upon awakening, a gossamer veil in a breeze. With this new clearness came a vague sense of guilt, a recollection of trying to murder her husband — or was that part of the dream, as well? She couldn't say.

She smiled as she remembered how the little boy held onto her hand firmly as they walked up the hill to her house, his little hand so warm and loving to the touch. Just like her son's hand. When she gave Riki the Coca-Cola and smiled at him, he had smiled back, with such a smile that would break any mother's heart. Perhaps it wasn't a really a smile, but it was close.

Yet, that drunken woman talked ugly to Riki! Once, she yelled at the child as if he were a yellow dog in the street! Clearly, this is a woman without shame. No question about that. Drunk, staggering about like the village whore, in front the whole world, not to mention little Riki. No shame at all! Clearly, she does not deserve to have a son. How could the Goddess Tonantzín, Goddess Ciuacuátl, and all the Catholic Saints possibly take my son, yet give *that* woman a son? How can the Gods permit this drunken whore to walk around impersonating a Saint?

Gradually, a vision drifted into Micaela's mind. It swirled around, effectively pushing all other thoughts away. A concept took shape, growing more and more logical the longer she considered it. The concept condensed into a plan, as sensible and practical as life itself.

The plan was simple: A heavy stone, smashed against the fallen angel's forehead, would fulfill the Will of God. *Of course! Then Riki would be mine!* The more the thought ripened in her brain, the more Micaela became convinced that the boy with the beautiful smile couldn't possibly belong to the drunken lady.

She *can't* be his mother! The boy has beautiful dark skin. Almost as dark as mine. But her skin is sickly white, like the underbelly of a lizard. And her hair is ugly yellow, like old corn husks — not black, dignified, like Riki's. Clearly, the Gods, in all their wisdom, sent this drunken woman, this fallen angel on a mission! She is destined to return my son! How can I dispute the will of the Gods? It must be the way of the Goddess Tonantzín! Yes, *a gift of the Black Goddess!*

Micaela smiled and enjoyed a warm glow in her belly as she envisioned the happiness and bliss she and her son Riki would enjoy in their new life together. She whispered softly to herself, "He will learn to help about the store. He will go with the men to gather resin on the mountainside. As soon as we save enough money, we will buy an elegant pickup truck, and go to Tlaxcala to buy fresh vegetables and sell them in the village.

"We will own a truck just like the one that belongs to that animal Culio Lázaro." She paused to smile. "Only bigger. We will sell vegetables and matches and things in *all* of the villages. We will be rich. With the help and blessings from the Gods, we will be rich! Just me, and my son Riki!"

A sudden touch of panic pushed her upright as she realized how late it was getting. The dawn's indigo rays leaked through cracks in the rock wall. She knew that if she were to finish the Goddess's mission, she must hurry.

She pulled her clothes on and slipped outside in search of a suitable stone. It had to be a heavy stone, because when she tried to kill her husband with the hatchet she found it much too light to do the job. It ricocheted off his skull instead of breaking through the brain case. It made a terrible mess, with blood all over the bed. This time it would be different. To truly murder an angel or a demon, drastic steps and careful planning are in order.

In the first place, the stone must be heavy enough to crush the woman's skull with one blow—second try at the most. Would the fallen angel disappear and go back to heaven after she was killed? That would be most convenient, for Micaela knew that villagers would make ugly comments about her if they suspected she had a dead body in her house. Villagers often said nasty things for much less than that. Some accused Micaela of being a witch — she knew that. Therefore, if the body didn't dissolve, she would have to find a good place to hide it.

The morning cloud cover was light, creating an exceptionally bright sky for this early in the morning. The sun seemed to be rising faster than usual. Before long, it would break over the mountain's crest. Then it would be too late. Hurry!

She searched frantically for a stone of just the proper size. Eventually, she found one next to the corral of upright sticks which she used as an outhouse.

Perfect! If I lift this one high enough, just one smash, and my son will be mine again!

She began to trot, hugging the stone to her breast. She heard Claudio Fernandez cursing a goat out of his hut. Someone on the other side of the village began singing an ancient tune left over from the days even before the Aztecs came.

The village is waking! I must hurry!

She pushed the door open with her foot. She stepped inside. The packed dirt floor felt like cement beneath her feet as she stalked toward the bedroom.

She pressed her ear against the plank door and listened. Nothing but a light snoring noise. She managed to hold the rock in one hand while she lifted the latch. The door opened quietly. The thumping of her heart sounded in her ears like a wooden drum.

The fallen angel lay sleeping on her side, her back toward little Riki.

Perfect. The weakest part of the Angel's skull, the temple, lay exposed. *Just one blow and the Will of the Gods is done!*

Micaela tiptoed to the side of the bed and mentally measured the spot where the rock should land. With Riki so near, the rock could bounce off the Angel's skull and injure him.

Must be very careful!

She lifted the rock chest high and paused. She closed her eyes for half a moment to recite a short prayer to Tonantzín, a plea to Ciuacuátl.

Help me, oh Goddess. Help me succeed in this sacred, heavenly mission!

Suddenly, the sound of a horn blowing outside in the street paralyzed her arms on high.

Culio Lázaro!

She hadn't heard his truck approaching. The dirty animal would be outside, with his truck loaded with a hog carcass and chicken parts. He would be waiting to leer at Micaela and, if he got the chance, to slip his hand inside her dress and rub his filthy fingertips across a nipple. Animal!

At the first blast of the horn, the village hounds broke into a frenzy of barking and snarling. The sound of the horn drew closer. It was now or never.

Micaela closed her eyes and readied herself for the act. Resolutely, she lifted the rock over her head. She moved next to the bed.

Diana was sound asleep when the horn raised its raucous disturbance. Her first instinct was to ignore it and return to a drug-like sleep. Suddenly she realized: *A car! We're saved! We can get out of here!*

She sat up quickly and threw the covers off. At that instant, something heavy slammed into the bed, creasing the pillow where her head had been a fraction of a second earlier. The bed shuddered and swayed crazily. Diana rocked back and forth and shook her head in a futile effort to clear the fuzziness from her brain. *What's going on?*

She turned to see the dark-skinned woman standing beside the bed, an odd look of horror on her face, her eyes twitching. Saliva drooled from one corner of the woman's slack mouth, and her hands clutched empty air, as if she were holding something invisible.

Diana rubbed her hands across her eyes, trying to bring them into focus. This was all very confusing. Enough alcohol coursed through her veins to keep her tipsy for several more hours.

She was about to ask what the hell was going on when the truck horn blared once more. She struggled from the bed and stared vaguely at Micaela, who was retrieving the rock, getting ready for another try.

"Did you hear that? A car! *We're saved!*"

Diana ran toward the door, pausing to step into her shoes, pulling them on as she hurried outside, shouting, "Wait! Don't go away! We need a ride!"

Micaela clutched the stone to her breast and started after

Diana. This was her last chance. But the sound of Riki's voice stopped her. She turned to look at him, and her heart filled with joyous pain. He was saying something she couldn't understand, but it didn't matter. She laid the rock in the corner and went to the bed and sat next to her son.

She smiled at him and smoothed her hand across his forehead. *"Como estás, mi niño?"* He must have guessed what she was asking, for he said something she assumed meant, *"Muy bien, gracias."* His strangely colored gray eyes met hers with a direct gaze, and although he didn't smile, Micaela imagined that he had.

Actually, Rickey had said, "Don't touch me! You dirty bitch!"

She leaned over to kiss his forehead, but he pulled away and crawled out of bed. He said something in English which she took for an expression of shyness. She returned his words with a loving smile.

Outside, Diana smiled at Culio Lázaro as he stood on the street, his hand through the open truck window, hitting the horn button rapidly. In Spanish, he shouted, "Vegetables! Fresh meat! Special price today!"

Diana hurried toward Culio with her hands held out in supplication. "Señor, can you please take me and my son to the next town? Understand? Next *cuidád* Please? I mean, *por favor?*"

Culio Lázaro looked first at Diana's breasts, which were loose and swaying provocatively under her light blouse. Then his eyes smoothed down her body, lingering on her crotch, before coming back to study her face. He nodded in approval. *"¿Ciudad? ¿Por favor?"* he said, mocking her Gringo accent while giving her a lecherous grin.

Culio had worked for a time in East Texas where he picked up some English and saved money to start a business. Then one day, he got lucky and managed to steal this truck.

He spoke in heavily accented English, "I es-speak the *inglés*, lady. Yes, I happy to go to town with you. Any time!" His

25

tongue flicked across his lips suggestively, but Diana Cranston-Barron was too muddled to catch the significance.

"Oh, thank God! I thought I might be stuck here for a week or so. I'll go get the boy and my luggage. I'll pay you well."

Culio looked at his truck then back at her with a disappointed frown.

"A boy? I don' wanna take no boy with us. Lady, look *dentro*, uh, inside truck — just two seats. One for you, one for me. Leave the kid here and you and me, we go to town. Okay?" He smiled in anticipation, his eyes trying to see through Diana's blouse, beyond the tantalizing thin fabric. "You want me to take you, I take you. Then we come back for the kid."

"Okay, okay. Just drive me to the nearest place where I can rent a car or a taxi. I'll come back here later."

She didn't want to argue, she only wanted to get to a telephone and present her side of the story before Alex Barron heard Lance Rexford's version about what happened. By now, Alex would be climbing walls, she was sure of that. She resolved not to have any more to drink so she would be sober by the time she reached Acapulco.

Culio grinned and said, "Get in. You and I go to town now. I can come back an' sell fuckin' pork chops any time. Let's go!"

"Wait. I'll be right back." Diana ran inside the store, pulled on her coat and grabbed her purse. She hastily kissed the boy on the forehead. "I'll rent a car and be right back, Rickey. So, you wait here, okay?" As she started for the door, the row of dusty bottles caught her eye.

Perhaps one more drink?

Diana looked about for Micaela, but she had gone outside, clutching the stone, hoping for a second chance.

Not wanting to waste time, Diana stepped up on a stool and grabbed two of the little rum bottles. "By the time I get to Acapulco, I'll be cold sober," she told herself confidently. "Meanwhile, I need something to clear my head."

Rickey followed her outside, a concerned frown on his face.

"Don't leave me here, Diana. It's dirty here. Everything stinks! And that woman is weird. Take me with you. Diana, *please*?"

"It's okay, honey, I'll be back in a jiffy." She noted that he had said *please* for the first time she could remember.

"Then can we go home? I want my dad."

"Yes, then we'll go home." She leaned over to kiss him on the lips, but he turned away from her stale breath. She frowned, and then kissed him lightly on the cheek.

"And, from now on, it's going to be 'mommy' or 'mother' — *not* Diana. Understand?" She sighed as he shrugged his shoulders and turned away from her.

Micaela abandoned her stone and now stood aside from the villagers who were waiting to buy meat from Culio. She rarely tasted meat since her husband fled — she couldn't really afford it — but perhaps today, she might buy a handful of calf intestines to cook for Riki's breakfast.

Then, Diana came running out of the house, her purse in one hand, two half-pint bottles of rum in the other. Micaela stared sullenly. *If only a few moments quicker with the stone, the boy would be mine. What disgusting luck!*

She felt her mind slipping back into the old, pitch-black tunnels of emptiness. Micaela breathed a deep, melancholy sigh as the scene started to replay itself, starting with the creak of a door opening.

She heard a whisper, raspy and tense: *"Mica? Mica, it's your turn now! Guess what I have for you..."*

Diana waved at Micaela as she hurried to the truck. "Take care of Rickey 'til I get back with a car," she shouted. Micaela's trance broke when she heard the word *Riki*. She shook her head and tried to concentrate.

She squinted her eyes at Diana, who pointed at Rickey, then at herself and then at the truck.

"Listen, I'm going to town to rent a car, and I'll be back right away. Understand? I'll be right back."

Diana remembered the two rum bottles and held them up so Micaela could see them.

"I'll pay for these bottles later. I don't have anything smaller than a fifty right now. Understand?"

She held up the bottles again and said, "I'll pay when I get back with the car." Then she pointed to her son and said, "Take care of the boy until I return. Okay? *Comprende?*"

Micaela nodded slowly. A pleased expression softened her face. Diana took this to mean that she understood. She then squeezed into the small pickup, slammed the door shut, and waved goodbye to Rickey. He returned a disgusted look and turned away even before Culio got the engine started.

Micaela watched the truck bounce down the road with a sense of wonder at the way of the Gods. She made the sign of the cross in the complicated way of the Indian/Christian ritual.

She traded the boy for two bottles of rum? Maybe that is Tonantzín's way of doing things. How curious. Who am I to question the ways of the Gods? As long as Tonantzín replaces my child, I shall never question.

The village people were shocked and scandalized. Could they believe their eyes? Was it possible that this woman was trading a boy for two bottles of rum? Clearly, Gringos were crazy, for everyone had heard stories and had seen movies of their *locuras*. But trading a boy for two bottles of cheap alcohol, this was something else. The villagers talked about this for months afterward, and some wondered if perhaps Micaela might be correct, that this was indeed the Will of the Gods.

Diana never returned with a taxi or rental car. As Culio Lázaro rounded a curve a few kilometers from the village, his right hand dropped to Diana's thigh. He squeezed it gently.

Astonished, she hesitated, turning to look at the man in disbelief. Before she could grab his wrist, his hand was slipping under her skirt, trying to force her legs apart.

She swung her purse with all her might. It split open as it slammed into the monster's mouth.

Blood colored his lips an angry red.

Furious, Culio balled his fist and swung a backhand at Diana's face. His wrist cracked her nose, breaking cartilage. Blood streamed as if he had turned on a faucet. Blinded with pain and fury, Diana began punching and clawing like a wildcat.

The truck's tire bumped as it caught the edge of the pavement. Culio twisted the steering wheel to regain control, but Diana clutched his sleeve and pulled with one hand, clawing with the other.

Finally, he jerked his arm loose. But it was too late.

The red truck careened over the side of the mountain. It rolled and bounced and rolled some more. Both doors flew open and the windshield glass shattered into a snow-like curtain.

Diana's body flew out on the third hit.

The truck continued rolling down the side of the mountain, crumpling like a wad of wastepaper.

Miraculously, it did not catch flame until it reached the bottom of the canyon, finally bursting into a mass of orange flame and soot-black smoke. Culio Lázaro's body fat added blackness to the smoke. Few people in the village could read without laboriously sounding out words letter by letter. Only don Rafael read very much. He used to be the schoolteacher, years ago, when there were still children in the village, before he accepted his pension from the government. His eyes were bad now and the only thing he could read were schoolbooks with large print left over from the days when the village had children and a school. But that didn't matter, because newspapers seldom found their way into the village; no one saw the headlines in the next day's papers.

When Culio Lázaro didn't return with fresh meat that week, everyone assumed he had run away with the gringa lady. The village women were scandalized, the men envious. The question of whether the woman had really traded the boy for the rum continued for a long time. Some speculated that there could have been a misunderstanding. Yet the fact was, everyone saw the transaction with their own eyes! Eventually they accepted the trade as fact. Gringos were crazy, that couldn't be denied.

People living in the capital couldn't escape the headlines that shouted the news across the front pages of the Mexico City newspapers. In the English-language Mexico City News, for example, the story read:

<u>Diana Cranston Dead</u>
MOVIE STAR KILLED
IN MOUNTAIN CRASH

Diana Cranston, actress and estranged wife of movie director Alexander Barron, died yesterday when a small truck in which she was riding went over the side of a mountain in the state of Tlascala. The driver, as yet not identified, apparently lost control of his vehicle on a curve and the truck burst into flames as it plunged down the mountainside. According to authorities, the truck had been stolen in Texas several years ago; its present ownership unknown. Ms. Cranston's body was identified by papers in her purse, which was found nearby.

Ms. Cranston was vacationing at the Acapulco home of her ex-husband, Alex Barron, where he lives with his son Richard Alexander Barron III. She and her husband recently had announced plans for a comeback, by making her first movie in almost five years. Mr. Barron was to produce and direct the movie. At press time, he had not been located for a statement.

Twice nominated for Academy awards, Diana Cranston was most remembered for her first starring role, in which she played the role of Madonna in the...

Chapter Three

Blue waves topped with white froth rolled in from the depths of the Pacific, curled hesitantly, and then crashed on Condesa Beach with a muffled thunder. The waves trailed foam to glisten in the tropical sunshine as they pulled back to repeat the endless cycle. Vendors trudged along the sand, offering cheap tourist goods to those lounging on beach chairs or spread-eagled on colorful beach towels. A steady salt-air breeze carried the balmy odor of the tropics.

"Acapulco never looked better," Alex Barron thought as he leaned back in his canvas chair and stretched luxuriously. A thatched ramada shaded him from the mid-day sun. He smiled pleasantly at the waiter when a cool drink appeared on the low table alongside his chair.

But as he sipped the Fernet Branco-and-Vermouth, his forehead creased into a frown of annoyance; a cloud of murky anxieties began taunting him. Diana was scheduled to return with Rickey two days ago. Although worried over what could have happened, Alex's strongest emotion at the moment was anger.

"Nothing ever happens to Diana," he tried to reassure himself. "If she's in another jam, gets her name smeared all over the front pages again, she's definitely through. That's it! What the hell was I thinking about, when I agreed to let her take Rickey on a trip?"

January's tropical sun glinted off of the strands of silver in Alex Barron's black hair, which contrasted handsomely with his tanned skin and intense, gray-blue eyes. Like his father and

31

grandfather before him, Alex inherited that strange combination of olive complexion and gray eyes, a mixture of southern Italy and northern Switzerland—dark Moors from North Africa and blue-eyed mountaineers from Austria. The Barron family eyes and dark skin had been passed on to Rickey. The tropical sunshine had burned both of their skins even darker, actually as dark as many native Mexicans.

"Too bad Rickey's not here to play in the surf," he thought. "The kid's crazy about the beach." Rickey also loved the swimming pool at their Acapulco winter home; and not quite four yet, he swam like an otter. Alex smiled with satisfaction. A swimming specialist started giving Rickey lessons while the boy was still in diapers. Every winter, when Alex moved his headquarters to Acapulco, the instructor worked with Rickey.

"Your son's a natural athlete," the instructor said last week, "Before the season's out, he'll be a championship-class diver."

Lately Alex's whole life seemed to revolve about Rickey. His plans for the future involved the boy in one way or another. Rickey had changed Alex Barron's life many ways. For one thing, the boy's birth was the final blow that shattered his infatuation with Diana. He and Robin Summerhill were married within weeks after Rickey's birth.

It was also the beginning of a new direction in his film career; Alex no longer felt driven to produce a movie simply to promote Diana Cranston's career. Today his emphasis is on quality and artistic content. He now planned no more than one project every other year, allowing time to relax and be with his son.

Again, he mentally cursed himself for agreeing to help Diana get her career back on track. Robin had been right all along. "You're making a mistake. She isn't going to change," Robin had insisted, "But I suppose if you don't give it a try, you'll forever feel guilty you didn't give her a boost her when she needed help. I'm going to step aside and let you handle this next picture. When it crashes, I don't want any gossip that jealousy of my husband's ex-lover had anything to do with the disaster."

Alex felt a tight feeling of chagrin and guilt as he thought of how correct Robin had been. He forced himself not to think of the money they'd sunk into pre-production costs. He begged Robin to stay in Mexico while the picture was underway, but she had refused. "I want to be totally in the clear on this one. We've got things I should be doing in California anyway. I have the feeling this won't take long."

Another wave crashed on shore, sending tongues of bubbling water toward Alex's feet, only to disappear quietly into the thirsty sand.

Diana had seemed okay for the first month. Then she began to fall back into the old pattern, arriving late for meetings and conferences, looking haggard, the lack of sleep aging her face. She denied drinking or pills had anything to do with this. "It's some kind of allergy, something in the Acapulco air," she insisted. "Maybe those damned Jacaranda trees. I'll be okay once we get going. I promise."

When Alex expressed doubt over the viability of the project, Diana took a new, almost desperate tack. She acquired a sudden interest in Rickey, the son she abandoned at birth in return for a guarantee that the movie she was working on would be released. In effect, she had traded her son for a career boost.

Now she insisted on seeing Rickey at every opportunity, finding pretexts to bring him presents or to take him somewhere. This left Alex in a quandary. She was, after all, Rickey's mother. It would be an injustice to deprive the boy of the opportunity to know his real mother.

Rickey, however, didn't see this as an opportunity. He obviously didn't like Diana and made no effort to conceal his feelings. Part of the problem was the superficial and phony quality of Diana's newfound maternal instinct.

Clearly, Diana *tried* to like Rickey, but Rickey didn't make it easy. He knew all the right buttons to push to set her off and delighted in doing so. Alex had to admit that Rickey was a somewhat high-spirited child—and well, perhaps even a spoiled, impossible brat as some claimed. He smiled as he thought about this, confident this was just a stage kids go through. Well, maybe a *little* spoiled, but why not?

Alex reached for the drink, sipping at it as he looked out over the ocean's curving horizon. "Where the hell can she be?" he grumbled aloud. "I must have been crazy to let her take my son on an overnight trip. I swear, she screws up this time, she'll never see Rickey again." Then he thought, "Probably be a blessing for both of them."

His stomach twisted when he thought about Diana's latest boyfriend, Lance Rexford Jr., an insipid Hollywood character whose father directed Diana's first picture. How foolish to have allowed them to take the Rolls on this trip. But Rexford promised he would keep Diana sober.

"Lance Rexford, my ass! A no-talent phony just like his father. Just as phony as their names. A half-baked, nowhere actor—looks more like a girl than a man."

His thoughts were interrupted by the approaching bulk of Johnny Gregorio, treading clumsily through the sand. Johnny's face bore a worried frown. Alex narrowed his eyes and tried to guess what might be wrong. In addition to being Alex Barron's right-hand man in the Barron family enterprises, Johnny Gregorio was his best friend. They'd gone to Stanford together, played football on the same team and competed for the same girls. Including Diana. In their own way, each lost.

Johnny stepped around sunbathers, swatting his knee with a folded newspaper as if punishing himself for some unforgivable sin. When he saw Alex, he broke into a run, looking like the quarterback he used to be, pulling the famous sneak play that made him the sensation of his senior year at Stanford.

"What's wrong, Johnny?" Alex stared at the folded newspaper and suddenly felt something strange stirring in the pit of his stomach. "Diana made the papers again?"

Johnny nodded. He tried to say something but ended up clearing his throat as if there were something choking him. He looked at his boss with a look of agony.

"Sit down and have a drink. What did she do this time? Punch out a cop? Dance naked on a bar? Go ahead, sit down. I've been expecting trouble."

He shook his head and remained standing. "Worse than any of that, Alex. She's dead." He slowly unfolded the newspaper to uncover the headlines.

"Dead?" Alex struggled to get out of the slant-backed chair, then fell back in a dazed paralysis. "Dead? When? How?" Suddenly he sat up. "*Oh, my God!* What about Rickey?"

He struggled to his feet. "*Where's Rickey?*"

"Here. Read this first."

"Goddammit! What about my son? Is he okay?"

"No one knows yet. Read!"

When he finished, Alex wadded the paper and threw it toward the surf. It blew back at his feet and he kicked it away. "Where's my son?"

"Got a bunch of people working on it, Alex. All we know is, they haven't found him. So maybe he wasn't in the truck when it went over the side. He could be safe."

"What about Rexford?"

"He wasn't in the accident. But he was with Rickey and Diana the day before it happened. We know that for sure."

"Then, maybe Rickey's with Rexford. Maybe he's okay."

"No, Rickey's not with Rexford. I'm sure of that 'cause I've got Rexford on ice. In jail not far from where the accident happened. The driver of the truck was a Mexican, probably a local. Still hasn't been identified. Tough enough for them to identify Diana, what with the damage going down the mountain side. The truck was so messed up, they can't even tell who owned it. One of those stolen jobs they bring down here from the States."

"If Rickey was with Rexford the day before, he must know where Rickey is. Right?"

Johnny Gregorio shrugged and said, "Best we can figure, night before the accident, they stayed at a hotel in Jalapa. They had a couple of knockdown fights, yelling and screaming at each other, breaking things. Diana's usual thing when she gets swacked. And we know Rexford hit a telephone pole with your Rolls, then he sideswiped an ox cart and finally clipped a kid on a bicycle. That's why he's in jail."

"Drunken bastards! Where's Rickey? That's all I want to know. Where?"

"We're looking, Alex. We're looking. I've got half a dozen guys scouring the road between Jalapa and Tlaxcala. Rexford claims he let her out of the car at a little village somewhere between those two towns. But he was drunk and doesn't remember exactly where."

"How do we *know* Rickey wasn't in the truck when it went over the side?"

"We don't know for sure. Cops have been searching all over the mountainside, thinking he might have been thrown clear. He could be okay, you know. Maybe just stunned, or maybe confused and got up and started walking. And maybe he wasn't even with her. She could have left him in that village for some reason."

"Does Robin know?"

"No, she's on a windjammer cruise around the Greek Isles. Completely out of touch with the world."

"Find him, Johnny. We have to find him!" Alex stood now, pacing back and forth, kicking sand angrily with each step. He whispered hoarsely, "Find my son!"

"If he's alive I'll find him. That's a promise."

"If he's not alive?"

"Don't talk that way. I'll get another team to comb that mountain. We'll offer a bigger reward. Okay?"

Lance Rexford was in jail in a place called Apizaco. A news writer for a Mexico City paper had spotted the Rolls Royce in the police parking lot and notified Johnny Gregorio. Johnny promised the Apizaco police chief a bonus to keep Rexford locked up until Alex Barron could get there.

They flew to Mexico City; a rental car waited at the airport for the drive to Apizaco. They had no trouble locating the cement block jail building.

A paunchy police sergeant pulled Rexford from his cell and shoved him roughly into the small room where Alex Barron and Johnny Gregorio waited. Rexford's expensive clothes were rumpled from sleeping in them and pouches under his eyes spoke of the rough time he'd had in a Mexican jail. He needed a shave and was obviously terrified to face Alex.

"Jesus Christ, Mr. Barron, I swear, none of this was my fault! I *wanted* to get back to Acapulco, but she went crazy. I mean, like she needed a drink in her hand from the time she got up until..."

Alex cut off his words with a slap across the mouth that stunned Rexford into silence.

"Where's my son, you sleazy creep? What did you two do with Rickey?"

"*She* took him, Mr. Barron. That's the truth. She insisted on getting out of the car. You know how she can get, don't you? She demanded to get out of the car, but I wouldn't let her out until we at least came to a town. I couldn't just leave her out in the country, could I? Well, I stopped the car in this little village. I begged her not to get out. I tried to reason with her. But she pulled Rickey out of the back seat and ran away. I hung around for two hours, waiting for her to return. But she never came back. I tried to take care of her, Mr. Barron, I honestly did."

Johnny said dryly, "Sure you did. You took good care of her. Like you took care of Mr. Barron's Rolls Royce."

"That was her fault, too," Rexford protested. "Know how I got into this mess? She slapped a contact lens out of my right eye, and I couldn't see where the hell I was going. I hit a few things, and when I got to this town, they tell me I hit a kid on a bicycle. I thought someone thumped the car with a rock or something, so I kept on going. Until the cops stopped me."

"Where is Rickey? Rexford, if I don't find my son, I'll..." He couldn't finish; he clasped his hands against his face. His body shook with emotion.

"I swear to you, *I don't know!* The last I saw of them was in that little village. Seems to me it was the only village on that part of the road. It should be easy to find. Get me out of here and I'll show you where it is."

As Johnny drove, Alex followed the route on the road map. Lance Rexford studied each village they came to. He shook his head desperately after they had traversed the road for the third time.

"I just don't understand. I know there was a cobblestone road, or trail, because I remember the Rolls spinning its wheels on the wet stones. And there were a bunch of black huts with thatch roofs. And a church—but it looked like it was abandoned. Yeah, I remember, the church didn't have a roof."

Alex felt a red flash of anger that he couldn't control. He slapped Rexford's mouth with the back of his hand. He would have punched him had Johnny not caught his hand. Alex took a couple of deep breaths, until he was able to talk more or less calmly.

"We'll drive the road one more time, Rexford. This time we'd better find Rickey."

They stopped at every village and went off the pavement to look at other villages on the map. They hired a teenager who spoke a little English and brought him along as an interpreter. The search went on for three days. Every police station, every store, every person they saw walking along the road was questioned.

"A gray-eyed little boy? A *gringuito* wearing suit and a tie?

No, señor. If I had, I would have remembered. I am sorry."

They passed the turnoff to Tezcatlipocas many times. By this time, the detour road leading up to the village had been sliced away by the bulldozer that was repairing the slide. The dirt was needed to fill the part of the highway that had been carried to the bottom of the barranca.

For several days—possibly a week or two—the village would be cut off from the highway, until the road crew got around to grading the old route up to the village and opening the road once more. It really didn't matter much, because no one in the village owned an automobile. Later, when there was nothing else to do, the bulldozer would leisurely cut a new approach to the village. That's the way it worked on that stretch of highway. Alex couldn't find the village on the map because it wasn't on the map. Tezcatlipocas had fallen so low that the map makers forgot it was there.

Eight times in all, Alex Barron passed 100 meters below Tezcatlipocas.

Once as he passed, Rickey Barron was playing in the dirt in front of Micaela's store, digging holes with a machete and covering them over with the flat part of the blade. Three elderly women and two wrinkled men squatted in a circle to observe the youngest of the Barron dynasty as he played with the long, sharp blade. It had been years since a child other than Micaela's had been in the village, and hers didn't really count since her boy had been sickly and seldom strayed outside the store.

It seemed correct for a boy-child to have such a practical toy, for a machete would be essential later on in life when he became a man. But they all realized that this boy-child was different. He had a rich family somewhere who would most certainly return to take him from the village, once the woman realized her mistake in trading the boy for two bottles of rum. If not tomorrow, maybe the day after.

When the unusual-looking boy became a man, he would no

doubt be rich and hire others to wield machetes for him. This was too bad, for they would have liked to see the boy stay. They wished that Micaela could be correct about his being a gift from the Goddess Tonantzín. They wondered if Micaela would give the boy up without a fight.

But two bottles of rum? What a cheap price God places on a boy! Gustavo Sanchez, who had no respect for religion, pointed out that the woman could have at least held out for two large *garafones* instead of the little eighth-liter bottles. He also pointed out that the lady had nice pair of chichis. Not that that had anything to do with the trade; it was just that Gustavo liked to talk about chichis.

That first day had been very difficult for Rickey. But now he felt a bit more at ease with the gathering around him. He sensed that they liked him. He still thought they were incredibly ugly and dirty-looking people, but he enjoyed the attention they showered on him. At least, none of them smelled of the revolting sour-pungent odor that Diana often exuded, the odor that turned her into a mean, vindictive person. If anything, he was happy that she wasn't around, with her unpredictable outbursts of anger, alternating with strange professions of love.

But he truly missed his father and wondered why it was taking so long for him to come and take him away from this stupid place.

He thought of how his father's beard was rough and how it tickled when it was rubbed the wrong way, making both of them laugh and giggle. He thought about how his father carried him on his shoulders, and how he would pretend he was a horse and gallop around the house, and how they would sometimes jump into the swimming pool like that, while sitting on his daddy's shoulders. He wanted to go home. He wanted to see his father. But he felt calm because he knew that eventually his father would come and get him.

He lifted the machete above his head and chopped at the ground, throwing a chunk of clay a full meter away. The people around him applauded and a man touched him on the back, smiling in approval.

"*Muy bueno! Que fuerza!*" they said, making Rickey feel the warmth of their approval, so he did another swing at the earth, to test whether this was the cause of all the good cheer. Again, they applauded, and he felt good.

"*Muy bueno,*" he whispered. Thus, he learned his first Spanish words. *Muy bueno!*

A few hours later, Rickey became overwhelmed with despair and guilt. Have I done something wrong? he kept asking himself. Why have they left me here? He couldn't help wondering what he might have done to make his father punish him by leaving him here. He searched his mind for something naughty he'd done. The list was long, but nothing serious enough for this. The only possible incident was when he'd accidentally broken the crystal statue that always perched on the edge of his father's desk.

"Be careful Rickey," his father had pleaded. "I'd rather you didn't play with that. Why don't you just put it back on the desk?"

Rickey ignored him and turned the object in his hands to see how it sparkled in the light. The crystal depicted a huntress with a delicate bow poised, an arrow notched into an imaginary string. He turned it in his hands once more to watch the colored light flash from the statue's crystal interior.

When he finally tried to place it on the desk, something went wrong. The statue teetered briefly, then crashed to the floor, shattering into a thousand crystals, each with its own musical tinkle.

For a moment there had been a dreadful silence. "Oh, Rickey, no..." were the only words his father said, but they were full of anguish and sorrow. The distress on his father's face, as he stared at the crystal shards on the floor, puzzled Rickey. He had never seen his father so upset. Tears welled from his eyes

41

and glistened on his cheeks.

Yet there had been no punishment, not even a scolding. Just the strange look of pain. Perhaps this is the punishment? That's why he didn't come to take me home?

Alex Barron's search for his son reached a frenzy by the end of that first week. Hundreds of local people were hired to climb the hill, to search around the wreckage, probing for the body of Richard Alexander Barron III. They found nothing.

Alex hired several private investigators. Between the detectives, Johnny Gregorio, and himself, they asked hundreds of questions, all of the wrong people. No one could imagine which village could be the one where Diana and Rickey got out of the Rolls Royce. It never occurred to anyone to think of Tezcatlipocas. The highway didn't go through the village. Now, in fact, there was no road of any kind going through the village.

"The *luggage!* What happened to Diana's luggage?" Alex paced up and down the tiled hotel room floor, clenching his fists in frustration. "She had a big leather suitcase that couldn't possibly have been overlooked on that hill. She carried a small fortune in jewelry in that suitcase. Where is it?"

"Maybe someone stole it before she got into the truck," Johnny suggested timidly. His boss was getting very testy lately, and often he didn't know what to say. "Maybe someone found the suitcase on the hill and decided to keep it when they found the jewelry. Or maybe she left the suitcase in the village."

"We have to offer a reward for the jewelry, Johnny. A big reward. Then when someone claims it, we'll know where Rexford left Rickey and Diana. Maybe Rickey is still in that village. I can't get that thought out of my mind. I'm convinced my son is alive. I have this feeling, as if he's trying to communicate with me."

"I already posted a reward, Alex. I sent a description of each piece of jewelry on her insurance inventory to the *Monte de Piedad* and to every police station in every little town from here to Veracruz. When the thief tries to sell even one piece, we'll have him immediately. Money talks down here. I didn't put a time limit on the reward, either. I figured you wouldn't mind my putting your money on the line."

"Whatever it takes."

"I'm in this thing all the way, Alex. I love Rickey as much as if he were my own son. Almost was, you know."

Alex looked up sharply and Johnny Gregorio flinched. "Sorry. I didn't mean that the way it sounded. Look, we're both under a lot of strain."

"Forget it. You're right. We're under pressure, and we can't be taking it out on each other. God, how I wish Robin were here. If I'd only listened to her. None of this would have happened if I'd have just listened."

"I tried to contact her again this morning. The yacht still hasn't returned. Left word for her to contact us here."

Alex resumed pacing, staring at his knuckles and the back of his hands as if he had never seen them before. Common sense told him something terrible had happened to his son, yet his heart couldn't allow this to be true. For a long time to come, sleepless nights and fitful dreams would torture him. Every time he saw a child Rickey's age he would stare, having to make certain.

Before they left Mexico, Alex made a decision. "I can't just leave things hanging, Johnny. I want you to hire someone to keep working on this, full time. I *have* to know what happened that day."

That afternoon they interviewed Enrique Morales. Morales held the rank of lieutenant in the Mexican Secret Service. He was an intense man with the tenacity of a pit bull. Alex decided he liked him even before he heard him say a word. Then, after the man spoke, Alex was totally convinced that if anyone could solve the mystery, it would be Enrique Morales.

"If conditions are as Mr. Gregorio indicated," Morales said

evenly, "I shall be honored to accept the job. I promise you I will spend every minute of my waking hours looking for your boy. I promise you I will locate the jewelry as well, for as you know, that is the key to this mystery. We find the jewelry, we find your son. Simple."

"And your job with the Ministry of Justice?"

"If you agree to the contract Mr. Gregorio suggested, I shall resign. If I solve this case, there is no question but I can return to the Ministry at a much higher position. Who knows? Maybe next time as a Colonel. However, I hope that won't be necessary."

Alex looked quizzically at Johnny Gee, who explained, "I told him we'll double his salary until Rickey has been found. Then a bonus of $50,000 plus a security job with Barron-Summerhill Productions. That okay?"

"Whatever you say, Johnny. We have to clear this up. I'll lose my mind if I don't."

Enrique Morales smiled, the thin moustache broadening, making his face seem wider than it was. His eyes became mere slits in his face, glittering in anticipation of this easy money. Morales loved money even more than things money could buy. Enrique Morales would, without hesitation, kill for money, although he had never been given the opportunity. With such a perfect combination, greed and total lack of principles, everyone agreed that Enrique Morales had the makings of a successful Mexican politician.

Later, he told his girlfriend, "This will be the easiest money a man like me can earn. It's like *finding* money! I don't even have to steal it!"

"Oh? Nobody else can find the boy, so why you? You were a stupid burro to quit such a fine job at the Ministry for this ghost-chasing business."

Enrique smiled tolerantly. "The boy is dead, that's obvious. Whoever stole the jewelry must have killed the little bastard and buried him somewhere. That's only logical. When I find the thief, I simply make him show me the grave. Then I collect the reward plus a lucrative job in California. Would you like that? Living in Hollywood?"

"You think finding the jewelry will be easy?"

"Don't laugh. If there is one thing I know, it's the ways of criminals. No way on earth can a Mexican thief keep that jewelry hidden. The thought of all the pesos the jewelry will bring is too much for anyone to stand. And jewelry is the hardest thing in the world to sell and not get caught. Sooner or later, probably sooner, the thief will start selling. When he does, the news will come directly to me. You see, all of the reward notices list only my name. Only my telephone. I am in charge of everything!"

"So? Maybe the boy wasn't with the jewel thief. Maybe he was killed in the accident and a pack of wild dogs ate him. That's happened before in those mountains. What then?"

Enrique smiled, although he didn't feel quite as confident now. That was a possibility he hadn't considered.

"It won't matter. While I'm waiting for the jewelry, I get paid the same if he is buried in a shallow grave or if he is passing through some dog's stomach. Once I find the jewelry, I can find a grave—*any* grave will do. Then I collect the reward for finding the kid's body. Just that will be enough to keep us in luxury for all our lives. But that's not all."

She gave him a sidelong glance and said, "You're going to keep the jewelry, aren't you?"

A broad grin stretched his moustache into a thin stripe across his face. "If it works out that way, of course. I only need to turn in a couple of pieces, to prove that I've found the killer and the body. Once the search for the missing jewelry is over, I can sell the rest to a friend in Bogotá. We'll be rich, Susana! Rich beyond our dreams!"

He put his hand on her shoulder and began smoothing it back and forth, but she shrugged his hand away and moved aside.

"But suppose the boy is alive? Suppose he has the jewelry

with him when you find him. You won't be able to steal it. That would be a big joke on you, Enrique."

A frown darkened his face only momentarily, replaced by a confident smile.

"Look, I get paid as much for a dead boy as a live one. If it gets complicated, I'll simply produce a dead body. So, one way or another, I will have the jewelry, *and* the job in Hollywood. I have a list of the treasure, and I guarantee you that in South America it'll bring a million dollars, even from the stingiest buyer. And, who knows, I might decide to keep a bauble or two for your pretty little wrist, and perhaps something glittering to place around your neck so it can hang just like so..."

She slapped his hand away from the breast he tried to fondle and tossed the hair back from her face with a look of contempt.

"Ha! You think I'm going to leave a perfectly good husband to go with you? After you quit your job with the Ministry? Don't make me laugh. You could have moved into politics and been somebody important. Just look at you! You don't even have a regular job. You won't ever find the boy or the jewelry. When this is over, you will be back in a police car, chasing speeders for 100-peso *mordidas*."

Enrique's eyebrows lifted in painful imploration. "Please Susana, don't talk that way. This job will pay more than I could ever hope to make working for the *pinche* Ministry. We have a great future, you and me. Even if I don't find the jewelry, I'll find the boy's grave—or make a grave—and I get the job with Barron Productions. We can live in California! In Hollywood! Would you like that? Money? Expensive cars? You and I? *Money?*"

She shrugged and gave him a distant look that neither promised nor refused. She examined her face in her compact once more and stood up to leave.

"When you find the kid and the jewelry, give me a call. Until then, good luck."

Morales got good and drunk that day. But he knew Mexican personalities, and he knew the psychology of thieves. The jewelry would surface. He would find both the jewelry and the kid's grave.

"Susana will be sorry she humiliated me." He spilled a drink and cursed at the bartender who cleaned it up. "God, what a stupid fool I am when it comes to beautiful women. The worse they treat me, the more I love them. Will I ever learn?"

From that moment, Enrique Morales developed a resentment toward Richard Alexander Barron III. Intellectually, he realized that it was foolish to dislike a dead child, but the longer he was to search for him the deeper the resentment was to become, until it developed into total hatred.

Chapter Four

The morning of that first day, after Diana went away in the red truck, Rickey waited outside the stone hut, hoping to see his father coming to take him home. Even Diana would have been welcome. To his dismay, the bizarre Mexican woman followed him outside. He didn't like the color of her skin. It looked dirty. Her hair was coarse and greasy looking as well. Her clothes smelled of sweat and mildew.

She kept putting her hands on him and jabbering words he didn't understand. This made him feel extremely uneasy. No matter how he tried to pull away, her hands followed. The Mexican servants in his father's Acapulco home rarely spoke to Rickey, much less touched him. Only Robin and his father ever did that. Again, he tried to move away, but it was no use. She kept smoothing her hands over his hair and looking down into his face, repeating words he couldn't understand. "*Mi hijo, mi hijo...*" Whatever that meant.

At the moment, his biggest concern was finding a bathroom. After Diana left in the truck, he had looked around the woman's house, but couldn't find the bathroom. His stomach felt like it would burst if he didn't find a bathroom soon.

"Hey, I have to pee," he had said, loudly, hoping volume would help her understand. When she just smiled, he said it again, louder. This time he pointed at his crotch and pressed his knees together. The dark woman's face brightened with understanding as she smothered a giggle behind her fingers.

She took his hand and led him behind the house and pointed to a rocky patch of ground where some upright sticks formed an irregular circle. She said something incomprehensible and again pointed toward the ring of sticks.

"No! I have to go to the *bathroom*, stupid! Understand bathroom?"

She looked perplexed for a moment, then firmly took his hand and led him toward an opening in the circle of sticks. Suddenly he understood. Inside the corral lay feces in varying stages of decomposition attended by the odor of stale urine. Metallic blue-and-gold flies buzzed about ominously.

Rickey stepped back, shaking his head in horror. He ran around behind the house and relieved himself against a black lava boulder. The dark-skinned woman was obviously upset, but he didn't care. He shivered in disgust at the thought of entering the ring of sticks.

When evening arrived, and still no father, he reluctantly allowed the dark lady to put him into her bed. He was hungry but couldn't bring himself to taste the food she handed him. The tin plate held something that looked like misshapen chunks of sausage, and it smelled like vomit.

He found it difficult to go to sleep that night, because the woman kept hugging him and murmuring words in a strange language. He didn't like being here at all. Everything in the house smelled of mildew. In the morning, for breakfast, the weird woman gave him a bowl of something that looked like watery cottage cheese. He pushed it away in disgust.

"I won't eat that!" he said angrily. "Don't you have any Coco Puffs or Sugar Crisps?" But the weird woman just stared at him and tried to stuff the stupid gruel into his mouth. He knocked the spoon from her hand and ran outside the house.

But Rickey's stomach demanded nourishment. When he returned to the room, the woman was starting a charcoal fire between three stones. When it was going well, she placed a piece of iron sheeting over the glowing coals. Then, on one edge of the iron plate she set a clay pot of beans, and in the center, she began cooking something that looked like pancakes. But, before she put them on the stove, she slapped them between her palms with a rhythmic slip-slap, slip-slap noise. That sound would become familiar in the days to come, but for now it was a mystery.

The food smelled delicious. Micaela scooped some beans from the pot, plopped them onto one of the pancake things, rolled it up and handed it to Rickey. He grudgingly nodded his thanks and took a large bite. Suddenly his eyes widened. The scalding, chili-spiked beans ripped at his tongue and throat. He spit the mouthful onto the dirt floor and gasped for breath. He ran outside; Micaela followed.

"*Que pasa mi amor?*" She took his hand and tried to console him, but he pulled away angrily.

"That tastes like dirt! I burned my mouth! I want to go home! I don't like it here at all!" The hurt look on her face only made him more angry and resentful. "I *hate* it here! I *hate* you!"

That evening, when Diana still hadn't returned, Rickey forced himself to taste and finally eat one of the rolled-up pancakes with beans inside. The chili warmed his stomach, and miraculously, after the first bite, he was hungry no longer! At noon, he was able to eat three of the things she called *tortillas*. After some time, the combination of tortilla, beans, chili—and sometimes boiled meat—would become as natural as veal or pizza had been before.

After supper he went outside to go to the bathroom again but couldn't go near that ring of sticks. It was several days before he could bring himself to enter the corral to "go poop." After a few weeks, however, it seemed perfectly natural.

He cried himself to sleep the first few nights, wondering why his father didn't come to get him. The dark woman lay next to him in the bed, whispering softly in Spanish and caressing him until he finally managed to drift off to sleep.

He discerned that her name was *Micaela*, which had a pretty sound to it. After a while, he got used to her continually fussing over him. There was nothing he could do about it anyway. The days dragged on slowly, for life in the village was quiet and boring, each day stretching into an eternity. He had no other children to play with, no toys except a machete and a bone-handled knife one of the old men had given him. The man tried to show him how to carve wooden whistles, which along with his knife, were to be his only toys for the rest of his childhood.

Gradually he began to understand much of what was being said, and he learned enough words to make his wants known. After a while, he stopped crying himself to sleep when he realized that this made Micaela feel sad. He tried not to cry when she was around, but he kept repeating under his breath, *I want to go home. I want my father. I want to go home.*

He had a recurring dream in which he was playing in the swimming pool in his back yard, and that his father was in the house trying to piece the crystal statue back together, but it kept falling apart. When he went inside to help, the slivers of glass began shattering into even smaller pieces.

Some memories lingered longer. For example, he remembered that the Acapulco house fronted a garden with a pretty blue swimming pool and a swing-and-slide set. But as time crept on, he wasn't clear as to what part of his dreams were true. Or whether his memories of the dream house were real. Eventually, the Acapulco house became just another imaginary place in a gradually dimming past.

Micaela fussed over Riki as if he were a proud jewel to be continually polished. She didn't wonder where the lady had gone, or why she hadn't returned, at least not at first. Micaela simply said a prayer of thanks to Tonantzín for every day she was allowed to keep Riki, and each additional day reinforced her belief that it was undoubtedly the Will of God that Riki should replace her lost child.

Since her son had returned to her, the veil of semi-consciousness lifted, bringing the world into focus. She only vaguely remembered trying to kill the woman who claimed to be Riki's mother. Like the attacks on her husband, the incident was a half-dream, like something she had seen in a *cine* projected on the Church wall. Exactly how she obtained Riki wasn't clear, except for a muddled memory of trading two bottles of rum for him. Yet, in this new state of consciousness, that seemed absurd. Why would someone trade a treasure like Riki for two little bottles? Yet, several villagers confirmed this; they had witnessed the transaction with their own eyes.

A premonition lurked in the back of her mind warning Micaela that something was wrong with this situation. Someday, if not the mother, then relatives of the child could come looking for him.

She resolved to protect her interest in her son. She regularly darkened his skin with a mixture of kerosene and black walnut husks to disguise him, in the event strangers came through the village searching for a white *ladino*. Once, when an itinerant trader entered the village with a vanload of wares, Micaela splurged and purchased a pair of plastic sunglasses to disguise the boy's odd-looking gray eyes.

"His eyes are weak," she explained to the villagers. "He must wear dark glasses to protect them from the light." The villagers accepted this because the eyes did indeed look weak — sickly-looking gray, surrounded by ghastly white.

Riki accepted the fact that his eyes were weak; he wore the sunshades as he was told. Fortunately, few strangers ever entered the village. But when they did, Micaela managed to keep Riki out of sight.

Starting from the first day of Riki's arrival, the villagers noticed a profound difference in Micaela. Her distracted, strange mannerisms gradually gave way to normal behavior. Her eyes, instead of staring blankly, gazing at something no one else could see, began focusing on reality.

The child had obviously cured her madness. Neighbors no

longer crossed themselves when passing in front of her store. They no longer feared her. Micaela smiled now, something she had rarely done before her child died. Before her husband abandoned her in fear of his life. Now Micaela laughed at jokes, and even made some of her own. Instead of looking like and behaving like a crazy old woman, she gradually became a vivacious, 19-year-old girl. She put on weight and her cheeks filled out to a cheerful puffiness.

Only occasionally she behaved irrationally; that was when being fiercely possessive of her new son. "Riki is a gift from the Goddess Tonantzín," she insisted. "I prayed for him, and the Saints willed that Riki be mine."

The villagers said nothing to contradict her, at least not to her face. After a while, they began to speculate that perhaps there was something to this.

"Is it possible that Micaela is correct about the Saints sending the boy to her?" said doña Ramirez one day. "Riki's been in the village for two months now, and the drunken woman still hasn't returned."

"The ways of the Gods are mysterious," was the reply. "At first, I thought Micaela crazy when she said those things, but more and more I see how she is cured of the *locura* and how happy she is. Then, too, we all saw the business transaction with our own eyes. The woman clearly traded the boy for the rum. Did the Gods have anything to do with that? Well, who knows? Mysterious ways! Mysterious!"

Micaela worried about clothing for little Riki. The only clothes he possessed were those he wore that first afternoon when he appeared in the village, the bizarre clothes of a man on a little boy. Somehow, that seemed obscene, but exactly why, she could not say.

His shoes were of fine leather. Everything he wore seemed expensive; they wouldn't do at all for the village. Besides, extravagant clothing would surely attract strangers' attention.

One day, Micaela gathered the courage to open the lady's suitcase. Disappointed, she found not one article of clothing for a little boy. Apparently, the woman hadn't thought of Riki's things when she snatched her suitcase from the fancy automobile. Probably his clothes remained in the Rolls Royce, in another suitcase.

However, what she *did* find in the suitcase jarred her mind and chilled her body with a wave of apprehension. She extracted cocktail dresses, soft sweaters and flimsy underthings, laying them aside one by one until she came across the dangerous surprise. The surprise lay hidden in the bottom of the suitcase, inside a long, quilted box. It was heavier than it looked. When she opened the lid, strange music filled the room with a tinkling sound. She gasped in surprise when the glittering contents of the music box seemed to leap out at her.

Her fingers touched a diamond necklace as she stared in fearful astonishment. When she lifted the strand in trembling hands, it sparkled marvelously in the light of the kerosene lamp. She held up a double handful of watches, necklaces, rings, chains and pendants to the light. Gold, silver, and transparent stones with liquid fire in their hearts.

Micaela had never in her life seen anything so beautiful or rich, not even when she was a little girl, the time she visited the ornate church in Orizaba. A shiver chilled her spine at the sight of flashing white fire inside the diamonds.

"*Madre de Dios,*" she whispered in awe, "there must be a fortune in jewelry here. Maybe ten fortunes!" She examined each piece carefully and noted that some bore engraved inscriptions, words she couldn't decipher. She had trouble enough reading Spanish, but these words didn't seem to be Spanish.

Micaela knew little about such things, but she was convinced that the glittering, fiery stones must be diamonds. And she recognized gold when she saw it, for she owned a heavy gold crucifix and chain which had belonged to her great grandmother, her only piece of jewelry. With trembling hands, she packed the precious cache back into the music box, closing the lid to shut off the annoying music.

"This means trouble," she said softly to herself. "*Real trouble.*" The woman leaving the child here is one thing, but someone, someday, will surely come looking for the jewelry. This wasn't part of Tonantzín's bargain. Micaela replaced the music box, covering it with a piece of flimsy lingerie as she shuddered with fearful realization. "Suppose the woman claims that I *stole* the suitcase? I would be punished, thrown in the *cárcel*, and my son would be taken away, gift from the Black Goddess or no. A business trade or no."

She searched through the suitcase contents once again. Nothing Riki could wear. Nothing. Just scandalous underwear and gaudy clothing like that worn by the licentious women who walked the streets of the *zona de prostitución* that time Micaela visited her cousin in Veracruz. The clothing emitted strong fragrances of perfume, adding to the sense of wickedness. One cocktail dress was covered with gold sequins that shimmered like liquid metal in the lamp's orange light. She held it in front of her and drew a breath of delight when she saw the effect of the light flashing off the sequins.

"But there is almost nothing to cover the front! If I wore this, my *chichis* would probably fall out!" She giggled sinfully at the thought as she folded the dress into the suitcase. She snapped the latches and carried it to the corner of the kitchen where she boosted it up into its hiding place beneath the overhanging roof where it would remain out of sight to anyone entering the room.

The next day she discussed the jewelry with don Rafael, the retired schoolteacher. Don Rafael twisted at his moustache ends thoughtfully as he listened to her story. "Riki needs clothing," she ended up saying, "Perhaps I can sell one small piece to buy things for him? Just one necklace?"

"You *cannot* sell the jewelry," he warned sternly. "Not one piece! You must keep it safe for that day when the police come to the village looking for it and looking for the boy."

"But Riki is mine! It was the *Will of God!* A business deal! You saw the trade yourself, didn't you? Everybody saw."

Don Rafael smiled patiently and nodded in understanding. "Mica, you must remember that authorities rarely accept 'the Will of God' as a valid excuse for anything. Yes, they might believe that the woman sold you the child. Just maybe. But the idea of trading a boy and valuable jewelry for only two bottles of rum would be impossible for them to accept.

"No. You must keep the jewelry safe. That is your only protection. If the woman changes her mind about the trade and accuses you of being a thief, you can point out that you didn't steal the jewelry. You were merely saving it for her. That proves you didn't steal the child either. You were just saving both for his mother's return. Your protection is: never sell even one piece of the jewelry. *Never!* And never tell anyone about this. Not even Riki."

She nodded in agreement and thanked don Rafael by kissing his hand in respect.

But she still needed clothing for Riki. She inquired about the village, but of course no one had clothes to fit a four-year-old. So, Micaela cut, stitched, and patched castoff village clothes to make warm things for Riki. His shoes would soon wear out, for his exuberant running about the cobblestone trail and his exploring the raspy lava hillsides were taking a harsh toll on the once-shiny leather shoes.

"He has the energy of a bantam rooster," Mica thought proudly. She found a piece of automobile tire down on the highway and began cutting out a pair of homemade *huaraches* to fit his little feet. She loved doing things for her son. "*Mi niño, mi niño,*" she repeated to herself with warm pleasure. He was truly her son now. She crossed herself and said, "Thank you, Tonantzín, thank you and say my thanks to your son *Jesús* for bringing the boy into my life. If you hadn't arranged the trade, I might have murdered that woman."

The villagers found the boy to be a delightful ray of sunshine to brighten their dull lives. Each morning before breakfast, he scampered across the way to look in on the Ramirez house, then next door to don Rafael's place, and on down the street from one hut to another, until Micaela came after him and brought him home for breakfast. All teased him about his early morning visits, but all looked forward to his brightening the day for them.

"Here comes *the bantam rooster, our alarm clock*," they would say. He enjoyed helping with chores and learning. He held skeins of wool while doña Matilda rolled the yarn into balls. He helped the men process resin. He became an expert at keeping livestock away from gardens, chasing chickens, pigs, and goats with lusty shouts, threats, and an occasional well-aimed pebble.

He learned to chatter away in Spanish and surprised everyone with the adult words he used. Of course, he didn't speak like a typical Mexican child—he couldn't—he had no children to imitate. He heard neither "baby talk" nor the *tu* or *vos* forms of Spanish. He spoke with the reserved formality of an adult. He acquired the only Spanish accent he'd ever heard, the soft slurring speech of mountain Indians, colored with *Nahuatl* and *Azteca* words left over from the days before the Conquest.

At first it seemed humorous to hear a little boy speak like a grownup, but after a while people tended to forget that Riki was a child. They conversed with him as if talking to another adult, speaking with solemn dignity of the village. He absorbed customs of respect and the value of personal honor. These were his first lessons, but there were more to follow. Many more lessons.

The months passed. Riki's clothes became thoroughly Mexican-Indian right down to the leather-strap huaraches with rubber soles that Micaela bought from a passing vendor. A woven reed hat kept cold mist and burning mountain sunshine from his head.

With the hat and the Indian style clothing, a passerby would notice nothing unusual about Riki. Unless one looked into those startling eyes, Riki appeared to be an ordinary urchin from an ordinary *Indio* village. Even though his skin lost its Acapulco sun-burned darkness, he was still dark enough to be within the range of many Mestizo children seen playing in the streets of other villages, even without the artificial darkening applied religiously by Micaela. The rare outsider who chanced to visit Tezcatlipocas noticed nothing odd about the boy.

As the months passed, Riki couldn't remember exactly what his mother's face looked like; he began to wonder if he would recognize her when she returned for him. Probably not, because she had only been visiting the Acapulco house for a short time before she took him on the ill-fated trip to Veracruz. He barely knew her and found it hard to believe that Diana could really be his mother.

But his father's face, he was sure he could never forget. Every night, just before he drifted off to sleep, he visualized his father and the games they used to play. He tried to picture each item of furniture in the Pebble Beach home, each of his toys in his room, and the interesting things in his father's studio-office.

He remembered that the Acapulco beach house was much smaller than the Pebble Beach place, with just three bedrooms: one for his father, one for Riki and one for guests. Robin slept in his father's room. Occasionally Diana stayed overnight in the guest room, but it was obvious that this displeased Robin.

He continually puzzled over why his father didn't come to the village to get him. Every night, just before he drifted off to sleep, he searched his memory to recall what he had done to displease his father. *Why am I abandoned? Why? Does my father hate me?*

As the months dragged by, turned into years, memories grew fainter. Images of both houses became fragile dreams, then absurd abstractions, blurred, until the only thing that remained clear in Riki's mind was an image of his father sitting behind his paper-cluttered desk, writing on a yellow pad. The crystal statue sat on one corner of the desk, a lamp with a stained-glass shade balanced the other corner. Each night, the visions became a little more difficult to remember, a little more dreamlike. His love for his father gradually turned to resentment and finally, anger at his rejection from his father's world.

Don Rafael, who lived almost directly across the trail, particularly enjoyed Riki's visits. Don Rafael was one of the few villagers who did not have to gather resin or firewood, nor did he knit sweaters. He lived on a small pension from the government for his years of service as a schoolmaster. Deep wrinkles lined his face—his hair was snowy white, with a handlebar moustache that curled up on the ends like the horns of scrub cattle. His round eyeglasses were so thick they magnified his eyes. Don Rafael's face seemed to be all eyes and moustache. Many years had passed since don Rafael last taught children; he delighted in having a pupil once more, a pupil who enjoyed learning. Sitting on the teacher's lap, Riki would turn the pages of the books and listen while don Rafael explained the pictures and pointed out the letters and their sounds. Riki loved this; he remembered his father doing the same thing.

Because don Rafael had a large collection of history books, Riki soon knew the names of many revolutionary generals, even though he hadn't the slightest idea what a revolution was or what a general did. Obregón, Francisco Villa, Felipe Angeles, and other names came readily to his lips when talking to don Rafael. The boy learned so quickly that the old man couldn't contain his amazement. He bragged about Riki all over the village.

"Can you believe it? The boy can read many words! Just from looking at the words and the pictures, he can spell out the meaning!"

The villagers smiled warmly, sharing don Rafael's pride.

Riki became part of everyone's family, a surrogate grandchild.

It was don Rafael who helped Riki over much of his original confusion over being abandoned. He tried to draw the boy out about his family. "Where is your home?" he asked.

"Across the road. In Micaela's house."

"No. I mean where does your family live? Your mother and father? Your brothers and sisters?"

Riki furrowed his brow in a very adult way and tried to explain. "My father lives someplace called *Pebble Beach*. And we have another house, too, in a place called *Acapulco*, or something like that. But I don't have any brothers or sisters. At least I don't think I do. I don't remember any." The way Riki pronounced the words, don Rafael heard: *Pebbabeech* and *Apuco*.

"And your mother?"

"You mean Diana?" He shrugged. "I don't know where she lives. Sometimes she lives with my father. Mostly we live with a lady named Robin in our house. And there's a swimming pool in the back yard. I have my own room, and Robin sleeps in my daddy's room."

"A woman who is *not* your mother sleeps with your father?" Don Rafael had difficulty keeping the indignation from his voice. "More than one woman?"

Riki nodded happily. "I like Robin a lot. And I had hamsters and white rats in my room, too." Riki didn't have the Spanish word for "swimming pool" in his vocabulary, so he tried to explain to don Rafael, using the words he'd learned thus far. And he tried to describe hamsters and white rats to don Rafael.

Finally, the old man understood that there was a cesspool, or something of that nature, very close to the house where Riki lived, and that his father allowed him to wade in it. The father evidently was rather immoral, because he slept with any trollop he could lure into his bedroom, sometimes two at a time! Don Rafael decided that *Pebbabeetch* and *Apuco* must be rather squalid places to live.

He shuddered at the thought of children playing in open

cesspools. But the worst part was that the child had been forced to sleep in a room infested with rats and other vermin, where horrid beasts called *jamsters* ran about freely during the night, sometimes even creeping into the poor boy's bed to sleep with him. The very thought made don Rafael's skin crawl.

When don Rafael told the villagers, they shared his revulsion. "Clearly, Riki is far better off living with Micaela than in such an unhealthy place as Pebabeetch," don Rafael observed. "I'm not a believer in religion, and I can't swallow that manure about gods and saints, but it is a miracle that the child ended up in Micaela's loving care."

Doña Leonora pointed out, "The boy is good for Micaela. He cured her *locura*. That's something all the prayers in the world couldn't do."

"Let us pray that the drunken woman doesn't come to take the boy back," doña Maria worried out loud. "That would be a sin of unspeakable consequences. Imagine the horror of living with rats, vermin, cesspools—such an immoral life! Here, at least, he has a clean house and a loving village to take care of him."

The villagers, without putting the idea into words, unanimously resolved to protect the boy from having to return to the filth and squalor of Pebabeetch or Apuco. After that, strangers would have a better chance of getting money from a villager than getting information about a lost boy. Needless to say, the villagers were quite protective of their money. The scandal of the drunken woman running away with the vegetable seller and trading the child for two bottles of rum never quite faded in the village. As Velia Jiménez remarked, "It certainly seems strange about gringos, that they dress so rich and drive such expensive autos, yet they live like pigs at home. Don't they know about keeping cats around to chase the rats away?"

"Maybe they spend all their money on clothes and autos and can't afford to feed cats," suggested her husband. "Or maybe the *jamsters* eat cats. I wish Gustavo Sanchez hadn't moved to Mexico City, for he once worked in *Califa* and could tell us more about how gringos live."

The economy of Tezcatlipocas was simple. Men climbed high on the mountain slope each morning to gather resin and firewood. The women tended small gardens planted in the sparse soil among black lava formations. At night the men joined their wives around sooty fires in the center of the hut and together they knitted sweaters. A stingy entrepreneur from Orizaba came once a month to pick up the finished sweaters, heavy and warm, which he sold for a scandalous profit in the city markets. Another dealer bought the accumulated resin stocks about every three weeks or so.

Every month, life in Tezcatlipocas became more precarious, a little harsher than the last month. Someday, they feared, all must leave—one way or another. Then the village would be abandoned, gradually crumbling into rubble and oblivion. The village at the top of the mountain pass was about to end three thousand years of continuous existence.

The only viable alternative to this cruel existence was moving to Mexico City. The younger people had already done exactly that, leaving Tezcatlipocas to the middle-aged and the elderly who feared the specter of starvation in that crowded metropolis of twenty million souls.

"But they tell me there is work in *la capital*," mused Santiago Rodriguez.

His *compadre* snorted in derision. "Work? You have over 65 years under your skin. You are an old man. What kind of work could you do?"

Santiago shrugged. "Something. Maybe sweeping streets or something. They say that women have an easier time getting jobs than men, because they can work in the houses of the rich. My wife could work, and we could save our wages and..."

"Don't be a fool. Rich people hire young *muchachas*, not

worn out *viejas*. Think about it, man, we are not young anymore. Soon we won't be worth a broken cup. Here, at least we can collect resin and trade it for food. Here, we pay no rent. Here, we can trap rabbits and raise a few beans in our yards. Maybe we don't eat well, but we eat."

As time went on, Riki became a cog in the village mechanism. Every morning he accompanied the men as they climbed the mountain to collect resin; he quickly became a proficient collector for his age. Jorge Márquez made him a machete just his size. He imitated the men, swinging the machete in a wide arc, to bury the blade deep into a black pine trunk to start resin oozing down the trunk like streams of honey. He worked with the determination of a grown man. He learned to trim dead branches into hearth-sized pieces of firewood with quick slashes of the sharp blade. He tied them into bundles, hoisted them on his back, and carried them down the trail to the village, placing each foot just right to balance the load, sidestepping from stone to dirt like a mountain goat making his way down the trail. He enjoyed physical labor.

As he grew taller, his body acquired muscle and tone far beyond his years. The thin air of the sierra required huge lungs and a broad chest to take in sufficient oxygen. His body widened as he grew taller. His arms and chest rippled with muscle, taut as rawhide. He worked equally with the men and they respected him. He became thoroughly Mexican-Indian.

He never stopped wondering why his father hadn't come to take him home, but he kept these thoughts to himself. Although the villagers tried to keep the shameful story of his abandonment a secret, he was acutely aware that it was a common font of conversation. This became his private agony. His resentment toward his mother and father grew silently along with his humiliation. He tried to avoid thinking of his parents, to avoid the feeling of shame, to avoid feeling worth so little as a human being. Two small bottles of rum! *¡A la chingada!*

63

While don Rafael attended to teaching Riki to read, the village women saw to it that Riki's religious education wasn't neglected. They taught him to make the sign of the cross in the elaborate and complicated manner the Indians evolved from the early Christian invaders. He learned to be humble in the face of the Gods, to perform the proper rituals necessary to ensure good luck for the village. All this was complicated, because although villagers accepted some principles of medieval Catholicism, they still worshiped the ancient pantheon of gods. Just in case.

They observed the ancient calendar system, which recognized a different god in charge of each day of the month. To further complicate matters, the year had thirteen months, each of twenty-seven days, plus some "unlucky days" to fill out the year. As if that weren't enough, each month had its own proprietary god, so every day in the year ended up with a different name, that is, a combination of several gods' names. The different names wouldn't repeat for fifty-two years, when a new round began.

"I'll never be able to remember this," Riki complained. "Why is it important?"

"Don't worry. You will grow up to be a man," replied doña Maria, "and men aren't expected to remember religious things. Just women. But the month gods are important, you must be familiar with them, at least. They control your life. If the month gods are angry, you will be punished. If they are respected and pleased, you will have food to eat and sunshine on your head."

Riki wasn't eager to learn about religion, but finally he was able to recite the month gods and also the day gods without missing too many. This pleased the village women.

Doña Maria was the oldest woman in the village, toothless, with gray hair the color of freshly broken cast iron. Some said she was a *bruja*, a witch, therefore the best qualified to teach the youngster about the proper rituals and ways of religion. "Every god has two faces," explained doña Maria. "When the good face looks on the village, we prosper. But when the ritual is forsaken, or when the god is angry, the evil face looks upon us.

"Gods also have two names — one for each face. For instance, the god Tezcatlipocas, for whom this village was named, is *Smoking Mirror of Death*, the god of war. His other image is Huitzilopochtli, *the Hummingbird Wizard*, the god of peace and life. Huitzilopochtli and Tezcatlipocas of course, have a sister. Her name is Ciuacuátl. The evil side of both brothers. Only one god has one name: *Tonantzín*, the Earth Mother. She is the mother of Jesūs. The priests call her 'The Blessed Virgin', but that's the white man's name. Before the Spanish came, she was simply Tonantzín, the Earth Mother. She is the God above all Gods."

Riki tried to remember everything. He wanted to perform rituals properly and not bring bad luck to the village. He learned to place stones of the correct color and right size along the edges of a cornfield, pointing to the sacred directions, north, south, east and west. He learned how and why men plant a few *tonzontli* stalks to grow around the field in a way pleasing to the gods. He learned the hierarchy of gods, from the very ordinary one that regulated bowel movements, to the top one, Tonantzín, who held the power of life or death in her hands.

"In the old days, before white men," doña Maria explained, "our priests used to sacrifice human hearts to Tonantzín. This was the proper way. But the white man's priests stopped this. Today, we burn candles instead. Clearly you can see Tonantzín isn't happy about this. We are poor, hungry, and suffer because of the substitution. Just look what She did to our village church; she made the roof burn away."

Doña Maria smiled as she told of the foolish Protestants who come evangelizing to the village from time to time. "They believe *Jesūs* is the most powerful, most important god! How stupid. Just think about it... has anyone seen pictures of Jesūs when he was not either a little boy, obeying his mother, or else

65

as a weak, bloody man nailed to a cross?

"No man would ever touch his mother, for Tonantzín would rip him to shreds for even thinking such an abomination. She would tear his heart from his chest and feed his entrails to the vultures!"

Sex education in most villages the size of Tezcatlipocas would have meant listening to the whispering of other boys and guessing at certain rustling noises that sometimes take place in the dark cover of night when children are supposed to be asleep in their corner of the hut. But in Tezcatlipocas, there were no children to whisper. Certainly, no rustling noises in Micaela's house disturbed the evening's tranquility. For that matter in few of the other huts either, given the age of the villagers.

Village men, of course, seldom speak of sex, unless it is to make oblique, obscene jokes. Men were not a source of information about sex.

Village women traditionally lecture their daughters on the sin and pain connected with the sexual act. They explain how they must submit to God's will; they must submit to the animal instincts of a man once they are married. Painful and distasteful as it may be, sex must be accepted a part of the punishment of original sin. For a woman to enjoy sex would be a sin, something only done by wanton, unrespectable women, *putas*. Armed with this knowledge, village girls willingly go along with the strict system of segregation of the sexes in the village, and almost all girls manage to maintain their virginity until the marriage ceremony. Convinced that sex was painful and revolting, some women protected virginity far beyond the marriage ceremony.

However, Tezcatlipocas had no village girls to tempt Riki or to teach him the complicated courtship patterns. Still, he somehow absorbed knowledge about the dangers of sexual misbehavior.

His first lesson came when he saw two elderly village women bathing in the little stream, in the pool where they washed clothes. Riki, used to swimming nude in his own swimming pool, immediately stripped off his clothes and scampered toward the water. Shouts and angry gestures stopped him at the water's edge. Puzzled, he backed away, wondering what he had done wrong.

After the women pulled on their dry clothes, they took him by the hand and began explaining the facts of life as they walked back to the village.

"The Gods will punish you severely for going naked in front of women, just as they punish women for going naked in front of men. You can lose your ability to have children when you are grown. And even worse, you can be struck blind if you see a naked woman."

Because Riki had a grown-up's way of speaking, the women tended to forget that he was but a boy and had a limited vocabulary. They outlined a complicated set of rules, much as they would have given a daughter, using many words that Riki couldn't even guess at. He was told that "doing things unnaturally" merited the worst punishment, that of blindness and paralysis. Since he hadn't the vaguest notion of what "things" they were referring to, doing them unnaturally remained a mystery. Obviously, the matter of going naked violated some kind of religious taboos that doña Maria had neglected to tell him about.

After Riki had been living with Micaela for three years, something happened that made him wonder if he had neglected a religious ritual.

He had climbed the mountain to collect resin on this day. Micaela opened the store at her usual time, shortly after daybreak. She was sitting behind the counter of the store, pulling strings of boiled beef to make *machaca*, when doña Concepci6n came running to the door. She was out of breath.

"Be careful, Mica! There is a stranger in the village—he's looking for Riki!" She pointed in the direction of the highway.

"He's coming this way. Asking everyone he sees about that day when..."

Micaela dropped the bowl of machaca in her hurry to get to the door. Then she saw him. The man had a mean face, sharp cheekbones and narrow slits for eyes. A thin ferret moustache added to the impression of coldness and danger. He wore a black felt hat with a white band, the style of city folks, a striped suit and a white tie. Micaela stepped back from the door in horror.

"Who is he? What does he want?"

"I don't know. He may be a criminal, because he is carrying a gun in his waistband. Don Luis Alberto saw it. Where is Riki?"

"Up on the mountain."

"Good. Don't worry, no one will tell the man about Riki. Oh yes, there's someone else with him — someone waiting in an automobile, by the highway."

Micaela drew in a sharp breath. "Is it... is it a woman?"

"No. A man, probably a gringo. He was just sitting there, looking around. He might be a criminal, too."

Doña Concepción suddenly frowned and pulled her reboso tight around her chest. "*Dios mio!* He's coming this way!"

Micaela ran behind the counter and crouched down. "Get rid of him! I don't want to talk to him!"

When she heard footsteps scuffling on the cobblestones of the trail, she stiffened and braced herself for the man to appear. Concepción edged away from the door and hurried away when the man reached the door. He looked at the fleeing Concepción with a suspicious eye. Then he turned his attention to Micaela.

"My name is Enrique Morales," the man said in a surprisingly soft voice. "Here is my identification — As you can see, I am a private investigator, licensed by the Ministry of Justice." He paused while Micaela pretended to read the document the man held out. She was too nervous to read anything, particularly such small print.

"I'm looking for a boy — a gringo boy who was lost in these

mountains three years ago." Morales unfolded a piece of paper. It had Riki's picture on it. "Recognize him?"

Micaela felt her throat tighten. She shook her head nervously. "No lost boys in this village."

The man rubbed his chin and seemed to be absorbed in thought. Then he asked, "Who owns this store?"

She hesitated only briefly before saying, "I own the store. Why do you ask?"

"Many people from these mountains come to this store to buy supplies, right? Maybe not every week, I understand, but eventually they all come here. Is that correct?"

"I suppose so."

"Take another look at this poster. Are you sure you haven't seen him? This photo was taken when he was four years old. If he is still alive, he would look older, of course. Has he ever been in your store?"

Micaela's chest felt as if it were paralyzed. She wanted to breathe, but nothing was happening. Finally, she swallowed hard and studied the picture of Riki on the poster. She knew she couldn't speak without giving herself away; she just shook her head.

"Then, would you mind if I posted this on your wall? If the boy is anywhere in this area, someone will see this poster and he will claim the reward."

"Reward?"

"A *big* reward. This boy's father, Mr. Barron, will pay the amount listed on this poster. Here, read it." He held the poster out to Micaela, but she shook her head and backed away.

"I can't read much. What does it say?"

"It says there is enough reward offered to make every family here rich for the rest of their lives. Not only that, if the person who turns up the missing child mentions seeing the poster in your store, you get 1,000 pesos. Just for showing it. How do you like that?"

She watched anxiously as the man pulled the pistol from his

belt and used the butt as a hammer to tack the poster against the plastered portion of the wall where the official notices from the government were displayed. The pistol seemed enormous. When he finished, he turned to look closely at Micaela. She felt as if his eyes were piercing into her very soul.

"Remember, there is a lot of money involved. You could be rich if you only find this boy. The whole village could be rich."

She nodded dully. When he finally left, she closed the door and leaned her back against it. She forced herself to breathe deeply until the dizziness went away. Then she went to examine the poster. She tore it from the wall and began sounding out the words letter by letter.

She read very poorly but did understand that a man named *Alexander Barron* was willing to pay to find a lost boy, and also to recover some lost jewelry. There could be no question that the picture was of Riki. And the jewelry could be none other than the cache hidden under the rafters in the kitchen.

Her hands shook so badly that she had a hard time lighting the match. It sputtered in her hand and soon touched off a yellow flame that consumed the reward poster. Micaela dropped it to the earthen floor while it flamed. When it was nothing but a sheet of black ash, she ground the poster's remains into the clay and smoothed it over with her shoe until there was nothing left of it but a dark smear, like a dirty conscience.

Then she gathered some food into a knitted rebozo, locked the store and hurried to look for Riki.

She found him trudging down the trail with a trumpline of resin slung across his forehead.

"Come with me," she ordered. "You can't return to the village. It's dangerous there."

"Why? Where are we going?"

"To hide. It's dangerous in the village. You must understand that there are bad people in this world. You must always be careful that they don't grab you and take you from me."

He adjusted the trumpline and turned around on the trail, waiting for her to take the lead. "Why would they take me away? What would they do?"

"Never mind why. You must be very careful. When you see a stranger, you must turn your face and never let him see your eyes. That is most important. If they see your eyes, they will take you from me."

"But what if my father comes here someday? Maybe he will come to take me home."

Micaela's look of horror told Riki that he had said something terrible. He followed her dutifully as she climbed higher and higher into the mountain brush. They hid there for two days. It was cold and they shivered at night. Riki couldn't help but feel more resentment against his father for abandoning him.

After Enrique Morales posted the reward notice at the store, he walked back to the jeep. Alexander Barron paced about impatiently, studying the village through a pair of powerful binoculars. When he saw Morales, he pointed at the roofless church.

"Look! An abandoned church, like the one Rexford described! This could be the place!"

Morales wrinkled his brow and looked about with skepticism. "Not necessarily. You see, many churches around here are roofless. Government soldiers burned them during the *Cristero Rey* revolt back in the 1920s. There was a lot of fighting in this area. Many churches were never rebuilt. So, the church doesn't prove anything. Besides, I've been looking at maps of this area, and as best as I can figure, the road through here has been closed off for over twenty years. They *couldn't* have driven this way. Best we can hope for is that someone will step forward with information."

"Nobody remembers seeing Rickey? Nobody remembers a Rolls Royce coming through here that day?"

The detective shook his head in frustration. "No one will even talk to me. When I ask about your son, tell them about the reward, they just shrug their shoulders and turn away. Most mountain *indios* tend to show tight mouths to strangers, but this place is the worst.

"However, I posted a reward notice at the only store in town. If anyone knows anything about the boy or the jewelry, you can be sure they will get in touch with me once they see the reward money. It's more than ten men here could earn in a lifetime."

"But I can't shake this feeling..."

"Believe me, señor Barron, the news of the poster will travel into the deepest canyons of these mountains as quickly as if you had painted it on the sky. Gossip is the only form of communication in these parts, but it's efficient. The store owner is no doubt telling her neighbors all the details. At this very moment their stomachs are growling with hunger for the reward."

Alex leaned dejectedly against the jeep. "Rickey couldn't have just disappeared! *Someone* must have seen him, heard of him. Dead or alive, somebody must know something."

"I agree. What puzzles me most, Mr. Barron, is the jewelry. It is remotely possible someone might steal a boy and raise him as a son. Things like that happen. People have been known to kill..." Morales caught himself in time, and said, "But it is *not* reasonable to think someone would steal valuable jewelry and not try to sell it. The jewelry is the key. When we find that, we'll know what happened to your son."

"Maybe the jewelry is here, in this village."

"Look around you, sir. With poverty like this, do you think these people would keep valuable jewelry for their personal use? Perhaps to wear to dinner parties? Or to the opera?"

Alex trained the binoculars on the church. One of the walls had eroded until it was no more than a meter high in some places. Only one wall corner was complete — the corner supporting the bell tower front, the one that made the old structure look like a church. That was the wall where the village had seen Diana Cranston's movie, just before Richard Alexander Barron III had come to the village.

"I think we should go, sir. We have three more of these mountain villages to visit before it gets too dark to maneuver these trails."

Alex nodded reluctantly and looked about once more before returning to the vehicle. Something about this village bothered him. It was as if some sixth sense were being agitated. He felt a strange familiarity with the place, as if he'd been here before. Then he realized that perhaps he had been here — right after the accident — when he and Johnny Gee had visited many, many villages.

Enrique Morales started the engine and motioned for Alex to get in. But a sudden movement on a trail above the village caught Alex's eye. He lifted the binoculars and adjusted them. Two figures climbed a steep trail of black volcanic ash. One was a woman with a colored sack over her shoulder. The other figure was doubled over under a bulky load which he carried on his back with a trumpline over his forehead. Alex lifted the binoculars to take a closer look.

The woman looked back at the village below, and Alex could see her face. Even from this distance he could tell that she was rather young. The other figure was smaller, perhaps a boy. It was hard to tell. If a boy, he could have been Rickey's age. The woman turned to look up the trail and must have said something to urge her companion along, because he started climbing more quickly. Suddenly, Alex felt a strange crawling sensation on the back of his neck. Something about the way the boy moved...

"Please, Mr. Barron, we must go now."

"Wait!"

He steadied his elbows on the Jeep top and fine-tuned the binoculars. The smaller figure climbed the steep trail steadily, without any trace of fatigue. Something about the way he walked, something about the way he swung his body when he lifted himself up over a boulder...

"Come here, Enrique! Quickly!" He handed the detective the binoculars. "Up there... On that trail!"

Morales peered through the glasses. Then he shook his head, saying, "I'm sorry Mr. Barron, but I'm sure those are *indios*. You can tell by the way they walk, by the way they carry bundles. That smaller one may look like a boy, but I'm sure he's much older. Look at the way he carries that bundle, the way he steps from rock to rock. Pure Indian."

He handed the binoculars back to Alex with an apologetic shrug. "Most of these Indians are short, Mr. Barron. A grown man can look like a boy from a distance."

Alex grabbed the binoculars and tried to look again. But at that moment, the couple disappeared around a large outcropping of gnarled, cinnamon-colored lava. He stared through the glasses for several long moments, hoping they would reappear. They never did.

"Damn! Every time I see a boy Rickey's age, I think..."

Then he climbed into the Jeep and settled back against the hard seat. "Okay, let's go."

On the way back to Mexico City, Enrique Morales asked for more money. "My expenses are quite high, Mr. Barron. I spend every weekend in the country, asking questions, searching, always searching. And during the week I haunt the jewelry stores and the police delegations, always looking for some trace of the jewels and the thieves. Furthermore, every day in the week there are at least five false leads, impostors who wish to collect the reward, or who want to pass a common Indian boy as your son."

Enrique hated to have to plead with a rich Gringo for a few more pesos, but his new girlfriend was quite expensive and demanding. Not that she wasn't worth every centavo he spent on her, but the idea of playing beggar in front of Barron made him wish he had never met this new dream woman. He took a deep breath, as if to inhale the odor of her body, and released it with a long sigh of melancholy.

Alex granted the request with a disinterested shrug of his shoulders. This made Morales angry. He thought: *This Barron guy treats me as if I were some kind of taxi driver, boosting the fares without conscience. I swear, on the day I find the grave of the little Barron bastard, I am going to piss on it!* The thought made him feel a little better. The bonus that Alex Barron gave him, when they reached the Mexico City Airport, also improved his disposition. But each day his frustration level increased by not finding the jewelry. He needed to find the grave of the dead brat.

Chapter Five

The Wedding

San Francisco...August 19, 1972

From the far side of the restaurant, a piano rippled softly through a bolero, competing with the whirring of a cocktail mixer from behind the bar. A faint aroma of cigarette smoke mingled with expensive perfume, hors d'oeuvres, and cocktail conversations. Far below, the lights of San Francisco sparkled like a mantle of stars, spreading down Nob Hill, then up and over Russian Hill in the distance. The usual summer overcast failed to arrive that night. The City's sky glittered under a ceiling of real stars that took over where the floor of city lights ended. The date was August 19, 1972. Across the Pacific, a war simmered in the tiny country of Vietnam, while three people celebrated in Nob Hill's Top of the Mark.

Alex Barron lifted his champagne glass and waited until Johnny Gee and Diana touched their glasses to his. A glint of moisture dampened his eyes as he struggled to control his emotions. He knew this evening could very well be the last time the three of them would ever be together. Alex didn't want to spoil the magic of the evening by making a fool of himself — bursting into tears or saying something stupid. He tried to keep his voice light. "A toast to our fearless warrior, Johnny Gregorio." Three glasses clinked, spilling a drop or two on the tablecloth. "May he do as well on the battlefields of Vietnam as on the football fields of Stanford. May Johnny Gee make the world safe for democracy and apple pie, uphold the honor of our great nation, and all that kind of horseshit."

Johnny grinned happily as he refilled the glasses. A stray lock of coarse black hair curled across his forehead, accenting the little-boy innocence that belied the solid strength and muscle packed away beneath an amiable exterior. Although he didn't look like a football hero, he was one of the best quarterbacks in Stanford's history. An adoring alumni and enthusiastic fans called him "Johnny Gee."

However, Johnny Gee's promising career in pro football was temporarily out of the picture. Instead, he was embarking on another adventure, although somewhat unwillingly. He was on his way to Vietnam. He'd made the mistake of joining the Air Force Reserve before anyone dreamed of war in Asia. Now, he was being called up for two years of overseas duty.

Tonight, his voice slurred from too much of Alex's champagne, which — like everything Alex Barron bought — was the finest available.

"Okay, now's my turn." He held his glass high and thought for a moment. "Here's to Diana Cranston, the most beautiful and talented actress in the whole damned country. No! In the whole damned *world!* Hollywood's gonna be lucky to have her."

Once again, glasses touched.

Alex smiled at Diana and felt a bittersweet pain in his chest. He longed to tell her how much he loved her. For years he had wanted to tell her, but he didn't know how to start. Anything he said would come out like a lovesick high school kid. As long as Diana loved Johnny Gee, Alex was doomed to suffer in silence.

He adored Diana from the very first moment they met. When that happened, he and Johnny Gregorio were Atherton high school sophomores, both playing football, Alex just hanging on, and Johnny well on his way to being the school hero, and Diana a giddy freshman. At first, she dated Alex, but predictably fell in love with Johnny Gregorio, the hero. The three remained close friends, but this was small consolation to Alex. Over the years, Alex nursed this high school crush on Diana in silence.

Diana took Johnny's large hand in both of hers and touched her lips to his knuckles. "Thanks, sweetheart. I only hope you are half right about Hollywood. Every time I think about my audition, I freeze up. Even though it's a very minor part, it's scary."

"You'll knock 'em dead."

She tossed her head to shake a soft wave of light brown hair from her cheek and smiled at Johnny with a look of total love and adoration. Alex always felt a painful jealousy when she smiled "that way," because she never smiled at him like that — only at Johnny.

The Diana Cranston smile was one day to become the hallmark of her career, along with subtle dimples that somehow turned even the hint of the smile into an enticing promise of ecstasy. When Diana smiled into the camera, men couldn't help feeling convinced she was smiling for them alone. As an actress, she radiated an innocent calmness, a mixture of wantonness and innocence, promise and denial. This mixture of contradictions was to be a key element in her rise to stardom.

She said, "Fill 'em up again, boys. It's my turn to toast." She held the glass in both hands and stared with fleeting melancholy into the bubbling champagne. She wasn't used to drinking. As far as Alex knew she never before tackled more than three drinks in one evening. Her voice sounded husky as she said: "Here's to the *three* of us. May we meet here again — in this very place — when this war is over. We will then drink to the day Johnny Gee comes marching home. May we celebrate exactly as tonight. May our friendship live forever."

Alex forced himself to nod enthusiastically. He was determined to be casual. He tossed down the champagne in his glass, then motioned to the waiter and pointed at the almost empty Dom Perignon bottle.

"Are you okay, Alex?" Diana asked.

"Of course. It's just... Well, I have a feeling that this is the end of something special. A turning point in our lives."

Johnny Gee nodded. "Things change fast, don't they? Alex is the only one whose plans aren't going to change much. Gonna stay with the Barron Agency, right?"

"What else? Besides, I *like* advertising. When Dad died, they put me on the board of directors. Can't fire me now." He smiled sheepishly and finished his champagne. "Seriously, I hope each of us makes an effort to keep our friendship alive. Johnny in Vietnam, Diana in Hollywood, me in San Francisco — we could lose touch."

Johnny narrowed his eyelids as an idea suddenly struck home. He grabbed Diana's hand, his eyes sparkling with boyish excitement. "Hey! Why wait? Why not get married before I go?" He grinned impishly. "We could drive to Reno tonight! Tell me that's a good idea."

She shook her head, giggling at the idea. "You're goofy. I mean, we know we're going to be married someday, we've always known that. But why complicate things? Wait 'til you get back."

Johnny appealed to Alex, asking, "What do you think ol' pal? Don't you agree? Can you think of a *better* time to get married? Hey Alex, how long would it take to drive to Reno in that big ol' Continental of yours?"

"Reno? Tonight?" Alex's throat tightened and a sick feeling punched him in the stomach. He managed to sputter a few words, surprised to hear himself saying, "Sure, we could make it to Reno easily enough, but Diana's right. It just doesn't make any sense to..."

"There, you see?" Johnny said to Diana. "We can make it easily." His huge hand clasped Alex's shoulder and squeezed tightly. "Thanks, Alex. You'll *always* be our best man. Always."

"But, Johnny," Diana protested, "We can't simply..."

"The hell we can't. Just watch us! We'll find one of those all-night marriage mills and we'll just *do* it!"

Diana looked skeptical and turned to Alex for support. "Tell him, Alex, tell him he's crazy and idiotic. If that isn't enough, remind him that he's stinking drunk."

"Come on, Alex, doesn't it sound like a great idea? Besides, we'll hit the crap tables while we're at it. Have a million laughs. We'll make it back in time for me to report at Travis Field tomorrow. Right? Say right!"

Alex desperately searched for something to say to get this thing off the track. He tried to joke about it by saying, "If you two just want to make honest *citizens* of yourselves, you don't have to do it tonight. If you want my opinion..."

Diana straightened up imperiously as if she had been insulted. "Sir, I resent that snide remark about making honest citizens of ourselves. You are talking to a virgin, sir. Well, *practically* a virgin — because Johnny and I don't do it that much. Not as much as I'd like to. Besides, when he's been drinking, he has trouble getting..."

Johnny clamped a hand over her mouth and pulled her close to him. "Let's do it, Alex? Okay?"

"Look, if you really want to go to Reno and party, I suppose we could do that. Final celebration. But marriage is a bad, *bad* idea. Suppose something happens to you, Johnny?" Alex was angry with himself for having said anything positive about the crazy idea of marriage. "Where would that leave Diana? Don't you think that..."

"Nothin's going to happen. Ol' Henry Kissinger's negotiating with the Viet Cong right now, as we speak. Anyway, I have so much training coming, the goddamn war'll be over long before my two years are up. Then, when I get back, we'll all meet at this same bar, order from the same menu, listen to the same music, and then..."

Diana smiled at him and in a forced stage whisper said, "And then? And then?"

"And then... Diana and I will get a room and screw our

brains out."

She punched him on the arm and pulled at his hair. "Just my luck, you'll have too much to drink again, you bum!" Then she smiled, a dazed look in her eye, and said, "Well, I wouldn't mind going to Reno. But I *don't* wanna get married! Okay? I wanna play slot machines. Hate crap tables."

Alex signaled a hovering waiter for the bill, indicating that he'd take the almost-full champagne bottle with him. "Okay, as long as everyone behaves. No fighting, no farting, no getting married. Got it?"

Had Diana not been so high on champagne, and had they not picked up more bottles to sustain them on the trip, she would never have married Johnny. Not that night anyway. Alex thought it over many times afterward and he felt convinced of this. *And, of all things, I had to be the one to drive them to Reno!*

They casino-hopped in downtown Reno, with Diana winning consistently on the slots while Alex and Johnny lost at the crap tables. She started drinking scotch. This was the first time either of them had seen her intoxicated. In fact, she was gloriously drunk.

The actual wedding ceremony was a farce — at five a.m. — with the justice of the peace suffering from a hangover, and the bride and groom so sloshed they had to cling to each other to keep from falling.

Immediately after the ceremony, while Johnny was paying the bill, Diana ran outside to throw up. Alex followed and held onto her, cleaning her face with his handkerchief. She was sick all that next day and slept through most of the drive down the mountains to Travis Air Force Base. When they went as near to the embarkation point as they were allowed, Diana looked pale and drawn.

"How are you doing, baby?" Johnny asked. "You gonna be okay?"

She rubbed her forehead and said, "With any luck at all, I'll be dead by midnight. Remind me never, ever, to drink again. It turns my brain into tapioca pudding."

"I mean, will you be okay by yourself? After all, you're a married woman now. Will you get lonely?"

She shook her head. "I'll be just fine. Alex will be around. Any time I get lonely, we'll get together and talk."

Johnny put an arm around Alex's shoulder and squeezed tightly. "Take care of her, will you pal?"

"I'll try. I'll sure as hell try." He wished he'd said something more appropriate.

After Johnny Gregorio disappeared into the terminal, Diana hooked an arm under Alex's and stared at the empty sky for a while. "Getting married was a mistake," she said. "Not that way. Whose idea was it, anyway? I don't even remember."

"I think we were all guilty," Alex replied softly.

He had so many things to say to her, things that stuck in his throat. Finally, as they walked back to Alex's car, he asked, "When's your flight to L.A.?"

"Friday. Dammit, I'm scared." She looked at him speculatively, and said, "Alex, could you... could you come with me? For moral support?"

His heart skipped a beat as he said, "I was hoping you'd ask. But don't worry, you'll do fine. With the experience you've had modeling, TV commercials, not to mention those two stage plays, Hollywood will be a pushover."

"I'm scared, Alex. Anyone can model, that has nothing to do with acting. As for the commercials, if it hadn't been for the Barron Agency insisting on casting me, those would never have happened. And, commercials aren't really acting, either."

"Look, when we get to L.A. I'll talk to the producer. I know him. He's done several commercials for the Barron Agency." He paused a moment, wondering if he dare say more, then added, "Diana, let me say something. If you don't like Hollywood and decide to return to San Francisco, I'll really be happy. I'm going to miss you. A lot."

She kissed him on the cheek. "You're sweet, Alex. You'll always be special."

He put his arm around her shoulder and pulled her close for a delicious instant. It was then that he decided that if Diana succeeded, he'd transfer to the Beverly Hills branch of the Barron Agency.

Chapter Six

It was the day of the screen test. Diana's stomach fluttered. She tried to suppress a nervous twitch in her cheek. She pressed her hand tightly against her face, but the muscles continued to jerk convulsively.

"Please don't let that happen when I'm on camera," she thought in panic. "I think I'm going to be sick. Wouldn't that be lovely on camera? Diana Cranston vomits — take one!"

An effeminate makeup technician named "Ralphie" fussed with her eyelids, begging her to hold still while he finished.

"Which one's the producer," she whispered, "which one's the director?"

"The rather handsome one wearing that ghastly Hawaiian shirt. That's Mr. Wigglestone, the producer. Isn't that an outrageous name, Wigglestone? He is such a dear man, but they say he's a lecher. Absolute lecher. Sleeps with all of the cast, they say. Have you slept with him yet?"

"Which one's the director?" she asked, ignoring Ralphie's question.

"Not here yet. His name is Lance Rexford. Now there's *another* outrageous name. Can you imagine anyone actually named *Lance Rexford?* I'd give a nickel to know his real name. He is an old fart left over from the early days, and not much of a director if you ask me. And he has a son, probably about your age, Lance Rexford Junior, whom they're trying to palm off as an actor. Isn't that hilarious? Lance Rexford *Junior?* Like Rin-Tin-Tin Junior. However, they say he's not nearly as talented an actor as Rin-Tin-Tin."

"What's my competition? How many are going to be tested for this part?"

Ralphie stood back and smiled as if he knew some secret and would like to be teased out of it. Finally, he resumed working, saying, "It wouldn't matter if there were ten-thousand or if there were only two taking this screen test, dearie. The winner for your part will be Carole Lyndon—Mr. Wigglestone's latest passion. Probably fantastic at fellatio. On the other hand, maybe if you entice Mr. Wigglestone into bed and convince him you give better sex than Carole, then maybe. Just maybe."

"I don't believe that. It isn't as if this were a starring role; it's just a minor supporting part. Why would..."

"Please hold still. How do you expect me to work if you are going to bounce about like a cocker spaniel?"

"Why would they fly me down here for a screen test if the part's already been given out? That doesn't make sense."

"Well, it makes sense to the people putting venture money into this project. They want to think they're getting the best cast, the best director, the best technicians and all that kind of whoop-dee-do. But the truth is, the actors they have in mind are either over the hill or inexperienced, and as I told you, the director is still thinking 1940s. Consider yourself lucky, dearie; the picture's going to be a disaster. Wait for the next one, and you may have a career. God knows, you're pretty enough. Are you any good at fellatio?"

"I can't believe you. I just can't."

"Have it your way. I understand how I'd feel in your place. But there's one thing about this movie that's good. The screenplay. I've seen copies of the master script and the shooting script. They're great. The author is a dear friend of mine. Too bad it's all going to be loused up by Rexford and Wigglestone's sex partners. That is, if they ever get into production."

"What does that mean?"

"Rumor is, they're short of capital. You know, you ought to

consider going to bed with Wiggie. Lord knows I'd love to, but I doubt if he's bisexual." With one final touch of powder on her forehead, Ralphie finished and left without so much as a "good luck."

Diana jumped nervously when Alex touched her on the shoulder. "God, I'm nervous. How do I look?"

"If I thought I wouldn't smear your makeup, I'd give you a big kiss to tell you how good you look." He noticed a frown on her face. "What's the matter?"

As she repeated her conversation with Ralphie, Alex rubbed a hand over his chin thoughtfully. Then he said, "Go ahead and give it all you've got, Diana. We'll check this out later if it looks like a phony setup. I've been watching the screen tests so far, and I can't believe you aren't going to do great."

"Kiss me for luck, Alex. To hell with the makeup."

After touching lips lightly, Alex held her in his arms for a long time, patting her back with his hand as if she were a little child in need of reassurance. Then she was gone. He returned to the studio viewing room and sat next to Dan Wigglestone to watch the audition.

"How many are you testing for this part, Dan?" he asked casually.

"Four or five, I would guess." Dan paused as if embarrassed before asking, "Do you have an interest in the casting? A friend, perhaps?"

Alex shrugged. "In a way," he replied, not wanting to tip his hand. He wanted to see how Diana's performance stacked up against the others and then see how the selection process worked. He didn't want to use his position with Barron Advertising to influence anyone. Not yet anyway.

A voice called out, "Test twelve, take one—are we ready?"

The applicant—a thin, fashion-model type—studied the two-page script until the last moment. She was given a few seconds verbal instructions and then shoved toward the center of the set. The lights snapped on, baking the set with white heat. Alex watched the short performance, not more than a minute. While the woman did all right, the sharp slenderness of her body was distracting and not in accord with the character. Diana's turn came next. She didn't look nervous, but Alex knew that inside she must have been quivering. Alex clenched his hands anxiously as Diana moved in front of the camera. She looked so beautiful that he sighed involuntarily. She moved about the small set with a confidence and natural skill that obviously impressed even the technicians and the assistant director. She improvised hand gestures and head movements, gracefully, instinctively, never having to refer to the script. The scene ended with her smiling sadly at the camera. For the first time, Hollywood basked in the sexy warmth of Diana Cranston's smile.

When the lights faded, the technical crew murmured appreciatively, something they hadn't done for any of the other actresses. Alex grinned happily. He sneaked a glance at Dan Wigglestone whose eyebrows were lifted with surprise and concern as he glanced nervously at Carole Lyndon.

Carole Lyndon came on last. A platinum blonde with an empty face and jiggling boobs, she waved at Dan Wigglestone while she waited for the technicians to set up. Wigglestone looked away and squirmed uncomfortably, his face coloring slightly. When the camera lights blinked on, Carole held up the script and began reading. She moved about the set awkwardly, almost bumping into a wall flat because her eyes were fixed on the script. She read word for word; had the story been about Dick and Jane and Spot, the intonation would have been perfect.

"Nice figure, yes, an actress she is not," thought Alex with a great deal of satisfaction. When it was over, the technicians exchanged humorous glances and barely managed to keep from laughing.

At that point in his life Alex knew little about movies, but it seemed clear that Diana had captured her first Hollywood part.

He felt mixed emotions, happy for her, yet knowing this might be her first step out of his life forever. As he ambled toward her dressing room, he tried to arrange the future in some sort of order.

She answered his knock and threw her arms around him with a flood of excitement. "I think I did okay, Alex! What do you think? Was I all right?" Before he had a chance to reply, she began waltzing him about, smearing his lips and cheeks with kisses.

"You were terrific! I knew you would be." He didn't know which would be worse, her succeeding or failing.

She threw her arms around him again and he felt the ecstasy of her body pressed against his. He kissed her on the neck and was astounded to hear himself whisper, "I love you Diana."

"Thanks Alex, I'll always appreciate your sticking with me." She squeezed him again and suddenly stepped back, looking serious. "Tell me the truth: Was it because the others were so bad? Or do you think I'm really Hollywood material?"

"They were bad, but you were fantastic! Absolutely professional and totally fantastic. We'll celebrate tonight."

"Marvelous idea, Alex! Only no champagne. After the other night, I know I'll never drink again." She whirled about like a ballerina and grabbed Alex again for another hug. "I'm so glad you're here to share this with me. I'll never forget this moment!" She kissed him lightly on the lips, then again, with a lingering, voluptuous, dampness.

Alex blushed with happiness. "Wait! I almost forgot! I have a gift for you." He went to the closet and took out a box with gold-and-silver wrappings. "It's something I found at Neiman-Marcus this morning. I thought it appropriate to the occasion."

She tore the wrapping away and opened the protective box, revealing a smoke crystal figurine of the *Huntress Diana*. The sculpture sparkled dramatically in the dressing table lights, crystal magnifying reflections as if made from a dusky diamond.

"It's beautiful, Alex! It really is." She placed it on the

dressing table, too overwhelmed by events to fully appreciate such a gift. She said, "What a marvelous day! I'll never forget a moment!"

"It's a, uh... a statue of Diana, the Goddess of the Hunt," he explained weakly. "Somehow I thought it would be... I mean, it looks sort of like an 'Oscar,' doesn't it?" His words faded in embarrassment.

She squeezed his hand. "You're sweet, Alex, you really are. But here, you keep it for me 'til I've really earned it. After I finish the picture, we'll have a victory celebration. You can give it to me then."

She sat at the dressing table and started removing makeup. "What time are you going to pick me up for dinner?"

He replaced the delicate artwork in the box, disappointed that it hadn't added to her ecstatic happiness. But what the hell, he thought, a piece of crystal is nothing compared to today's triumph and successes yet to come.

The dining room was quiet except for the subdued clinking of tableware, as if customers (mostly tourists) were intimidated by the famous-name Hollywood restaurant. All spoke in whispers, including the stiff waiters with French accents who bowed from the hips, accepting dinner orders as if bestowing great favors. Alex took Diana's hand and gently touched his lips to each of her fingers in turn and ended with a prolonged kiss on the back of her hand.

"I love you, Diana," he said. "I'll stick by you, no matter what. I still don't see how Dan Wigglestone could have passed you over. Even if that blonde freak is his girlfriend."

She wiped a tear from her cheek with her wrist. "Thanks, Alex. You're a dear. But this has been a valuable lesson. Ralphie was right all along. Parts like that go to whoever performs best *off* the set."

Alex frowned thoughtfully for a long moment before he replied, "Maybe Ralphie was right about something else — the screenplay. I'd like to look at the script and see if it's as good as he claims."

"What good would that do? That big-titted cow got the part. And Wigglestone had the colossal nerve to put his filthy hand on my rear and say, 'Don't be disappointed, my dear, I have a *stunning part* in mind for you in my next picture'." She reached for Alex's drink, downed half of it and coughed slightly. "I know what kind of a stunning part he has in mind! He'd better keep his stunning part zipped up while I'm around or I'll belt him one."

"This project may not get off the ground anyway," Alex said thoughtfully. "I was talking to a couple of the investors and..."

"Order me another drink Alex! A double something. I don't care if I do get sick. Want to get Wigglestone off my mind. *Stunning part*! He can give his stunning part to Ralphie!"

Alex caught a waiter's eye and motioned for a drink. "Let's look up the screenwriter. If it's a possible winner, maybe I'll put some money into the production. Provided I have a say-so about casting."

"But the director? Ralphie claims Lance Rexford's a loser."

"If *my* money goes into the project, I'll make sure we get a new director."

Diana tipped the glass until the last of the drink drizzled through the ice. She replaced the glass on the table and signaled the waiter with one motion.

They located the author the next afternoon. He was a young man, erudite, rather homely, and not nearly as flamboyant as his friend Ralphie. While Alex and Diana studied the scripts, the screenwriter mixed drinks and tiptoed about his apartment with nervous excitement. He knew the future of his screenplay had been nebulous up to this moment. It was no secret that the project was shy of financing, and it was rumored that some investors were on the verge of pulling out, especially after seeing the cast. Since Wigglestone hadn't paid for the screenplay option as yet—everything was on spec—the author had been going through agony and uncertainty. And now, here was the heir to the Barron Advertising empire reading his script!

When Diana emptied her glass, the author took it from her hand and quickly filled it with a fresh drink. After a couple of hours, it became obvious that her brain missed a beat now and then.

Before they left his apartment, the author had a check in his hand for the standard Screenwriters' Guild advance. He smiled dreamily at his benefactors and kissed the check.

"We've got Wigglestone and the others between the proverbial rock and a hard place," Alex said, "the screenplay is our property now. Either the investors go along, or the project goes down the toilet. And I'm glad, because I have the feeling that you're going to really run with this part."

As they left the author's apartment, Alex and Diana realized they had zoomed from the depths of depression to the heights of elation. Time to celebrate Alex's entry into the motion picture industry and Diana's first role as a film actress. They went straight to the Brown Derby, what more appropriate place to toast their entry into Hollywood? Over champagne and Russian caviar, they leafed through their copies of the script and chattered like a pair of giddy children.

Diana held the script in one hand and a flute of champagne in the other and was reading one of her lines when Alex interrupted, saying, "Wait! I have a terrific idea! Instead of giving you Carole Lyndon's role, why not move you into the second lead! You can play the *Madonna*! Why not?"

At first, she was too dazed to reply. "I don't know, Alex." She shook her head uncertainly. "That's a major role. You should have a big name for that."

"So? It's my screenplay now—I can do whatever the hell I want. Besides, if all we need is a big name, we'll add a few letters. How about we bill you as, 'Diana Cranstonkowsky'? That a big enough name?"

"But, the Madonna is a big supporting role. I don't know if I can handle it, Alex. What kind of experience do I have to qualify as a co-star? This could be a major mistake."

He shook his head vigorously. "It's my money, you're a fine actress, and I'm the goddamn producer. So, that's that!"

Diana rested her head against the booth's leather back and gazed at the chandelier for a moment. A smile slowly replaced the frown. She giggled and touched her glass to Alex's in a toast. Her eyes were having difficulty focusing. "Here's to us, Mr. Goddamn Producer."

Closing time was drawing near. Alex said, "I'd better get you back to the hotel. You're going to feel like hell in the morning."

"Do I care? Ask me if I give a shit. Tomorrow, I'll be too happy to feel bad. Let's order a drink to go and we'll head for my good ol' hotel." She put an arm around his neck and let him pull her to her feet. He helped her into the taxi, then hurried around to get in on the other side. She slid over to fall against him, resting her head on his shoulder, saying, "Sleepy. Awful sleepy. Take me home, Mr. Goddamn Producer."

The next morning, the sun burned through the window, causing Diana to flutter her eyelids and turn her head away. She wondered what time it might be and whether there was any compelling reason to wake up. Then as she tried to force her eyes to open, she became aware of body heat from someone next to her. She shook her head gently, but a searing pain ripped through her brain.

Oh God! Someone's in bed with me! She lay still as she desperately dredged her foggy memory for clues. *Where am I? Why am I laying naked in bed? And who the bell is this person next to me?*

Resolutely, she forced her eyes open and tried to sit up. She cringed when a hand slid softly across her back and began caressing her skin. A voice said, "Good morning."

She recognized Alex's voice. Suddenly she remembered, at least some of it. She allowed her head to sink back into the pillow, eyes closed, mouth half open.

"Are you okay, Diana? You had a horrific amount to drink last night."

She snatched the sheet from around her waist and bunched it against her breast. She glanced at Alex in embarrassment. He smiled timidly, his hair hanging over his forehead giving him a little-boy look. Now her eyes opened wide as she tried to swallow to clear her throat.

"My God! Alex! What did we do? Why didn't we stop when..."

"It just happened, Diana. We love each other, don't we? Did we do so very wrong?" His hand eased around her waist now and her loins began to tingle as his fingers teased across her stomach and toyed with her navel. "Remember what you said?"

She pushed his hand away and lay back, pulling the sheet up to her chin. "I think so, but I didn't mean to..." She lay silent for a moment. Then she said, "It's okay, I suppose. I mean, it happened. No harm done."

He slipped an arm underneath her shoulder and moved closer.

"Wait, Alex. We shouldn't. Last night was a mistake. It shouldn't happen again."

He pulled the sheet away to uncover her breasts. She tried to cover them again, but he gripped the sheet firmly. She placed a palm lightly against his cheek as if to discourage him. But without resistance. His tongue persisted until finally, it reached a nipple. The tingle in her thighs grew stronger, overwhelming her sense of discretion. She moved her hand away from his cheek, to cup it behind his head, smoothing it over the back of his neck as she arched her body closer to his.

That afternoon Alex rented an apartment in Burbank, close to the studio rental lots. They began their new lives that evening with Alex cooking dinner, Diana setting the table and the refrigerator cooling a bottle of French champagne.

Chapter Seven

Alex Barron started his career in motion pictures at the top, as executive producer. He paid for his position with a mortgage on his Hillsdale property, flushing his bank accounts, and selling equities inherited from his father. He found someone to take over his accounts at the Barron Agency and he immersed himself totally in learning the film business. Before production got underway, he had time to spend two months asking questions, reading, and hiring experts to provide technical backup.

Getting rid of Dan Wigglestone and Carole Lyndon was surprisingly easy. When the word circulated that Alex had picked up the screenplay option, the investors were furious with Wigglestone for having misled them into thinking it was his property. After threats of lawsuits, he offered to sell Alex his share for a fraction of the actual amount invested. Although Carole Lyndon's I.Q. wasn't much larger than her brassiere size, she was bright enough to realize her days were numbered. She didn't bother to show up for the contract signings.

Getting rid of Lance Rexford was another story. He held a solid contract to direct this picture, and he wasn't about to let go.

Ralphie came up with the solution to this problem, although they didn't realize it at the time. "Robin Summerhill," he whispered in Diana's ear as he was doing her hair one afternoon. "Robin can work around Rexford. Knows editing, directing, and everything one needs to know about this business. Trust me, lovey-cakes, Robin Summerhill can handle

Rexford. Tell you what—I'll ask Robin to drop around and talk to Mr. Barron."

Alex was in over his head at the time, trying to understand what was going on around him. Diana assumed that Robin Summerhill was just another of Ralphie's many gay friends. At this point, Alex didn't need to be bothered with that. She dismissed Ralphie's suggestion and didn't mention it to Alex.

A week before production was to begin, Alex rented a furnished house on Wentworth Circle, a narrow street of expensive homes that winds high up into the foothills, yet only a twenty-minute drive from the studio. The large A-frame perched on a cliff overlooking Los Angeles, the view overwhelming. A glass wall reached to the peak of the two-story roof, opening to a panorama of stars on high and a lawn of sparkling city lights below, reminding Alex of that night in San Francisco, of Johnny Gee's farewell party. They quickly settled into a routine, Alex working on next day's shooting script—usually with the screenwriter, sometimes also Rexford, sometimes alone—often until past midnight. Diana began sleeping in her own room, toward the back of the house, insulated from noise. Their together-time became rare.

One night, after returning from dinner at Chez Fleur, Alex and Diana adjourned to the deck for a nightcap. Diana's drinking was beginning to worry Alex, but he tried to excuse it as a reaction to the tremendous amount of hours they spent working on scripts, learning the business and planning.

They leaned their forearms across the railing and stared down at the flickering light show below. Diana hummed a tuneless melody for a while, then looked quizzically at Alex.

"Why so quiet? Is something wrong?" She moved closer. "What are you staring at, Alex?"

"Nothing. Nothing wrong, I suppose. Just remembering that night in San Francisco. The night you, and Johnny, and I, were..." Diana slipped her arm around his waist and joined him in staring at the carpet of lights below and said nothing. Alex assumed that her conscience was kicking in.

"I've been thinking," he said. "We both know that someday... Someday Johnny Gee will be through in Vietnam. He'll be coming back." A long silence followed before he added, "What happens then? How do we handle it?"

Her hand tightened around his waist as she snuggled closer. "I don't know, Alex. I really don't. Let's don't borrow trouble. Let's not worry ourselves at a time like this. I'm too excited, too happy." She touched her glass to his and quieted his anxieties with the famous Diana Cranston smile. "I'll never forget what you've done for me, Alex. Never."

"Better go slow on the drinks, Diana. We have to get up early tomorrow. Trust me."

She answered by tossing the glass out over the cliff below and listening for the tinkle as it crashed against the rocks. She smirked in self-satisfaction and smothered him with a moist kiss. "You worry too much, Alex. I'll be fresh as a daisy tomorrow."

"I'm concerned, Diana. About us. We've become almost like strangers lately. And seriously, you've been drinking a lot. Too much."

Her reply was to kiss him on the ear. "You're being terribly serious, Alex. But then, you're the boss, and I'm awfully glad you are. One more little drink and I'll call it a night." She went inside, poured another glass, and took it into her bedroom, leaving Alex to continue staring down the hill, at the carpet of lights that stretched as far as the mountains.

When Alex arrived at his office the next morning, his secretary stopped him and nodded toward the open door. "Someone named Robin Summerhill is waiting for you, Mr. Barron, in your office." Her voice clearly signaled disapproval.

"Who the hell is Robin Summerhill?"

"A first-assistant director, I think. Looking for a job, I suppose. *Insisted* on barging into your office instead of waiting out here!" Alex pushed through the door to his office with a growing feeling of annoyance. He hadn't been able to put Diana to bed until after 2 a.m. He wasn't in the mood for dealing with a pushy job applicant.

Robin Summerhill sat on the corner of Alex's desk, toying with the crystal huntress when he entered. She was tall for a woman, almost as tall as Alex, and looked very much the outdoor type. She wore mannish-looking riding togs and a red scarf tied around her neck which tucked into a tailored khaki blouse. The blouse subtly revealed curves, obviously unrestrained by a bra. Robin's hair was pulled back and fastened in a careless bun that allowed several honey-blonde strands to fall over her forehead and one down the side of her cheek.

When Alex entered the room, she took one more look at the Huntress and replaced it on the desk. Her smile was confident and impudent at the same time.

"Robin Summerhill here," she said in a surprisingly husky voice. "Director, editor, and consultant. One of the best in the business. I imagine we'll be working together on your project. So, let's talk about it, shall we?"

"Would you mind waiting 'til you've been hired before we make any momentous decisions?"

"You'll hire me. You need me. Without me, you'll fall on your ass. It's that simple." She smiled smugly, clasped her hands together and leaned back on the edge of his desk.

Alex sighed in exasperation as he glared into her eyes. Then he folded his arms and said sarcastically, "I see. Suppose you tell me just how you're going to save me from total destruction."

She tilted her head and smiled seductively. "God, but you're a nice hunk of man! I think I'm going to enjoy working with you." She picked up the statue again and held it up to a beam of morning sunlight. She smiled at the colors streaming through the crystal.

Abruptly, her face lost its smile. Her voice took on a

business-like edge. "The problem is, Alex my man, you don't know fuck-all about the movie industry. You're going to be fast food for the sharks out there. They know how to chew you up without you ever knowing you've been tasted."

"I'm new, but I'll learn."

"By the time you learn, you'll be bankrupt." Her eyes followed him as he walked around the desk to sit in his leather chair. He sat down and glowered at the intruder. She wasn't beautiful; the tilt of her nose and splotchy freckles placed her in the category of "attractive" instead of gorgeous. Yet there was something undeniably sexy about her. Perhaps it was the husky way she talked, the way she held her body, or the way she sometimes looked at you with her head turned, watching from the corner of her eye. He idly wondered if she might be lesbian. *Robin? Maybe they call her "Bobby"?* "And just who are these sharks?"

"Everyone from the delivery boys to the union reps. Beginning with that shit-head you hired as a director."

"I didn't hire Rexford, I inherited him. But tell me, how do you propose to save the day?"

"You're going to make me co-director and you're going to give me veto power over Rexford."

"He won't stand for it."

"I've worked with him before. Worked *around* him is more accurate." She stood up and walked to the window to stare outside for a moment. Then she turned to face him, and her voice softened. "Believe me, Mr. Barron, you need someone like me. Your director is living in a world of film production that faded away with Shirley Temple's virginity. The fact is Rexford wasn't very good even back then. You allow him to do things the old way, you'll end up with a monster that even I couldn't pull together in the cutting room. Give me the authority, and I'll keep things on track. I'll be your teacher."

He thought about this for a few moments. Robin Summerhill did sound as if she knew what she was doing. He liked her style, even if she was pushy and antagonistic.

He shrugged. "What have I got to lose? Maybe I do need a teacher."

True to her word, Robin sped up production, rounded off the edges and had things flowing smoothly before the end of the first month. They spent working hours together and sometimes worked late at the studio. Alex was a quick learner and absorbed her knowledge and experience with enthusiasm. Robin had ways of making things clear. To his amazement, they began to come in close to budget. Her suggestions — orders, in fact — were feebly resisted by Rexford, but made worlds of difference in both quality and cost-cutting. As the film neared completion, they were actually well below budget.

Alex and Diana celebrated the film's progress with a reception held at their Sunset Circle house one Saturday evening. The screenwriter showed up accompanied by Ralphie the makeup artist; they held hands most of the evening. Most major cast members were there. Many seemed too nervous and ill-at-ease to really enjoy themselves. Robin Summerhill was an exception. She buzzed from one person to another, joking, cajoling, acting as excited as a kid packing for summer camp. Alex knew better. Robin was playing to an audience, but he couldn't figure out why.

"She's attractive, isn't she?" Diana asked. "I assume she's a lesbian. And I can see why women could be drawn to her. There's something special there. If I were to be inclined 'that way', I'd probably be attracted to Robin, too."

Toward the end of the evening, Alex stepped outside to breathe fresh air on the deck. He leaned on the railing and looked over the panorama of twinkling lights below. As it often did, his mind drifted back to that night in San Francisco, and then to the future, with Johnny Gee looming ominously on the horizon.

He became aware of someone standing beside him, then an

arm around his waist. At first, he thought it was Diana. Then he recognized Robin's understated cologne. When he turned to look at her, she took his hands in hers and squeezed them softly.

"We're going to make it, aren't we?" she said with a glowing smile. "We're actually going to be finishing in a few weeks. Incredible. We have some problems, of course. We'll need to talk about that before long."

"Problems?"

"Not tonight. We have a conference scheduled for Monday." She moved closer and placed her hands on his shoulder. "You can't believe how many times I've seen a picture go this far and suddenly, everything goes sour. But this one is going to make it."

"Thanks to you, Robin. I mean that. It was a lucky day for me when you charged into my office and took me in tow."

She replied with a kiss on his neck. Then, to his surprise, she placed her hands on his cheeks and turned his face to kiss him on the lips. "I've enjoyed every minute of it," she said huskily. Another kiss, this one longer, with more than a hint of passion, her tongue darting against his.

Embarrassed, Alex fumbled for something to say. "What... What are your plans after this is over?"

She leaned against the railing, the lights of Los Angeles framing her body, smiled and said, "You mean what are *our* plans, don't you? We're a team. I think we should be looking at other properties for our next film."

"Another film? I hadn't really thought about... I mean, this is not my business. I'm an amateur, Robin, a rank amateur."

"Not anymore. This film is going to make money. Believe it. Maybe not a lot of money, but together, we can pyramid the profits into some great productions. We can't stop now, Alex — not when we're on a roll."

Alex searched for an appropriate response, but the right words eluded him. Instead, he said nothing.

"Come with me." She took his hand and led him toward the

far end of the deck, where it was quite dark. "I need to tell you something important."

When they reached the end of the deck, the darkest part, she slipped her hand over his shoulder and rubbed the nape of his neck in a very sexy way.

"I have to tell you that I am in love with you. Like it or not, I have fallen head over heels, as they say. I think it happened the moment I walked into your office that first day."

He started to say something, but she stopped him by putting a finger against his lips.

"I'm well-known for falling in love with someone on every production I've worked on. But this time, I think it's for real. I really do love you." He tried to keep his voice light as he said, "Robin, I know you're kidding around, but please remember, Diana and I are very close. I'd never do anything to compromise our relationship. I like you; I admire you; I recognize your ability. I admit that I desperately need your help. But it has to be a different kind of relationship between us."

She pulled him close, drawing their bodies together. She whispered in his ear, "Don't you feel *anything* for me, Alex?"

He put his arms around her and returned the embrace. "I'd be a liar if I said there is *nothing*. I'm only human, an ordinary man, with instincts and feelings that go berserk when I'm with someone like you."

"Then love me. Love me as if there were no tomorrow. Forget about everything else but love. Just for tonight."

Alex felt a surge of spice inside when she kissed him, her tongue exploring his lips. He felt an animal urge to draw her even closer. But he pulled back before events could get out of control.

Alex swallowed thickly and said, "Robin, you are a very attractive woman, a very sexy and desirable woman, but you don't seem to understand. I mean, I can't just..."

She breathed deeply and fluffed at her hair for a second. Then she smiled knowingly and said, "I understand perfectly.

You will too, in time. Diana doesn't love you, and I do. You'll see." Before Alex could reply, she disappeared back inside the house.

Again, he leaned his arms on the balcony railing and waited for his heart to slow down. The electricity of her kiss stayed with him far longer than he expected. A brief fantasy of taking Robin to bed flitted through his head, but he pushed it away quickly. Then he felt a wave of sympathy for her, an embarrassment for her lowering herself to such obvious, transparent tactics. Her manipulative behavior lowered his image of her as a business partner. Not for a moment did he consider that what she had said about Diana was true. Diana loved him.

The party broke up before ten o'clock. Robin left with an emaciated literary agent—the one who represented the screenplay's author. They walked out the door, arm in arm, laughing, teasing each other, headed for another party in Redondo Beach. Alex waved good-bye, relieved that Robin had found another amorous interest, and hoping she would forget tonight once she sobered up. Yet he surprised himself by feeling jealous of the agent and wondered how close he was with Robin. An illogical sexual fantasy started playing in his head, but he forced it from his mind.

The last guests hung around until almost 2 a.m. Diana said weary good-byes and dropped, exhausted, onto the sofa. Alex sat next to her, grateful that she had controlled her drinking for once. She had behaved perfectly, and he was proud.

"What did you and Robin have to talk about so long on the deck? Was she making a pass at you?"

Despite his weariness, Alex laughed. "Yes, as a matter of fact, she did proposition me. But don't make a big deal about it. She had a couple of drinks too many."

"Not at all. It just shows that she has good taste. What was your reaction?"

"What do you think? I defended my honor to the utmost.

103

Actually, I told her that I love you and that she was wasting her time. Did I handle that correctly?"

Diana pulled him close and rubbed her nose against his cheek. "You did good." Then she relaxed and let her head fall back against the sofa's headrest.

She lay quietly for a long while, then she said softly, "Alex, there's something I've been thinking about lately. About the two of us, and I hope you take it the right way." He didn't reply, so she continued, "As soon as possible, I need to move into my own apartment. It isn't right for us to be living together, not when production is almost over and promotion starting soon."

"If it's Hollywood gossip you're worrying about..."

"Not just that, although the wrong publicity could be harmful. After all, I *am* married. You know how that looks, with a husband in Vietnam, and all."

"But Diana, we can..."

She interrupted, saying, "Look, Johnny could drop in at any time. His last letter hinted something to that effect. Our situation would not only hurt him, but it would be extremely embarrassing for us. If Johnny makes a scene, publicity could be disastrous."

Alex stared at her as if she were speaking some incomprehensible foreign language.

She continued, "I need to settle things with Johnny before we get any more deeply involved."

"But I've been wanting to talk this out for the past several months! You kept pushing me away. Why couldn't we have discussed this before?" His voice rose and he felt his face turning crimson.

She moved next to him and kissed him lightly on the cheek. "Try to understand, Alex. I care for you, a lot. But I need to do this my way. When Johnny makes it home, I want to let him down easy. Getting married was a mistake from the beginning. I knew that then, and I know it now more than ever."

He swallowed tightly before asking, "Okay, you let him

down easy. Then what? Then do we get married? That's what I want, you know. In case you don't recognize it, this is a proposal."

She didn't answer immediately. The hesitation said more than a thousand words. "I don't know. I care for you, Alex. I deeply appreciate all you're doing for me, but... I'm not sure we are right for marriage. Not just yet. But in any event, we aren't being fair to Johnny. I'd hate to have him discover our secret by reading it in the scandal sheets. See what I mean?"

Diana moved out the following afternoon. Just by chance, according to her, she found the perfect apartment with the first phone call. Alex discovered later that she'd arranged the lease almost two months earlier. Although she found time to have dinner with him once a week, she kept him at full arm's length. "Just until after the film's released, and after I deal with Johnny's homecoming," she promised.

Monday morning, Robin waited for him in the office. She smiled warmly as he entered.

"I seem to have gotten sidetracked the other night," she said. "Actually, there was something else I wanted to talk to you about. A production problem. A serious problem."

"What is it?"

"In a word, booze."

Alex looked at her with slightly narrowed eyes. "What does *that* mean?"

"I mean Diana and booze. Surely you can tell she's hungover almost every morning. That thermos she carries isn't for orange juice. Furthermore, I suspect she's discovered the secret of downers before bed and crank for waking up in the morning. Bad combo."

"So, she drinks a little. This picture's a strain on everybody. I've known Diana since high school, and I can guarantee she's not an alcoholic." He frowned and shrugged helplessly as Robin stared at him with sarcasm in her eyes. He added, "What could I do about it anyway?"

"You could cut her part down to a manageable size. She's in over her head, trying to be a star in her first picture. I talked to the screenwriter about it this morning. It isn't too late to scale her role down and beef up Linda Holmes' scenes. If we cut Diana from the palace sequences, and..."

Alex slapped his palm on the table. "No way! Diana is going to keep the part exactly as is. I won't hear any more about it."

"Well, don't say I didn't warn you. Alex, you're in love. You can't think clearly about this." She stood behind him and put her arms around his chest to pull him tightly to her. "I'm crazy about you, Alex. I want to make this picture a success for you. I want nothing but the best for you. But, if you really want the best for Diana, you'll listen to me."

"I promised Diana that—"

"She doesn't love you, Alex. Women can tell things like that. Diana doesn't love anyone but herself." She eased her body around until she faced him and began touching his face with light kisses. "Give me half a chance, and I'll show you what real love is."

She didn't give him a chance to reply; she pressed her lips against his and began undoing the buttons of his shirt. Without sex for some time, his reactions to Robin's advances were largely uncontrollable, natural responses. His arms gradually circled her body and excitement built until they fell back on the sofa. His fingers trembled as they fumbled with the buttons on Robin's blouse. He knew it was wrong, like something out of a daytime soap opera, but he had no control over the scene. Her breasts felt smooth, firm, tantalizing to caresses. She moved passionately with each touch, increasing his fervor.

He pulled her blouse off and she helped him with the rest of his clothes. "My God, but you're beautiful," he whispered huskily. "I never realized... You're even better than I imagined." She cut off his words with a kiss. Robin's body felt like firm velvet next to his. He lost all sense of time and place. Sensations of warmth, mystery and pleasure flitted through his being, in a way he had never felt with any other woman.

Suddenly, Robin was on her feet, pulling on her clothes. "I think my teaching days are over, Alex. You are on your own now."

"And what does that mean?"

"It means I'm checking out until you do something about Diana. And I doubt that will happen. Call me when editing is done."

Before he could protest, Robin Summerhill walked out of the office and out of the picture.

Toward the end, Alex was doing most of the directing himself. With Robin out of the production end, he began to lean heavily on Bill Vanderhoft, the first assistant director. But costs continued an upward spiral. Dinners with Diana became less frequent, until they stopped entirely. "For appearances sake," she said. Alex tried several times to contact Robin, but he couldn't get past her snippy house maid.

When production finally drew to a close, he was satisfied that the picture had a chance of being good. He began thinking seriously about starting on another. "Providing this one makes money," he reminded himself. Even though he had done everything possible to watch costs, there had been a considerable overrun. A few miscalculations, he realized, would drain the last of his cash, forcing him to borrow even more. He was immensely thankful when the final week of shooting was over.

There remained only a couple of weeks of final editing and assembly before the film would be ready for its first screening. Even then, no one knew for sure whether the public would accept it. After all, the movie had a strong religious theme, something always unpredictable with ticket buyers. The more he thought about it, the more dubious he became. His self-confidence began to ebb like water from a tide pool.

At the cast party, Alex's doubts grew stronger. As he stopped by the portable bar to order a drink, he overheard part of a conversation between two women. Alex recognized one as a wardrobe clerk, the other was a stranger. Neither saw him approach. One was saying:

"What a downer! This is supposed to be a cast party, not a funeral."

"It *is* a funeral, sweetie. Wait 'til you see the finals on this picture. It is going to be a disaster."

"Why?"

"Can you imagine people paying money to see a stupid religious picture with Lance Rexford directing? His style went out with silent films."

"Yeah, and the cast! What do you think of that amateur playing the part of the Madonna? A Madonna with sex appeal? With a hangover, yet?" The woman snickered and said, "She came in half-swacked every morning, and she shook like a vibrator by noon. She was supposed to have a supporting role, but 'Boy Wonder' made her into a co-star." Alex turned away quickly. He didn't want to hear any more. He found Bill Vanderhoft and asked, "What do you think, Bill? Did we do it right? Will it sell?"

Vanderhoft seemed embarrassed and toyed with his drink self-consciously before answering. "Well, to be perfectly honest with you Mr. Barron, we may have some problems."

"Problems? Why didn't you say something before?"

"No one asked me. I'm only an assistant. You and Rexford called the shots. But maybe we can fix it. Let's wait 'til we see the final takes." He tried to locate Robin again. Her maid said, "Miss Summerhill is working on some TV stuff back east, Mr. Barron. I can't give you her phone number. She told me to tell you not to bother her 'til you finished your picture."

"Tell her it's finished."

Chapter Eight

Alex pushed the editing crew and anxiously awaited the finished product. Diana went into seclusion and refused to answer the telephone. The day finally came for the official studio previewing; Alex felt tension building until he felt as if he were going to shatter. He tried once more to contact Diana but again her maid claimed that she was out and didn't know when she would return.

"Tell her the studio preview is set for two o'clock. If she's not too busy, maybe she'd like to attend." He slammed the telephone down as anger and frustration choked at his throat.

A light knock sounded at the door. He growled, "Come on in, the goddamned door's not locked."

The door opened slowly, and Robin stuck her head around the edge. "My, but you sound grumpy. Is it safe here?"

He jumped to his feet and hurried to take her by both hands. "Robin! Where the hell have you been? I needed you. God, how I needed you."

"Aren't you going to say you missed me? Or did you just miss my help?"

He pulled her forward to kiss her, but she turned her head so his lips touched her cheek. "You don't know how much I missed you, Robin. I'm so sorry I drove you away. I thought about you a lot. Every day and every night. Why didn't you answer my calls?"

"You made it perfectly clear, Alex. It was Diana, right or wrong. I can't see butting my head against that old stone wall. By the way, did she ever straighten up, or did she get worse?

Are you still, well... *that way* over her?"

He sighed. "I'm not sure of anything. But you were right about several things. For one thing, Diana doesn't give a damn about anyone but herself. Toward the end of production, the drinking got worse." He tried to pull Robin closer. "I've thought about you a lot."

She kissed him lightly as she pulled away. "Don't like to say I told you so. But I told you so. How does it feel to have a disaster on your hands?"

"You sure as hell aren't doing anything for my self-confidence. You haven't seen the finals. How can you be so sure?"

"I'm not sure about anything. I thought I'd go to the previewing with you, if that's okay. Like to see for myself."

"Want to see Diana flop, right?"

"No. I want to see you succeed. Alex, you have a natural talent for this business, but you let personal feelings color your judgment. At one point, I used to dream about you and I working together. We could have been a fine team, Alex. Maybe it'll happen somewhere out there in the future. Let's just hope this picture doesn't fall on its ass."

"Say soothing things to me, Robin. Don't even talk about failure today." His forehead creased into deep lines.

Some of the stiffness melted from Robin, and she covered his hand with hers. "It isn't the end of the world, Alex. You've just finished a picture, and you can't help but be nervous about it. Let's wait and see how the showing goes. Will Diana be going with you?"

"I doubt it. She won't answer her phone. I think she's been drinking. What if the picture flops? I'm losing faith quickly."

She brushed her hand over his shoulder and smiled confidently. "Things will be okay. Believe me." She kissed him gently and he felt some of his tension ease.

"The screening won't start for an hour," he said as he caressed her hand gently. "We have plenty of time to..."

She pushed him away. "We did that once, remember? It ruined our relationship for a long time, so let's don't start again. Not until you and Diana have been squared away."

"Robin, I care for you. I didn't realize how much until you left. At first, I thought it was because I needed you. Then it dawned on me that I love you. I want you to come back. I need you in so many ways."

"Come back? Come back until Diana sobers up? Gets tired of playing hard to get?" He struggled for an answer, one that would be truthful and yet not hurt her. He couldn't find one.

Robin smiled sadly. "Okay, I'll come back as a business relationship, if that's what you want. I told you I fall in love on every picture. We'll make another picture, and maybe I'll fall madly in love with a muscle-bound stagehand and finally forget you. But I doubt it."

Several independent distributors arrived early and stood around talking with Lance Rexford and some production people, but they stayed away from Alex. Actually, few knew who he was; he looked young enough to be a second assistant director, or a low-level executive. He felt relieved, for he didn't feel up to any additional pressures. Let the picture sell itself, he kept saying under his breath.

He went outside to stand in the sunshine, hoping the warmth against his face might evaporate some of his fears. The words of the wardrobe mistress kept echoing in his ear like a voice of doom: *Wait 'til you see the finals on this picture; it's going to be a disaster*. He took a deep breath and tried to push the words from his memory. From the corner of his eye, he watched people arriving. Robin joined him.

Diana's Lincoln pulled into the parking lot. She sat in the passenger seat; someone else was driving. It was Johnny Gregorio.

Johnny stepped out of the car, walked around and opened the door for Diana. She smiled up at him like a little girl and accepted his hand. Johnny grinned broadly when he saw Alex. He waved and started toward him, but Diana pulled firmly on his arm.

Johnny Gregorio grinned as he shouted, "Hey, Alex! Just got home. See you after the screening!" He smiled happily as Diana guided him inside.

Robin put her arm around Alex's waist, and said, "Looks like judgment day is here, in more ways than one."

"She said she was going to let him down easy."

"She didn't say *where* she was going to let him down easy. She meant in bed, Alex. In bed."

"Don't joke. Not now, I'm too tense."

"Well, let's go inside and see how you did without me." The theater lights went down, and Alex's stomach began tying itself into knots even before the credits finished. Johnny and Diana sat on the other edge of the room on a small sofa, she snuggled against him. Alex could see her arm moving slightly as she brushed her hand around Johnny's chest. Now he had jealousy piling on top of his anxiety. He felt nauseated. Robin seemed to understand. She took his hand into her lap and whispered, "Relax, just watch the film. Think about changes we might have to make."

Suddenly the opening scene splashed on the screen. He forced himself to settle back and watch as the individual takes, now spliced into one whole, came to life on the screen. He began to lose his nervousness as the story unfolded, fairly smooth, with acceptable continuity. Diana looked absolutely beautiful as the Madonna, and although he could see what the women meant about a Madonna with sex appeal, he couldn't agree that it distracted from the picture. He felt better and better. It was as if spring had unexpectedly arrived, and his self-assurance returned like swallows to Capistrano.

Then it was over. The lights came on, Alex looked at Robin. "Well? What's the verdict?"

She raised her eyebrows and started to speak, then she

hesitated for a few moments. "Why don't you see how the distributors liked it first? They're the ones who count right now."

"It's good, isn't it? Diana was great."

"You love her, Alex. She would look good to you if she had acne and talked with a lisp." She gave him a gentle shove. "Go on over and talk to the jury."

Now he felt the confidence to approach the distributors' reps, who were gathered about in a circle discussing the film. "What do you think?" he asked abruptly. "Wasn't it great?"

The representative from the largest distributor adjusted his glasses and looked at Alex with a question on his face. Then he said, "Oh, you must be the producer. Well, I don't like to deal with a producer directly; much rather keep at arm's length, so to say. But since you asked, I doubt very much if anyone will touch this one. Slow paced. Too many clichés. The casting, well..." Alex looked at the other distributors and each avoided eye contact as they self-consciously made their way toward the exit. One of them mumbled, "I'll contact your business manager tomorrow with our decision."

Another said, "Good luck with your film, young man." Then they were gone.

Alex felt alone, as the audience fled silently from the screening room, all avoiding looking at Alex. A slow, sick feeling seeped through his body leaving a bad taste in his mouth. Johnny and Diana slipped out a side door, holding hands like high school kids. They seemed to be completely unaware of the disaster.

Then he felt Robin standing beside him. He looked her in the eye and demanded, "How bad was it, Robin? The truth."

"Very bad. Worse than I expected."

"Oh, Jesus... I should have listened."

She took his hand and squeezed gently. "Diana invited me to a party for Johnny Gregorio this evening. She asked me to bring you. She wants to celebrate his homecoming and the success of the picture. She seems to think the picture is a smash hit. I didn't have the heart to tell her."

"She couldn't invite me herself? I'm not going."

Robin stepped close and kissed him on the cheek, saying, "Yes, we're going. You have to face her and tell her the truth about the picture. You have to confront the truth about many things. She loves him, Alex. I can tell these things. She loves him every bit as much as you love her. I'll come by for you at seven. Be ready and don't try to get out of it."

The party was at Diana's small apartment just off Wilshire. Only a few friends were invited, and she mentioned to no one that Johnny was her husband, trying to leave the impression that they were just close friends. But Hollywood being what it is, few people were fooled, and fewer would have cared in the first place. Alex found it difficult to pretend to be anything but despondent. When the guests attempted to talk about the picture, he avoided them and retreated to the small balcony overlooking the pool. Johnny followed, handed him a drink and slapped him on the back playfully.

"Snap out of it, Alex! Let's celebrate."

"Celebrate what?"

"You finished your first picture, and the Air Force is about to be finished with me. I get out in a couple of months. Hell, I'm married to a movie star now. That's enough to celebrate, isn't it?"

"Yeah, sure. My first picture is already finished," he replied morosely. "It's a bomb. A flop." He told him of the distributors' reaction.

Johnny made him accept the drink. Then he said, "That can't be. I saw the picture, and it was great! Pure dynamite!"

"Be honest, Johnny. It wasn't great."

"Okay, so maybe it was just okay. Look, you and I have seen plenty of pictures that were really bad, yet they made it at the box office. Why not this one?"

"Who is going to distribute it? Shall I go around and sell it to the theaters myself?"

Johnny thought about this for a moment and then suddenly began talking excitedly. "Why not? Think about it, Alex, you're a board member of Barron Advertising, right? Put the agency to work on the picture. Get TV spots every hour on every TV network. Saturate the country until every goddamn moviegoer will have to run to the box office. The distributors'll have to handle the picture. They'll be fighting for copies."

"Won't work. You can't sell a movie like you sell a bar of soap."

"Try it. You have Barron Advertising behind you. If you guys can market that crap your clients push off on the public, you can sure as hell sell a damned good movie to the public. I'll be needing a job soon, and you can hire me as your promotion director."

"I don't have any control at the agency. Yes, I'm on the board of directors, only because I inherited stock. I've never attended any meetings." He sipped his drink and looked at Johnny as if he just noticed him. "But you have an idea. Maybe we could swing it."

"Goddamn right we can!"

"Okay. When you're free, come and work with me, Johnny. We'll map out a campaign. It just might work."

"Do it. Do it for Diana, Alex. Don't let her down."

Alex cleared his throat and hesitated a moment before saying, "Johnny, there's something I have to tell you about Diana and me. Something that is very difficult to..."

Johnny's large hand slapped him gently on the shoulder, cutting him off in mid-sentence. "I know all about it. The word got back to me in Japan, and I've discussed it with Diana. She told me everything. It's okay. In a way, I'm happy it was with you instead of stranger, but I knew she wouldn't be able to hold out for long. She likes sex too much."

"It wasn't her, it was me, Johnny. I was the one who..."

"Don't kid yourself, Alex. I know Diana better than she knows herself. That's just the way she is. So, forget it. Let's think about how we can help save this picture. She's going to need a lot of help."

Robin had been standing in the open doorway, listening. When Alex tried to say something and the words stuck in his throat, Robin walked to his side. She put on arm around Alex's neck and the other around Johnny Gee's.

She said, "We'll do it together. I'll take over re-edit. Alex will work with the agency and stay away from the studio. Johnny will make sure Diana is sober and ready for the new takes."

Robin took Alex to her place that night. The next morning, they decided to form Barron-Summerhill Productions, and begin repair work on the film.

The chairman of the board — an old family friend — looked at Alex as if he couldn't believe his ears. "Do you have any idea what a campaign like this could cost? It's impossible. You can't afford it and the agency can't afford to give you much more than token support. It isn't like the old days; competition has pared us down to skin and bones."

"I own a good percentage of the agency," he reminded the portly old gentleman. "I should have something to say."

The chairman put a hand on Alex's shoulder, much the same way his father would have done. "Son, I helped Tony get this agency going when you were just a little tyke. I know precisely what your father would have said in a case like this; 'Cut your losses.' Tony would be the last person to let you throw good money after bad. True, you have stock, but the majority of the board will vote against anything like this. It could ruin the agency."

"How much would it cost?"

"Who knows? Several million, and that cheap only because you'd be getting agency work at cost. So, you see..."

"How much is my thirty percent worth if I were to sell my stock?"

116

The chairman looked shocked. "Son, I couldn't allow you to..."

"I asked you, how much?"

"We can do it, Alex! I'm sure we can do it," Robin said as she looked over her notes for the fifth time. "I've been thinking it over and I think I see what is basically wrong. We need to cut about half of Diana's dialogue and re-shoot the scenes in the temple, using the same actors. At least the ones who aren't working elsewhere."

"I don't agree. Why can't we shoot the footage using Diana?"

"We can't. She's getting worse—drinking and pills. She couldn't stay straight long enough to do us any good. But the real problem is that she is already has too much footage. Look, if you really want to help her, you'll make her look as good as possible. The blunt truth is that we have to tone her down and keep her the hell away from the action. You've trampled over the major premise of the screenplay by pushing Diana to center stage. To be even more blunt, even if we do what I'm suggesting, we still won't have a hit. But at least it won't be embarrassing."

"There isn't enough money left for all that. All my new money is allocated for advertising. Won't advertising alone move this thing?"

"No. Look, I have plenty of cash. I'll pay for revamping the film, you pay for promotion. We'll write up that partnership agreement we discussed. Okay?"

"What about Johnny Gee? We promised him a job."

"He's still in—as an employee. But not Diana. Okay?"

Robin started to work the next day, spending eight hours a day directing, and another eight hours in the cutting room. Alex went to work with the agency, writing ad copy and launching the campaign. Johnny wasn't successful getting Diana's cooperation. They forged ahead without her.

Although Alex wanted to start a simultaneous push all over the country, he allowed wiser heads to prevail. The campaign kicked off only in Atlanta and Milwaukee, at the board chairman's insistence. "If it falls on its ass in those two places," he pointed out, "we can chop off the campaign before you bleed to death."

TV film strips, thirty seconds long, were scheduled for every half hour on each of the television stations, starting at 6 a.m. and ending with the 11:30 p.m. news. "Beginning August 1st at your local theaters! The movie of the century! Don't miss it!" A quarter-page ad in each of the daily newspapers featured Diana Cranston smiling her sexy smile through a gauze background that darkened to black around the borders. In bold, reverse type, the ad read: "Dramatic breakthrough in entertainment. A must-see movie for every member of the family. Actress of the year in a soaring spectacle."

After the ads had run for a week, other distributors began to ask to see the film. Alex called the agency headquarters in Beverly Hills. "It's working! Let it go full tilt for an October 1 opening in the rest of the country." The chairman objected, but Alex insisted. After all, it was his money. He had pawned all of his resources for this promotion. If it failed, he was broke. Alex tried to contact Diana. He wanted her to be in Atlanta for the opening. Since the ad campaign started, she hadn't been seen in public.

It looked as if the promotion was working, at least in Atlanta. Opening day, a Saturday afternoon, produced long lines outside the theaters. Alex felt anxious, hoping against hope that people would like the film. He stopped in a pay telephone booth and tried once more to contact Diana in California. Her maid answered and sounded weary as she said:

"Miss Diana's not here, Mr. Barron. Last I heard, she was staying in Palm Springs or someplace like that." She paused for a moment in embarrassment, then added, "She said that if you called, I was supposed to tell you to... Well, she said 'drop dead', Mr. Barron. Those were her words, not mine. She's angry because you cut her best scenes out of the film."

He slammed the phone into its hook and stormed out of the booth. "Goddamn it all," he whispered fiercely, "After all I've done for her, the least she could do is help me worry about this." He hit his fist into his palm and stalked angrily to the end of the line of movie patrons. Her absence became more painful as he thought of her abandoning him.

The theater was crowded. He had to sit in the fourth row from the front and look up at an angle to see the screen. He tuned in on bits of conversations around him, hoping to pick up some clue as to what the audience was thinking. He heard nothing significant. His heart began pounding when the lights dimmed and the chattering voices began to subside. He slumped down in the plush seat and waited for the credits to end; they seemed to go on forever.

The revamping that he and Robin had done in the cutting room made an obvious difference, yet Alex fully realized that although it quickened the pace of the film somewhat, there were still some basic flaws that all the editing in the world couldn't patch. It was slow, painfully slow. The more he saw, the more ill he felt and the more anger toward Diana for deserting him at this crucial moment.

Suddenly, it was over. He walked slowly toward the exit, listening for comment. One man, who walked arm in arm with his wife said, "What was so great about that? I expected something else." Another woman turned around to her husband and said, "What did you think?" The answer was a shrug. Alex slowed, waiting for others to pass him. A young couple discussed where to go for dinner. The ones who talked about the movie did nothing to cheer Alex. Most seemed to be disappointed. He felt as if he could throw up.

Outside, the line for the next showing was even longer than the first. At least the movie will make money for the first week, he thought. He drove back to his hotel and ordered dinner sent to his room. And a bottle of scotch.

He awoke the next morning to a loud knocking at the door and to a hangover pounding at his skull. "Newspaper, as you ordered, sir," said the bellboy as he handed Alex a thick Sunday edition. He tossed the sections aside until he came to the fine arts and theater section. Yes, there was a review, just as he expected.

MUST SEE' MOVIE A 'WHY SEE' AFFAIR

After all the news media blitz and Madison Avenue promotion, one would clearly expect a bombshell of a movie, but this one turned out to be a dud of a different caliber...

Alex read no more. He twisted the paper, threw it at the window, then fell backwards onto the bed. A voice seemed to echo, "You failed!"

A knock at the door brought him to his feet. He shuffled dejectedly to see who was there.

Robin burst into the room, whooping like a maniac. She grabbed Alex around the waist and began waltzing him around the room.

"We did it, Alex! We did it!"

"What do you mean? Haven't you read today's reviews?"

"Oh, screw the reviews! No one pays any attention to critics. The important thing is the box office! I called Milwaukee a few minutes ago, and there are sold-out houses everywhere the film is running. Distributors and operators are burning up the phones. It's a hit! Oh, the power of advertising. A shitty film, but a money-maker!" She pressed her body against his and said, "We did it, Alex. We really did it!"

"I want to call Diana."

Robin suddenly relaxed her arms and stepped back. She stared with a dour expression as she said, "You really don't want to do that, Alex."

"Yes! I want to be the first to give her the good news."

She paused a moment before saying, "You won't be the first. I understand that Sam Goodman visited her in Palm Springs. Signed her to a three-picture deal with Pacific Studios."

Chapter Nine

Robin took the initiative in getting Barron-Summerhill productions underway. She found a suite of offices located next to a large warehouse in the El Segundo industrial area. "We'll save a bundle by converting the warehouse into sound stages," she pointed out. "We only need to rent commercial studios in Burbank for special effects."

She bought a small house in Redondo Beach and suggested that it would be best if Alex moved in with her, because of the convenience to their new production facility.

"You don't have to feel pressured," she said soothingly, "I won't endanger your singularity. Marriage isn't in our deal." Not yet, she added under her breath.

All that was needed now was a suitable script. Robin's confidence that Barron-Summerhill Productions would make it big began infecting others in the industry; cooperation of agents and other studios was encouraging. Fortunately, box office receipts from the first film provided comfortable financing. Barron-Summerhill became the production company to watch, according to industry gossip.

Their first production, *Fight for Glory*, was pretty much a success. The story dealt with a prizefighter who had fallen in love with his manager's wife. Somehow it avoided the customary first picture clichés. A second picture was underway even before *Fight for Glory* hit the theaters. When it did, the money started flowing in; production costs on the new project were covered from the beginning.

Meanwhile, Diana finished a picture for Goodman and started another. Johnny Gregorio went with her. Before long, rumors about Diana's drinking began swirling through the Hollywood gossip currents. Alex couldn't help wonder about Diana's career. He asked a friend to go to the Goodman studios to see what he could learn.

"It's a disaster, Mr. Barron," the informant said, "Goodman is way over budget and the investors are crying their eyes out. Miss Cranston is most of the problem. Everyone on the set is disgusted with her, including her husband. They say Johnny Gee walked out on her, and she's filed for divorce."

"When did that happen?"

"Almost a year ago."

Robin also heard the rumors and felt uneasy when she heard Alex was making inquiries. She brought up the subject on one of their beach walks. "Let her make her own mistakes, Alex. You've done what you could. You gave her a start, and now she has to stand on her own or fail on her own."

He nodded glumly. "Still, I can't help wanting to help her. She and Johnny Gee are my friends. We go back a long way."

"You gave her a start. That's all you can do. Even Johnny gave up on her."

He didn't reply; he simply nodded in agreement.

On a hunch, Robin optioned a modern western screenplay titled *Chino*. The plot was fresh, with action galore—a natural for the resurgent western box office boom at that time. The story line was about an Apache half-breed who falls in love with a dance-hall prostitute who is being held prisoner by the Apaches in Mexico.

The part of Chino was given to Rafael Galán, a talented young actor from Puerto Rico, hot in the market. The dancehall girl part was contracted to Marilyn Montel. Robin made arrangements for all outdoor action to be shot in Mexico, near San Miguel de Allende, and found a sound stage in Queretero left over from an old John Wayne set.

"It's perfect, Alex. We have miles and miles of empty land with mountain backdrops, cactus, canyons, just everything we need. And almost no tourists to interfere."

Production started on schedule and the project looked like Barron-Summerville had launched another success. However, two events changed the direction of Alex and Robin's lives.

The first event was Marylin Montel's illness. She came down with typhoid fever after a visit to Lake Patzcuaro—the week before shooting was scheduled to begin.

The second event was an unexpected visitor to San Miguel de Allende the week after Montel entered the hospital, too weak to hold her head up and her hair falling out by the handfuls. When Alex opened the hotel room door to see who was knocking, he found himself face to face with Diana Cranston. Her famous smile spread across her face, radiant and inviting. Alex felt his body melt with desire as he reached out to Diana and took her into his arms. As they kissed passionately, Alex pulled her into the room. Diana kicked the door closed with the heel of her shoe and snuggled her body even closer to his.

Robin was furious at first and refused to consider casting Diana in the picture. "Not just because I'm jealous of her, although that's part of it—but she wrecked the last production. Turned into shambles. Almost ruined Goodman. We're not going to risk my part of Barron-Summerville simply to help out your girlfriend. Not for old times sake. Not to keep you supplied with sex. She's a lush and a pillhead. We can't afford her. If you want to keep her as a bed partner, you do it on your own money, but she doesn't get a part in my productions."

"How many times do I have to apologize for that night, Robin? I swear, it won't happen again. I just lost my head when I saw her standing in the doorway."

"I suppose she found your head quickly enough and gave it back to you?"

"Please, Robin, don't make me apologize again. Diana and

I are through. But she would be perfect for this part. And I promise she'll stay clean. She agrees to have someone monitor every move she makes, twenty-four hours a day until production is completed."

"Who's going to monitor you, Alex?"

"You are. I'm asking you to marry me. This weekend. We can fly back to Las Vegas, do it and be back in time to start working over the script on Monday."

Robin eyed him suspiciously, but with obvious hesitation. After a few moments, she said, "Some marriage proposal. Very romantic."

"I mean it, Robin. I really love you and I want us to make a true commitment. Let's get married as soon as we can."

"Better wait until after this next production is complete. In the meantime, let's see how you and Miss Juicehead handle yourselves. See if you can keep your hands off each other."

"Thanks, Robin. I'll call Diana's agent and schedule her to start rehearsals — in February?"

Robin shuffled through the papers on her desk and thought for a moment before saying, "Make it the first of March."

Yet a third event, connected with Diana, suddenly altered Alex's life. After scrupulously staying away from each other through the production, Diana burst into his office one day, with tears streaming down her cheeks.

Alex felt uneasy as he asked, "What's the matter?"

"The matter? I'm pregnant, that's what's the matter!" She kicked at a floor vase, sending it shattering into the corner, a jumble of red shards. "Isn't that great? I thought I was just having problems because of all those fucking horses you've been making me ride. I got the news this afternoon. I'm knocked up!"

Alex shook his head in confusion. "Whose is it? Is it mine?"

"Yes, it has to be. But don't worry. I'm scheduling an abortion in Mexico City. I need to ask you to reschedule around me so I can get this over with."

"Wait a minute! Let me think about that. If that's my child, too, then I have a right to —"

"It's your child, Alex, but it's my body! It's my career! I'm not throwing my career away for a snot-nosed kid."

Alex stared at Diana in disbelief. Then he turned to gaze out the window and thought over the implications of this news. He felt weak, slightly nauseous as he thought of his child being murdered. Then he said:

"Don't worry about your career. We'll shoot all of your scenes now and work around you later. We'll save the closeups for last." When he saw the look of determination on her face, he felt a surge of cold anger. "Look, Diana, if you want to finish this picture, if you want to make a comeback —"

"Is that a threat?"

"Not a threat. A promise. I'll scrap this picture. You'll be finished."

She jumped to her feet in a rage. She glared angrily, then stalked to the bar. She picked up a bottle of scotch and sloshed a couple of ounces into a glass. She lifted the glass to her lip and started to drink. But suddenly she threw the glass crashing against the fireplace, sending slivers of crystal and droplets of scotch over the tiled floor.

"For the love of God, Alex! Don't you see what a kid will do to me? Look at what happened to Susanna Winter's career when the newspapers found out she had a bastard kid. She's all but finished!"

"We'll have a quick civil ceremony, and a divorce as soon as the baby is born." Alex's voice sounded cold, even to himself, cold and determined.

"I'm a selfish person, not a mother. Don't make me go through with it. And I'm scared stiff. What will a baby do to my figure? Make my tits hang down like beagle ears? I'm not a mother, Alex. I'm an *actress*. I don't want to be tied down with a kid."

"You don't have to be tied down, Diana. Give me custody, and Robin and I will take over."

They were married in Ajijic, by a judge who saw neither the bride nor the groom. It was done by mail, pre-dated by six months and the marriage certificate mailed to Queretero. At the same time, the judge conveniently enclosed a divorce decree, dated three months after the baby was due. This was costly, but worth it. Even before the papers arrived, Robin and Alex began making plans for their own ceremony, but in this case, they would do it in person, a week after the divorce papers were valid.

The picture came along nicely. With Robin's editing and Alex's directing, Diana was a success. There was talk of an Oscar nomination, and she would have received it had the movie not been a western. Westerns were in danger of becoming a glut on the market once more — a timing problem. Diana insisted on going to San Francisco to have the baby. She felt that being with her family there, she might keep publicity to a minimum. Alex and Robin picked up the newborn baby at the hospital and took him to their Pebble Beach home. Diana didn't even ask to see the child. She asked for and received release from her contract with Barron-Summerhill productions. Once again, she was in demand. However, it didn't last long. Without supervision she began drinking again.

Rickey was Alex's baby, there could be no doubting that, for the light eyes and dark skin could have come only from the Barron family's Italian-Swiss genes. And the smile — it was as if little Rickey had practiced imitating his father, for there was no mistaking the confident way he curled one corner of his mouth.

When Rickey was a year old, they bought the Acapulco house, spending six months of the year there. It was during their third stay in Acapulco, shortly after Rickey's fourth birthday, that Alex and Robin heard from Diana. Actually, it was her agent who called.

"Two things," he said, his voice full of business. "She wants to see her son. And also we'd like to see if you can't find a place for her in your new production. I understand that you're casting for a woman to play..."

Alex cut him off in mid-sentence. "She can see Rickey any time she wants to. But as far as working for us, I don't see that in the cards."

"You don't understand. She's sober now. She's undergone treatment, therapy, everything. Just talk to her. That's all I ask."

Chapter Ten

Life in the village increased in severity as the years passed. Micaela finally closed her store when she ran out of money to replenish her stocks. People had stopped buying anyway. She learned to knit sweaters and began climbing up the mountain slope to help Riki collect resin and cut firewood. From time to time, she considered leaving the village to search for an easier life for herself and Riki, but the idea filled her with dread. If she were to take Riki to the outside world, he could be recognized. Better to go hungry in Tezcatlipocas than risk losing her son. Yet she knew that for his sake, they must leave someday. She began saving each spare centavo for that "someday."

Riki had grown fast. By the time he was twelve he was as tall as she. Working like a man in the pine forest, cutting wood and packing heavy loads down the mountain trails turned him into a solid, muscular youth. The thin, crisp air of the high altitude enlarged his lungs and broadened his chest. With a mother's pride, Micaela watched him develop and grow even taller. By the time he was thirteen, he was a man in every respect. He was taller than any of the men in the village and still growing.

Deprived of childhood companions and playmates, he knew nothing of frivolous games, toys or make-believe. Life in Tezcatlipocas was serious; Riki had little time to fantasize or to play.

His manner of speaking and his behavior patterns were

identical to those of the village men—stoic, poor men who knew no other life than constant struggle against the elements— whose only salvation in this world was honor, dignity and hard work. Food on the table measured success. Meat in the stew meant luxury. Respect and dignity were the highest possible forms of wealth a man could hope to achieve in this humble world of Tezcatlipocas.

Micaela herself had grown—from the confused nineteen-year-old child who was willing to kill to obtain a son, to a handsome woman in the prime of life. Although she felt stronger now, she realized that Riki was her tenuous thread to sanity. Often, she wished they could live in Córdoba, where she spent a few months as a child. If she lived there, she might find a husband, a strong, hardworking man who would be a father to Riki.

It made her blush to think about it, but she also would like to have a man to sleep with. She recognized that she wasn't supposed to enjoy doing "that", because as a child she had been taught that it was sinful to enjoy sex. But even if it was sinful, she felt good doing it. Not with her husband, of course, but before she met him. It had been years since... But she pushed all thoughts of men from her conscious mind. Best stay here as long as possible, she convinced herself.

One day, shortly after Riki's fifteenth birthday, a stranger came into his life. His name was Epifamio López. Exceptionally short and stocky, Epifamio had powerful arms of solid muscle. His face looked as if it had been pounded to a pulp over and over. It had been, as a matter of fact. Epifamio López was a prizefighter—a tough, gnarled fighter at the end of a sad career.

Epifamio had been born in this very village some thirty-two years earlier and was returning for the first time since he was fifteen years old. Because he was so short and so aggressive, his ring name was *El Perrón* (the bulldog); at one time he contended for the featherweight crown of Mexico. That was before too many brain-scrambling punches ended his career. He now returned to Tezcatlipocas to visit his widowed grandmother, the señora Larín de López, who lived four houses down the trail from Micaela.

Epifamio appeared one morning, a misshapen man trudging along the trail, climbing up from the highway. He shuffled as he walked, the strange gait of a punchy fighter, unsteady and wobbly. He carried a grimy canvas bag slung over his shoulder and his eyes were cast toward the ground, a classic picture of dejection. Riki sensed that the little man was no danger, so he didn't hide as he was supposed to do when strangers enter the village.

When Epifamio reached Micaela's place, he shifted the bag to the other shoulder and tried to smile at Riki. Old scar tissue around his mouth and eyes turned the smile into a mask-like grimace.

"Does doña Larín still li-li-live up the road?" he asked in a halting voice. The words came out slurred, with a pronounced stutter, something Riki never heard before.

He nodded and pointed toward doña Larín's hut. The man mumbled thanks, shifted the canvas bag and trudged on. Riki got to his feet and followed. When the fighter reached his grandmother's house, he laid the bag on the ground and pounded on the door with a knobby hand.

"Grandmother! It's me, Epifamio López!"

Larín was one of the oldest women in the village. Her mind had become weak and forgetful lately; sometimes she didn't recognize Riki or Micaela, even though she'd talked to them the day before. So it came as no surprise that she didn't recognize the gnarled man who was slapping his palm against the door. She peered out of the window suspiciously, and then slammed the shutters closed.

"Go away," she said in her cracking voice. "I don't know you!"

"Grandmother! It's me! Epifamio! Your grandson! I need a place to sleep. Open up!"

She opened the shutter again, just a crack, and looked out. Her dark eyes were narrowed and her lips pursed with suspicion. She shook her head and pulled the shutters closed with a sharp cracking noise. "I must have a dozen grandsons," she called through the shutters, "but I don't know you. You are ugly. Go away or I'll make you sorry you didn't!"

El Perrón's shoulders slumped even more as he turned and tried to smile at Riki. Tears brimmed in his eyes. This made Riki uncomfortable. He had never seen a man cry before; only women, when someone died and was being buried behind the old church.

"Sometimes, doña Larín cannot remember things," he tried to explain, wishing the man would stop crying. "Maybe tomorrow. Look, stop doing that! Men don't cry. Maybe... Maybe, if you need a place to stay, I could ask Micaela to let you sleep in our storeroom. It's empty nowadays." El Perrón swallowed, mumbled a few words of thanks, and followed Riki as he uneasily led the way to Micaela's house.

For several days, El Perrón spoke very little. He was used to people making fun of him, of the way he walked, and talked, at the way he would forget what he was saying in the middle of a sentence. But when he found that Riki didn't ridicule him, he began to open up. Shyly at first, he would talk about the weather and things of little consequence. Then he became more comfortable and began to tell about his days in the ring. He had fought everywhere from Ciudad Juarez to the Chiapas. Once he even had a bout in faraway Texas, in a city called Dallas.

Riki didn't understand fighting at all. He asked, "Why do you fight? It's not dignified."

"I had a good life," he explained. "Always plenty to eat, and lots of *chavalas*, everything. I even had a convertible once... an automobile with a top that folded back, into itself."

"It doesn't sound worth it."

"I remember when I first went to *la capital*," El Perrón reminisced, a vague smile spreading across his face. "*Jijole*, but it's a big city! I was only fifteen years old, and I can tell you I was frightened. And I was hungry. I didn't know how to get food there, and I wasn't smart enough to steal. I noticed other kids shining shoes, so I made myself a box, borrowed some polish and went to work. It wasn't easy because there were a million shoeshine boys."

"How did you start fighting?"

"I was the littlest puppy on the street, and I had to learn quickly how to handle myself. Then one day, I was shining the shoes of don Crespi, the boxing promoter. He saw that my shoulders were wide and my chest was big, like all men from this village. Also, he realized that I was little enough to fight as a flyweight, so he took me to his gymnasium. After that, he gave me money and made sure I had all I ever wanted to eat."

"The city sounds bad."

"No, it's a great place to be if you have money. If you have money, there is no end of things to buy... food, clothes, women, and they sell pulque and beer almost anywhere you look! But one thing you have to watch out for, is *la policía*. When you see them, you run. Understand?"

"*La policía*? Who is she?"

El Perrón chuckled; he had begun to laugh more often now. "You will know la policía when you see them. they are men, bad men, who carry pistols in leather cases on their belts, and clubs to knock you around. You know they're dangerous by the evil way they look at you. Never trust them. I learned that from my first day in the City."

"Why do they hit you with clubs?"

"I don't know. Maybe because people are poor. They don't bother rich people. If you have money and you do something wrong, you just pay la policía. But if you don't have money — away you go to the *calaboso*."

"They sound terrible."

"They are. But if you think they are bad, you never want to see the policía in *los Estados*. When I had my fight in Texas, in a place called Dallas, I almost didn't make it to the arena. La policía arrested me for just walking down the street. They put me in a cage and turned a water hose on me, as if I were an animal. My manager got me out of jail just in time to make the fight. I lost because I was feeling sick from all that cold water."

"Why did they put you in jail?"

"They don't like Mexicans there. They only like Gringos. People on the streets give you dirty looks and say nasty things if you are not Gringo. One time, I went into a restaurant with my manager, and they wouldn't let us even sit down. *Los Estados* is not a good place for Mexicans."

Riki tried to picture such a place where people could be so impolite. He knew this could never happen in Tezcatlipocas. "I don't understand. Why do these people, these Gringos as you call them, why do they behave so impolitely?"

Epifamio shrugged. "I suppose because they are full of hate. Gringos are very rich, but they are also very stingy and try to cheat you. They seem to hate everyone who is not one of them. Take my advice and never go up there, and never have anything to do with Gringos. I do my fighting in Mexico, where people are honorable."

Riki nodded gravely and filed this information away in the back of his mind. The villagers had told him that his mother was a Gringa, so his father must be a Gringo. This helped him realize why they abandoned him in the village. Obviously, Gringos have no honor.

"But if you liked fighting, why did you quit?"

"Look at me and you should know. I didn't quit. I used to be on top, but when I slowed down, nobody knew me. They wouldn't even lend me money for food. I decided to come home." Tears welled up in his eyes and he looked as if he were going to weep again, which made Riki feel embarrassed.

The little fighter helped Riki cut wood, climbing up to the forest with him every morning. Even though he was almost a foot shorter than Riki, he could carry twice as much wood down the rocky trail to the village. They finished early every day, giving Riki more time to rest. But El Perrón couldn't rest. He found a braided horsehair rope and would jump several hundred times without stopping. Riki helped him make a goatskin bag which he filled with wet pine needles and hung it from the bough of a black pine tree. The fighter pounded the bag with furious thumps that showered pine needles through the loose seams.

When Riki asked why he did all of this, el Perrón replied, "Maybe, if I work hard enough, I can get back in the ring. I used to be good. Very good. Maybe if I work hard enough... Maybe I can get back my senses and think clearly again. Maybe that's more important than fighting. I don't know." He feinted a right to Riki's head and rolled away to throw another. "Come on, puppy, let's spar. I'll show you how!"

Riki stepped back in surprise. El Perrón threw two more punches that stopped a breath of air short of landing. "Like this!" He threw a flurry of punches that flailed away at an imaginary opponent.

Then he stepped back and eyed Riki from head to toe. He squeezed the boy's arms, prodded his belly and nodded approvingly. "I bet you could be a fighter. A good one, even better than me. Come on, let's spar."

Riki didn't like sparring, but he went along with it — partly because he felt it would be insulting to refuse, and partly because for the first time he could remember, he had a companion, someone to "play" with. Nevertheless, he told the little boxer quite firmly, "I'll never fight. I don't understand why anybody would."

"Because you could be rich and famous. You can have all of the good-looking *chavalas* you want and drive beautiful cars. I could still do that, if I only hadn't gotten hit so much. Maybe if I work hard..."

Riki wasn't sure what "rich and famous" meant, he wasn't sure what a "good-looking chavala" was, and wasn't sure he wanted to know, either. But he did enjoy the game of trying to dodge out of the way of the light punches and open-handed slaps the little fighter threw at him. This, plus the exercise—running, rope skipping and bag punching—supplied something missing from the confining life in the village.

El Perrón admired Riki's height. "*Jijole, manito,* if I only had four inches of that height, I could have been champion. If I were as tall as you, and with those arms, I would be king of the world! Let me make us some soft gloves, and I'll teach you to fight."

Riki sighed and said, "I've told you before, I don't ever want to fight."

"Someday, little puppy, you are going to leave Tezcatlipocas. When you do, you will find you *have* to fight once in a while. You must learn." He hesitated for a moment, and then said, "Fighting is the only thing I know, the only thing I was ever good at. I need to show this to someone. I need to feel important, just for a little while."

El Perrón reached down and picked up a broken piece of wood. He handed it to Riki and said, "Look, pretend this is a knife, and that you are going to stab me."

Riki took the pretend knife and stood up to face El Perr6n.

"Come on—come at me fast. You can't hurt me."

Riki moved in closer. Without warning, he lunged forward, the weapon flashing toward the fighter's chest. But the wooden knife cut through an empty space where El Perr6n had been just a second ago. The boxer twisted, then feinted with his left hand. Riki tried to counter, but El Perrón's foot suddenly lashed out to knock Riki's hand sharply upward. The wooden knife sailed into the air and clattered to the ground.

"You see? If that had been a real knife, it would have been flying to the moon. Now you try it again."

This started a new game that Riki enjoyed: practicing tricks that El Perrón showed him —punching, feinting and slipping in a kick when it was least expected. Yet, even though he had the reach advantage, and even though he was almost as strong as

El Perrón, he was seldom able to touch the agile little man. On the other hand, El Perrón could land a volley of light slaps and touches any time he pleased.

Riki became frustrated. "Why is it that you can move out of the way every time I try to hit you? Yet, I can't learn to duck? I don't understand."

El Perrón's eyes gleamed in delight. "I hoped you would ask that question. Now is when I give you the final secret. I'm going to teach you to read eyes."

"Read eyes?"

"Exactly." He dropped his arms to his sides and crouched over slightly. Now, try to hit me. As hard as you can." When Riki hesitated, he repeated, "As hard as you can. Don't worry, you won't even touch me."

Presented with this challenge, Riki stepped forward and feinted a couple of times to prevent his adversary from knowing which hand he was going to throw. Then he unleashed a left hook that should have torn El Perrón's head from his shoulders. Instead, it swished harmlessly through the air. Before he knew what happened, El Perrón landed a flurry of soft slaps to the midsection, finishing off with a touch on Riki's temple.

El Perrón grinned happily. "If that had been a real fight you would have been laying on your back. So now comes the lesson on reading eyes and counter-punching."

He pulled on the soft gloves and motioned for Riki to face him. "Watch my eyes while I try to hit you. The secret is this: Most people, just before they throw a punch or a kick, their eyes shift toward the hand they're going to use. It's something a person can't help, not unless he trains. The shift isn't very much, and it comes quick. When you see the movement, you duck in the same direction as the eyes move."

"The same direction?"

"Yes. When he looks one way, you shift the same way. Then you don't catch the fist or the foot. It flies past you. Remember, keep your attention on the eyes. Let your body do the counter punching. Don't think about a thing but the eyes. When you move to the side, the enemy's arm is forward, leaving his body wide open, face unprotected."

Riki took a hundred soft punches until he caught on to El Perrón's secret. Soon he drew grunts of approval as he slammed his gloves into his teacher's exposed side. After three weeks, Riki was scoring almost as many points as El Perrón, sometimes even more.

Next came practice in keeping the eyes from moving. "You won't often meet someone who can read eyes," the fighter said, "but when you do, you have an advantage if you can fool him by making him think you are going to give him a left hand, but instead, you kick him in the kidney as he is leaning away from the blow. When you are really good, your eyes can give false signals."

This was much harder, and Riki never quite mastered this new skill. However, he became quite adept at varying his attack, throwing left-left-right combinations, and just when the right hand was expected, a left foot would connect with at El Perrón's solid body.

"Higher! You must learn to kick higher! You will never fight anyone as short as me."

Micaela watched all this with disapproving eyes. But the villagers kept her from putting an end to it all. Doña Matilda pointed out one day: "Don't you see? Riki is curing Epifamio of his illness, just as he cured your illness. He is driving out the evil spirits. Haven't you noticed the change in Epifamio? He doesn't drag his feet when he walks, and he has practically stopped stuttering. It's another miracle. The strange ways of Tonantzín!"

This was true, Micaela had to admit, "But he is turning Riki into a ruffian."

"Not so. It's simply God's way of curing Epifamio. It's even affected doña Larín—she remembers her grandson now and remembers better than she has in a long time."

So, Micaela kept quiet. If it was God's Will, then there was nothing to be done.

El Perrón stayed in Tezcatlipocas almost six months. By the time he was ready to leave, Riki was well on his way to being a hardened athlete, one with skills he didn't appreciate and had no intention of ever using. No one ever fought in the village. It would be unthinkable. By the time El Perrón was ready to leave, the little fighter was a different person. He still slurred his words somewhat, and he was still forgetful, but this was normal for a retired prizefighter. However, his thinking was much clearer. His words made sense and his eyes focused when he talked.

Riki was sad when El Perrón told him he was leaving. The little man was as close to a child's playmate that Riki was ever to know. The day his friend packed his canvas bag and started down the road to the highway, Riki walked with him and struggled to keep tears from his eyes. He was determined to be a man, and not weep like a woman.

El Perrón walked slowly past the far side of the church, along the cobbled road that gradually gave way to damp earth, without saying a word until they reached the black rock cliff that jutted over the highway below. This was the farthest that Riki was permitted to go.

Suddenly El Perrón grabbed Riki in a tight embrace. "Adios, amigo! We'll probably never see each other again. But remember all I've taught you, okay?" He kissed Riki on the cheek and gave him another bone-crushing *abrazo* before he turned him loose and picked up his canvas bag.

Riki was mortified to see tears streaming down El Perrón's scarred cheeks. He tried hard to keep his own tears from flowing, but they came anyway. "Where are you going?"

"To Veracruz."

"Are you going to fight?"

"No. I can't do that again. I know that now. You helped convince me of that. But I can teach. I taught you, didn't I? I'm

139

not worthless as I thought. I can be a trainer. I know a promoter in Veracruz who might give me a job as a trainer. If not him, then someone else."

"Will you return?"

"Probably not."

Riki wiped the tears from his face with his sleeve. "I'm sorry to be crying. It's just that you are the only real friend I've ever had, and...and I'll miss you."

"Never be ashamed to weep. It takes a man to cry, because to cry is to face the truth. It takes a man to face the truth about himself and about the world."

One more abrazo, and El Perrón was gone.

Riki trudged back to the village. He sat on a flat stone midst the ruins of the church and wept for a long time. He didn't know exactly why he was crying, but it felt like the right thing to do. The thick walls of the church cut off the sound, so he bawled like a calf and wept copiously. This was the first time he ever remembered crying out loud. He thought of his mother and his father abandoning him, and the price of two bottles of rum. It was almost dark before he had no energy left for tears.

It wasn't long after El Perrón's departure that conditions in Tezcatlipocas grew worse. For some reason, the market for resin disappeared, and no one came buying sweaters anymore. The village was in its last stages of rigor mortis. Micaela knew that soon there would be no choice but leave. She counted and recounted her tiny horde of coins and worn-out bills. Not enough, she knew, and there would be even less the longer they stayed. But fear of the unknown kept her there, helplessly watching the money dwindle away.

The lady's suitcase was still in its hiding place beneath the eaves. Its tantalizing heap of jewelry — enough to fill two hands — could make her wealthy, she knew that. Several times she had been tempted to take some of the treasure, perhaps just one of the watches, and sell it in Córdoba. One watch or a bracelet would keep Riki in food and nice clothes for a year. But she realized only too well, this would not only be theft of the lady's property, it would place her and Riki in great jeopardy. If the police should question her about the jewelry, she would be forced to tell the whole story and she would lose Riki.

She remembered her last conversation with don Rafael, only a few days before he died. "Don't dare sell a thing," he had whispered. "The police seldom understand the mysterious ways of Tonantzín. They'll think you are crazy as a raccoon if you try to explain it that way. No, do not sell any jewelry unless you are prepared to go to jail." She agreed. The jewelry would remain in the suitcase, she resolved, come what may.

She began climbing the mountain every day to dig for roots while Riki hunted rabbits and quail. Even these were becoming scarce, and more often they came home empty-handed. Finally, one night, there was nothing in the house to eat but a small handful of beans that the Martinez family gave her. She laced them with chili to give that warm glow to the belly, to fool it into thinking that it had just enjoyed a full meal.

"I'm not feeling well tonight," she said as she pushed her plate across the table at Riki. "You eat it all. We mustn't waste."

Riki shrugged and said, "Better you eat it. I'm not feeling well either." He picked up a dried red chili and rolled it between his hands and tossed the dust into his mouth. He started to leave the table, and then he realized that she was crying.

"What's wrong? Are you really sick?"

"We must leave this place," she said weakly. "Very soon. We have to find work."

He put his hand on her shoulder and tried to think of something to say. But she pushed away from the table and ran into the bedroom. He sat down at the table and slowly began to eat the cold beans. The implications of leaving were too much to take in all at once. He unrolled his *petate* and spread out the goats-wool blanket to make his bed. Then he blew out the lamp and lay down to think about this sudden change in his future.

He tried to imagine what the world would be like away from the village, but it was impossible, the only images he could conjure up were second-hand ones, fear-inspiring images created by El Perrón and by don Rafael.

As he thought of leaving Tezcatlipocas, he felt a curious mixture of excitement and terror. Since that day he arrived in the village—that misty day he only half remembered—he had never left the mountainside. Never. Micaela had prohibited him from going near the highway down below. The farthest he was allowed was the cliff, where a large flat rock balanced and projected out over the edge. Often, he went there to lie on the rock and gaze down on the automobiles and trucks as they hummed along the black ribbon of asphalt below. Where are they going? Where are they coming from? Why are they driving about, hurrying here and there all the time? He tried to imagine where the drivers lived, what sort of houses an automobile driver would live in.

He knew two kinds of houses, Micaela's house on the one hand, and those strange dream houses in *Pebabeetch* or the house in *Puco*, with its swimming place and green lawns. He seemed to remember soft carpets on the floors and a special room with a shiny white bowl where you were expected to urinate and defecate. It was *inside* the house too, as he recalled, although this seemed a little unnatural. Or was that a dream, as well? It was hard to believe that anyone would shit *inside* a house.

He drifted off to sleep unable to picture what his new life might be.

Chapter Eleven

Riki was fifteen when Micaela decided they could stay no longer. The highway repair crew needed landfill and had taken so much of the hillside that the road down to the highway had been cut away permanently and no one had been to the village in over a month to buy resin. The remaining villagers had run out of money to buy wool long ago, so few sweaters were being knitted. Micaela didn't say anything, but Riki knew something world-shattering was about to happen when she began selling things from the house, putting the coins into her wool knit purse.

Then, early one morning, she started folding up their clothes and placing them into two net bags. "Today, we leave Tezcatlipocas," she said simply. "Help pack our things."

He helped in silence, sensing the terror and dread that she tried to suppress. He tested the larger of the bundles by squatting in front of the bundle and arranging the straps over his forehead, then lifting to his feet. This is the normal way the village men carry their burdens, the way Riki carried firewood, on his back with a trumpline slung across his forehead, the only way he knew. Yes, it was heavy, but he pretended it wasn't; he didn't want Micaela to overload her bundle. He put it down and helped her pack the other bag.

When she finished, she shoved the table against the wall and climbed up on it. Riki was puzzled. He couldn't imagine what she was up to. She pulled and yanked until a brown leather suitcase slipped from under the eaves of the house where it had been hidden these eleven years. With a damp rag, she wiped off a thick coat of dust and mice droppings, then

143

placed it beside the two bundles of clothes. Riki ran his hand over the cracked leather and felt a small tug of memory, recalling a foggy afternoon when he sat in the back seat of an automobile, his feet resting on this suitcase. The leather smelled moldy and musty. It felt rough against his hand and against his memory. No, that was just part of the dream, he decided.

"What's inside? Can I open it and see?"

"No!" The sharpness of her voice startled him. She pulled him away and said, "Someday, we will both open this, but not until you are older. Much older. There's nothing but trouble inside there."

"Don't you know what's inside?"

"Yes. I've looked. Enough questions. Get ready to leave. We must find jobs."

He wanted to ask where, but he suspected that she didn't know where. It wouldn't have meant anything to him anyway. Although don Rafael had shown him pictures of Mexico City and had told him tales of faraway places such as Durango and Torreón. And El Perrón had spoken of the dangers and pleasures of the city, and of the horrors of the United States. Riki's imagery was very incomplete. He had built a picture in his mind about these places, a picture of miraculous tall buildings, millions of automobiles and uncaring people. The excitement built to a fever pitch, but a lid of anxiety kept the fervor from boiling over.

"Have we packed everything we will need?" she asked solemnly. "We won't be back."

The only thing he wanted to add to the bundle was his machete, well worn, sharpened on a rock to a razor fineness. He wrapped it in a piece of frayed canvas and slipped inside the large bundle with the machete's sweat-stained handle sticking out, ready to be grasped if necessary. Then he lifted the bundle to his forehead again and stood up.

"I'm ready," he said in a brave, calm voice that he didn't feel. He stooped down and hefted the suitcase. It wasn't as heavy as it looked. "What about the house? Will it be safe here, empty like this?"

She nodded sadly and tried unsuccessfully to keep from crying. A tear glistened on her cheek as she lifted the bundle and adjusted the trumpline across her forehead. "More than half of the houses are abandoned now. No one is moving in. If we were to come back here ten years from now, we would have our choice of almost any house in the village. But... We won't be returning to Tezcatlipocas."

"Where are we going?"

"To Mexico City. Doña Herencia lives in a fancy house there. She works for rich people and I am going to ask her to find us jobs."

She squared her shoulders, walked out of the house and paused only long enough to snap the heavy padlock onto the door. Then she took Riki's free hand as they marched forward, heading down the road to the highway. She didn't look back. Riki followed close behind. He felt thrills of elation at finally going down to the highway, past the lower end of the village. His body tingled with anticipation as he wondered what life would be like away from Tezcatlipocas.

He turned around for one last look at the village as the trail turned around a huge granite boulder. The houses and the cobblestone street seemed desolate, as if they knew no one ever returns. Micaela's house seemed particularly sad that it was being abandoned. He wondered if they would find a house as nice as this one in Mexico City. It had the driest roof in the entire village.

The descent from the sliced off trail down to the highway was somewhat precarious because of the loose dirt and rock left over from the bulldozer's latest theft of the old cobblestone roadbed. Riki slipped and slid down first and waited for Micaela to lower the bundles to him with a thin cord. Then she picked her way through the stones, dirt and rubble until she too, stood on the edge of the asphalt pavement. Without a word,

Micaela crossed the highway and waited for a *camión* to come by.

Camión can mean either 'truck' or 'bus' in colloquial Spanish, and Riki hoped it would be one of the large buses he had seen driving along the highway. From his vantage point on the black cliff, the autos looked like bugs racing one after another, but the powerful-looking buses were clearly the kings of the road down here, as they roared down the broad highway like monster animals of steel and glass.

Micaela waved her hand at each bus, but none stopped. Riki could occasionally see a face peering through a moistured window and he tried to imagine what it would be like, sitting up high and looking through the window as the bus roared about the world. It seemed so glamorous.

"Why don't they stop?"

Micaela sighed deeply. "I think they are all full, coming back from the Veracruz Carnival. We may have to wait a long time for a bus to come through empty."

Hours passed slowly. The cool shadow of the mountain crept over them as the sun crawled toward its resting place in the western underworld. Finally, Micaela made a decision. "Come on," she said abruptly as she crossed the highway. "We'll go to the other side of the road and stop a bus going to Córdoba. Buses going that way are empty. I think Don Crescencio moved to Córdoba. Maybe he will help us find work."

Riki hefted the bundle with his forehead again and trotted after her with quick, short footsteps. Less than half an hour later a blue and red bus coasted to a stop and its doors swung open. Micaela pushed at Riki's back and urged him to climb aboard. He slung his bags aboard first, then reached down to help Micaela get on. It was a second-class bus with as many people as could be squeezed in.

Odors of unwashed bodies and bad breath mixed with the aromatic scent of cilantro, cured tobacco, and strings of garlic on the way to market. From the back of the vehicle came the distressed sound of a piglet grunting, struggling against its bindings of jute twine. The air was tired, used, foul; Riki breathed through his mouth to avoid the unfamiliar odors. From where he stood, there was no way to see out a window. But they were on their way to some marvelous place called Córdoba and the overpowering excitement soon made him ignore the discomfort. He wondered if people on the bus could tell how excited and happy he was.

It was dark when the bus stopped in front of the shabby restaurant that served as a bus terminal. The mob of people leaving the bus carried Riki and Micaela outside to the sidewalk, breathing cool, fresh air once again. Micaela looked about with uncertainty. Finally, she said, "What do we do now? How do I look for a job?" She unfolded a handkerchief and took out the thin roll of pesos, the money she received from the sale of everything left in the house. "Not enough to buy two kilos of beans," she said softly. "All those years in Tezcatlipocas and all I have to show is two kilos of beans. I must find a job right away. I must!"

"I can get a job, too. I am strong. I can cut wood as well as any man."

She smiled at him proudly. "We'll see. Right now we need a place to sleep."

"Where?"

"When I was a little girl, my family used to come here to sell things in the market. I remember that there were some good places to sleep there. And they were free. Come on."

With Riki at her side, both leaning forward under their burdens, they walked toward the market area. She tried to remember where were the good places to sleep, on the sidewalk, as she recalled, where other women slept, waiting for market to open. "Tomorrow, I will find a job with a rich family and we will have a beautiful place to sleep, in real beds."

The unfamiliar odors and confused jumble of noise in

Córdoba overwhelmed Riki. He wasn't prepared for such a hodgepodge of sensations. As they passed a bakery, delicious odors of warm, yeasty bread aroused brief memory flashes of long ago—of chewy bread and melting butter, sitting at a table with white linen, and sparkling silverware. The vision evaporated when the smell of death assailed his nostrils as they passed the decaying body of a dog laying in the gutter. Pungent smoke from Delicado cigarettes mixed with thick greasy diesel fumes and flowers blooming in a nearby garden. The sweet perfume of *dama de noche* blossoms covered all else for a while. The night was warm, something unthinkable in Tezcatlipocas. Riki inhaled deeply of thick, scented air and smiled in delight.

Radios and TVs blared from every window and doorway, mixing with the roar of unmuffled trucks and the constant yelping of dogs. Riki looked this way and that, nervously absorbing each new sound. Electric lights were everywhere, magically turning the night into small islands of brittle daylight. He stopped suddenly by an open window which looked into a family's living room. There, on a small table, sat a TV set, a black and white picture moving across the screen. He stood in open mouth amazement until Micaela nudged him to move along. He swallowed with difficulty. Memories of resting on his stomach on a thick, soft carpet watching endless TV cartoons began to confuse his head. Nothing seemed real.

Ahead was the outline of a domed church. The street opened onto the square of the zócalo with trees and a bandstand in the center. Micaela said, "On the other side of the zócalo is the market. That is where don Crescencio had his vegetable stand. He will know where we can find jobs. If we find him. We'll sleep in the market tonight and tomorrow..." She couldn't finish the sentence; her throat clutched with uncertainty.

A new smell drifted through the air now, the savory odor of cooking grease and frying foods. Riki breathed deep as if trying to take nourishment through the delicious smelling air. He slowed his walk to a shuffle as they passed a row of curbside stands offering potato pancakes, pork-stuffed empanadas, crispy fried calf entrails, and tacos of chopped beef tongue al vapor. His mouth watered. His legs trembled. They hadn't eaten since breakfast that morning. He glanced at Micaela, but her neck was bowed against the weight of her burden, her face solid stone. She stared ahead, as if not wanting to look at Riki, not to see the hunger on his face, not to cry out in hunger for herself.

"This to too expensive," she finally whispered. "When we get to the market, I'll buy some tortillas. And sometimes one finds perfectly good food thrown away there, free for the taking." She tried to take the leather suitcase from him, but he wouldn't allow it.

He felt her anguish cut through him like a knife. He was embarrassed for her, and angry with himself for so obviously showing hunger. He knew she had no money to be wasted on fancy cooking. He leaned forward against his burden. "I'm not very hungry anyway," he said, trying to convince himself this was true. "Tortillas will be fine." *When I get a job, the first thing I am going to do is take Micaela here and eat something from each one of these stands.* He forced his eyes to look down at the sidewalk and not torture himself by staring at any more frying food, but the crackling of the grease and the tantalizing odors mocked him as they trudged past the row of food stands.

The market was in a large, tin-roofed building. Small stands, knocked together with two by fours and castoff plywood, crowded together, forming a maze where customers wandered about in search of the best bargains. It was late now, and most stands were either closed or in the process of closing. Riki followed Micaela through the narrow aisles as she asked people about don Crescencio. Finally she found someone who knew him. An old lady with no teeth grinned mirthlessly and said, "don Crescencio? Yes, he used to have a stand over there, where he sold tomatoes and onions. But he is gone. Months ago. Where? Only God knows."

"We need jobs. Do you know where we can find work?"

The old woman laughed in a cackling voice that reminded Riki of a hen laying an egg. "You need jobs? Just got in from the country, did you? Well, good luck, because there are so many people out of work now, what with the trouble at the auto plant. And you ignorant country people don't help things at all. Why don't you stay home where you have family and friends?"

Micaela turned away from the old lady. She found a lady putting away her stock of tortillas in preparation for ending the day's business. Micaela pointed out that they were stale and would be even worse in the morning and talked her into letting half a kilo go for four pesos. The lady threw in a handful of wilting green chili peppers. The tortillas were indeed stale and tasted of soapy lye, but Riki stuffed his mouth and felt his hunger pains ease up. He munched on a green chili and watched while Micaela arranged some old newspapers on the ground, next to the market wall.

"We'll sleep here," she said quietly, as if she were ashamed of something, "and in the morning, we'll find a job. It will be all right, you'll see." She took two blankets from her pack and spread them over the newspapers. He sat next to her as they finished the rest of the tortillas, washing them down with the last of the water from a gourd she carried in her net bag.

Sleep was impossible for Riki; he was too excited. He leaned against the wall, wondering what would happen next, what kind of job could he find, wondering what kind of work he could do that someone might pay him pesos. Eventually he dozed some, but he was too excited to drop off to sound sleep.

He was starting to nod when he thought he saw something move. Yes, something near Micaela's feet. At first, he thought it was a trick of the darkness, then he saw it again. A large rat, its tail curled over its back like a weapon, was sniffing at Micaela's toes. Riki jumped to his feet and made an involuntary sound of disgust.

The rat reared back on its haunches and bared a set of

gleaming teeth. Its claws flared as it threatened with long-fingered forepaws. Riki tried to kick it away, but the animal leaped deftly aside, then lunged for his ankle. He pulled his foot back quickly. The rat missed and landed on Micaela's stomach. When she pulled the blanket away to see what was going on, she found herself looking eye to eye with the rat. Her piercing scream did the trick. The rat scurried away to disappear in the darkness.

They quickly replaced their blankets inside the net bag. Several other rats moved about the enclosure, insolent and unfrightened as they watched the intruders leave. Riki and Micaela headed for the zócalo, now deserted and silent. They placed the bags and the suitcase on a bench and sat down. But before they could any more than catch their breath, a man wearing an ill-fitting khaki uniform approached. Riki realized that he must be a *policía* because he wore a pistol hooked onto a belt and carried a black club, just as El Perrón had described. Riki felt a thrill of fear in his abdomen and grabbed Micaela's hand and made her get up from the bench.

The policeman eyed them suspiciously until they hefted their burdens and crossed the square toward the church. A light drizzling rain began falling.

It was an old church, probably constructed in the late 1600s, with massive walls and columns of hewn stone. Inside, gilt angels clung to a high, domed ceiling of creamy marble. An altar glittered with candles yet was somber with ancient paintings of Christ bleeding on a cross and a statue of the Virgin Maria Tonantzín. Micaela kissed the gold crucifix she always wore about her neck and prayed silently to Tonantzín. Riki gazed about the inside of the church in wonder. The only church he had ever known was the one at Tezcatlipocas; it had no roof, no paintings, no statues, and it smelled of the garbage the villagers often threw there. This one had no odor except for a faint drift of incense. The statue of Tonantzín glittered in the candlelight. She looked formidable, but unless She found them a job, Riki decided he couldn't feel like praying to Her.

After a while, they went outside and noticed several sleeping figures huddled under the dark shelter of the church's portal. They found a clear space and Micaela spread her blankets once more. The rain fell heavier against the flagstone courtyard, but they felt snug and secure and dry here. Soon exhaustion overcame them and they slept, Micaela with her head against the suitcase, her feet touching her net bag. Riki leaned across his own bag, using it as a pillow. The machete handle felt hard and uncomfortable, but he didn't move it, because if necessary, he could pull it out of the bag to defend Micaela.

In the morning, they discovered that the net bag, the one Micaela had been guarding—the one with her clothes and personal belongings—had been stolen.

And the suitcase was gone!

Chapter Twelve

Micaela tried to be brave about the theft of the bag and the suitcase. It would do no good to weep now, she told herself, it would only make Riki feel bad. She led him to a street stand and used most of her precious money to order a large bowl of steaming *menudo*, which they shared, picking succulent chunks of meat from the stew with their fingers and alternately sipping from the crockery bowl. The chewy pieces of tripe, piquant with chili, sent shivers of delight through Riki's body.

When it was finished, he wished they could afford another. As they wiped the last of the juice from the bowl with pieces of tortilla, a man approached them. He had a friendly smile on his face, and for a moment Riki thought he might be one of those who left Tezcatlipocas and made it rich in the city, for he wore a suit, although rather threadbare, and he had real shoes of polished leather. He was taller than any of the men from the village, taller even than Riki.

"Just in from the country?" he asked pleasantly. "Looking for a job, I would guess."

Micaela nodded eagerly. "Yes, we'll work at anything. Do you know of a job?"

"Well, now there is a possibility. Just a possibility, mind you. It would be working for a rich family. The both of you. But it will cost you some pesos. You do have pesos, don't you?"

Micaela's face turned dark with despair. "Not many. Almost none."

The man's smile disappeared; a look of boredom replaced it. "How much do you have?" When she unwrapped the small

153

fold of money, he mentally counted them and made a wry face. "That's all? My God, woman, that won't buy a decent meal."

He started to walk away, but she pulled at his sleeve. "Wait! I have this crucifix. It's of real gold. Maybe I could borrow money on it." She lifted the chain from her neck and held it out to the man, who now seemed interested again, the smile slowly returning to his face. Riki knew this was her most valuable possession, for the crucifix had belonged to her mother, and to her grandmother before her.

"Well, now that's better. Now, here's the way it works: You don't have to pay me a thing until *after* you get your first wages. But I have to be sure you're going to pay me. You understand that, don't you? Well, we will put your money and your crucifix into this paper bag, and you must hold it in plain sight so that I know you don't have any bad intentions of keeping them. Then you hand me the bag when you are accepted for the job. I will hold it until you get paid, then I return it for my commission. Understand?"

Micaela looked puzzled, but she carefully placed the crucifix and the money into the paper bag.

The man's eyes twinkled as he nodded his head in approval. "Here, let me write my name and address on the bag so you know where to reach me, should you not get the job and want to contact me later." He took the bag and scribbled something on it and handed it back to her with a smile of satisfaction. "Now follow me, and we will have you working by this afternoon."

Micaela grinned and dug her fingers into Riki's arm in excitement. After a few blocks the man stopped at a busy street corner.

He said, "Wait right here a few minutes. I am going to bring the *patron* here to interview you for your job. Hold onto the bag, so no one can steal the crucifix and money." He disappeared into the swirling crowd of people.

Riki and Micaela waited for some time, over an hour. They

began worrying that the man had changed his mind about the job. She reached in the bag to take out the crucifix to use it in a prayer to Tonantzín. Suddenly, her face lost its color. She swayed as if she were going to faint; Riki put his arms around her waist to steady her.

"Thief! He was a *thief*." Her voice was husky and thick. "There's nothing here but torn paper and some nails! Madre de Dios, what do we do now?" She started to weep, sinking down to kneel on the sidewalk, her shoulders shaking uncontrollably. Riki tried to comfort her as he looked around, hoping to spot the smiling man in the crowd. It was no use. At that moment the man was several blocks away, in a second-hand jewelry store, watching with greedy satisfaction as the owner of the store counted twenty-peso bills onto the glass countertop.

As Micaela slumped on the sidewalk, several well-dressed citizens passed by and saw what they assumed to a beggar woman. Two of them dropped copper coins by Micaela's side and continued on. When Micaela looked up with tears streaming down her cheeks, a group of passing tourists looked down at her in disgust.

One said in English: "God, beggars are like ants at a picnic around here!"

Another replied, "Dirty, too. I wonder if they ever wash?"

"I doubt it. They look too stupid to do anything but beg. Too lazy to work for a living. I never give anything. God helps those who help themselves, I always say."

One tourist, a heavy man with a Gringo-pink face, slowed his walk and fished a 50-centavo copper coin from his pocket. He flipped it with his thumb, sending it spinning high in the air. It hit the ground in front of Micaela, spun for a moment then went tumbling into the gutter, coming to rest in a pad of dog vomit. The tourist shrugged and hurried to catch up with his companions.

Riki looked after the Gringos with hate and anger smoldering inside. He spit in their direction. Those were the first words in English he had heard in more than eleven years, and although they sounded strange, he had understood perfectly, and he hated them—both the words and the people.

Micaela picked up the coins from the sidewalk and stared at them. "A beggar! They think I'm a *beggar!*" She dropped the coins and started weeping again. A street urchin retrieved the coin from the gutter and went running away with his sticky prize.

Riki helped Micaela up and then hoisted the remaining net bag to his forehead. He guided her toward the zócalo and made her sit on a stone bench. They sat quietly for a long time.

"We have no clothes, no money, no food." Her voice sounded very strange now, a weary monotone. "Not even my grandmother's crucifix." She stared vacantly toward the church at the end of the zócalo. "And the suitcase... I lost the suitcase!"

To Riki's dismay, her mouth assumed the slack, half-open appearance of long ago, when Riki first came into her life.

"Don't worry," he said as calmly as he could. "I'll do something. Things will be just fine, you'll see." He felt panic gathering in his stomach, a fear that Micaela was returning to the strange being he had heard about. He couldn't remember exactly how she had been before, but he'd often overheard the villagers discussing Micaela and the miraculous change in her personality. He put his palm against her cheek and asked, "Are you feeling all right?"

She continued staring straight ahead as if she were deaf, and a line of saliva began running from the corner of her mouth. Riki shook her gently and kissed her on the cheek. "Don't act like this, please."

She turned to stare at him, dull, corpse-like eyes that sent despair flooding through Riki's body. For a brief moment she started to come out of it, a brightness flickered in her eyes, then it slipped away. "Sleep. I need sleep." Her voice was now a ragged whisper.

He urged her to get to her feet. Then, hooking the strap of

the bag over his forehead, he guided her toward the church courtyard where they stayed last night. At the rear of the structure, where some renovation had been going on, he found a pile of worm-eaten lumber and some oiled canvas tarpaulins. Micaela stared listlessly at the ground while Riki pulled a square of canvas next to the church wall and made her sit down. Then he leaned some boards against the masonry and covered them with another piece of tarpaulin. She was sleeping soundly by the time he had finished.

At least she will be dry here, he thought. *Next thing is, how do we get food? She can't find a job like this, so I must.* She slept for most of the day. Toward evening she stirred and sat up. Riki took her hand and said, "Are you feeling better now? Can you watch the bags while I get something for us to eat?"

She stared at her hands for a long time before replying. "Eat? Yes, I am very hungry." Then she slumped against the wall and began humming a nonsense tune.

"Watch the bag, don't let anyone take it. I'll be right back."

He walked around the zócalo first trying to think of a way to get some money or some food. He thought about stealing some but didn't know how to begin. His legs were feeling weak, and he remembered El Perrón's story about being hungry in Mexico City.

The street with the food stands lining the gutters had plenty of food, and he thought he could reach over and grab some and run. But, there were too many people standing about. They would stop him, or maybe beat him, or put him away someplace, maybe in that *calaboso* place El Perrón had mentioned. Then who would take care of Micaela?

The market! Of course. Didn't Micaela say that they throw away food there? He hurried back across the square and into the maze of food stands. Again, it was late; vendors were closing down for the evening.

He found the woman who had sold them the tortillas last night and asked her if she knew where people threw food away.

She looked at him for a moment and then said, "Nothing they throw away here is fit for anything but rats. But you are hungry and you have no money..." She looked at her small pile of unsold tortillas for a moment, then back at the boy. She measured half of the stack. "Take these. I'll take half, you and your mother eat the other half." She smiled sadly as he murmured humiliated words of thanks. "*Vaya con Diós mi hijito,*" she whispered when he hurried away with precious food for Micaela.

He was stuffing another tortilla into his mouth after only half swallowing the first when he saw the man. He was stocky, with a beard that seemed to cover all his face except for his eyes and nose; he wore ragged clothes and a knit cap. He hurried furtively through the church gate and began trotting up the street, leaning forward under the weight of a burden. Suddenly, Riki realized: the man carried Micaela's leather suitcase!

"Stop! That belongs to my mother!" Riki began running after the man. When the thief turned and saw the youth coming after him, he gripped his loot tighter and began running. He sprinted a few meters, then disappeared around a corner.

Clutching the precious tortillas, Riki ran after the thief. Never before had he felt anger like this, never before such hatred. The bearded stranger symbolized all misfortune and evil in the world. Riki ran so fast that he almost fell as he turned the corner in pursuit of the thief.

The street was empty. He slowed a bit, wondering where the man could have gone. As he was passing a narrow alley, he heard a dog barking angrily as though some audacious intruder dared enter his sacred territory.

Riki wiped the sweat from his forehead with the back of his hand and slipped into the narrow passage. It was dark, and the place smelled of old garbage and stale urine.

The alley ended at the rear of a large building where a light bulb cast a faint pool of light. Riki kept walking, wary and alert. Then he saw the man. He was leaning over the suitcase trying to pry it open with Riki's machete. When he saw Riki coming, he spit on the ground threateningly.

"Get away from me you ignorant brat, or I'll cut you like a pig."

"Those things belong to me. You stole them."

"They belong to me now. Now get going, or else!" He turned his attention back to the suitcase, expecting the boy to be cowed. Mexican boys usually respect authority and power. He was surprised when he looked up to see the boy approaching. "Are you crazy? Do I have to slice you to bits? Now go!" He grasped the machete, stepped forward and stamped his foot as he would to scare a dog or a frightened boy away.

But Riki kept coming. "Get away from my belongings, or I will hurt you." His voice surprised him, it was calm and matter of fact. Blinding anger precluded any feelings of rational fear.

The man laughed with disdainful amusement. Then, when the boy kept coming, he tightened his grip on the machete, and again stamped his foot. Again, he felt surprise, that this had no effect.

"Don't say I didn't warn you."

He brandished the machete, expertly switching it from right hand to left. He stepped forward to meet Riki with rapid tossing and clutching ploys. The semi-polished blade reflected flashes of yellow light, until he finally grasped it in his fist—ready for a flat-sided blow.

"This is your last chance, puppy. You better run, fast!"

Enough light spilled though the alley from a distant streetlight to allow Riki to lock onto the man's eyes. The bearded one stepped closer, now within chopping range. Then, an abrupt shift of eyes told Riki which direction to duck.

The flat of the blade flashed toward its victim. The man gasped in surprise. Instead of slapping against Riki's ear, the machete missed its target, pulling the man half around. He grunted and fell sprawling backward when Riki's fist cracked against his unprotected jaw. His mouth opened in indignant astonishment.

"You! Why you young bastard! You broke my tooth!"

"Get away from my *maleta.*"

The man jumped to his feet, clutching the weapon with both hands. He charged forward, the machete ready, this time the cutting edge of the blade held ready.

Riki stood his ground. He didn't look at the blade, only at the man's wide, flaring eyes. He waited for a message. It came quickly. Riki's foot flashed upward with the full force of his frustrations. It found its mark with a satisfying jolt against the thief's wrist. The machete flew upward, into an arc, falling with a sharp crash against a metal garbage can. A fraction of a second later, the man felt Riki's sandal-clad foot itself deep into his belly.

The man doubled over and fell to the ground. He moaned and clutched his hand to his chest. "My wrist! Look what you did! You broke my wrist!"

"What did you do with the bag you stole last night? You took it, too, didn't you?"

The man said between gasps of pain: "I sold it. There wasn't much there. Not enough for a full bottle of aguardiente." He struggled to regain his feet without the help of his hands.

"Then give me the money."

"But..." he dropped his objection when Riki stepped closer. "Okay, okay!" With his good hand, he reached into his pocket and pulled out a greasy wallet. He tried to take some money out, but Riki said:

"Throw it here and then leave."

"But the rest is *my* money. I earned it, and it's mine." His voice was no longer threatening but instead, whining and pleading. When he saw that Riki wasn't wavering, he threw the wallet on the ground.

Riki sensed power and it felt good. He put his foot on the wallet where it fell. He waited until the man crept down the alleyway. Then he placed the wallet in his waistband. Gripping the suitcase, he started back to the church.

He didn't look inside the wallet until he had everything stored underneath the tarpaulin. Micaela was snoring lightly. He felt through the net bag until he found a box of waxed string matches. By the flickering light he counted the money. Almost 100 pesos. Would it be enough rent a house? Or even a room? He had no idea how much anything cost, but he knew he needed a safe place for Micaela.

He started when he heard approaching footsteps. Abruptly, a brilliant light flashed into the shelter. Someone was holding a flashlight on his face. A rough, angry voice cut through the night.

"You can't stay here! You either sleep with the others on the church steps, or away you go." It was the policeman from the other night. Riki felt an involuntary fear grip his stomach. He remembered El Perrón's warnings about policemen. "My mother is sick. We have no place to stay."

"Can you afford 50 pesos? If you can, then get her to the hotel, otherwise you go up front with the others where you're supposed to be."

"I have money. Help me."

The hotel room was large and even had a bathroom at the end of the hallway, with porcelain fixtures like Riki remembered from dreams. Even a white tub with two faucets, one dispensing cold water and the other hot water! The room clerk showed him how to use the key, and how to flush the toilet. Riki shook his head in awe at this miracle.

Their room had two small beds and a window that looked out into the street. But the most exciting thing about the room was an electric bulb that dangled from the ceiling. It had a string that hung down and the light could be turned on and off simply by pulling it! Riki flicked the light on and off several times to experience the magical power of electricity. For eleven years, the only lights he had seen were kerosene lamps and candles.

As soon as he was sure Micaela would be all right by herself, he locked the door and hurried to the street to see how much food the money would buy. He ordered something from each stand until the money was almost gone. Then, carrying a bundle of hot food wrapped in newspaper, he ran triumphantly back to the hotel.

While she absently toyed with the pile of fried tacos and flautas, Riki gnawed at a piece of tough *carne asada* and contemplated the suitcase. When he finished eating as much as his stomach would allow, he placed the suitcase on his bed and examined the locking mechanism. The thief had already broken one hasp, and other didn't look too difficult. Micaela was staring at the wall and not paying any attention. The hasp opened with a single twist of the machete edge.

He lifted the lid slowly. A folded dress lay on top, purple with a fur collar. It was the most beautiful piece of clothing he'd ever seen. He half remembered a woman wearing something like that at one time. His mother? He wondered how Micaela would look wearing it. Then he began lifting clothing items out one at a time. Micaela would not have to worry about clothes now; these would do fine.

Then, he came upon a padded box resting on the bottom of the suitcase. His brow lifted in mild surprise at the weight of the box. He pressed a button on the front and surprisingly, the top flipped open. A strange tune began to play from somewhere inside the box, high pitched and melodic. Micaela looked puzzled, and, for a brief moment frightened. Then she sank back into her wall-staring lethargy. Riki's eyes grew wide as he inspected the box.

Gold and silver and pieces of colored glass sparkled under the naked light bulb that hung overhead. He knew instinctively that he was looking at something very valuable. He picked out a wristwatch, gleaming gold with stones set in the band like glittering stars. On the back were some tiny words engraved, but they weren't in Spanish and Riki couldn't make them out except for one word which he guessed might be someone's name, *Diana*. The name was vaguely familiar, as though he'd known someone named Diana, long ago, back in that dream world of before he came to the village.

Maybe that woman who...

This didn't make sense! Where did Micaela get this jewelry? Why hadn't she sold it? The questions kept rolling around his head as he examined the treasure with increasing excitement. The answers to this puzzle would have to wait until she regained her senses.

There seemed to be only one thing to do: sell some of the jewelry. But how? Where? To whom? He selected a gold wristwatch. Glittering stones encrusted in the gold band sparkled wickedly in the bare electric light. He looked at the other jewelry once more before slipping the watch into his pocket. Then he replaced the music box and shoved the suitcase under the bed.

He left the room early the next morning to sell the watch. He had no idea of how to go about it. He stopped a rich-looking man and held out the fancy bauble. But the man's reaction was puzzling. Before Riki could say a word, the man's mouth turned sour as if he had tasted something spoiled. "I don't buy stolen property," he said tersely, "and I am going to report you to the first policeman I see." He stalked away angrily. Riki hurried down a side street, looking for a place to hide.

Then, on a back street, not too far from the market, he came across a small shop with a sign in the window: *Gold and Silver Bought Here*. It was closed, so he waited across the street, squatting on his heels as the men in Tezcatlipocas do when they have time to nullify. Finally, a well-dressed man approached the door, adjusted his thick eyeglasses, and fumbled with the lock until it opened.

Riki waited a few minutes, then cautiously peered inside before entering. The man frowned. "Well? What do you want?"

"I have something to sell. Your sign says you buy..."

"I know what the sign says. What do you have, and where did you steal it? You'd better have something good, or I'll cuff you about the ears."

The man was using the familiar "tu" form of Spanish with Riki as is the village custom when speaking to children, inferior people or when ordering animals about. But in Tezcatlipocas, since there were no children, and since everyone was equal, the familiar form was only used for cursing at animals. Riki felt anger, burning in his face. Except for the bearded stranger in the alley, no one had ever used the *tu* form with him before. He was being insulted, but he needed money. He tried to ignore the insult.

"I didn't steal anything. This belongs to my mother." He held out his hand and slowly opened it to reveal the watch. He kept his eyes on the jeweler, hoping for some clue as to the worth of the watch. He naturally expected to be cheated; by how much was the question.

Behind the thick glasses, the jeweler's eyes seemed to grow as large as the glasses themselves. He reached slowly for the watch as if he thought it might disappear. Then he snatched away his glasses and replaced them with a strong eyepiece which he put close to the watch's band. He looked at each of the diamonds in turn, nodding slowly all the time. Then he turned the watch to study the engraving on the back. His hands quivered, and he looked oddly at Riki, then read engraving once more. He replaced his glasses and his lower lip jutted out as he tried to look disinterested. But the man had given himself away. He pushed the watch to one side, sneering as if it were a piece of garbage.

"All of you thieves are alike. You steal worthless trash and try to take advantage of me. By law, I am supposed to call the police. Do you know why I don't? Because I feel sorry for you grimy little street urchins. I know you are making a living the best you can. Because of my soft heart, I rarely turn your kind into the police."

When Riki didn't answer, the man became uncomfortable. "What's the matter with you? Why are you staring at me?"

"Please don't talk to me like that?"

"Talk to you like what?" The jeweler was taken aback by a youth who spoke to him like a man, who looked him squarely in the eye as if an equal.

"As if I were a burro or a dog. Don't say *tu* when you speak to me. Say *usted*! And the watch is not stolen. If you don't want to buy it, give it back."

"Don't be clever. I don't have to buy the watch, and I don't have to give it back. The law says I must call the police." He sighed apologetically and continued, "But it's as just as I said: I feel sorry for street kids—I mean men—like you. Of course, I will buy it."

He reached under the counter and brought out a heavy metal box and removed a padlock. He held a sheaf of bills and looked speculatively at Riki. "You can tell me the truth, where did you *find* this watch? There's a lot more where this came from, isn't there?"

Riki shook his head quickly. "How much?"

The man narrowed his eyes and studied Riki for a few moments. Finally, he said, "Tell me how much you want."

Riki tried to think how much he should ask. He had no way of knowing how much the watch was worth. He'd observed enough bargaining in the village to know that no one gives their final price first. But how much should he ask? "You tell me how much you will give."

The jeweler looked at the watch and set it aside carelessly. "It isn't worth as much as you think. Those aren't real diamonds, just glass. But maybe I can give you... maybe 200 pesos."

Riki frowned as he tried to think. Obviously the first price was low, but by how much. Two times the offer? Three times? He chewed at the back of his thumb nervously.

Then he saw it! Hanging on the wall, behind a sliding glass shield, next to some necklaces and chains, was Micaela's crucifix! It looked mournful and pathetic, out of place.

"That crucifix. How much is it?"

The old man looked at the crucifix and shrugged. "Very expensive. Pure gold. Easy worth 1,500 pesos. But for you I could let it go for 1,200. Now, I know that you have a lot more jewelry around, or you know where to get more. So, maybe we could make a trade? Eh? The jewelry for the crucifix. Or for money."

"Why do you think I have more jewelry?"

A conspirator's smile crept across the jeweler's thick face. "Because this watch is famous. The police have been looking for it for years. You know that as well as I. Where did you get it? You know, we could make good business, you and I, if only you..."

Riki cut him off in mid-sentence. "I don't know what you are talking about. Two hundred pesos isn't enough for the watch. I need more."

"I could call the police, but instead, I'll give you 250, and not a peso more."

Riki remembered how bargaining in the village went, and he made his next move. "I want 1,500 pesos *and* the crucifix." He watched the man's eyes closely for a reaction. He caught a glint of excitement and he knew he'd asked too little. He felt angry with himself.

The man smiled and shook his head sadly. "Maybe 700 and the crucifix, but..."

Suddenly Riki grabbed the watch and backed away, poised, ready to run out the door. The man raised his hands pleadingly and a look of desperation crossed his face.

"No. Wait! I'll pay. Don't leave." He reached for the wooden box again and slammed it on the counter. "I'll pay the 1,500 pesos, and you can have the crucifix. Here, I'll get it for you right now." He almost ran to the glass display case to get the gold crucifix. He held it out, letting it dangle temptingly. "Now hand me the watch and I'll hand you the money and the crucifix."

Riki shook his head coldly. He realized that he was in control now and he was enjoying it. "The price is now 2,500 pesos and the crucifix."

The jeweler gasped and was about to protest, but something in Riki's eyes told him not to argue. He nodded hastily and began counting banknotes onto the glass countertop. Riki picked them up, then the crucifix, and only when they were safely tucked into his pocket did he lay the watch on the counter. Then he started to back away, keeping his eyes on the man as he felt behind him for the door.

"Wait! Don't leave! You and I can make a lot of money. Just tell me where you stole that watch and where the rest of the stuff is. I can sell it all for you, and we will both become rich!"

Riki shook his head and kept backing toward the door. When he reached it, the jeweler called out, "Don't be a fool! Tell me!" But Riki stepped outside and hurried away.

The jeweler picked up the watch and hefted it in his hand. "The lost Barron jewelry!" he whispered in awe, "Why, a watch like this would go for fortune at the *Monte de Piedad*. Just the diamonds are worth 50 thousand each. And just think about the reward! But wait! I don't want the reward for just this one piece. I want it all!"

Chapter Thirteen

The jeweler called out: "Nephew! Hurry! Follow after that boy. Find out where he lives."

The nephew, an idle youth of eighteen whose main interest in life was finding a girl to whom he could sacrifice his virginity, came to the door with a total lack of enthusiasm. He caught a glimpse of Riki as he hurried down the street and ducked around the corner. Ruben casually pulled on a green soccer shirt and started for the door. His uncle hurried him along with a cuff on the back of his neck.

"Get going, you lazy burro! Don't let him get away. He has the jewelry the whole world has been looking for! It's worth a fortune just in rewards!"

Ruben stepped into the street and reluctantly broke into a forced trot. He knew the boy would be easy to find, what with the stupid straw hat and the peasant clothes. Why the hurry? He turned the corner and saw the boy pause in front of the hotel, as if he were going to enter. But when the boy caught sight of Ruben, he must have sensed that he was being followed, for he broke into a run, turning the corner, heading for the marketplace. Ruben now had to run fast to keep up with him. In a way, Ruben hoped the boy would get away, partially because he detested his uncle, and partly because the boy was bigger than he, and they would probably have to fight if and when he caught up with him.

Riki suspected from the outset that he wouldn't get away with all that money so easily. As he hurried from the jeweler's shop,

168

he kept glancing behind to see if he was being followed. He noticed a youth wearing a green shirt step around the corner and stare belligerently at him. Riki broke into a run, heading toward the market. It was the only place he could think of, where he could hide amidst the market's confusion.

Green shirt began running after him. Riki turned into the broad gateway opening in the wall, which was the market's main entrance, and he glanced about frantically. A maze of passageways ran between the vendors' stalls like tunnels in a rabbit warren. Riki darted into the rows of stalls and headed for the darker interior of the market.

He dodged this way and that like a hunted animal, hoping to elude his pursuer. As he rounded the corner of a used clothing stand, he suddenly stepped back. There was green shirt, looking around intently.

Riki ducked down, ran a few steps and then crept behind a display of blankets. He crouched low, his heart pounding as he peered through an opening between the blankets. Green shirt came closer and closer. Riki drew back and huddled against a wooden stand, holding himself as still as a rabbit. He heard a voice say: "Did you see a boy, an *Indio*, come through here just now?"

The weary blanket seller replied, "I see lots of indios here."

"This one is wearing a ragged straw hat and those stupid-looking white Indian clothes, and..."

Riki pulled the hat off and threw it under the stall. He stayed hidden until green shirt moved on. Then he crept from his hiding place and looked around to make sure his pursuer was not in sight. A stand of second-hand clothing caught his eye. The lady sitting behind the counter frowned at him, wondering if he were a potential customer or a potential thief. She stood up, ready for either event. "You want to buy something?" she asked suspiciously.

For a moment Riki fingered the money in his pocket, then he made a decision. He pointed to a bright red shirt. "How much is that shirt?" he asked timidly, "and that pair of green pants, and that hat... the yellow one." The woman allowed him to change into his new finery behind her stand. When he finished dressing, she held up a cracked mirror so he could admire his new image. His eyes were dazzled by the beautiful colors. Never had he seen anything so beautiful. He grinned proudly at the woman and counted out the money. She smiled and raised her eyebrows, for she had never seen anyone make such a horrible selection of colors. He looks like a parrot, she thought, and almost felt guilty at overcharging him so.

He hurried home to show Micaela, hoping it would surprise her enough to make her smile. She was lying in bed as usual, her stare fixed upon the ceiling.

"Mica! I have surprises for you. Look! Look at my new clothes."

Her eyes drifted slowly to where he was standing, where the afternoon's sunlight through the window did the best for the colors. Immediately, her eyes opened wide and she pushed herself to a sitting position. She studied him from head to foot with a look of amazement on her face. Her mouth hung partly open in astonishment.

"How do you like them? Pretty, eh?" When she didn't reply, he held up a newspaper-wrapped package. "The next surprise is food!"

She watched with interest as he unwrapped the newspaper to reveal a plate of steaming pork chunks. The delicious odor of hot grease wafted through the room. Micaela smiled in approval and accepted a cardboard plate piled high with the meat. As she ate, she kept looking at Riki's new clothes, and once almost said something.

Then, as her stomach filled, the lethargy started to return. She dropped the cardboard plate and lay back on the bed. Her eyes once again focused on nothing. Some of Riki's enthusiasm drained at this. He sounded desperate as he dangled the crucifix in front of her eyes, saying:

"One more surprise. Look at this, Mica, look, look." He swung the crucifix back and forth like a pendulum. "It's yours. The one that was stolen from you. Remember?"

She sat up again and looked closely at the golden cross. She lifted it from his hand and held it to the light of the window and slowly nodded. A shy smile spread over her face. "Yes. I remember. Where has it been? I've been looking all over for it."

"Everything's going to be all right now, Mica. You'll see." But he felt discouraged when the dull look returned to Micaela's eyes; she started to lay back to stare at the ceiling once again.

He grabbed her by her arms and pulled her up to a sitting position. "Come on! You're going to get dressed, and we're going to the cinema. There's one on the corner of the square."

A slight look of interest brightened her face, stirring Riki's hopes. "Get up! We'll find something for you to wear from the leather suitcase."

Reluctantly, she stood up and allowed Riki to select a dress for her to wear. It was of white wool, now yellowed and smelling strongly of mildew. But it looked elegant on her. She giggled and pirouetted in front of the scabby mirror, for an instant, a whole woman. Just for an instant. Then, as she tried to go back to bed, Riki firmly took her by the arm and said:

"Let's go."

"Go where?"

"To the cinema. We'll both enjoy it. I've never been to one, and I want to see what it's like." He had to push her firmly through the door to keep her from returning to the bed.

The movie theater was an old one, with hard wooden seats that creaked when people shifted about and a ventilation fan that clattered in the wall above the screen. But to Riki, it was pure luxury; a carpet covered the aisle floors and curtains hung from the ceiling clear down to the floor. He waited excitedly for the show to begin. Several times he had seen movies in Tezcatlipocas when a traveling entrepreneur brought a projector and showed Mexican cowboy films on the church wall.

But the image was weak against the rough, yellowing wall and the picture flickered erratically. This was going to be different. This was a real theater, something he had never expected to see.

The film was American, the dialogue in English with Spanish subtitles below the picture. The story was about a prizefighter who was in love with his manager's daughter. To Riki's amazement, he discovered that he understood much of what was being said, despite the squeaking seats, the rattling fan, and people talking and whispering all around him. Those who could read, translated for those who couldn't. Many words he didn't understand, but the Spanish subtitles at the bottom of the screen made them clear.

Totally absorbed, he watched the story unfold. He was shocked at the boxing scenes where the opponents pounded each other without mercy. Riki now realized what El Perrón had been through, and why his head was no longer right. He found himself caught up in the plot, his heart skipping beats during the exciting parts, and tears in his eyes when it was sad. Then he noticed that Micaela was leaning forward in her seat, her eyes on the screen in fascination. Her lips moved as she tried to sound out the subtitles, and she laughed in the appropriate places. She even wept at the ending. Riki squeezed her hand in joy. She seemed to be coming out of her depression. They remained in their seats through the intermission and watched the movie for the second time.

Once outside the theater, Micaela reverted to her listless, distracted mannerisms. Riki tried to draw her out, to get her talking about the movie, but she didn't seem to hear him. He decided to bring her back tomorrow.

They returned every night for the rest of the week, watching the movie twice each night. Riki learned many English words he didn't recognize at first, either by matching them with Spanish equivalents in the subtitles or through the context of the action. Then, on Friday, the film changed. It was another Hollywood production with Spanish subtitles. This one was a gangster movie, with plenty of shooting scenes and automobile chases. But the most thrilling moment was a scene where the hero dove into a swimming pool and rescued a drowning child."

"That's it," he whispered excitedly and nudged Micaela. "That's what I told don Rafael about! There was one of those ponds at my father's house in 'Puco'."

He soon knew every line by heart. At night, while waiting to go to sleep, he repeated the phrases under his breath, tasting the sounds of English, wondering if he would ever hear the words spoken by real people. Through watching the film over and over, Riki discovered that there are several ways of saying the same thing, several levels of behavior. Gangsters — the ones who carried guns — spoke one way, their victims another. He noted the calm, yet threatening way the bad guys treated their victims in order to instill fear in them. He stored these ways of behaving into the back of his mind, along with the new words.

The best part about the cinema was that it had a slow, beneficial effect on Micaela. Every day, she seemed to take a little more notice of her surroundings. She even began looking at the fancy dresses in the suitcase, holding them in front of her and looking at herself in the mirror. Riki now felt better about leaving her alone for longer periods of time while he went looking for work. He knew he would have to find a job they could do together. She still wasn't capable of functioning by herself.

The money began running low after the third week. Riki set out one day, determined to find some way of earning money. Before he left the hotel, he pocketed a gold and emerald bracelet with the idea of selling it if necessary. He found no work that day. When he approached the jeweler's shop, he lost his nerve. Green shirt was inside, being scolded by the jeweler. Riki pulled his hat down over his face and hurried on past. He heard the jeweler shouting:

"You *must* find him, you lazy dog. He has to be somewhere in this town!"

173

Riki breathed easier when he rounded the corner and found himself on the zócalo once more. He started to cross the park when he saw something that sent shivers of horror down his spine.

Across the square, stood Micaela and a policeman. She was dressed in a low-cut sequined cocktail dress which she had taken from the suitcase. Her bosom glittered with a string of diamonds as the afternoon's sun played against them with sharp stabs of light. Long pearl strands of a necklace hung down, looping below her breasts, which were scarcely covered by the sequined dress material. The uniformed cop had her by the arm and was pulling her toward the *municipio* which was directly across from the church. Riki ran across the square. Micaela's puzzled expression revealed that she didn't quite realize what was happening. The cocktail dress was cut so low that one of her nipples had popped out as the cop pulled on her arm roughly.

"What's wrong? What did she do?"

The cop glared at Riki and then at Micaela. "This *puta* is going to spend three days in jail, that's what's wrong. She can't sell her wares right here in the zócalo! That's what the red zone is for."

"Wait! She's my mother, and she's sick. Please let her go." Riki grabbed her free hand and held on tightly.

The cop snorted in disgust. "Just look at her! Parading around the zócalo, drunk, showing her *chichis* like a shameless sow."

Riki reached over and pulled the dress up to cover Micaela's breast. "She isn't drunk. She's sick." Then he remembered what El Perrón had said about the *chota*: "They can be bought."

"How much to let her go?"

The cop relaxed his grip on his prisoner's arm and the frown eased from his face. "Well, I don't know what the fine for something like this will be, but I suppose I could take the money and pay the fine for you. How much do you have?"

Riki fingered the slender fold of banknotes in his pocket. "I only have 95 pesos," he said softly.

The cop started to frown again. "The fine should be much more than that. Well... Okay, plus I'll just take some of this junk jewelry she's wearing. My little daughter likes to play with stuff like that." He reached for the diamond necklace.

Riki's eyes narrowed and his voice growled, "Don't touch that!"

His voice surprised him, for it sounded strong, threatening, like the gangsters in the movies. It must have surprised the cop too, because he hesitated and thought for a moment before saying. "Okay, okay. Give me the money, and don't let me catch her selling *pinche* in the square again." He counted the pesos and stuffed them into his uniform pocket. All the while, Micaela hummed an ancient melody she had learned years ago in Tezcatlipocas.

Micaela was still humming when Riki opened the door to their room and led her inside. Carefully, he unhooked the jewelry and returned it to the music box case. After he put it safely under the bed, he tried to lecture Micaela about her adventure in the zócalo. But it was useless, for she lay on the bed, her eyes staring at the ceiling.

He slipped his hand under the mattress and felt around until he found a small fold of pesos, the last of the money from the jeweler. He counted them several times. Not enough to last more than a couple of days. What comes next? A job?

The next morning, he paced the floor, wondering how he could find some way to earn money without leaving Micaela alone. The only solution seemed to be in selling more of the jewelry. But how? Then, as he passed by the window, he looked through the broken shutter slats and drew in a sharp breath. More trouble!

Standing across the street, pointing at the hotel, was the youth in the green soccer shirt. With him were the pudgy man

175

who had bought the watch and two men wearing smart brown and tan uniforms, holstered guns and polished boots. Riki had never seen uniforms like that, but he didn't need to be told that they were policía. The zócalo cop with the tired-looking khaki uniform was also there, talking and motioning toward the hotel.

"Mica! Get up! We have to leave!" He slapped her on the arm, and then on the cheek until she began to move. "Hurry!"

Riki began throwing clothes into the leather suitcase. Clearly, there would not be room for everything, and Micaela couldn't be trusted to carry anything. He pulled her from the bed and pointed to the pile of Diana's clothes that were piled in the corner of the room. "Get dressed. Now!"

Something in his voice directed her to obey, as a child obeys its parents. She picked up the sequined dress from the top of the pile and pulled it over her head. "Where are we going?"

"To Mexico City, if I can figure out how to get there. Maybe doña Herencia can help us. And make sure your front things are covered by your dress."

He had found Herencia's address in Micaela's bag one day, and he recalled that when she left Tezcatlipocas she had urged Micaela to join her in looking for a new life in the capital. "If you should change your mind," she had said, "come see me and I'll help you find work."

Riki snapped the locks on the suitcase. Then he pulled Micaela by the arm to hurry her along. No one was in the hall. He held her hand tightly and started for the stairs.

He stopped when he heard steps and the voice of the hotel owner echoing in the narrow hallway.

"I thought it was strange that a young boy like that should have so much money, could afford to stay in a fine hotel like this. But how was I to know he is a thief and she a prostitute?"

The steps grew closer. Riki and Micaela hurried down the hall, trying the doors one after another until finally, one swung opened. The room was empty save for a broken bed and some rubbish piled in one corner. He eased the door shut and listened.

A voice cried out, "They're gone! How could they have gotten away?"

The jeweler said, "That one is a clever thief. I told you he was a professional criminal. He's capable of eluding any trap you can set."

"Why didn't you report him to us, then? Why did you have your nephew follow him instead of calling the police?"

"But... but, I didn't *know* the watch was stolen," the jeweler protested weakly. "Not until you showed up looking for the thief. Anyway, I think I should be entitled to at least *part* of the reward. After all, if it hadn't been for my..."

"Shut up, you idiot! Is there a telephone here that works? I have to call my superiors in the capital and report this stupidity. There have been reward posters out on these pieces of jewelry for the last eleven years. You should have recognized that watch immediately."

"But I didn't, I swear that..."

"Because of you and your greed, the thief got away with the rest of the pieces. I could lose a fortune in reward money."

"Yes, payable in pure gringo greenbacks, too," the hotel owner added sadly. "Maybe they're still in town. That woman is so *chiflada* that she can't get very far. There are other hotels not far from here. Maybe..."

The local cop said, "I'll check the other hotels. We can't let that reward money slip away."

When the footsteps faded, Riki dared to re-enter the hall. No one was downstairs. All were out combing the streets, looking for the thief and his prostitute friend. Riki led Micaela through back alleys until they came to the bus station. A bus with the letters "Mexico D.F." marked on the window was revving up its engine while passengers climbed aboard. Riki tugged at Micaela's hand and they hurried to join the tail end of the line.

Chapter Fourteen

Johnny Gee brought the news. Alex Barron was presiding in the conference room, a brace of studio executives sitting around the polished walnut table. Johnny brushed past the receptionist and threw the door open, letting it bang against the wall loudly. He ignored the astonished faces and went directly to Alex.

"They found a piece of Diana's jewelry, Alex! Her watch! The one you gave her when she finished *Chestnut River*."

"Where? Where did they find it?"

"It showed up in the National Pawn Shop in Mexico City. They traced it to a shady jeweler in Córdoba. He bought it from a local thief."

Alex waved the others from the conference room and sat back in his chair with a stunned look on his face. "After all these years. What do you think, Johnny? Could he be alive?"

"I think we ought to get our asses down to Córdoba and find out where that watch has been hiding. I have a charter plane waiting for us at the airport. Enrique Morales will meet us there. He's the one who located the watch when it turned up in the Mexico City pawn shop."

Enrique Morales waited as they disembarked from the Cessna. He escorted them to his auto, proudly exaggerating his role in the jewelry's discovery.

"This is a tough case, Mr. Barron. Never would I have guessed that the thief would wait so long before selling a piece of the jewelry. But now that the ice is broken, we will see action. I can guarantee you that. We'll have answers before long."

"Let's hope so," was Barron's only reply. After several

178

attempts at conversation, Morales shrugged and drove in silence toward the center of Córdoba. Although he felt happy that the first piece of jewelry had finally surfaced, the suspense about where the rest of it could be was about to drive him crazy. This was a delicate situation. He needed to find the kid's grave and the jewelry before Barron did. That way, he could deliver the burial spot and collect the reward and keep at least some jewelry. Morales desperately needed money. His latest girlfriend left him, practically spit in his face, because he couldn't afford to keep up the rent on her house in the Lomas de Chapultepec. The bonuses from Barron had stopped long ago, and his salary wasn't enough to keep even a girlfriend, plus a wife and six children, in proper style. He had the distinct feeling that he was going to be fired if something didn't turn up this time.

When they came to the stretch of road where Diana died, Alex and Johnny tensed. They studied each path and foot trail, just as they had so long ago, wondering if one might lead to the lost village. They passed below Tezcatlipocas without noticing the earthen bank and the stair-like foot path where the old cobblestone road once had climbed to the village, before the bulldozers had cut it away for the final time.

It was afternoon when they arrived in Córdoba. They went straight to the jewelry shop. Enrique Morales interrogated the jeweler, who sweated nervously as Enrique translated his answers into English.

"Tell those gringos that I had nothing to do with the theft," the jeweler pleaded as he wiped his forehead with a damp handkerchief. "The Secret Service questioned me; the Federal Police questioned me; the local police browbeat me; the insurance investigators threatened me! Tell those gringos I don't know a blessed thing. All I know is that a thief sold me a watch. That's all! I didn't even get the reward that was promised."

Enrique Morales translated. Alex nodded as if he were in

complete sympathy with the distraught shopkeeper. "Tell him I understand, and that I am willing to compensate him for his troubles, but that I need to find out exactly where the watch came from. Ask him how to locate the thief. And tell him not to hand us any bullshit about him not knowing who the thief is. A cheap fence like him will know. Explain that we don't threaten; we'll *pay* for the information."

The shopkeeper looked at the stack of 1000 peso bills Alex placed on the glass-top counter. He swallowed thickly as Enrique relayed the message. "By the grave of my mother, I would tell you if I knew. Oh, how quickly I would tell you! For that much money, I would sell you the grave itself."

He fingered the bills fervently, saying, "All I know is this: a young hoodlum came in here one day and showed me this watch. He asked me to buy it from him, and when I refused — for I suspected it might be stolen — he threatened me. Of course, the police scoffed at this, but the pure truth is that this thief is not the ordinary street ruffian you see coming in here every day. No señor! This one has eyes like the Devil himself; they bore into your very guts and send fear creeping through your body. This one has violence and death written on his face. I told him that I must call the police and he said he would kill me if I didn't buy the watch. I paid 10,000 pesos for it, plus a handful of valuable gold chains and crucifixes, not because it was valuable, but only because he threatened my life. Can you imagine the brilliance of this criminal? If he gets caught, he can claim that he didn't rob me, but just 'pawned' a watch, and that he intended coming back later to purchase back the watch. Clever, eh?"

Morales translated, adding, "He's exaggerating, of course, trying to cover up his part in the transaction. He's probably telling the truth about selling his mother's grave, though."

"Ask him what the thief looked like," Alex ordered. "Could he possibly have been an American?"

The shopkeeper smiled sarcastically when he heard the

translation. "American? Don't make me laugh. This one had guts of a killer — he was pure Mexican. Who else could have the nerve of a Pancho Villa plus the larceny of a Mexican politician? If he is not Mexican, then I must be an Eskimo."

"Describe him. Was he dark like an *Indio* or light like a *ladino*? What about his eyes? The color of his eyes."

The pudgy man rubbed the back of his neck before answering. "His eyes? Truthfully, I don't know, because he wore sunglasses. His skin color was lighter than a pure Indio, more like a mestizo. Yet he spoke with an Indio accent. Pronounced his words like those campesinos who live in the mountains near here. You know what I mean? With a soft, slurry way of talking. And he was dressed like a back-mountain Indian, wearing those old-fashioned white clothes and *huaraches* made of old automobile tires. He sure didn't talk or act like a city-type person, yet he knew enough to steal good jewelry and to extort 50,000 pesos from me! A professional thief, no question about that."

"You said 10,000 pesos earlier."

"I did? Well, I meant to say 50,000. Also, the crucifixes were worth at least 50,000. Pure gold. I think you should pay me 100,000 pesos for my information."

Alex interrupted impatiently. "What's he saying? I can't understand a word."

"He is telling how tough this thief is. I asked if there is a chance that he might have been an American, but he says no. Says the thief was an Indian, probably from around here. That means we're close to finding the rest of the jewelry."

"How old was the boy? How tall?"

Morales put the question to the jeweler. He answered, "About as tall as you. He looked to be young, and at first I thought he might be only a youngster. But when he became angry at my using *tu* forms of language with him as we always do with children, and when he looked me squarely in the eye man-to-man, I suddenly realized that he had to be much older

181

than he looked. Much older."

"How old?"

"Only God knows. Maybe twenty years old. Maybe even older than that. Maybe even thirty. It's hard to tell ages of these *Indios*. Certainly, I was dealing with a grown man who perhaps looked a little younger than he is." He rubbed his hands together and smiled hopefully. "And now about that reward? After all, if it hadn't been for me buying the watch, well..."

Enrique cut him off by picking up the stack of banknotes and folding them in his hands. "The reward is for the capture of the thief, not the jewelry. You made your mistake by selling the watch instead of contacting me."

Alex frowned as Morales explained about the thief's probable age and the improbability of his being anything other than an Indian from the mountains. "About twenty years old, or maybe older. I'm sorry."

"Any chance he's lying?"

"This guy does a lot of exaggerating, but I doubt that he's out and out lying. The Secret Service was in on the questioning, and they usually get answers."

Johnny Gee sighed deeply and said, "Then, you're absolutely sure the thief was Mexican?"

"It certainly looks that way. Do we give him any reward money?"

Alex pressed his hand against the glass counter, stared at the jeweler in the eye as he said, "Tell him he earns his reward when he tells us where and how the thief stole the watch. If we can trace the watch back in time, maybe we can figure out where Rickey and Diana were on that day. We will know what happened to Rickey."

When this was translated, the shopkeeper looked crest fallen. Alex started to leave, but then said to Enrique, "Oh, hell. Give him the money. Tell him I'll triple it if he can find where the jewelry's been hidden all these years."

The jeweler's eyes brightened when Morales gave him the

money and repeated the triple-bonus offer. Morales said, "This man would turn somersaults and set fire to his children for the reward. If he learns anything, I believe he'll contact us."

As they walked down the street, Johnny held the watch in his palm, letting the sunshine sparkle from the diamonds. He said, "This thing is in perfect shape. We know the jewelry couldn't have been lost on the mountainside, and then just found lying around. The silver parts would have corroded at least some. Someone's been keeping the jewelry hidden."

The local chief of police was eager to please. He offered his huge leather chair to Alex and called in three uniformed cops who stood at attention while the chief questioned them. They paused after each sentence while Morales translated into English.

One said, "I first saw them in the square, just a few nights before the watch turned up in the jewelers. I thought they were ordinary wretches from the country who were looking for jobs. There are lots of them coming here lately. I chased them away. The next night, I found them trying to make a house in back of the church. Again, I made them move. They had enough money to get a room at the Palacio Hotel, a rundown place on the square, so I made them go there. But I had no idea they were thieves. I saw the woman later, coming out of the hotel, dressed in flashy clothes. The kind prostitutes wear. That's when I realized there might be something wrong. Another thing, every time I saw the boy, or man, he was wearing sunglasses, even at night."

"Why didn't you arrest them?"

"They hadn't done anything wrong as far as I knew. Dressing like a whore isn't a crime. When the news came from Mexico City about the watch, it was too late."

"They were gone?"

"Yes. Felix Sanchez, who owns the hotel, said they left not an hour before I got there. It must have been about noon. I asked him where they went, and he thought they headed for the bus station. They weren't there, so I looked all over town for them. They weren't anywhere. I couldn't miss them, not the way they were dressed, the *puta* in a gold sequin dress and the hoodlum in a bright red shirt, green pants and yellow hat. He bought the clothes in the market—we talked to the woman who sold them. She said he was pure Indian. Changed clothes in the market and threw the old things away."

"Ask him the thief's age," Alex demanded.

"Maybe twenty, maybe thirty, who knows?" was the reply. "He was wearing a ragged straw hat the first time I saw him, and the yellow hat the second time. I never got a good look at his face. He seemed to be mature, though. I mean, he didn't talk like a youth—more like an adult, like an Indian man from the mountains."

"How do you think they escaped?"

"Probably caught a bus while I was searching the streets around the hotel." The chief of police nodded agreement. In heavily accented English, he added: "A bus for Mexico City stops here at noon. Leaves fifteen minutes later. The bus to Veracruz doesn't arrive until after 1:00. We know they weren't on that one. They must be in the Capital."

Morales translated, adding, "Mexico City is a monstrously large place. There are barrios of professional criminals there where a thief can disappear like a cockroach in a garbage can."

Alex again asked, "Any question he might *not* have been Mexican? That he might *not* be a criminal?"

Morales posed the question in Spanish and one of the other cops replied, "No question in my mind. The evening before the watch incident, he attacked one of the local criminals, breaking his hand and robbing him of his wallet. We have the thug he attacked in jail right now if you'd like to talk to him."

The cell was in the back of the police delegation, a cave-like room with no windows and a solid wooden door. When he was brought out, the prisoner rubbed his eyes and squinted from the bright light. He answered questions vaguely, protesting that a mistake was made and that he was an honest man. He rubbed his hand over his rough beard as he talked.

"They've arrested me before by error," he explained. "Reason I was in the Rodriguez house was not to rob it. Truth is, I noticed the door open and I just stepped inside to make sure there weren't any thieves in there. You see, I..."

"Don't feed us that shit," Morales snapped impatiently. "Tell us about the man who robbed you. That must have been a change."

He pulled at his beard and glared at Morales with hurt feelings. "I'm minding my own business, and from out of nowhere comes this animal, threatening me with a machete. He corners me in a blind alley, and I stop to defend myself. I tried, but look here..." He pulled his lip up to expose a vacant space in his teeth. "He hit me with the flat of the machete and knocked the tooth out. And look at this wrist, broken! It will never be the same."

Morales translated to Alex and Johnny. "So, what happened next?"

"What could I do? He was fast and expert. I tried to defend myself, but *zas!* Before I could think, he kicked me and broke my wrist. Knocks me down, stomps my stomach before I know what's happening. This one's a professional. You don't fight with someone like that. So, I give him my money. Money I worked for and earned by the honest sweat of my..."

"Yes, yes. Describe this person. How tall, how old, color hair, everything."

"Taller than I, about as tall as that man." He pointed to Alex. "At first I thought he was a boy. But when I heard him talk, I knew he was no youngster. He worked with his feet and hands like a professional, like those kickboxers you see on television. He dressed like an *Indio* from the mountains and his accent was Indio. But an ordinary Indio could never fight with such skills. Best street fighter I've ever seen. Dangerous!"

Alex said wearily, "Explain about my missing son. Ask him

if there's any chance, any chance at all that..." He stared at the floor morosely while Morales put questions to the man in Spanish. There was nothing further to learn.

The bus station was just a small restaurant where four rickety tables with tin covers and a dozen crude wooden chairs provided bus passengers a place to sip soft drinks while waiting. Only when the bus was stopping or passing through would anyone have an excuse to eat here. A fat woman, greasy with perspiration and steam, came from behind the counter to talk to Alex through Enrique's interpretations.

"Yes, I remember the woman and the young man. The reason I remember, she was dressed like a whore, in a dress made of gold sequins. She looked as if she had been smoking marijuana because she acted strange. Her eyes didn't focus, and she kept humming to herself. Her friend held her hand and led her about as if she were a child. She was a pretty woman. Even for a *puta*, she was pretty. So sad to see someone ruin their lives with *drogas*."

"You say she was with a young man? Not a boy?"

"Didn't look like a boy. He was a man. He had on a yellow hat that he kept pulled over his forehead, like gangsters do in gringo movies. He looked very hard, dangerous. But I could see his face clearly. He was taller than the woman, and he acted protective, as if he were her pimp. He could have been twenty years old, maybe even thirty. Oh yes, he wore sunglasses."

"Ask her if he could possibly have been an American," Alex said urgently. "Ask her if there's any chance of that."

She shook her head slowly with indecision. "I don't think so. No. Because when he bought the tickets, I heard that accent. I know it well, because my husband was from that part of the mountains and he talks the same way. No. He couldn't be Gringo."

"They went to Mexico City?"

"Yes. The boy bought two tickets and paid for them with

186

two hundred-peso notes. I remember, because I didn't have change and had to borrow some from my husband."

The woman remembered nothing more. The three men bought some tepid beer and waited for the noon bus to come in from Veracruz on its way to Mexico City. They needed to talk with the bus driver when he arrived.

The bus driver was a handsome man with a pencil-line moustache. He looked as if he should be an airline pilot rather than a bus driver. He remembered the couple because of the dress the woman was wearing.

"I thought she might be a loose woman. She was pretty and looked like a good thing to have in bed. I wanted to see about getting her to my hotel room when we arrived in Capital," he said, "but she seemed to be *chiflada* and didn't hear my words. I figured drugs. So, I didn't bother asking her to my room. They are more trouble than they're worth when they're like that."

"What about the person with her. Was he a boy or a man? Could he possibly have been American?"

"I'm sorry, I don't remember much about him. If it weren't for the whore, I wouldn't even remember him at all. He was just an ordinary type, except for the parrot-colored clothes. Built pretty good, too, with wide shoulders like an athlete. It seems to me that I saw them talking to a taxi driver in the station in Mexico City later on, after I checked my bus in with the dispatcher."

"Did they leave in a taxi? Can you describe the driver?"

He shrugged. "I didn't see if they left with him or not. You see those kind of cab drivers all the time hanging around the station, trying to hustle tourists and strangers. His kind never have regular taxi permits. They usually have an old car and try to hook people who don't know what the right fare should be. Sometimes they are pure criminal types. You know, they roll drunks, pick pockets, maybe even rob passengers at gunpoint. They all look alike to me."

On the flight back to Mexico City they discussed how to

begin their search. Johnny Gee shook his head sadly. "The Capital has maybe fifteen million people. No one knows for sure. Maybe twenty million. Where do we begin?"

"First, locate that cab driver at the bus terminal."

A police lieutenant eagerly assigned himself to work on the investigation, delighted at the opportunity to serve a rich man and share in the reward.

The lieutenant drove the three searchers to the bus station and officiously questioned employees and the entrepreneurs with small concessions in the large bus station. Several taxi drivers fit the description given by the bus driver.

Morales and the lieutenant questioned the drivers in a small storage room in the terminal. The lieutenant's method of questioning involved delivering sharp punches to tender parts of the body when he didn't get an answer he liked. Morales did his share in the softening process, until the lieutenant stopped him.

"Easy. You must not be angry when questioning, it isn't professional. I think you may have broken some ribs on this man."

"Sorry. It's just that this investigation has been so frustrating for me. Ten years of nothing, then when something begins to break, the clues fade away like smoke in the wind."

But no one remembered talking to a woman wearing a gold sequined dress who was with a youth dressed in Indian clothing. Although Alex and Johnny Gee didn't realize it, the drivers wouldn't have told the police the day of the week, no matter how much pain was dished out. The harder the interrogation, the weaker the memory. Street survival.

The police structure in Mexico City is organized along the lines of an army, with generals at the top and patrolmen at the bottom. For an ordinary man with an ordinary child disappearance, nothing would have been done. But in this case, the distraught father was rich. With that difference clearly in

188

mind, the police took an intense interest in the case. They distributed photos of Rickey Barron, taken when he was four years old, along with the description of the boy or man who sold the watch in Córdoba, and a list of the missing jewelry. The notice of reward wet many lips in anticipation.

Alex and Johnny passed the next few days wandering aimlessly around the city, from one barrio to another, always asking questions, looking at crowds of people, always searching for a 16-year-old with gray eyes. Enrique Morales called them daily, but with no news. Each day he sounded more despondent.

Robin flew in from Dallas where she had been filming a TV special. "I got here as soon as I could, Alex. Have you found anything?"

"Nothing. It's like looking for that famous needle in the haystack." He told her of the jewelry shop in Córdoba and of the investigation to date. She gently massaged the back of his neck while he brought her up to date on the search. She felt his pain and anxiety as if it were her own. She desperately wished there were some way she could help him, but she knew there was nothing she could do.

"I was hoping so much that you could put this to rest once and for all. You are killing yourself with worry, Alex. There's nothing more you can do."

"I was almost over this. I'd convinced myself that Rickey was dead, and now... the nightmares are back again. Haven't had a good night's sleep in over a week. It's that same old dream, Rickey is being held against his will, that he is being abused, tortured."

"He's dead, Alex. You must believe he's dead, because that's the only way it can possibly be."

"But where did the watch come from? After all these years? Who sold it? It could have been Rickey. Why not? Maybe he needed money. Maybe he..."

"Look at it this way. Whoever sold the watch certainly

wasn't being held prisoner, was he? The police claim he's a hoodlum. He even robbed a local criminal the night before. Right? Okay, so there was a falling out between thieves. One robs the other and takes a watch from him. The next day he sells the watch to the jeweler."

"But where did the watch come from in the first place?"

"Stole it from someone else, who robbed it from someone else. If he weren't a criminal, why would he run from the police? Look, for the sake of the argument let's suppose that it *was* Rickey. That he needed money. Once he *had* money, wouldn't he have tried to contact you? Would he run?"

"I don't know. He was only four when we lost him. Would he remember where he lived? Would he even remember me?"

Robin put her arms around him and held him tight for a long while. "Let's go to our place in Acapulco. Let's let the police do their work and wait."

Every night, instead of sleeping, Alex tossed and fought off nightmares. Robin comforted him, walking around the house with him, trying to calm him down so he could get some needed sleep. Often, she found him standing in Rickey's room. He had kept it exactly the way it had been when he disappeared. Some stuffed animals sprawled on the bed. Books and crayons lay about on the floor. The servants had instructions to dust around them, and not move them under threat of discharge.

"Come on, Alex," she said gently. "You're killing yourself. Let's go to bed and try to sleep."

Tears streaked his face and he nodded weakly. "If I could only go back in time. Just for that one day when I allowed him to go with Diana."

"You can't go back in time. Now, lay down, and try to sleep."

"I feel so damned helpless—so useless. Just when I almost had myself convinced that he died in the wreck... Just when the nightmares were fading, this happens. What can I do? There must be something."

Robin turned him to lay on his stomach and she gently massaged his back, her fingers working the muscles to disperse tension.

"The police are working on it, Alex. We'll clear everything up before long. I don't like to see you this way, sweetheart. I wish there were something I could do. I love you too much to see you suffer."

The next day the three of them flew back to Mexico City. They renewed their aimless wandering through neighborhoods and barrios. They realized the odds were astronomical that they might find one boy in a city teeming with humanity. Yet, it was the only plan of action they could imagine. Day after day they left the hotel early in the morning and returned late at night. After two weeks they recognized the futility of it all and reluctantly returned to the United States.

Chapter Fifteen

The fare to Mexico City consumed most of the remaining pesos. Riki counted the remaining few tattered bills over and over during the long bus ride. The windows were grimed over with a coat of highway dust. He couldn't see much of the countryside blurring past, yet he kept his face to the window and tried to absorb some of the strange sights during the eight-hour journey. He could hardly contain his excitement. Twice they stopped while the passengers went for food and to the restrooms, but there was no money for food, and he didn't suspect luxuries like toilets in bus stations.

The bus seemed marvelous, much different from the other bus he had ridden. This one was first-class. Every passenger had a reserved seat, no one crowded into the aisle, and there were no livestock or produce aboard. He felt self-conscious, because he suddenly realized how he and Micaela stood out, because of their clothes. He wished he'd had time to make Micaela wear something besides the flashy sequin dress. Fortunately, she had a dark reboso which covered much of the dress, as long as she kept it wrapped around her. He also realized that people who were rich enough to ride first-class buses didn't wear bright clothes such as his red shirt and green pants. He began to feel shame.

He also felt a growing need to urinate. Then he noticed that from time to time, someone would get up from their seat and walk to the back of the bus and go through a small door. After a while the person would exit and another would enter. His curiosity got the better of him, and he self-consciously stepped into the aisle and went to the door. It said *baño*. Bath? Were these people taking baths on a bus? He started to return to his seat when the door opened. A heavy woman stepped out, adjusting her skirt around her hips as she came. Then Riki saw what was inside the room: a porcelain stool, similar to the one at the hotel! He gasped in surprise. He hadn't realized the full extent of the luxury of the bus. Self-consciously, he entered the room and relieved himself with a wondrous grin on his face. He could hardly wait to share his discovery with Micaela.

Finally, just about dusk, he caught his first glimpse of the Valley of Mexico and *la capital*. It happened when the bus rounded a curve and started down a long grade and a marvelous panorama appeared through the windshield. The city spread out to fill the valley below like an enormous lake of lights, some lights in strings like glowing frog eggs in a pond, others flashing, some glittering with color. It was a feast for the eyes, one that made his heart pump with excitement.

He nudged Micaela and whispered, "Look! It's even bigger than I'd imagined. El Perrón said it was huge, but..."

She leaned over to peer through the window and a worried frown came over her face. He rubbed his palm across her back and said, "We'll do just fine, don't worry. I'll find a job and we'll live like rich people." The excitement kept Micaela alert for the rest of the drive; Riki felt encouraged by this.

When the bus finished the long downhill grade into the valley of Mexico, it plunged fearlessly into the lake of lights. Glowing bulbs and colored signs flashed by the bus window to confuse Riki's eyes. Brilliant whites, reds, blues, greens, some blinking and some moving with animation — blurred past while amber glows of streetlights arched over the wide boulevard like ghostly multiple suns. Riki's throat grew thick with anticipation of the unknown. He said a silent prayer to the ancient gods of Tezcatlipocas.

The sky was black by the time the bus maneuvered into its narrow stall at the rear of the bus terminal. Its diesel engine shut down with a sigh of relief and the passengers began moving slowly for the exit.

The first-class section bustled with commerce and milling crowds of passengers. Stands selling food, candy and magazines filled the edges and corners of the building. Riki sniffed the tantalizing odors of cooking and felt his mouth water helplessly at the sight of people eating chicken *tortas* and slices of honey-sweet melon. The little money left must be conserved, he told himself as he turned his mind away from his stomach. The terminal seemed like a cement beehive, with people buzzing in and out of the entrances, hovering about the exits momentarily, then flying off to unknown destinations.

Riki stared about in awe. He gripped the leather suitcase tightly, determined that no thief would get another chance at stealing it. Micaela clung to his arm as he lifted the net bag to his shoulder and moved with the crowd toward one of the street exits. She looked around at the confusion. Then a slight smile played on her lips. She squeezed Riki's arm with excitement. Then for the first time in weeks, she spoke rationally, clearly:

"If there are this many people just in the bus station, what is it going to be like outside?" She was talking just as before; the distant, vacant stare replaced by eager anticipation.

Riki stared at Micaela in surprise and then broke into a happy smile. He would have hugged her had not his hands been full of luggage. He felt as if a fifty-kilo bundle of wood had just been lifted from his back. *If she is cured, nothing will be too hard*, he said to himself. *The city will be good for us.*

"Come on, Mica, let's go find doña Herencia!" She returned his smile, her first rational smile in a long time.

They struggled against a cross current of people to get to the exit. "How do we find doña Herencia's house?" he asked. He studied the address he had found among Micaela's things.

"This doesn't tell much. There are some numbers and the words *Calle de Flores* and the word *Pedregal*."

Micaela shrugged her shoulders helplessly. "She told me it

was a long way from the bus station. She said she had to go on a *Metro*, whatever that is."

A tall, stringy man wearing a frayed pin-striped suit and a red baseball cap elbowed his way through the crowd. He smiled, revealing crooked and yellowed teeth. "Taxi? You want a taxi?" He fingered a thin moustache as he waited for an answer.

Riki tightened his grip on the suitcase. Something about the man reminded him of the swindler in Córdoba. Maybe it was the moustache, or the striped suit, or maybe that shifty look one has when forcing oneself to be polite.

"What's a taxi?"

The man lifted his hands and let them drop by his side. "Oh *Puta Madre*! More ignorant Indians from the country! You probably don't even have the price of a bus, much less a taxi."

"I don't know. How much does a bus cost? I only have a few pesos left."

"That depends on where you are going. Do you even have an idea?"

Riki handed him the piece of paper with doña Herencia's address. "We have a friend who lives here. She said she would help us if we ever came to the capital."

The man studied the address and whistled through his teeth. "This is a high-class neighborhood. I would guess your friend works for a rich family. Well, it will cost the two of you 60 pesos to go in my taxi. Do you have that much?"

Riki pulled the thin fold of bills from his pocket and showed them to the man. The man glanced at them and shook his head and snorted sarcastically.

"Don't make me laugh. That wouldn't buy enough gasoline to take you to the corner. Come on, bring out the rest of the money you have hidden in your shoes. I know how you *indios* are. I came from the country myself, years ago."

"This is all I have. Just tell us which direction it is? We can walk."

The man suddenly lost interest. He removed the baseball

cap to scratch his stiff black hair as he looked about the terminal for paying customers. He said contemptuously, "Sure. You could walk, but it would take you about three days to do it. The Pedregal is on the other side of town." Then he walked away. Riki followed. "Which direction?"

The cab driver made a face of annoyance. "Ask someone about a bus; it will only cost you four pesos. Now quit bothering me." Suddenly he spied two gringo-looking tourists struggling with heavy luggage. He hurried to snare the prospective customers.

Riki picked up the bags and motioned for Micaela to follow him. They walked outside onto the sidewalk. A stream of autos, trucks and buses flowed past, headlights glaring, horns blaring, and exhaust fumes tinting the air blue. They paused in fascination for a few moments as they marveled at the confusion, lights, noise, and the bustling crowd of people. Micaela clapped her hands in delight.

"Riki, this is wonderful! I never thought I'd ever see anything like this! So many people... so many lights... the noise... Isn't it exciting?"

He nodded. "Just as El Perrón said. Only more than I expected." He looked around in awe. "Where do we find a bus?"

A line of taxicabs pulled to the curb one by one, and before the doors could open, a crowd of boys in dirty clothes would be waiting, clamoring to carry the luggage. The boys were about Riki's age, some much younger. He sensed that they were doing this to make money, and then he saw a woman give one of the boys some coins for carrying a light-looking bag. "What an easy way to make money," he thought. "This isn't going to be so hard." He wondered how one gets a job like this. How to get any job?

Just then, a bus pulled next to the sidewalk and people began crowding to get on. It was a clean, modern bus of chrome and orange plastic. Somehow Riki felt sure the bus would take them to doña Herencia's house. Riki noticed the people were putting money into a glass box by the driver's seat. When everyone had climbed aboard, he took Micaela's hand and started to board.

The driver shook his head emphatically. "Not with that junk you're carrying, you don't. There's not even enough room for people in this bus." The doors swung shut with a strange whooshing of air. The bus pulled away, trailing a cloud of greasy diesel smoke. Pressure built in his stomach. Panic clawed at him, a feeling of being crowded from all sides. He looked to Micaela for some help, but she returned a puzzled stare.

Before long, another bus stopped. A clot of humanity began to push and shove at the same time as passengers inside were struggling to get out of the door, causing a temporary impasse. Riki knew it would be hopeless to attempt to board.

"Come on, Mica, we'll walk."

At that moment, the taxi driver in the striped suit and baseball cap came struggling through the door trying to manage four valises. The gringo couple woman ambled along behind, carrying nothing.

Then, Riki had an idea. He dropped the leather suitcase beside Micaela. "Guard this closely," he said. "I'm going to see if I can make some money." He imitated the boys he had seen and ran to the cab driver and asked, "Can I help you?"

"*Hijo de la puta madre!* Is it you again? Get away from me! Can't you see I'm busy?"

"Can't you at least tell me which direction to walk? They won't let us on the bus with our bag of clothes and the suitcase."

The driver grumbled under his breath for a moment as he struggled with the suitcases. Finally, he said, "Here, carry a couple of these to the car and I'll tell you how to get there. But it will take you two days to walk, because it's at the far end of the city."

"We'll make it. My mother was sick, but she seems better now. We can walk all right."

The taxi driver snorted sarcastically. He opened the trunk of the old Buick and began stacking the gringos' luggage inside. Then he looked at Micaela, who was standing by the door, the suitcase grasped firmly in her hand. The taxi driver's eyes wandered up and down her body and seemed to pause significantly when he looked at her bosom, where the inadvertently opened rebozo showed generous areas of breast.

"She's not your mother. She's too young. Who is she?"

"My step-mother. She's going to try and find a job with a rich family."

When he slammed the trunk closed, the driver looked at Micaela again, his eyes squinting speculatively. "Nice looking woman. Why is she dressed like that?"

"That's all she has to wear. Someone stole her clothes and we... We found these."

The driver shrugged and said, "She is too pretty to dress up like a whore. Take my advice, as soon as you find a job, buy her some decent clothes. You don't want your stepmother looking that way."

Riki narrowed his eyes and wasn't sure if the man was insulting Micaela or not. "Save your advice. If you won't tell us which direction to walk, we'll ask someone else."

The driver looked at Micaela again, and then sighed in resignation. "Wait, come back here. These rich gringo bastards are going to San Angel, which isn't too far from the Pedregal. I'll tell you what... If they don't squawk, maybe you can ride up front with me. Do you have any money at all you can pay me?"

"No. We can walk. If you just..."

"Get inside, esquintle, before I change my mind."

"No."

"What? I offer to help you, and you say no?"

"Don't call me *esquintle*. I am not a dog."

The taxi driver threw back his head and laughed. "Here in the city, when we say *esquintle*, we mean 'little one,' not 'dog' like you indios say in the mountains." He slapped Riki on the shoulder. "I understand, my friend. When I was about your age, I came to the capital, without money, without friends. I felt as lost as you do now. Put your mother inside the taxi and we'll go."

The male gringo, a soft-looking man with a paunch and a shiny face nodded amiably when the driver explained about his passengers. The explanation was in Spanish and the gringo obviously knew nothing but a few memorized phrases of the language and didn't want to admit that he couldn't understand. His wife frowned and said, "What the hell is he saying? Can't he speak English?"

"Beats the hell out of me. I think he wants to take these people in the cab with us. Doesn't matter, I suppose, as long as we get to our hotel."

"Yes. I want to get an early start tomorrow and get all of the sightseeing out of the way as quick as we can, so we can start enjoying our trip."

Riki and Micaela slid into the wide front seat. Riki refused to relinquish his grip on the suitcase; he held it on his lap. The ride took them down past Bellas Artes with its marble statues of half-naked women, pale and cool and lit by floodlights, then along the Alameda past thousands of strolling people, past the huge, impressive monument of Reforma and then to Insurgentes and its rows of elegant shops, fancy restaurants and tall buildings of mirrored glass. Both Micaela and Riki stared at the incredible sights with an ever-increasing sense of awe. Micaela was now as alert as ever in her life. Riki began to feel an overwhelming sense of well-being and at the same time, thrills of excitement. Yes, El Perrón was correct. The city *is* exciting!

As they rode, Riki listened to the couple in the backseat conversing in English. The words sounded strange, sometimes blurring all together in a clump, occasionally making no sense at all. Yet he understood most of what they said. They didn't talk smoothly as people did in the movies. They repeated words and phrases, using lots of 'uhs' and 'ahs', something done neither in Spanish, nor in the movies. Riki found it fascinating that he could understand so much.

The woman was asking, "How much is this taxi supposed to cost?"

"I don't know for sure."

To Riki, it sounded as if the man said, *Ay-uh-naw-f'shu* — one lump of a word — and he was surprised that he understood.

"I showed him the address and he said something in Spanish. I think he said 65 pesos, or was it 650?"

"How much is that in real money?"

"Let's see... 65 would be about five bucks, I think. Or is it twenty?" He asked for something called a "calculator." When his wife dug the object from her purse, he began pressing buttons on its face.

His wife said, "Just give him a twenty-dollar bill, and act if you expect change. It shouldn't cost more than $20."

The driver mumbled, "Those gringos and their *calculadoras*! Every time they get one out, I know I'm going to be in trouble. I sure wish I understood what they are saying back there. Then I'd know how much to over-charge them."

Riki said, "The man is wondering if he is going to have to pay more than twenty dollars for this trip. The woman is saying it is worth it because they'd have to pay more than that at home."

The cab driver looked at Riki and laughed contemptuously. "I suppose you understand English. Don't make me laugh."

"Why would you laugh? I understand what they are saying. That doesn't seem funny to me."

"Oh, you understand, do you? And how did you learn all of this? In the university?"

Riki didn't like being made fun of, so he didn't answer. He turned his attention to the colored lights of Mexico City.

Then the driver looked at Riki from the corner of his eye. "You can't really understand the gringos, can you?"

"Yes."

"Do you think I could get away with asking more than I told him? I told him 65 pesos."

"How much is 20 dollars? The man is saying that he has a $20 bill, whatever that is, and he is going to offer that to you and see if that's enough."

"*Jijole!* Don't I wish that were true!"

The cab driver was properly impressed when indeed, the tourist handed him a $20 bill and waited tentatively to see if any change was forthcoming. Forewarned, the driver saluted as if the amount were just right and hurried to open the trunk. Riki grabbed three of the suitcases before the cab driver had a chance, and he went running to the hotel lobby.

The gringo marched to the registration desk and called to his wife, "I suppose the kid will want a tip. Give him something, will you?"

"How much?"

"Shit, I don't know. I can't figure out this play money. Just make sure he doesn't steal anything." She frowned in confusion as she fished a handful of bills out of her purse. She handed Riki the first piece of money she found, which was happened to be a 100-peso bill. She thrust it into Riki's outstretched hand and looked at him to see if it were enough.

He stared at the bill in disbelief, then up at the woman. He was about to give fervent thanks, when she said, "He looks pissed off, Herbert. I guess I didn't give him enough." She took two more bills out of her purse, both 20-peso notes. "Is that enough?"

Riki nodded dumbly, unable to speak. He started backing away, afraid that she would want the money back. Then he broke into a run and didn't stop until he reached the taxi. The driver was grinning at him happily.

"How much did you get?"

"140 pesos! No wonder those kids at the bus station want to carry luggage. I'll be rich before long."

The driver laughed so hard, he had difficulty getting the

key into the ignition. When they arrived at the address in the Pedregal, he was still breaking into laughter periodically. The house was large, with a tall iron fence about the grounds and a lean Doberman glaring through the bars.

"I should charge you for the trip," he said, "but since you helped me get the $20 dollars, it's free."

As Riki and Micaela got out of the old Buick, a young, Indian-looking girl was opening the gate to the house. For the first time since that tragic day in Córdoba, Micaela spoke to a stranger on her own. She called out, "We've come to see doña Herencia. Does she live in this house?"

The girl smiled shyly. "No. She did, but last month she lost her job. The owner of the house died and all of the servants except my mother and me were fired."

'Where did she go? How can I find her?"

"Who knows? She went away. They all did."

Micaela looked at Riki with a stunned look on her face. He grabbed her hand, afraid she would slip back into her illness, and said eagerly, "It's all right. We'll find jobs and make a lot of money. Look here. Look how much money I made in just a few minutes of work? We will be rich here."

The cab driver started to drive away but hesitated and then backed the car to where Riki and Micaela were standing. "Oh, come on. Get back in. I'm finished for the night anyway. I'll take you to my barrio and you can find a place to stay. I know a place. It isn't a mansion, but it is cheap. By the way, my name is Manuel Salas. Maybe someday you and I can do some business, son. It would be a big help to have you ride around with me and tell me what's being said in the back seat."

"My name is Riki Montalvo, and this is my mother, Micaela."

"It is with great pleasure to meet such a charming lady," Manuel said as he touched the bill of the baseball cap. His crooked teeth gleamed in the light of a passing automobile as he smiled at Micaela. "I am at your service."

She hung her head and didn't reply. A blush turned her face

dark, but despite her efforts, a shy smile broke through. She kept glancing at Manual Salas for the rest of the trip to the barrio. Whenever the smile flickered on, she compressed her lips to drive it away. But it kept coming back. Riki noticed all of this but determined to keep out of it. He wasn't sure what he could do or say anyway.

Chapter Sixteen

The barrio was all but deserted by the time Manuel Salas wheeled the Buick into a narrow street of red-and-black lava stone buildings. The streetlamps cast pools of yellow light where schools of insects fluttered and pulsated, rising toward the globes and falling back to the darkness.

"This is it," said Manuel Salas. "The owner is a friend of mine. Maybe he'll give you a reduction in price." He parked the cab on the sidewalk and said, "Follow me. I'm sure he has a vacant apartment."

They entered a narrow passageway filled with black shadows and made their way toward the faint shape of a door opening at the far end. They stepped into a courtyard. and followed Manuel to a doorway where he knocked loudly.

"Compadre, open up! It's me, Manuel Salas."

After a while the door opened and a sullen, grouchy face peered through the crack. "What the hell do you want? Why are you getting me out of bed so late?"

"My friends here want to rent an apartment."

The manager gave Manuel a dirty look. He pointed to an open door on the other side of the courtyard. "It's that one," he said. "Come back in the morning and I'll let you look at it." Then he closed the door.

Manuel Salas smiled triumphantly. "You see? I told you he has a place for you." He took Micaela's hand and looked her up and down, a pleased smile playing about his lips. "I think maybe you and I will be seeing more of each other." Then he said goodbye and left them standing in the dark courtyard.

Riki and Micaela waited all night, sometimes dozing, while sitting on two wooden benches that faced each other across from the community faucet. When dawn made it light enough, Micaela tiptoed to the open door of the vacant rooms and timidly looked inside. She beckoned excitedly. "Come here and look, Riki! This is going to be perfect. See... There's even a table and three chairs. And look! There's an electric light, just like we had in Córdoba." She stepped inside to pull the string and watch the yellow bulb blink on and off. She giggled like a child, and Riki felt good despite the all-night wait on the hard wooden bench.

Except for the odor from the toilets, Riki had to agree with Micaela. It was as good as the house in Tezcatlipocas, maybe even better, because this one had cement floors instead of packed clay. He knew that soon the smell would become so common as to disappear as bad odors have a way of doing.

Finally, daylight came—people began lining up for the toilets, and children lethargically played in the crowded patio. A dozen cooking breakfasts sent odors of reheated beans and steaming tortillas to stir up the stomach juices. Riki and Micaela revisited the apartment for a closer inspection.

The apartment consisted of two tiny rooms. The sleeping room, without windows, was dark as a cavern and smelled of dust and body odor. The sleeping room contained no furniture except for two wooden crates that served as clothing storage. Two cane petates stood in one corner of the room, to be rolled out on the cement floor for sleeping. The room in front was a kitchen. It boasted a small window—with glass long ago broken—that permitted a shaft of light to penetrate the darkness of the kitchen. An iron grate covered the window to keep out uninvited guests. A kerosene stove rested on a grease-soaked wooden box; above that an orange crate had been nailed to the wall to store food out of the range of foraging mice. A cement sink clung to the wall next to the stove. There was no running water, but the sink could drain away dirty wash water, if one waited long enough. When the wood-planked door stood ajar the room was light enough to cook or eat in without using the light bulb that hung from the ceiling. The light in the bedroom suffered from incurably corroded wires, so whoever rented the apartment needed to purchase wax tapers to light that room.

"It's so much better than I expected," Micaela said excitedly. With an electric light, and a toilet close by!"

In all, twenty of these two-room apartments formed a squared horseshoe around the open concrete patio where children played and fought during the day, where adults gossiped and argued politics in the evening. It seemed that each of the apartments had children living in them, some a lot of children. They ran, screamed, kicked at dogs and sometimes toddled into the open doors of anyone's apartment. No one seemed to mind. A common faucet in the center of the cement patio provided water for the women to carry back to their apartments using five-gallon oil cans that were thoughtfully provided by the landlord.

The latrine occupied a corner of the patio, the only services in the complex. Two of the three showers worked, and the toilets (four of them) flushed as long as you brought a can of water to fill the bowl to start the siphon action. Everyone waited for someone else to flush, so the odor from the toilets was so thick it was almost visible.

The manager insisted on two months' rent in advance, but Micaela convinced him that Manuel Salas would pay later. This satisfied the manager, and he permitted them to move in. Micaela borrowed a broom from a neighbor and was soon happily sending clouds of gray dust through the door and onto the patio.

"Is there any money left?" she asked. "If there is, I'd like to buy some food and cook a first meal in our new house." She looked around proudly, as if she'd won the fattest prize in the lottery.

He handed her the small fold of money and said, "I'm going to look for a job."

"I'm sure you'll find a good job. You made so much last night, just carrying two suitcases that I know you'll be rich in no time."

He smiled at her with a confidence that he didn't feel. Manuel Salas had explained about the tip the Gringa had given him last night. "That won't happen again in a million years," Salas had said. "Usually, gringos think they are giving away dollars when they give you pesos. One or two pesos is the usual tip for what you did."

Riki wondered, how does one find a job? In Tezcatlipocas, if someone wanted to hire a man to help him, he simply went to the zócalo and looked around to see who was loafing that day, and then offered him so many pesos to help clear a field or repair a wall, whatever. This didn't happen very often of course, but Riki had occasionally earned some money that way. He wandered up one street and down he next, always remembering how many blocks he was away from the apartment. Everyone seemed to be busy doing something. He observed people working in little grocery stores, in an electrical repair shop, driving trucks, washing store windows, running errands, shopping. It was a miracle—everyone seemed to have a niche, a job, a way to earn a living, all these millions of people who crowded into the city, all working, eating, living, paying rent...

Riki wondered what his place in the miracle was to be. When and how shall I find my job? He felt excitement and fear at the same time.

A man sat on the sidewalk hammering at a chisel, cutting chips and shaping a limestone building block. Riki watched him work for a few minutes, and finally he gathered the courage to ask, "How can I find work like you're doing? I need a job."

The worker's eyes, red with the agitation of rock dust and

poverty, stared at Riki for a moment. Then he spit contemptuously and went back to work without saying a word.

Riki backed away in bewilderment and resumed his explorations through the barrio. El Perrón had been right about one thing: People in the city aren't as friendly as those in the country. Some streets were wider, with businesses and stores filling entire blocks. Automobiles honked and trucks growled and whined through the gears. People were everywhere, hurrying here and there, each intent on his own mission, each invisible to the others. Sometimes a passerby would take a second look at Riki's colorful clothes, but otherwise people were totally oblivious of a hungry lad searching for work. They all seemed to have jobs. They earned money somehow. They were well fed and well dressed.

He kept walking, trying to make sense of the strange sights and smells of the city. He walked as far as the center of the city, to the huge square that stretched in front of the Cathedral and the imposing National Palace—where once Aztec pyramids stood, where once people worshiped Tezcatlipocas, Tonantzín, Huitzlipocas, and others. Riki gasped in surprise when he saw this enormous paved zócalo. "Why, ten villages the size of Tezcatlipocas could fit here," he said to himself. "And the churches! Why are they so big? What are they used for?"

He walked around the two large churches to see if he could find a clue as to their use. In Tezcatlipocas, the church was a place to burn trash and occasionally watch a movie. Then, on a street behind the cathedral, he found what he was looking for. Lined along the sidewalk were at least a hundred men, obviously waiting for jobs. Each had a box of tools for his particular trade and a sign... "electrician, I repair everything"; "plumber, good work, cheap"; "carpentry and bricklaying". Riki walked along the street twice but could think of nothing he could put on a sign. All he knew was wood-cutting, resin preparation or perhaps minding a herd of goats. None of those skills seemed much in demand here.

He was very hungry when he returned home and was looking forward to a stomach-warming plate of beans and chili pods. When he stepped through the kitchen door, he found Manuel Salas sitting at the kitchen table. Micaela looked embarrassed when Riki entered the door. She jumped up to busy herself at the stove. She called over her shoulder, "Sit down Riki, and I'll bring you some food." Something about the tone of her voice said she felt like a child caught doing something naughty. "Manuel brought me a chicken as a gift!"

Manuel Salas looked at Riki in a very strange way, lifting one eyebrow as if expecting to be scolded. He awkwardly stood up and offered his hand to Riki. "I just came by to see if everything's going all right."

Riki shook his hand briefly and sat on one of the wood slat chairs. "Things are fine, except I need to find a job."

"You will, with a little luck. I could use a little luck myself. Like last night, the police were looking for jewel thieves, offering a reward. Big reward. If I had been lucky, I would have picked them up for fares instead of you. I could have been wealthy today."

"What do you mean, *reward*?"

Micaela cleared her throat anxiously and made some noises with the pan and metal food plates. "This chicken will be ready in a minute. Are you both hungry?"

"Tell me about the reward," Riki insisted.

"They say some criminal stole some jewelry from a rich gringo named 'Barrón.' He's offering a mountain of money to anyone who finds the thief and the jewelry."

Riki glanced at Micaela, who turned away quickly and busied herself stirring the chicken stew. "The gringo's name is Barrón?"

"Yes. Alexander Barrón. One of those rich bastards who wouldn't miss a little jewelry, but he's going to make it tough for somebody. Too bad it wasn't you—I could use the reward money." Salas smiled lazily and studied the curves of Micaela's buttocks.

Riki frowned as he tried to think. The name "Alex Barrón" seemed to bring pictures to a dim, half-lighted past. *Alex... Alex Barrón...* But the images were faded, blurred. Something dark and uneasy brooded inside his chest as he repeated the name under his breath. "Barrón!"

Manuel Salas was saying, "The cops tried to question me about whether I'd seen them. But I sidestepped and got away before they could collar me. Anyway, I wouldn't tell them if I knew. That's a rule of this barrio. You don't tell la policía anything. One really bad guy called Enrique Morales was doing the questioning. Jórge Caraval got two broken ribs, so the story goes." Micaela brought a dish of steaming chicken and rice and nervously placed it front of Salas. "Here, you try this first, and tell me if it is good or no."

They both noticed the jumpy way Micaela was acting. She nervously wiped her hands on her apron and hurried back to the stove to serve up a portion for Riki. Salas picked up a wing and sucked the meat from the bone. He smiled at Micaela in approval.

"Too bad you two aren't jewel thieves. I could use the reward." He smiled at his little joke and didn't notice the looks of concern that Riki exchanged with Micaela.

"I don't steal," Riki said with a worried voice.

Laughing, Manuel Salas tore a piece from a tortilla and used it to pick up a chunk of chicken thigh. "That's just my luck. A fortune in jewels and rewards goes running around the bus station for the finding, and I have to find you. But in truth, my reward is meeting such a beautiful woman."

Manuel's lips exposed his yellow-and-brown teeth in a leering smile. Micaela's face burned darkly. She unsuccessfully attempted to suppress a pleased smile.

Riki rolled a portion of refried beans in a double tortilla. He kept his eyes on Manuel's face as he chewed. "You would turn someone to the police for a reward? I thought you said you

210

wouldn't do favors for the police."

"Not for the police, no. But for me... Well, that's different." Manuel smiled slyly. "One thing you must learn about the city is, take care of yourself first. Here, few people have family or close friends to help them. You are on your own. You do what you have to."

"Well, I don't lie, and I don't steal."

The cab driver laughed bitterly. "I can see that. Or you wouldn't be living in a pigpen like this. But you will learn to lie and to steal before you've lived here for long. You will learn."

Micaela joined them at the table. "Pigpen? What's wrong with this place? Look, it has a cement floor, and an electric light. What more could you want?"

"You will learn to want much more, pretty one." Then he paused as he looked her over appraisingly. "You know, I think I know where you might get a job, Mica. In a restaurant I know of. Someone as good looking as you shouldn't have a problem. I can't promise anything but..."

Micaela giggled and dipped her head toward her plate.

Riki said, "Where can I look for work? I walked all day long, but I don't know where to start. I'll have to find something tomorrow, or we won't have money for food."

"How does anyone find work? Go around and ask. Make a pest of yourself." Manuel thought for a moment as he smoothed his fingers absent-mindedly across his moustache. "Maybe go to those places on Calle de Abril where they're tearing down buildings. They always need extra people to work in places like that."

After dinner, Manuel Salas wanted to stay around and talk with Micaela. "Why don't you take a walk around the barrio," he suggested to Riki, "maybe you will meet a sexy little chavala."

Riki didn't reply other than shaking his head. He sensed that Micaela might want to be alone with Manuel, but wasn't going to allow that just yet, although he wasn't sure why he felt that way.

When Manuel finally left, Riki bolted the door and turned to look at Micaela. "I think it's time you tell me about the jewelry. Where did you get it, and who is this Barrón person?"

She turned away from him and went to the sink. She began to slosh water over the tin dinner plates. Finally she replied, "I don't know anyone named Barrón."

"Tell me! Where did you get the suitcase? Did you steal it?"

She shook her head hurriedly. "No! Never think that I stole it. Never."

"Then where?"

Suddenly she spun around to face him. Her eyes fixed upon his with a determined, defiant gaze. "This is a religious matter. Those jewels were entrusted to my care by Tonantzín. The Black Goddess told me to keep them safe, and never sell even one of them. You broke the trust by selling the watch, so if anything happens it is your fault."

Riki shook his head in disbelief. He didn't like to see her acting this way, because he knew how stubborn she could be, particularly in religious matters. "But Mica, why would Tonantzín give you a suitcase with those strange clothes, and with all of that jewelry? They must belong to someone, probably this Barrón person. Why would..."

"I am *not* going to talk about it. This is the Will of the Black Goddess, and I am going to obey." She threw the tin pan she was holding and left it clatter on the cement drainboard of the sink. She turned and went into the bedroom, slamming the door behind her. Riki knew it would be a waste of time to question her further.

The next morning, Riki drew a bucket of water and sponged himself off by the kitchen sink. Micaela heated the rest of the chicken, beans and tortillas. That was the last of the food, and little of it. He'd have to find a job today. He began pulling on his clothes.

"First thing, I'm going to look for a job where they're tearing down the buildings."

"Are you going to wear your good clothes? Why not put on your white muslins?"

He shook his head and looked down at his red pants and the green shirt. "Too country looking. No one wears them here. Besides, once I start a job, it won't matter how dirty these clothes get, because I'll be able to buy something a lot better." He picked up the yellow hat and put it on.

As he was leaving, Micaela kissed him on the cheek. "I hope you have good luck today. Maybe I will, too. Manuel promised to ask about a job for me, and if he finds something, he'll pick me up in his taxi and take me to talk to the employer. I'd like to work for a restaurant. They'll probably let me bring home leftovers."

Riki tried not to show his displeasure. He still didn't trust Manuel Salas, perhaps, he thought, because he is so much like that swindler in Córdoba. There's something about him...

Even though it was early in the morning, the children playing in the patio were boisterous. Riki had to dodge in order not to be bowled over by a boy who was running head down, pretending to be a bull. Calle de Abril was only six blocks from the apartment. Still, he felt pressured. He wanted to be the first on the job, and maybe he could go to work that very day. He broke into a half-trot. At the corner, where his street intersected with one slightly wider, a white wagon stood by the curb. A sign hanging from it said, *tripas de leche*. A man stood behind the wagon stirring succulent pieces of milk tripe in sizzling grease. The beans and chicken for breakfast had been pitifully inadequate, so his mouth watered at the delicious aroma. Several youths about his age, some older, some younger, stood waiting for the man to chop the tripe into tiny pieces and fold it into a steamed tortilla with cilantro and onion.

Riki slowed his pace and finally stopped at the wagon and sniffed the air. But he didn't have money for this now. Maybe later. As he turned to leave, a youth about his size, perhaps a couple of years older, caught him by the sleeve.

"Hey, look! Look at this guy's clothes! I think I found a parrot! A *papagayo*." The others laughed, and the youth basked in their encouragement. "Where are you going, Papagayo? To learn some new parrot jokes?"

Riki shook his sleeve loose and backed away. His face burned with shame. No one had ever laughed at him like this before. His tormentor was taller than the rest, the oldest of the group, obviously a leader. He had the arrogant air of approaching manhood, a need to prove his manliness. He looked strong and confident. His hand shot out and again grabbed Riki's sleeve.

"Come on, now Papagayo, make some parrot sounds for us. Whistle *La Adelita* for us. All parrots know that one." The laughter was louder, aggressive.

The other boys yelled encouragement. They called the older boy *Comanche*. Comanche's grin widened, when Riki again pulled away and began backing away. His heart beat furiously and his mind blurred with the puzzlement of what was happening.

Comanche swaggered and swung his shoulders exaggeratedly as he matched step for step as Riki backed away. The children snickered at the entertainment. Cold sweat formed in Riki's armpits. As he backed away the boys followed. "Come on, Papagayo, let's hear you whistle!"

Riki took a deep breath to control his anxiety. Although he was shaking inside, he forced his voice to be calm.

"I don't whistle."

He took one more step backward and was about to turn and run when he bumped into someone. He realized that they had formed a circle about him. His fingers trembled slightly, and his heart began pumping blood even faster. Comanche folded his arms across his chest, and the grin left his face, replaced by a scowl.

"What are you doing in our barrio?"

When Riki didn't answer, Comanche frowned menacingly. "When I ask you questions, you answer. Do you understand that? Perhaps I'll let things go this time, if you pay for our tacos."

Riki turned to look behind him. Only two boys, dirty and ragged—children really—stood between him and the street. Comanche now stood about three paces away.

Panicked, Riki pushed the nearest boy aside and began hurrying away. He glanced back to see if they were going to chase him.

Comanche yelled, "Wait, Parrot! I said stop!"

Riki started to flee, and he heard the sounds of running footsteps coming after him. He knew the boys could eventually run him down like dogs hunting a deer. He stopped. The villagers of Tezcatlipocas would be ashamed of him for running. He decided to try and get out of this with some dignity. He stopped and turned to face his pursuers.

An angry look twisted Comanche's face. "I told you to stop!"

"I'm not a parrot. I don't take orders from you. Leave me alone."

He stared at Comanche's eyes, watching for the tell-tale flicking of the eyes that signaled a punch.

When Comanche started to grab at his sleeve again, the eyes flicked. Riki moved quickly and smoothly. He easily ducked under a telegraphed left hook and clipped his tormentor lightly on the shoulder with the palm of his left hand to set him up. Then, without really meaning to—but exactly as El Perrón had taught—he swung his body around and placed a fist into that spot just above the stomach and just below the rib cage. The full weight of his mountain-muscled chest went into the blow.

Comanche gasped in pain and surprise as he dropped to his knees. His throat rasped as he struggled for breath.

The other boys stepped away in shocked silence. The boy on his knees stared at Riki with surprise and rage. Riki whirled about in time to see another boy moving toward his back. His foot flicked upward, catching the boy on his neck, sending him stumbling back in surprise. Riki held his hands in front of him as El Perrón had taught him, and he turned in a slow circle to see if anyone else was ready to press the attack.

No one did.

Riki turned and began walking slowly away. He wanted to run, but his dignity forbad it. Besides, his knees felt so weak, he didn't dare.

Comanche's voice was hoarse as he sent a threat following after Riki. "I'll get even with you, Papagayo. I'll get even."

Riki watched over his shoulder to see if any of the boys followed. But no one had moved after the second boy took the surprise kick. Riki felt better now, proud of himself for not having behaved cowardly, even though he felt some shame at fighting. He trotted all the way to the building site.

Workers trudged unenthusiastically into the dusty ruins like cattle entering a slaughterhouse. One by one they began taking their places to start the day. When Riki asked where to ask about work, one of the men pointed at a huge man, with arms like a hairless gorilla, who stood looking at the workers belligerently. "That's him. You have to ask the *jefe* for work. He's a rotten son of a dog."

Riki felt jittery as he approached the man, but he managed to appear calm. "I'd like to work here. I can work hard."

The big man turned to sneer down at Riki. "You want a job? Shit! So does half of Mexico. Do you think I have money to waste on lazy pachucos? This is man's work. Get your ass out of here, *esquintle*."

Riki lost his nervousness; he felt cold anger at the tone of the man's voice. "I'm not a pachuco. I can work as hard as anyone you have. I'm as strong as any."

The jefe's belly shook as he laughed sarcastically. "You're a goddamn punk, with baby fat instead of muscle. I ought to break your head open to teach you respect for real men. But I'll tell you what I'm willing to do. I'll give you a chance to prove yourself. I'll let you work today. If you can do a man's work, I'll pay you. If you can't, I'll kick your ass off the lot and down the street."

Riki eagerly ran to the crew the foreman pointed out. "I'm supposed to help you," he said to one of the men. "What do you want me to do?"

The men looked at his colored clothing contemptuously. One said, "Jesus, now *el jefe* is hiring Pachucos. He'll do anything to save a centavo."

Riki didn't look at the man. He repeated, "What am I supposed to do?"

The man he was speaking to replied, "We take turns. First, we clean the mortar off the bricks with these iron straps, then we stack them on that truck. You can start cleaning. Juan will show you how. Then you take your turn stacking."

The work was dusty, with clouds of dry, ancient mortar hovering over the decaying building. Riki imitated the others; he squatted by the pile of rubble and went to work. He tried to keep up, brick for brick with the others. After half an hour, he caught on and was building his stack of cleaned bricks higher than any on the crew. When his turn came to stack the bricks on the large flatbed truck, he carried twelve bricks at a time instead of ten as the others carried, and he trotted up the heavy plank instead of walking.

The crew broke for lunch. Most of the men had pails of food from home. Some brought out tortillas and cold soup, others unwrapped sandwiches of hard rolls and sliced pork. All began to eat. Riki moved away from them and sat on a stack of bricks so the sight of food wouldn't torture him. He looked away and stared at the traffic edging along the street. His legs quivered from hard work and lack of food, but he steeled his mind against it. He was startled when someone touched him on the shoulder. He turned to see one of the workmen. He held out half a sandwich. "I'm not really hungry," he said. "I don't want to throw this away." Then he was gone.

Riki was chewing the food, savoring every bite, when another of the workers handed him a tin pail half full of chicken soup. "Drink this," he said. "And do me the favor of finishing up this sausage. The old lady always puts more in my lunch than I can eat."

That afternoon he worked with a frenzy. He piled up almost as many cleaned bricks as any two of the others. When quitting time came, he was exhausted but the elation of succeeding on his first job masked the weariness. He could hardly wait to tell Micaela the good news.

He hurried to the foreman's shack. The workers had told him that if you need the money, the foreman will pay every day, but that he takes a discount for himself.

"He's a stingy son of a bitch. Be careful, or he'll cheat you out of your pants," said the man who gave Riki the soup at lunch. "Every centavo he doesn't have to pay us goes into his fat pockets."

He couldn't find the foreman around the shack. "The *jefe* went home twenty minutes ago," one of the men said. "He won't be back until morning."

Riki nodded in disappointment. "I need the money, but I suppose I'll have wait until tomorrow."

On the way home, he kept a wary eye out for the boy called Comanche. There was no sign of him. He recognized a boy who had been in the crowd that morning, but the boy looked away, pretending not to see Riki. When he opened the door to the apartment, the first thing he saw was Micaela. She was sitting at the table, her head laying on her arms. She was crying.

"What's wrong?"

At first, she refused to say anything. Finally said, "Manuel took me to look for a job."

"You couldn't find one?"

"Oh yes. I found one. But..."

He pulled a chair out and sat down. He waited for her weeping to subside. After a few moments she wiped her eyes and said, "He took me to a place called 'El Gato Negro'. He said it was a restaurant, and that I could work cleaning up."

"What was wrong?"

"It wasn't a restaurant. It was a *cabaret*. They wanted me to work as a *prostituta*. When I started crying, Manuel tried to force me into a little room. There was nothing there but a bed. I kicked him in his private parts and ran away."

She stopped talking while she cried some more. Then she sat up straight and pointed to a rip in the dress's bosom. "Look what he did. He ruined it. Then he yelled out the door that he was going to tell the police I am a puta if I don't go back. I tried to spit on him, but he was too far away."

The evening went slowly. Hunger has a way of making time drag. The next morning, he was up early. He thought that if he were first on the job it would make a good impression with the jefe. When he stepped into the street, he looked about to make sure none of the barrio toughs were waiting for him. Then he hurried down the street. When he came to the block where the tripas wagon had been yesterday, he detoured around to the next street.

The foreman stood in front of the construction shack, a steaming coffee cup in his hand, a sour expression on his face. Riki managed a smile when he caught the foreman's eye. He nodded humbly as the men in Tezcatlipocas did when greeting each other.

"I wanted to ask you for some money last night. You see, I don't have any, and I wanted to see if I couldn't get paid for yesterday by the end of today's work."

The man's lips puffed outward and his eyes narrowed. "Pay? Pay you for what you did yesterday? Don't make me laugh. You're lucky I don't kick your asshole up around your ears for loafing so much. Now get moving, and don't let me catch you around here again."

No one from Tezcatlipocas would ever permit these kinds

of insults. He was surprised at how calm he sounded when he said, "I worked yesterday, harder than anyone else. You're going to pay me." A trace of a smile came across the foreman's face. He flexed a muscle in his arm. "You're going to *take* the money from me? Want to try?"

He drew back his right hand as if to throw a punch. Riki shifted his weight and knew he could easily deflect the blow and land one on the man's mouth, but he hoped the man was only bluffing. He didn't want to fight; he wanted his money.

Then he saw it... the foreman's eyes flicked to the right. Quickly, without thinking, Riki shifted his weight away from the expected punch, and he readied himself to counter.

But from out of nowhere, the foreman's foot lashed out and thumped loudly against Riki's groin. The kick was aimed at the testicles, but missed by millimeters, spinning him around and off-balance. Then a left hand sneaked out and thumped against Riki's neck. He fell to the ground, landing on his back.

The foreman reads eyes!

Riki shook his head to clear his brain and got to his hands and knees. Suddenly, like a rattlesnake's strike, the foreman's foot shot toward Riki's head. Just in time, he managed to roll over, the heavy boot sending a puff of mortar dust in the air.

Riki rolled again and was on his feet just as the foreman closed in. The big man held both hands up, clinched together like a sledgehammer. He had a confident smile on his face.

Riki waited, his eyes riveted to his foe's, looking for a signal. He knew that it was almost impossible to control the eyes every time.

Then he saw the momentary shifting of eyes and ducked under a powerful, hammer-like blow. He stepped back just in time to miss the foot-combination.

When the next punch came, Riki was ready. He twisted to the right and then rammed his fist into the foreman's midsection. A cheer rang out from the circle of workers as Riki danced away. "Hit him again!" "Kill the stingy son of a bitch!"

But he knew that the punches couldn't have done much more than annoy the huge man. El Jefe let out an angry roar and bulled his way forward again. He towered over Riki by at least six inches and his long arms and street fighting skills should have given him an advantage.

But Riki's training and reflexes helped even the match, if only to a small degree. He peppered three quick jabs to the foreman's face, doing little damage, but arousing even more anger. The more frustrated the foreman became, the less control El Jefe seemed to have over his eyes. He charged at Riki in blind rage. A huge fist aimed for Riki's face.

He weaved aside and then landed two quick chops to the face, just as El Perrón and he had practiced so many times. The cheers seemed thunderous now.

Blood trickled from the foreman's nose. He charged forward like a furious bull.

Then, as Riki stepped back in retreat, he tripped on a chunk of concrete and fell backwards.

He landed on his elbows, but his head hit the ground with a splash of colors. He shook his head and tried to get up.

A gasp came from the workers. One started forward to help Riki, but he hesitated and stepped back when he considered the consequences.

The big man laughed as he closed in on his prey. He paused to pick up a cement block. He hefted it in his hands and lifted it in the air for all to see. He was enjoying this immensely, playing with his prey like a cat with a mouse. Riki pushed back with his feet, looking for an opening to get up. El jefe followed.

"I'm going to break both of your legs, *pendejo!*"

Riki shook his head again and tried to get to his feet. Then he noticed someone pushing through the crowd. He hoped it was one of the workers coming to his rescue.

To his dismay he realized that it was his new-found enemy, Comanche. The youth stopped to picked up a brick, tossed it a couple of inches in the air, caught it, and swaggered up to stand beside the foreman.

The foreman turned to see who was there. He stared at Comanche with a puzzled look on his face. The puzzled looked turned to astonishment when the brick in Comanche's hand broke over his forehead.

The big man's mouth opened in astonishment, then his eyes glazed over. The chunk of cement fell from his hands to thud heavily on his instep. He probably felt no pain because he was unconscious before he hit the ground. A chorus of happy whooping came from the workers.

Comanche reached down and offered Riki a hand to pull him to his feet.

"You have a lot of guts, Papagayo. This is one of the toughest mother molesters in Mexico City. Used to fight heavyweight! You would have taken him, too, if you hadn't tripped."

Chapter Seventeen

Riki started to thank Comanche, but the squealing of automobile tires made them turn away. A white and black car with a flashing red light came to a sliding stop across the street.

Comanche hissed, "*La chota!* Let's go!"

As Riki followed Comanche, he saw two uniformed police step out of the police cruiser. Both carried long black clubs. Comanche ducked into the shell of a half-demolished building and exited through a hole in the back. Riki followed close behind. They ran through a maze of alleys and narrow streets. Comanche knew every crevice of the barrio.

They halted in the mouth of an alley for a few moments while a police cruiser drifted past. The youth looked at Riki and smiled in conspiracy. "What's your name?"

"Riki Montalvo. Why do they call you Comanche? Is that really your name?"

He laughed. "Of course not. My name's Horacio. Everyone has a street name here. They'll probably call you 'Papagayo' because of those clothes you wear." He pulled Riki's arm and said, "Okay, it's safe to cross the street."

"Thanks for helping me."

"I watched you handle that guy, and you were pretty good," Comanche said. "I was mad at you for what you did to me, and I was planning on getting even. But I have to hand it to you. You were better than me. And it was beautiful to see you make a fool of that foreman. He's known as one tough bastard in this barrio. I can guarantee that your reputation is going to soar like an eagle."

"I didn't want to fight with him. I don't want a reputation. I just want my money. I didn't get it."

"Forget it. It's peanuts. Why don't you work for me? I have ways of earning money, and you don't have to carry dusty bricks. It would be good for my reputation to have a tough guy like you working for me."

Riki shook his head stubbornly. "I'm not a 'tough guy', and I don't want to make money by robbing from people as poor as me, like you were going to do yesterday."

Comanche laughed. "I was only playing *macho*. I wasn't going to take money from you. You know how it is—a new guy moves into the barrio—I've got to uphold my reputation. You looked pretty strong, so I thought it would do me good to put you down in front of the barrio pachucos. What a mistake! You made a donkey out of me."

"I want a real job, not a criminal one."

"You need money? Here, here's a handful of pesos. There's more where that came from."

Riki looked at the money with temptation but started to back away. Comanche grabbed him by the arm, his voice half pleading, half threatening. "You don't understand. My reputation is at risk now."

"At risk?"

"Yes. A newcomer to the barrio puts me down, makes a fool of me. Can't you see the problem? The only way I can salvage my reputation is if you become my friend, work for me"

"I want a job. I don't want to steal."

"I'm not asking you to steal. I'm asking you to be my friend. Just work for me for a while. Just pretend to work if you choose. If you don't, I'm in a mess. Either I let you go and let people think I'm a coward, or, I have to do something bad to you in order to prove to everyone that I'm still the *gran chingón*. Don't make me hurt you. I like you."

"I'm not afraid of you."

"I know that. I don't fear you, either. I think with a second chance maybe I could beat you in a street fight, but there's no question I can lay you in the gutter with a knife or a gun. I'd have to do that, you know."

"What do you want me to do?"

Comanche pointed across the street to a taco stand. "Come on, I'll buy you something to eat to make up for what I did yesterday, and I'll explain. What do I want you to do? Nothing at first. Just watch. Then later, when you understand what is going on, you can cover for me. You don't have to steal anything. Let's eat and I'll explain."

Riki walked to the taco stand with his stomach whirling at the thought of food. It wouldn't hurt to listen... and to eat.

It turned out that Comanche was the leader of a few boys who were experimenting, searching for a niche in the underworld economy. The gang was new, weak, a mere ripple in the current of stronger, older, organized groups. Half a dozen street urchins banded together with Comanche, not so much because they respected him, but because the older gangs would have nothing to do with beginners. They had to be satisfied with the leavings. Theirs was a very loose group, more or less centered about Comanche. Most had no homes, sleeping at night wherever they could, eating whenever their wits provided. When they had surplus, they shared. When they had nothing, they starved. Currently the boys were practicing robbing wallets on the buses that ran along Reforma to the Museo de Antropologia.

"There are nearly always *turistas* on the buses," Comanche explained. "The pickings are slim, and it's a little dangerous. But so far, no one has been nicked by the chota. Some days we spend most of our money on bus fares, and no wallets gathered. But we're getting better all the time."

"What are *turistas*?"

"Gringos. They have plenty of money and it doesn't hurt them to lose some of it."

Somehow it didn't seem quite as bad to think about Gringos

being robbed, because Riki remembered the things El Perrón had said about them; he remembered those in Córdoba. He listened carefully as Comanche explained how one of the gang members, a boy named Angel, had become fairly proficient in lifting the wallet from a victim's pocket. He would make the hit and immediately pass it on to Comanche who then slipped it to Pepe, a rather dull-witted little boy.

"You see, Pepe ends up with the wallet, and nobody knows it. If anything, they suspect Angel. It's Pepe's job to get off the bus at the next stop and wait for the gang to come together again. That's about all he can be trusted to do, since he can't remember anything more complicated than that," Comanche explained. "Where you and I have brains, Pepe has guacamole sauce."

"But what about Angel? The boy who steals the wallet? Doesn't he get caught?"

"Most of the time, the Gringo doesn't even suspect. But if he does, it's my job to keep the Gringo away from Angel. Since he doesn't have the wallet anymore, there's nothing can be done. But sometimes the turistas can get angry. With me there, I can keep things from getting out of hand. The only danger comes when undercover cops ride the bus, watching for games like this."

Riki shook his head dubiously. No matter how Comanche put it, it was stealing, and he couldn't help but think how the villagers in Tezcatlipocas would have disapproved.

"Come along tomorrow, and you'll see how it works. Trust me. We don't take money from anyone who can't afford it. Just from Gringos who, as everyone knows, are as rich as Mexican politicians. Do you think they would miss a few moldy dollar bills?"

"I don't like idea of stealing. Not even from rich Gringos."

Comanche shook his head impatiently and repeated very slowly: "You don't steal anything! Remember that. All you have to do is be there in case the Gringo catches on and sees me hand off the wallet to Pepe. You step in front of our 'client' and pretend to be clumsy, keep him blocked until Pepe is safely off the bus. You don't do anything wrong, and none of us has the wallet. You're big enough and strong enough that they'd have a hard time moving you aside. You pretend to be angry because the turista is trying to shove you around. If there are any chota on the bus, you back away and apologize. By that time Pepe will be standing on the street. You work with me and my boys and you will learn. Yes, you will learn."

Before he went home to Micaela that afternoon, he accepted the handful of pesos from Comanche and he bought vegetables and a knuckle of beef as well as a kilo of white rice.

She had been feeling dull that day, staring out the door for long periods, but she brightened when she saw the packages of food. She soon busied herself preparing dinner. "They paid you well for your work to be able to buy all of this in one day," she said happily, "and when I get a job too, we will be rich! Oh, how I wish we'd come to the city years ago."

He lied to her again, telling her that he was supposed to work the next day. He'd never deliberately deceived Micaela before and it bothered him. He felt apprehensive when thinking about what he had promised Comanche. He resolved that if he couldn't find a job soon, he'd sell a piece of the jewelry whether Micaela liked it or not. Maybe it was lucky that he met Comanche, because the gang leader would surely know where to sell jewelry.

The next morning two other boys besides Comanche met Riki at the designated place in front of Bellas Artes. Both were smaller, the smallest probably not much over twelve years old. Pepe, the boy entrusted with holding the wallet and waiting at the bus stop, was small, soft-looking, with huge brown eyes that made him look as innocent as the cherub statues on the facade of Bellas Artes. He didn't appear dull-witted, but before long Riki realized that the boy was innocent-looking because he had no evil thoughts, or any other kind of thoughts, for that matter.

The second boy was Angel. His skin was as dark as an olive

that had been in the brine too long, and there were rough pox marks on his cheeks. Standing almost as tall as Riki, Angel was stringy and hungry looking, with teeth much too large for his mouth, some of them twisted confusedly. He smiled seldom, as if he were ashamed of his crooked teeth. Pepe, on the other hand smiled continually and was obviously pleased that Riki was joining the group. Comanche handed Pepe a large sugar-coated *churro* and ruffled the boy's hair. "Where did you sleep last night?"

"In the pipes. Nice and warm there." Pepe bit into the pastry and began wolfing it down. His eyes sparkled and he smiled at the world with unlimited love.

When Riki looked puzzled, Angel explained, "There's a set of ventilation pipes from the Del Prado hotel that open into an alley, and Pepe found a way to pull the screen aside and get inside to sleep."

Pepe nodded and said through a full mouth of food, "Nice and warm. Smells nice, too, because the air comes from the kitchen."

They waited for Pepe to finish eating, then Comanche urged his friends to move on. "Maybe today will be our lucky day."

Riki felt nervous but began catching some of the excitement that Comanche had spoken of yesterday. The companionship of boys his own age was something new for him, and he felt warm and euphoric. Yet his stomach fluttered when he thought about their mission.

He didn't want to steal. It was against all of his background growing up in Tezcatlipocas, against everything the people in the village believed in. Still, he felt obligated, now that he had companions. He vowed to do no more than absolutely necessary.

Comanche was like a general on a campaign. "Pepe, run on down to the Zócalo and catch the bus when it's empty so you can get a seat by the door. Now remember, if I hand you something, you put it in your pocket and get off the bus as soon as it stops. And you wait right there. Can you remember that?"

"Sure. I'll remember."

"What else do you do?"

"I hold my hand out the window, so you know which bus to get on."

"Good! And Angel, you get on in front of the Juarez monument. Riki and I will go a few blocks further. We don't want anyone to guess that we're together."

Comanche and Riki waited until they saw the bus rolling to a stop, the one with Pepe's arm hanging from the window. They jumped on and worked their way to the back. Angel looked away when they squeezed past him. Pepe remembered not to smile at them.

As the bus rumbled through the streets of ancient Tenochtitlan, they observed each passenger who boarded the bus. Comanche evaluated the 'clients' as to possible business.

"See that one who just got on? I bet he has plenty of loot on him, but where? It isn't in his hip pocket, because there's no bulge there. So, he must keep his wallet in his front pockets or else in the coat pockets. Or even in a money belt. How are we to know? That's the toughest part of this business. If they would only wear a sign on their backs telling where they keep the wallet, it would be much easier for us."

They made three trips this way to Chapultepec and back before Angel tried to make a *golpe*. A stout American lady wearing thick glasses stood near the back door, and when the crowd started pushing to get off, Angel managed to open her purse and feel around inside. But before he could find the wallet, she pulled away from him. She noticed the open purse and snapped it shut, probably thinking she had carelessly left it open, yet suspecting something could be wrong. She shifted the purse to hold it tightly under her arm. Disappointment showed keenly on Angel's face.

Comanche shrugged in apology and whispered, "This could be another unlucky day. But we can't expect to have money fall in our laps. If not today, then tomorrow. We can't push our luck."

Then, when the bus stopped by the *Monumento de la Revolución*, a tourist couple, middle aged and talking loudly in English, climbed aboard.

Comanche nudged Riki and whispered, "Look, Gringos! And look, his wallet is in his hip pocket!"

The man was heavyset; his face reminded Riki of a pig's. The nose was uptilted and set in the middle of a wide, fat face. The woman had a pinched look. Her nose was so sharp it looked as if it could scratch glass. An unpleasant mouth curved down into permanent lines of disapproval. These two reminded Riki of the rude people in Córdoba, the ones who had called Micaela "dirty." So, these were Gringos! He felt a bad taste in his mouth as he inspected them. Their voices were loud and arrogant when they talked.

"Watch out for your wallet, Chester," the woman whispered. "You know how these thieving Mexicans are. Have you still got it?"

The man unconsciously felt his hip pocket, which was covered by a large checkered sport coat. "Yeah, yeah. Nobody's gonna steal my goddamned wallet. I ain't been a cop all these years for nuthin'. Anyway, I don't keep my money there. I ain't that stupid."

"Where is it?"

"Where it ain't gonna get stolen." Without thinking, his hand went to his front pants pocket and fingered something thick, a fold of banknotes. He smiled smugly.

Riki nudged Comanche and whispered, "His money isn't in the wallet. He keeps it in his front pocket."

"How could you know that?"

"I understand what they say. Don't ask how, I just do. In the front pocket. Can you signal Angel?"

It went off so smoothly that the tourist didn't feel a thing. A discrete bump when the bus swerved around a glorietta and it was all over. Comanche accepted the fat roll of banknotes and moved toward the door where he slipped it to Pepe. With the money stuffed safely into his pocket, Pepe hopped off the bus at the next corner. He obediently trotted to the shelter of the bus stop and waited for his friends to return.

As the boys hurried back to meet with Pepe, they laughed and sometimes skipped with delight. Comanche looked at Riki with admiration. "You really can understand *inglés*? How can that be?"

Riki shrugged. "It's easy. I learned it when I was a baby." He didn't want to talk about it, or even think about it.

"Can you speak that language, too?"

"I haven't tried since I was a little boy, but I think so. I can say the words I hear in the *cine*, but I've never practiced saying them to anyone. Not out loud."

Comanche thought a while, and then said, "I have an idea. Tomorrow, let's try something different."

When Riki came home that afternoon, Micaela was delighted to see the money he had earned. "You make so much working, and your clothes don't even get dirty! How lucky. I am so proud of you."

He insisted they go to a restaurant for dinner. He had never been in a real restaurant since Diana had left him in Tezcatlipocas, and that was beyond his memory. Micaela giggled with excitement and rummaged through Diana's suitcase for something suitable to wear.

"Forget that," Riki said. "Before we go to the restaurant, we'll buy you a new dress." He pushed Micaela out the door and insisted that they walk to the used clothing store on the corner. She selected a cotton dress, dark blue with a white lace collar. Riki found a pair of black trousers that, although worn and shiny, had no holes in the seat. Then he bought a white shirt with cuffs that buttoned at the wrist. Except for a yellow stain on one of the sleeves, it looked almost new. He paid for the clothes without even haggling over the price, and hurried back to the apartment, bubbling with anticipation.

Micaela tried on her dress and turned about the room in a whirlpool of happiness. "What do you think? I wish I could see myself in a mirror."

"You look like a city person. I like it a lot." He looked down at the white shirt and black pants he was wearing and nodded approval. He resolved to get rid of the *papagayo* clothes, to never wear them again. It felt good to dress like a city person. He put on his sunglasses out of force of habit, even though it was getting dark outside.

The restaurant they chose was around the corner, a narrow place with five tables and benches along one wall. A steamy kitchen closed off the back of the room. Hypnotic smells of boiling soup and frying meat made Riki's mouth begin watering. He followed Micaela inside and felt self-conscious. He had to look down at this elegant new clothing to reassure himself that he looked all right to be entering a real restaurant.

They sat on a wooden bench in front of the plank table and looked at the menu painted on the wall. A woman came out of the kitchen, mopped the sweat from her brow with her apron and then placed a knife, fork and spoon in front of each of them. She waited for them to make up their mind.

Riki touched the utensils and frowned thoughtfully. Some memory in the back of his mind stirred, trying to take him back to the time when he had used utensils like this before Tezcatlipocas. For village people, a tortilla served as fork and spoon. Beans and boiled meat don't require the use of a knife. He looked about the little restaurant and noticed how other people handled the fork and the spoon. It looked clumsy, but he was willing to give it a try.

"I think maybe I can look for a job now," Micaela said brightly as they waited for the girl to bring their plates of turkey mole. "With this new dress, I won't be ashamed to look for one."

"Maybe you won't need a job, just yet. If I can make this

much money every day, you won't have to work. Pretty soon, we can leave that small place we are living in and move to a better apartment — maybe one with glass windows."

Certainly, stealing money wasn't as difficult as he had imagined. And Comanche was correct; taking money from rich Gringos was easy on the conscience. Something about Gringos made it easy to believe they are less than human.

The next day, on the second bus trip, Riki decided to try his English as Comanche suggested. Half a dozen tourists rode the bus, most headed for the museum. A lanky Australian stood near the back door, leaning against a chrome pole. Riki swallowed tightly and said:

"Be careful, sir. There could be thieves here. Yesterday someone stole a wallet on this very bus."

The tourist obviously understood perfectly, for he nodded and reached for his inside pocket to make sure his wallet was intact. "Thanks for the warning, mate."

At the same time, the other tourists who understood English reached for their valuables, gently patting their pockets for reassurance. Now Angel knew precisely where to look. Within five minutes he lifted two wallets, each containing a respectable thickness of pesos and one with two one-hundred-dollar bills.

Later, they rendezvoused with Pepe at the bus stop, their eyes sparkling as they counted the multicolored pesos and the rich-looking dollar banknotes. This was the most money any had ever "earned" in one day.

Riki enjoyed himself as he joined them, running down the street, shouting at each other, laughing foolishly. They stopped at every food stand they found, ordering snacks and giving them away half-eaten to other street urchins, then running on to the next stand.

When they were full and could eat no more, they went to the Alameda and lay on the grass to talk. Pepe lay next to Riki, clinging to Riki's arm with one hand and holding a sweet rope of red candy with the other.

"With all this money, we don't need to take a chance on working for a week or two," Angel said with a pleased laugh. "We can take vacations."

"Good idea," Comanche said. "If we work the buses every day, it's a matter of time until we get caught. Let's lay low for two weeks, then try it again."

"Too bad we can't think of a way to work every day."

"Maybe Papagayo can teach us to speak English," Comanche suggested. "If we knew how to speak English, we could pick up lots of money as guides. They say that sometimes pays better than stealing."

Angel said, "Like, I know a kid named Raymundo, who's only a couple of years older than me, and he takes tourists to Teotihuacan and makes a lot of money in tips. You ought to do that, Papagayo, you know? Tourists like to look at pyramids and crappy old buildings while guides make up stories about them."

"Gringos are all crazy, you know. They can't come here without going to look at stupid old buildings," Comanche added. "I don't know why. I went there once and there's nothing there but piles of rock."

"How do you get guide jobs?" Riki asked.

"Raymundo says it's easy. If you know how to speak Gringo talk, you just go up to them and say, 'guide, mister?' And they give you money just to go with them. Sometimes, when they give him the money, he just puts it into his pocket and runs away. But you don't have to do that, because they usually give tips after you bring them back to town."

"Where are the pyramids?"

"Far away from the city. I think you have to take a taxi or a bus. But the tourists pay for this. You ought to try it, Papagayo."

"I don't know enough English," Riki protested. "And I don't know anything about the pyramids. Only what don

Ramon told me when I was little."

"Neither does Raymundo. He makes up stories about them. It's easy, because they believe everything he tells them. He says it's fun, because he makes up a different story each time. He had one lady believing that Pancho Villa destroyed the ruins when he and Maximiliano fought against General Zapata."

"Well, I don't like Gringos. I don't think I'd like to be with them very much."

They counted the money once more and laughed and talked about how easy it had been. But then came the problem of what to do with the $100 bills. Usually, large bills were sold to a man in the barrio, a man named Barragan who ran a surreptitious *casa de cambio*, buying foreign currency from anyone who couldn't afford the risk of going to a bank to change stolen money. But he also had the reputation of taking advantage of the weak, sometimes keeping most of the money for himself, knowing youngsters wouldn't dare complain.

"Too bad we can't just spend these big bills," Angel lamented. "When the tourist complains to the police, they'll be watching for Mexican pickpockets trying to cash these big green bills. Can you imagine how many pesos we could get for these things in a bank?"

Comanche agreed. "We'll have to sell them for a third of the value to that thief, Barragan."

"Maybe less."

Riki thought about this for a moment, and suddenly had an idea. "I look enough like a Gringo that maybe the bank wouldn't become suspicious. If you want, I could try to change them into pesos."

The boys looked at him in astonishment. Angel said, "I thought this guy came from the country! A couple of weeks with us, and already he is talking like a *gran chingón*. He'll be running for *presidente de la republica* before we know it."

Comanche looked amused, and at the same time, contemplative. "Sure, why not? We'll give you an extra share.

235

All we can lose is the money we probably wouldn't have anyway if you get caught."

It turned out to be rather easy. The boys found a sport shirt that looked like one a Gringo tourist might wear, and they hung a camera (that Angel had lifted from a tourist) around his neck to complete the disguise.

Riki watched how things worked in the bank. He noticed that people stood in one line to have their money counted and were given a slip of paper with the total written on it in exchange for the bills. This slip of paper was then presented to another cashier who exchanged the paper for a stack of pesos. He stood in line to obtain the paper, then he handed the receipt to Comanche, who went to the other line to collect the pesos.

Soon they were walking out of the bank with a thick wad of money in their pockets. That night, he and Micaela went to another restaurant, this time, one with checkered tablecloths on the table, and real chairs to sit on instead of backless benches. She couldn't conceal her delight at doing something so extravagant, and she kept telling Riki how proud she was of him and his job.

Every day for the next two weeks, Riki left home in the morning, telling Micaela he was going to work. He spent the mornings wandering about downtown, and the afternoons at the movies. He found the cinema a fascinating source of information about the world, how people behaved, what other places looked like. He was particularly interested in American films. His recognition vocabulary expanded daily until there were few situations he couldn't understand without having to read the subtitles. American gangster films fascinated him. He studied the way gangsters spoke, and how they could frighten people with a burning stare or facial expression

He noticed that Gringo people shook hands heartily in greeting instead of bowing politely as they did in the village of

Tezcatlipocas or the weak handshakes of the city. Apparently, unmarried men and women commonly go places together without chaperones — to nightclubs, for drives in open cars, and even kiss and fondle each other — without family approval. Obviously, Gringos must be rich, for they live in modern houses with carpets on the floors, servants and, best of all, have swimming pools everywhere. The women seemed to be rather loose, with little regard for modesty or morals, wearing skimpy swimsuits and continually allowing men to kiss them (sometimes even with their mouths open!). Occasionally, Riki would feel vaguely uneasy, as if something about the scene — the room or the furnishings — were familiar... memories of something he'd lost somewhere.

He began to recognize actors, and sometimes searched out a movie house where he could watch one that he particularly liked. One afternoon, he found a small theatre on San Juan de Letrán where an old western with John Wayne was showing. The second billing was also an old film, called *Chestnut River,* starring an actress named Diana Cranston. The feeling of uneasiness struck him particularly hard during the second show. He found his heart beating fast and beads of sweat popping out on his forehead. He didn't know why.

When the cine was over, and as he was walking toward home, he wondered what it was that had bothered him. The story had taken place in someplace called Scotland, where people talked strange, but he felt as if he had been there before. He went back the next day to see the film again and decided it must be something about Diana Cranston that caused the reaction. After that, he searched the theaters for some other picture with Diana Cranston. He found none. Each day he killed time until it was time to return to Micaela.

He felt very lonely, wandering the streets of downtown Mexico City. Everyone else seemed rich, which emphasized his poverty. As he walked the streets, he studied the passersby and envied their lives full of love and companionship. Children with their parents, brothers and sisters, some holding hands, all with the blessings of family love. Most of them wore new clothes with creases and pleats nicely ironed. Few of them ever knew what an empty stomach felt like. Few of them ever knew the humiliation of not being wanted. His abandonment was never far from his mind, and he wondered if the shame and humiliation of it showed in his face, as the love and pride showed in other's faces.

Especially poignant were the beautiful young ladies walking hand in hand with their well-dressed, debonair boyfriends, looking in shop windows and making imaginary purchases for their someday honeymoons.

Riki believed he was looking into a world that would forever be closed to him, and he felt sad. As long as he was poor, humble, a "street kid" he had no hope of joining the world of respectability, of courtship, maybe not even of marriage. He wondered what his future was to be, and whether he might ever move into a higher level of society. He wondered what it would be like to be a gangster.

Although they had planned on not making any *movidas* for another week, Comanche came by for Riki early. Apparently, he had spent more money than he had planned. Riki was glad to get back to work; movies were beginning to bore him.

They decided to work the bus to the airport instead of the Reforma bus. After two trips, Comanche looked worried.

"There's something wrong. I can smell *chota* on this bus."

Angel said, "I haven't seen a single tourist that looks like he could have more than 50 centavos in his pocket. Let's try once more, and then we ought to try the Reforma bus again."

They waited around the bus stop, waiting for tourists to exit from the terminal. Finally, a businessman with a hard-looking face came out, carrying a briefcase and looking for a taxi. Two passed but were already carrying passengers.

"Mexican," whispered Comanche. "I can tell by the shoes.

Too bad he isn't getting on the bus. I'll bet he's loaded."

Another taxi cruised past. Then the bus loomed around the corner and pulled to a stop. The businessman frowned, looked once more for the taxi, then came hurrying toward the bus.

"Maybe our lucky day," whispered Angel.

Riki smiled at the man and said in Spanish, "Be careful on the bus, señor, there are a lot of pickpockets around."

The man looked at Riki contemptuously and, as he walked past to climb on the bus, said, "I can take care of myself." But he tightened his grip on the briefcase, and his hand involuntarily moved up to pat his front pocket.

The boys boarded the bus behind their victim. Pepe went first and followed at the man's heels. The bus was crowded, and the man walked to the middle of the bus and stood by the door.

He looked around suspiciously and again touched the pocket. Then he braced himself against the metal rail with his pocket pressed tightly against the chrome pole.

Angel moved close, and Comanche took up his position, ready to stumble against the victim. Pepe stepped down into the door well, ready to do his part. The bus made several stops before Angel made his move. When the bus started up, a razor sliced through the fabric of the man's pants pocket.

Comanche gave the signal, and Riki pulled the cord to stop the bus at the corner. When the bus braked, Comanche fell against the man, pulling him momentarily away from the pole. Angel's fingers worked smoothly and fast. Riki barely saw the switch, and the wallet was now in Comanche's possession. All that remained was to hand it to Pepe.

Then, Riki noticed something odd. A pair of men, well dressed and both wearing hats, began edging their way through the crowd. If they were going to get off the bus, this didn't make sense, because they were closer to the front exit. Then he noticed bulges in their coats, both under their left armpits. *Chota!*

His heart began pounding wildly. He almost forgot to give the signal. Finally, he began coughing, as though something

239

were stuck in his throat.

Comanche looked at him sharply, then around the bus. He nodded when he spotted the two men. The bus was still rolling, but he kicked the doors open and leaped out.

By leaning away from the direction of travel and leading with his left foot crossed over his right, he ended up running a few steps. Then he stopped and turned to run the other direction.

"Stop! Stop, thief," one of the cops called out as they pushed their way through the crowd.

The victim suddenly reached for his pocket and found the gaping slice of fabric instead. "They stole my wallet!"

Angel pretended to stumble and knocked one of the men aside as he fell. Riki picked up the cue and went to help Angel get up. This blocked the second cop for another precious second. By the time the bus stopped, Comanche was disappearing into a narrow alley.

"Forget it," said one cop to the other. "We'll never catch him." He grabbed Angel by the arm. "This is the one who did the work. At least we got him."

The other cop brought out a pair of steel handcuffs. The sound of them snapping shut echoed in Riki's ears like cell doors.

Comanche and Pepe were waiting in the Alameda later that afternoon. The wallet was fat, with over five hundred dollars. Comanche counted it out, but the mood was somber.

'What will happen to Angel?"

Comanche shook his head in despair. "Thirty days, probably. But this is his second instance. Three instances and you go to prison. Sometimes for twenty years."

Pepe was crying, wiping his eyes with the grimy backs of his hands.

Comanche ran his hand through the boy's hair and said, "It's okay Pepe. Angel will be okay." Then to Riki, he said,

"We're out of business for a while. The police will be looking for me, and you won't be able to work on your own."

Riki nodded. "Maybe I'll look for a job."

"At least, with this score today, we'll have enough money to last us a while."

Chapter Eighteen

The money should have lasted Riki and Micaela for several months, but Riki insisted on moving into another apartment in a better barrio. This one not only had windows in every room, but it had a toilet and shower as well. When they moved into the apartment, they spent half an hour taking turns flushing the toilet and laughing in wondrous joy as they watched the water run out noisily and then fill up for another flush. There was also an oven and a kitchen sink with a faucet that worked.

But the sheer luxury of the apartment was *two* bedrooms. One was tiny, just enough space for Riki to spread a petate and goat-hair blanket, but the room was all Riki's. They felt proud of their new status, but also a bit intimidated by the new social environment. Most of the men in the apartment building had regular jobs. And even some of the women had jobs.

Just before the money ran out, Riki found a real job. One of the men in the apartment building told him about it. The job paid 40 pesos a day for moving stock in a factory not far from the apartment. It was hard work, lifting, pushing and running from one task to another, but by working Saturday and Sunday, it brought in enough to pay for the apartment rent and buy some food. Just barely enough.

Micaela made friends with one of the neighbors who asked her employer to hire Micaela when there was extra work to be done. Micaela was thrilled and was able to work two and sometimes three days a week. The work was hard. It involved cleaning ovens in the bakery. Between them, they earned enough to eat well, and Micaela was permitted to bring home last week's bread from the bakery. The thing that bothered Riki most was that he had neither time nor money to go to the cine.

The months began passing quickly. Twice, Comanche came by to visit. Each time, he asked Riki to go to work with him. Each time, the answer was no.

"Come on, Papagayo, why not? Angel is out of jail now, and we've been making some good moves, working the bullfights."

"I haven't felt good about stealing since I saw those cops beat up on Angel. He was handcuffed and couldn't do a thing. I wanted to help him, but I couldn't."

"You couldn't have done anything. Look, why not give us a try? Working isn't that good, is it?"

"No. Not good at all. But I don't want to go to jail."

"Have it your way, Papagayo. But if you change your mind, you know where to find me. I'm expanding my operations. Got four other guys working for me, now. I have a good move planned that needs an English-speaking person, and that's you."

As a matter of fact, Riki hated his new job. The foreman was a bully and a loafer and was continually threatening that he would fire Riki if he didn't work harder. Riki ended up doing both men's work and then some. He would have looked for another job, but working seven days a week until dark gave him no time to search.

He would have continued this way forever, had it not been for the factory and the warehouse closing. Suddenly he was out of a job, and they hadn't paid him for his last two weeks work. He didn't have the courage to tell Micaela.

He looked for a job for several days and found nothing. Rent was due and he was getting desperate. One day, he found himself in the old barrio. Comanche's place was in the next block, and without thinking about it further, he started walking in that direction. Comanche was delighted to see him. "This is the tourist season," he said. "The money is there to be harvested like cutting *leña*."

Angel added, "We need you, Papagayo. I'm glad you've come to your senses."

Pepe just smiled and held onto Riki's hand for a few moments. The boy's face was still cherubic and innocent. Riki had to admit that it felt good to be back with friends. The street meant freedom, companionship, and not having to cower before a foreman. He made a decision.

"I'm glad to be back. I'll never work in a warehouse or factory again."

Comanche said, "Come on, let's go to our new meeting place. You're going to be surprised." He began walking and the gang followed him.

He paused in front of an old building of red lava rock that had been part of an Aztec pyramid before the Spanish dismantled it for construction material. A dusty window had the word "Cantina" painted across it, in faded and chipped letters. Above the doorway was the usual sign, saying, "Women, minors, or soldiers in uniform not permitted."

Riki looked inside the dimly lit room and saw a dark brown bar and four tables, all looking quite rundown. Comanche explained, "My cousin owns this place. Come on in. I want you to meet somebody."

The bartender, a chubby man with a scar on the side of his face, smiled at Comanche when he entered. "*Quiúbele manito?* How's it going?"

"Matacuaz, I want you to meet my good friend, Papagayo. He's going to be working with us."

Matacuaz held out a hand that, although it looked as if it would be limp and sweaty, was hard as rock. The nickname *Matacuaz* meant "bricklayer," which Matacuaz had apparently been before buying this rundown cantina.

"Comanche was telling me about you, Papagayo. Yes, I think he's right. You do look like the picture."

"Picture?"

Matacuaz opened a drawer behind the bar and rummaged

through papers and books until he found it. He took out what looked like a small blue booklet. Then he threw it on the bar and explained, "It's a U.S. passport. Take a look at the picture inside. It isn't a perfect match, but it's close enough that you could get by."

On the inside page was a picture of a man. His hair hung down across his forehead and both his hair and skin seemed lighter than Riki's, and he also looked somewhat older. But other than that, Riki could see some resemblance. The name on the passport was Lawrence D. Ormand. He had been born someplace called Spokane, and he was twenty-three years old.

Riki handed the passport to Matacuaz. "What is it for?"

The bartender smiled, and his cheeks puffed up to almost close his eyes. He reached under the bar and took out a handful of travelers checks and placed them in front of Riki.

"Know what these are?"

"Sure. Travelers checks. But you can't cash them. We always throw them away when we get them."

Comanche said, "Not anymore. We've been keeping these for months, hoping you'd help us. With this passport, you can go to the bank, show it for identification, and *zas!* We're in business!"

Riki counted the checks. there were forty checks of $50 each. "Two thousand dollars?"

"That's right," said Matacuaz. "You cash them, and you can keep $500 for yourself. It's that easy."

"Why me?"

Patiently, Matacuaz explained, "Because you look like a Gringo, you can talk like a Gringo, and because you look like this passport. Without all of that, nobody would ever cash checks for you."

Angel said, "Another thing—we've been having to sell our $50 and $100 bills to Barragán at a discount. We can't take a chance on cashing them at a bank or casa de cambio. They get a reward for turning us in. And lately, banks have been asking for identification to cash even $20 bills. We really need you, Papagayo."

Riki shrugged and took a drink from the bottle of beer that Matacuaz placed in front of him.

"Sure. Why not?"

Matacuaz arranged for Gringo-type clothes for Riki to wear in order to look the part. First, with his heart in his throat, he tried just one traveler's check. The clerk glanced at the picture, then at Riki, and handed him the form to fill out. It was easy. The next bank took four checks without question. Soon they were all gone. *El Papagayo* was happy and he had plenty of rent money.

He told Micaela that he got a raise in pay. They went out to celebrate, and Riki ordered champagne, just as he had seen done in the movies. The restaurant had to send out for it.

He was slightly disappointed because champagne was warm, and it was sour, like beer or pulque, but he was drinking champagne, just like the movies. He felt truly sophisticated. The look of joy on Micaela's face was worth any risks.

The passport soon became a liability when word reached the police that someone was cashing stolen travelers checks with a passport issued to someone named Ormand.

Comanche and Riki talked this over and came to a decision. "We'll have to concentrate on stealing a new passport." Comanche ordered Angel, and a new gang member named Salvador, to monitor the bullfight crowds for someone who looked like Papagayo. "If we keep after them, we'll find someone with a passport who resembles Papagayo. Don't worry about money, just go after the passport."

It didn't take long. By the end of the week, they had three passports. Each of them looked enough like Riki that he could get by, even if the clerk looked very closely.

Matacuaz passed the word to other money brokers that Riki could cash large denomination bills. Riki kept ten percent for himself, and Matacuaz collected a ten percent commission. To explain his extra income and his irregular hours, he told Micaela that he was now working as a "salesman."

In between currency moves, the gang worked the bullfights, and from time-to-time buses on Reforma Avenue, depending where the police were concentrating at the time.

The word quickly got around the underworld population that Papagayo could speak English and could be trusted to change dollars at the bank without attracting attention, and without stealing the money for himself. Before long, the first of many customers approached Riki, asking him to convert stolen hundreds into pesos.

Others used him as a translator to negotiate with Gringo drug buyers and Colombian suppliers. At first this intimidated him, but he discovered that his practiced gangster stare and mannerisms made a big impression on both sides. The commissions were heartwarming.

Several times he made a stack of money simply by being the translator on the telephone end of several crooked deals. Money became plentiful. He bought an expensive suit for himself and a complete wardrobe and extras for Micaela. His suit was exactly like one he had seen a mobster wear in the movie, "*The Godfather*." He watched the movie a dozen times, studying the mannerisms and the Brooklyn accents the mobsters used.

As his income increased, he began thinking of upgrading their apartment. He located one on the third floor of a fairly new apartment building. Micaela was ecstatic when he took her there. "Oh, *Madre de Dios*! It has furniture and everything, even a television! And look! Windows that crank open! And the kitchen is a room all its own!"

At first, she refused to move, but when he convinced her that they could afford a better place because of his earnings as a "salesman," she relented.

"This costs ten times as much as the old one, Riki. What a

terrible waste of money." But she loved it. She spent a lot of time looking out the living room window, down onto the street, a broad smile on her face. Even more time went into exploring the mysteries of TV.

From time to time, Micaela tried to find work. But Riki discouraged her. "I earn enough," he said. "You stay home and keep the house for me." She never seriously questioned how Riki was earning his money. It somehow seemed natural, since she had seen how much money he earned just for carrying those suitcases the first night in Mexico City. By the time he turned eighteen, Riki had totally absorbed the ways of the city; he felt at home on the Mexico City pavements as he had on the mountain crevices of Tezcatlipocas. Instead of boulder-studded mountain slopes, there were streets and traffic. Instead of gossiping villagers, there were gossiping barrio people. One common denominator was poverty, the specter of hunger and a constant struggle for daily needs. Another commonality was the way the barrio people helped each other. They had no choice but to take care of each other, just as the villagers in Tezcatlipocas did.

He began to acquire a reputation around the northern barrios. Many knew him by sight; his sunglasses and gangster mannerisms were part of his image, as were his broad shoulders and barrel chest. He was treated with utmost respect.

Several times, when some cheap crook tried extortion on a barrio shop keeper, the owners appealed to Comanche and Papagayo for relief. It seldom took but a few choice words of advice to convince the blackmailers to move to another part of the city. Occasionally, it took bruises and few broken bones, but in the end, peace reigned.

Once, a sobbing housewife brought her problem to Papagayo, explaining how her husband beat her and her children when he was drunk. Riki tried to reason with the burly wife beater, but he was met with belligerence and threats.

"Keep your nose out of my business," he said. He made the

mistake of swinging a baseball bat at Papagayo's head.

After Riki finished the job, the husband saw the error of his ways. He agreed to quit drinking under penalty of another encounter with Papagayo.

"I mean, not even a bottle beer, or we will meet again!"

The man nodded humbly.

This lesson was not lost on other wife beaters in the barrio; Papagayo and Comanche were responsible for many unusually peaceful households.

By the time Riki was twenty years old, he had become a legend. His name was known in half a dozen barrios, as a man to be respected, to be feared. A man to be looked up to, to be respected. A desirable friend.

Of course, the police also heard stories of this criminal called Papagayo. This complicated Riki's life. He learned to avoid cops, and to spot plainclothes *chota* a block away. He stayed away from dangerous crimes like pickpocketing — dangerous in that chances of being caught were high. On occasion, he would join in a *movida* with his old friends, more to help them out than for the money.

Things went smoothly for a long while. Then disaster struck.

It happened on a Sunday afternoon when Riki, Comanche, Angel and Pepe were working a bullfight crowd. Riki hadn't wanted to go — pickpocket money didn't seem worth it anymore — but Comanche pleaded with him.

The *movida* was to purchase tickets for the cheaper, sunny side of the arena, then, when the crowd pressed toward the entrances, they quickly darted around the wooden barriers and made their way to the reserved sections on the shady side. People with money in their pockets always sat in the shade.

The crowd was heavy and sluggish as cold syrup that day, just the way Comanche liked it. The boys clung to the wall, allowing the crowd to flow past, waiting for a likely set of "clients" to come along.

They heard the Texans long before they could see them, for

they were laughing, shouting and passing a bottle of tequila back and forth as they shoved their way forward.

The four men wore wide-brimmed sombreros, the kind sold on street corners, the kind only a tourist would wear. They spoke with drawling East Texas accents. All four were tall and muscular looking, yet each sported a pot belly that came from too many good restaurants and plenty of Lone Star beer. They looked as if they were used to having their way, at ease pushing and shoving people out of their way.

Comanche signaled for Angel to work his way into the center of the crowd to intercept the Texans. Then he and Riki began moving closer with Pepe close at their heels.

Riki reached out to touch the Texan in the lead, the largest of the four.

"Excuse me, sir. But you'd better watch out for your belongings. There are pickpockets working around here." The man pushed his sombrero back on his head and grinned down at Riki. "Well, that's right nice of you to warn me, good buddy. But ain't nobody gonna get my wallet. No sir. Here, have a drink." At the same time, he reached to pat his wallet in his pocket, just to make sure it was still there. His companions did the same.

Riki shook his head at the proffered tequila bottle and he stepped aside to allow Comanche to step closer to Angel.

Pepe was trying to get into position, but it was difficult; the crowd whipsawed him back and forth. Riki planted his feet and waited for the little boy to catch up.

Angel slipped the wallet from the Texan's pocket so smoothly that Riki didn't see it happen. Then, as the crowd staggered past, he plucked the wallet from the second Texan.

This should have been enough, but Angel was caught up in the excitement. With two wallets in his left hand, he made a try for the third. He bumped into the victim and eased the wallet out of the hip pocket. With one swift move, all three wallets went to Comanche who passed them to Pepe.

But Angel's timing hadn't been the best. The Texan must have felt a silky movement against his buttock. He wheeled around in time to see Pepe trying to stuff three fat wallets into his one small pocket. It couldn't be done. Pepe panicked and tried to run, but he was hemmed in by the crowd.

"Hey! That asshole stole my wallet!" The Texan lunged through the crowd, shoving people aside. His long arm lashed out and his fingers caught Pepe by the back of his T-shirt, holding him as a bitch dog holds her puppy. "Got you, you little fucker."

Riki had to flail his way through the crowd. He had allowed himself to be pushed out of position!

Pepe's eyes grew wide with terror. His mouth dropped opened. He dropped the wallets to the ground. The other Texans began shoving people out of the way in order to join their companion.

One shouted, "Hey! They got mine too!"

The other screamed, "Me too! The *asshole!*"

The Texan kept his grip on Pepe as he reached down to scoop up the wallets. Then he said, "I'll teach you to steal, you greasy little bastard." He swung his foot back and kicked Pepe in the buttocks as hard as he could.

The sound of leather against the boy's flesh and snapping bones sounded clearly over the rumble of the crowd.

Pepe screamed and went flying forward to land an open space on the pavement as the crowd pressed back. His face scraped along the cement. He lay in a heap, moaning softly in pain, his body crumpled like a broken doll. The crowd gasped in horror.

The Texan stepped forward and brought his foot back for another kick. Riki grabbed his arm and said, "Don't! You'll kill him!"

"Get the fuck away from me. I'm gonna kick his head in, that's what I'm gonna do. Now let loose of me, asshole, or you'll get some too." He shook Riki's arm loose and poised like a football player ready to kick a field goal.

Suddenly, his head snapped around when Riki's fist connected with his jaw. He staggered sideways. "Why you... you bastard!" He straightened up and readied a kick at Riki. But Comanche dropped him with a kidney punch. Riki finished it off with a series of punches to the face before the Texan could hit the ground.

The crowd roared approval. The other Texans tried to help their comrade, but suddenly found themselves being pressured away by the crowd. Like poor swimmers in a strong current, they were swept away from where Pepe lay whimpering in pain.

Pepe never walked again. For the rest of his short life, he would need a set of crutches to drag his paralyzed leg along the streets of Mexico City. His bright smile never returned to his angelic little face because pain never left his back and leg.

Every day Riki visited the little boy, bringing him food and candies, massaging the leg in futile hopes that it might get better. He now lost his reservations about stealing. Stealing from Americans seemed justified, even moral. Each time he left Pepe's bedside he felt his hatred grow for those arrogant, rich, insensitive animals. It was an American who persecuted Micaela and it was an American who crippled gentle little Pepe. His Gringo father abandoned him as if he were an unwanted cat, and his Gringo mother sold him for two bottles of rum.

Part of every deal Riki made went to Pepe and his sister. He moved them to a nice apartment, where Pepe could have his own bed; he paid a doctor to visit regularly. If it weren't for Riki and Comanche's contributions, Pepe would have had to beg on street corners to eat. As it was, he chose to do that anyway, for the little guy couldn't stand the boredom of lying in bed. Whenever the pain slackened, he would drag himself down to the street and sit on a pillow and beg.

El Papagayo expanded his operations as he worked harder, as

if to compensate for Pepe's condition. His influence began to overwhelm that of Comanche's. He didn't want to push his friend aside; he wasn't trying to do that. Things just worked out that way. After Pepe was crippled, Comanche became a different person. He had little enthusiasm for "business."

"Papagayo, I've been thinking," he said one day, as they were drinking beer in a cantina. "I need to move out of this business. It's only a matter of time we get into some bad trouble. Maybe I should try something else. I'm not a kid anymore, I'll be twenty-four soon. There is a school in Colonia Heroes where they teach welding, and things like that. Besides, I've met a nice girl, and her family likes me, although they don't know much about me. Maybe it's time."

Riki knew that Pepe's condition weighed heavily on Comanche's mind because he blamed himself for getting Pepe involved with the scheme. But Riki shouldered his own share of guilt for letting Pepe down. It should have been his job to protect Pepe, yet it happened so fast.

Chapter Nineteen

Riki continued expanding his status in the barrio, and had it not been for a close call he had one day, he might have continued on the same path until his name became known throughout all of the City.

The incident happened on a quiet Sunday afternoon in the Colonia Nápoles area. He had set up an obnoxious tourist from Detroit for a *golpe*. The Gringo had hinted that he would like to buy some Quaaludes. After haggling over a price, Riki agreed to meet him on the steps of the Colorado Hotel with $2,000 worth of the pills.

Riki purchased a carton of sugar capsules from the corner *farmacia* and hurried to meet the appointment. Something about the victim stirred doubts in Riki's mind; some second sense began to warn him that something was wrong. This put him on guard.

The American was waiting, a friendly smile spread across his face when he saw Riki approaching. He furtively glanced across the street and then back at Riki before he waved his hand. Riki's eyes darted in the direction the American had looked, and he saw them just in time. Across the street stood two plainclothes detectives, waiting to close in on him. He pretended not to see the Gringo and kept on walking.

"Hey, wait," the American called out. "You promised me something."

Riki turned to look at the man as if he were crazy and continued on walking. When he turned the corner, he broke into a run. He crossed the street and ducked into the entrance to a neighborhood handball court, and he pressed himself against the wall, hoping the cops would pass by without looking inside. He waited a long time before venturing out on the street once more. There was no question — the police were after Papagayo.

This close call sobered him; he spent a long time rethinking his life. Several street kids he knew had already been jailed, a couple for the third and final time. So far, he'd been lucky, never having been arrested even once. He thought about this for a while, then decided to join Comanche in a crime-free life. Or try it, anyway.

He began looking for a real job. If not a totally honest job, then at least something that would allow him to ease gradually into a legitimate lifestyle.

He tried very hard. Things would have worked out much differently if he hadn't gone to jail. For over six months Riki hadn't stolen anything. He'd been making a fairly comfortable living working as a bartender at a hotel near the Bellas Artes. When he ran short of money, he would sell last night's opera tickets to Americans standing in line at Bellas Artes. He always found tickets on the floor when he swept up, and there were always plenty of tourists standing in the line who thought they smelled a bargain by buying "stolen" tickets.

This particular day started when Pepe's sister came to his house, weeping copiously. "He didn't come home last night," she said. "Something terrible has happened to him. I just know it."

"Where did he go?"

"To the Cathedral, to beg money by the gate. But he always comes home before dark. Always."

Riki didn't go to his hotel job that day. Instead, he searched the city for little Pepe. He combed the streets of downtown, inquiring of shopkeepers and passersby to ask if they'd seen anything of a crippled boy on crutches.

Finally, he gathered the courage to call on the *deligación de policía.* He could only hope that no one would recognize him as El Papagayo.

"Oh, that one," the sergeant said without interest. "Yes, a crippled boy got hit by an auto last night. Stupid little bastard was trying to cross Juarez against the red light. A diplomat from the U.S. consulate ran over the dumb little turd. Caught him between the wheel and a fender. Had to damn near ruin the car to get him free. It was a new Cadillac. Must have cost a fortune."

"Is he... Was he killed?"

"The boy? Just about. Last I heard, they took him to the clinic on Cinco de Mayo."

Pepe wasn't at the hospital. A white uniformed nurse with boredom permanently ironed onto her face said, "He only lived a couple of hours. Bleeding inside the stomach, I believe."

The noise of a siren in the distance assaulted Riki's thoughts and it took a moment before the truth began to take root in his consciousness. *Pepe, dead? Pepito, little Pepito? That can't be. He loved me. I loved him. No.*

A hazy fog began to soften his thinking; for a moment, he felt he was going to pass out, but the feeling faded, leaving him with acute, bitter reality.

Pepe was dead. The only person in the world who loved him as much as Micaela. Killed by a *Gringo!*

"If you're a relative, you're going to have to come up with some money for burial. Otherwise, they have to dispose of the body within a week."

"Dispose? What do they do with it?"

"How should I know? Get rid of it somehow."

"What about the Gringo who was driving the car?"

"The American? No, he wasn't hurt. Oh, you mean... Well, he's *diplomático*, you know. Can do no wrong. And besides, it was only a crippled beggar who had no business being in the middle of the street. What do you expect?"

Tears made the world bleary as Riki walked out of the sickly sweet, death odors of the hospital. Fucking Gringos! First, they cripple the little boy, then they run him down like an animal, and abandon him to be tossed on a garbage heap. He snapped a fist into his palm, wishing it could be a Gringo's face he was hitting.

Probably nothing would have happened had Riki been able to go someplace quiet where he could grieve and meditate, weep for his friend in the solitude of grief. But luck wouldn't have it that way. As he turned the corner at Isabel la Católica, someone grabbed him by the arm and spun him around. Instinctively he pulled away, throwing his hands into a defensive position.

He faced an angry woman, her face distorted with fury, her fingers like jaguar claws as she reached for his face. Riki ducked out of the way and stared at the woman in disbelief.

She was a tourist, dressed in fluorescent greens with pants ballooning at the knees in the latest American style. Her lips, painted the color of blood, amplified the fury distorting her face.

"You *bastard!*" she shouted as he again sidestepped her clutching hand. "You're the one who sold us those phony tickets the other night. You knew goddamned well they were for the night before."

Her husband came running out of a curio shop. "What is it, honey?" A bull of a man with thick shoulders, he had the ruddy complexion of a daily jogger and health nut. "What's going on here?"

"Recognize this crooked bastard? He's the one sold us the tickets. Made all of us miss the opera. Ruined the whole Goddamned evening!"

The man's mouth tightened in angry recognition. "Call the cops, Elsie," he said through gritted teeth, "I'll hold this cheap crook 'til they get here."

Riki sneered contemptuously. "Back off," he said. "You too, lady. Come at me one more time, I'll break your head."

He gave the two of them his gangster stare. They stepped

257

back momentarily

He turned to leave, keeping a wary eye on the woman, confident that he could handle her husband with no trouble.

But the man suddenly lunged at Riki and seized his arm in a steel-trap grip. Riki tried to pull away, but the man jerked him back, sending Riki's sunglasses flying into the street.

"No you don't! You're going to stay right here 'til the cops come! Try to get away, I'll kick your goddamn teeth out of your head."

Riki only vaguely remembered what happened next. His mind became a swirling storm of anger, frustration and hate.

Memories of Pepe on crutches mixed with images of a Gringo tossing a coin into dog vomit in Córdoba. Arrogant, over-fed Gringos. A Texas boot slamming into Pepe's spine. Abandonment by his Gringo father...

He was aware of a woman screaming and shouts from the man. He felt a cramping pain in his knuckles, and the jolt to his body from kicking something as hard as he could.

The next thing he remembered clearly was a police club glancing off his forehead. Then another cop pulling him away from the man lying on the sidewalk. The woman in fluorescent green bent over and tried to urge her husband to his feet.

"He *kicked* me," the man whimpered. "Knocked me down and kicked me."

Blood streamed down Riki's forehead and into his eyes. Another crack from the policeman's club sent him reeling and opened an additional split in his scalp.

He lifted his hands to ward off another blow and caught the rubber-covered weapon as it flashed toward his head. He twisted it away from the cop and held it threateningly. The man backed away. But a club came from another direction to drop him to his knees like a bull at the end of the fight. The world suddenly turned to blackness, shot through with streaks of red flash. The thunder of blood pounding in his temples gradually faded to nothingness.

Riki woke up with the sun blazing painfully against his eyes. His head throbbing with each heartbeat. He lay flat on his back on rough cement. Each joint of his body protested as he pushed himself to a sitting position. His eyes were mere slits of swollen flesh, and he could barely see.

Four men squatted in a half circle around him, watching intently. They smiled obsequiously when they realized that he'd regained consciousness. Each wore ragged cast-offs, the dirty uniform of the *pelado* — those perpetual losers who wander about Mexico City and all large cities of the world, searching garbage cans for food, stealing whatever is easy, finding temporary happiness in alcohol, paint thinner and occasional drugs.

Riki didn't have to look around to know he was in jail. And the blood on his clothes told him that the charge would be something serious.

One of the men, as old and gnarled as a black pine, smiled through a toothless mouth and said, "Welcome to the Grand Hotel. Your first visit?"

When Riki nodded, a man with a beard so dirty it looked stiff said, "If you have money, we can make things easier for you. We know the guards — we can get you the very best of anything, a bed, blanket, cooked food, anything."

Riki searched his pockets as best he could, with his muscles stiff and sore. He shook his head sadly and turned the pockets inside out. His wallet and even the loose change had disappeared. The toothless one said, "Oh, but you must have relatives? A brother or sister to bring you money for a bed? Some hot food once in a while. No? Not even a mother or a grandmother?"

The bearded one said, "You see, we're only in here for sniffing paint on the street. They always let us go after a couple of days. Just give me an address of a friend who'll pay me something for my trouble, I'll tell him you're here. He can help

259

you. Otherwise, you sleep here on the cement, without even a blanket. And it rains this time of year, and it gets very cold."

When Riki shook his head, the pelado pointed out, "They don't feed you here for the first three days, you know. And after that you have to buy food unless you like to eat yesterday's leftover tortillas. Hard as cardboard, but not as tasty."

Riki couldn't think straight at the moment, but he knew he didn't want Micaela to know anything about this. Not just yet. He shook his head with finality. The men abandoned their sympathetic smiles. One by one, they wandered back to the line of prisoners who were sitting in the shade of the high wall. Against the side of a small guard station an open latrine sent a foul odor through the jail courtyard like an invisible fog. The smell turned Riki's stomach sour, so the thought of food didn't mean much to him at that moment. A bed, however, would have been most welcome.

He spent the rest of that day leaning against the wall with a hundred others, like domestic field animals sullenly waiting for the night to fall and a new set of discomforts and boredoms. It seemed as if every part of his body ached and throbbed.

The only place to sleep was next to the urinal, for the spaces away from there were claimed by the strongest. He was too weak to fight for a better position. It didn't matter anyway, since all who had to sleep on the courtyard cement without cover suffered more or less equally. He slept little that night. He kept telling himself that he would not give in and let others know of his disgrace. Sometime after midnight, the bearded man crept up and covered Riki with a heavy wool serape.

"Too cold for a sick man to be without a blanket," he whispered. "Don't tell anyone I gave this to you. Tell them you paid for it." Then he was gone.

But in the morning—his body shivering with cold and pain—Riki changed his mind. The gashes on his head were beginning to fester, and he knew he would need money to pay for a doctor soon. He found the toothless one, who was getting out at noon that day, and instructed him to inform Comanche of his fate. "He'll pay you something. He knows I'm good for it."

Visitors weren't allowed inside the jail. If someone wanted to speak to a prisoner, one had to go to an opening in the wall and call through the thick bars until the message got through.

Comanche didn't arrive until almost dark, and Riki wolfed down the cheese sandwiches he brought, making four bites of each.

Comanche handed him a bottle of sugary orange soda to wash down the food and said, "*Jijole manito!* You've got yourself into a real mess! I talked to the commandante of the jail, and he says you are charged with fraud for selling the theater tickets, assault on the Gringo and his wife, and trying to attack a *chota*, the one who beat you up with his club. This makes you one bad guy."

Riki shrugged and finished the orange drink.

"They could throw the book at you, make it all three offenses — that would get you twenty years for certain. You need a lawyer with a lot of connections, and you need a mountain of money."

"I have neither."

"I know a lawyer. His godfather is also mine. He knows a lot of people in the courts. They say his brother-in-law is a judge. Maybe he can help."

"That costs money."

Comanche frowned as he nodded thoughtfully. "Let me see what I can do." Before he left, he pressed some pesos into Riki's hand and sounded embarrassed as he said, "That's all I have right now. You know, they say 'crime doesn't pay', but being honest doesn't pay worth a handful of shit."

"Better tell Micaela where I am. I don't like for her to know, but she would worry just as much not knowing what happened to me."

The next morning the Bearded One shook Riki awake. "Someone's calling for you at the visitor's place."

He gave the man a small tip and left his rented bed to go to the bars. It was Micaela.

Tears streamed down her cheeks and she was hysterical.

"Riki, Riki, what happened? Why are you in here?"

He did what he could to calm her down, but she was like a frightened child.

"Comanche is helping me. So, don't worry."

She returned that afternoon, and again in the evening, bringing a pot of hot soup and a small loaf of bread with bean paste spread inside.

"I talked with Comanche," she said. "The lawyer told him that he can combine all of the charges into just the one of the theater tickets, but it will take bribes for many people."

He thanked her for the food and said, "Whatever happens will happen. I won't die because of a little time in jail."

But both of them knew that he could get the full twenty years. Assaulting a policeman is not a trivial offense in Mexico City.

The days dragged by with excruciating slowness. The man with the beard was released. The day after that the toothless one was back in jail. Sniffing paint thinner in public again. Riki still had some money, so he bought the *pelado* food so he could get past the first three days of nothing to eat. They released him the following day, but Riki knew he'd be back soon.

About the fifth or sixth day — Riki had lost count — when the main gate swung open, a lawyer was permitted to enter the yard to look for Riki. He was a slender man, very short, with a head too large for his body, as if it should have gone to a heavyweight wrestler instead of to such a small man. His eyes were set so far apart that they seemed to be staring off in different directions, and Riki was never sure which eye was looking at him. "You must sign these papers," he said without any preliminary words. "You are admitting to selling tickets which you believed to be valid, but that you now realize were out of date. There is a problem, since the authorities know that you are the one known as 'El Papagayo,' and your reputation is not very high with the police. It will take money to make them forget about El Papagayo."

"How long will I have to stay in jail?"

"'Just sign the papers. Chances are I can have you out of here by the end of the week." As he handed Riki a ball-point pen, the sun's rays glinted sharply from a large diamond on the lawyer's little finger. After he'd signed the papers, Riki looked at the ring once more. The stone was set between a nest of green stones, emeralds — a woman's ring. He recognized that ring. It came from the musical jewel box.

His release came less than a week later.

Micaela and Comanche met him and took him home in a taxi. She had bought a small bottle of French brandy and was pouring a celebration drink for all three of them when an urgent knock at the door disrupted them. Riki answered the door.

There stood a barrio character known as *Mocho*. He was a man of about twenty-five who'd been active in barrio gangs as a youth, but now worked as a part-time police informer and part-time car thief. He was a handsome man in a way, with regular features and a perfect-toothed smile, except for one defect; he was missing an ear. For this, he was called El Mocho, "the mutilated one."

"Bad news," he said cryptically. "A private investigator, named Enrique Morales is on Micaela's trail. He knows that she gave a ring to your lawyer, and he claims the ring is stolen. He just found out about it and will be sending some *chota* here any time now to arrest her. Don't tell anyone how you found out. I have to keep on the good side of him, but you know how it is — I don't like to see my friends in trouble. Believe me, this is big trouble for your mother. It isn't an ordinary theft case. Morales is a wild man."

"Why is one piece of jewelry so important?"

"All I know is that there is a large reward for the arrest of whoever stole the ring. Not for recovery of the stuff, but the arrest of the thief. It belongs to some rich pig of a Gringo. They say he has a vendetta against the thief. Better get moving."

Comanche agreed. When Mocho left he said, "I told you about Morales before. He's no one to fool around with. Better pack up your things. Whatever you can't take with you now, I'll keep for you at my place until you get settled."

Riki turned to question Micaela about the ring, but she was on her knees in the corner of the room, praying to the lithographed picture of the Virgin of Guadalupe-Tonantzín and the flickering candle that illuminated it and made it jump in the light.

"For God's sake, can't you tell me how you got the Gringo's jewelry? Why is that Barrón person after you?"

She refused to answer. He pulled her to her feet and said, "Let's get going." He began stuffing clothing into a net bag while Comanche threw belongings into a large cardboard box. After a while, Micaela joined Riki and started putting her things into the old leather suitcase. She packed her underthings around the music box and looked defiantly at Riki when he looked as if he were going to ask again.

"I didn't ask why you were in jail, did I? I did what I had to get you out. Don't ask questions about the jewelry."

They weren't out of the apartment fifteen minutes when the neighbors heard a loud knocking at the door Then a crashing of wood as the door splintered off its hinges. The cops began a door-to-door search for Micaela Montalvo and her son, the street hoodlum known as El Papagayo. No one could tell them where the fugitives might be. In that barrio it was unlikely they would tell the police even if they knew.

Enrique Morales leaned back in the leather chair and looked about the office. He hated the place, and resented the psychological trap he'd built for himself, epitomized by this office. Still on the payroll of Alex Barron, unable to quit because of the tantalizing prize of the jewelry and the reward, he seemed to be forever on an endless treadmill of searching for a misty ghost.

He detested the ghost of Rickey Barron, a ponderous burden that held him captive in this office, in this treadmill of a job.

Another burden was Alex Barron's attitude this past year, an attitude of growing indifference, as if he had all but given up hope of ever finding a trace of the boy. This put Morales' income in grave jeopardy. If he should be cut off the payroll, it would be pure disaster. He was too old to return to his former position with the Ministry.

But now, things may just be changing. He frowned as he examined the ring in his hand, turning it this way and that, watching the sparkles of light from the large diamond and the cool glow of emeralds. He tossed the ring into the air and caught it with an angry, snapping motion of his hand.

"So, finally, more pieces of the loot surface! Damn! That means the thief has been here in Mexico City all the time."

Kiko Saavreda, the private investigator who shared the office, nodded as he shuffled through a stack of police reports. "According to these, the woman's name is Montalvo, and she came from a village called Tezcatlipocas. Not too far from the scene of the truck accident fourteen years ago."

"Yes. And her son is a street hoodlum known as 'El Papagayo'. A tough guy, from what I hear. So tough, nobody's willing to turn informer. Everybody knows him. Nobody will admit it. But at least we know who to look for. The case is moving. The thieves are out in the open."

Saavedra read through the arrest report on Papagayo, and a pensive look crossed his face. "What if — just for the sake of argument — what if this Papagayo turns out to be the lost boy? What if he has been here in Mexico City all along, right under our noses? What if Mr. Barron learns that after all these fourteen years, you failed to..."

"Keep your goddamn 'what ifs' to yourself!" Morales kicked at his desk and stood up. He strode to the window

Gift of the Black Goddess

angrily and began staring up at the smog-tinted afternoon sun. "Papagayo *can't* be the Barron kid. It's impossible. For my sake, he *has* to be dead. If Barron thought I'd spent all these years and not found the little bastard, he'd..."

Saavedra looked apologetic and got to his feet to leave. "Just curious. You needn't take offense."

"To satisfy your curiosity, I can tell you 'what if'. I would lose my chance at the rewards. I would lose my promised job in California, and I would be out of work, and *chau!*"

He didn't mention the biggest loss, the chance to pocket a fortune in jewelry. "If I had only solved this case, today I would be sitting in my own office in Hollywood, vice president of security of Barron Enterprises. I would have the prettiest women in the world at my beck and call. I would..." He couldn't continue, the *ifs* were so tragic.

"Now that the thieves are out in the open, you'll have no problem running them to the ground. Just let it be known that there is a stack of pesos to reward the person who points out El Papagayo's hiding place."

Morales sighed in despair. "What can I use to pay a reward? I'll have to get Barron interested again. Interested enough to lay out more money." He took the ring from his pocket and looked at it again. "On your way out, tell my secretary to come in here."

His secretary, a luscious figure with soft brown hair who was actually much more than a mere shorthand expert—came in and closed the door behind her. She walked to Enrique Morales' side and brushed a stray lock from his forehead to place a kiss there.

"Let me see the ring again, my love. I just get shivers from looking at it."

He shook his head and shoved the ring deep into his coat pocket. "Place a call to California and get Alexander Barron for me."

"You can't notify Barron, silly. He'll want the ring back, and the reward money he'll give you won't be worth a fraction of the ring. Keep the ring, make it into a setting for me, and Barron will never know. Then, if you ever do run down the thief, think what a hero you'll be and think about what we could do with that extra reward money."

One of the things he liked about Rosita was that she always made good sense when confronted with a problem. Also, she was much better in bed than his wife, another thing he liked. He patted her on the behind and said:

"Go ahead and place the call, my love. Señor Barron will be grateful for our news. I need his gratitude if I'm going to keep even this lowly job that I have. Besides, this case is the one major disappointment in my life—outside of my marriage—and I must resolve it or I'll never be able to live with myself."

"But this is a valuable ring! Who would ever know?"

"Don't worry, I wasn't planning on giving this to Barron, if you really want to know. Now make the call. When we capture the thief and the rest of the jewelry, there will be time enough to make a ring for you."

Chapter Twenty

Robin and Alex dropped everything and hurried to Mexico City. They arrived late in the evening. Inspector Morales met them at the airport. As he drove to their hotel, he filled them in on the details.

"There's no question but the same two people are involved, señor Barron. This time the *woman* produced the jewelry. She gave the diamond and emerald ring to El Papagayo's lawyer. The ruby and sapphire bracelet went to the prosecutor in return for dropping the case against El Papagayo. The prosecutor refuses to return the ring he took for his part in this thing."

"Who is El Papagayo?"

"An underworld character. The woman's son. He was in jail for assaulting a tourist and resisting arrest. I'm certain it's the same cheap crook who sold the watch in Córdoba a few years ago. The streets of Mexico City abound in rascals like El Papagayo, always living on the fringes of the law, stealing, hustling, occasionally working. This is the first time this one ever came to our attention—no police record of any kind. But on inquiry, we learn that he's a gang leader, and a very clever one, never having been caught before."

"How do we find him?"

"That's the problem. The people of the barrio are tight-mouthed when it comes to talking to police. Worse, it turns out that El Papagayo is highly respected in the barrio. I hope you don't mind, but I've posted a reward for information on El Papagayo and his mother. But news is slow in coming. Slow indeed. We have an informant who will be waiting for us at my office first thing in the morning. A taxi driver named Manuel Salas. He knew the pair when they first arrived in Mexico City, after they escaped from us in Córdoba."

Alex thought for a moment, trying to sort out the confusion from his mind. Finally, he said, "My son would be twenty-one years old this month. Is there any possibility, any possibility at all that..."

"None. My impression is that El Papagayo is much older than that. It is impossible that a twenty-one-year-old could gain so much influence in the barrio or become a gang leader with so much respect. Things like this takes years. I understand how you must feel, however, and we'll do everything in our power to find him and to set your mind at rest once and for all."

"Does this Papagayo person speak English?"

"My understanding is that he does. Look, it isn't unusual for a street character to make an effort to learn English. And many a poor family sneaks across the border into your country during the summer harvest seasons. Kids can pick up English in just one season."

"One way we could tell," Robin said, "would be to look at his eyes. Rickey Barron had most unusual eyes, exactly like his father. That could never change."

"No one seems to be sure about his eyes. The problem is, El Papagayo always wears sunglasses, a sort of trademark, you might say. Still, I am positive he can't be anything other than a street criminal."

Manuel Salas waited in the police delegación, anxiously twisting his baseball hat in his hands. He jumped to his feet when Morales entered. He followed anxiously into the police inspector's office.

"I am very nervous about this," he said in Spanish to the inspector. "El Papagayo is well-connected in the underworld. If the people in the barrio suspected that I am helping la policía, well..."

"Why *are* you helping? You could have told us about this before. You were the one who picked them up at the bus station when they first came to the city, weren't you? Tell the truth."

Manuel shrugged noncommittally. "That was a long time ago, señor Inspector. It might have happened, but I have so many passengers that I can't remember one particular fare. And well, to tell the truth I am here because I don't like to see criminals like El Papagayo go unpunished. I understand there is a lot of valuable jewelry involved in this case, and also there is a reward. Had I known this before..."

Morales translated for Alex. Robin knew enough Spanish to understand some of what Manuel Salas was saying, still she relied on Morales to make the meaning clear. "Ask him to describe El Papagayo and his mother."

Manuel nodded, eager to be of help. "El Papagayo is about as tall as señor Barron, perhaps a bit taller, and has arms and shoulders like a prizefighter. He sometimes walks with a bit of a swagger, but that is something he assumes to impress people with his rank in the barrio. He is also well-known as a fighter, entirely unbeatable in a street brawl."

"His eyes," Robin said directly to Manuel. "What color are his eyes?"

When Morales posed the question in Spanish, the cab driver twisted his face in concentration. "Hum-m... They're funny looking. You don't often see Papagayo without sunglasses. His mother says he has an eye weakness and must wear them. They look weak, too. That would be the only thing weak about El Papagayo!"

"But what color?"

Morales felt a cold chill of fear in his spine when the cab driver replied.

"They're a funny-looking gray color. Something like that man there." He nodded at Alex Barron.

Robin sat up straight, sharp tension in her voice as she asked, "Did he say something about *gray* eyes? Like Alex's eyes?"

Morales struggled to keep panic from his voice. "No. He said that... That he couldn't *tell* if they were gray. If they were gray like Mr. Barron's. The man doesn't know."

Morales quickly resumed questioning before Robin could pursue the point further.

"Was he wearing sunglasses that night when you picked them up at the bus station?" Morales asked innocently.

"Like I said, he always wore them. I wondered about that, it being dark that night and..."

Manuel knew he'd been trapped. He frowned guiltily. "All right. Yes, I picked them up. But I thought they were just stupid *indios* from the hills of Tlascala. I know, because once I was just as ignorant as they. Neither of them had ever been out of the village. I could tell, from the way they spoke."

Robin asked, "About the sunglasses? Could it be that they are to cover up something about his eyes that he doesn't want people to see?"

Morales shook his head. "You know how young people are nowadays. They think wearing dark glasses makes them look glamorous or tough. Sometimes they wear them because certain drugs make the eyes weak. Many drug addicts wear dark glasses, you know." A sick feeling swirled through his gut.

"He's a drug addict?"

"Who knows? From stories I heard in the barrios, El Papagayo deals with people who buy and sell drugs. Does he use drugs? Who knows?"

The inspector said, "All right. You picked them up at the bus station. Where did you take them?"

"I took them to a cheap housing place on calle Primavera, in Colonia Doctores. They stayed there for several months, and then moved to a place on avenida Compostela. I stayed away from them because the boy thought I was trying to take advantage of his mother. That wasn't true. I was trying to help her find a job."

"You knew where they lived, yet you didn't go to the police?"

"I didn't dream that they had any jewelry. They were poor, almost starving. Why should I go to the police? Besides, Papagayo has a reputation as a tough guy in the barrio. I could have been hurt."

Morales translated for Alex, explaining, "I had the police send three men to Papagayo's apartment as soon as I heard about the jewelry exchange. But he and his mother cleared out moments before my men arrived."

Then to the taxi driver he said, "Tell us what you know about the jewelry. How much does he have? Where is he getting it?"

"I only wish I knew. I would get some for myself! The way they were living when they first came here, they couldn't have had any jewelry, or they would have sold some. For a while it looked as if they might starve to death. I tried to help them, but she was too proud, and he was ungrateful. Therefore, if he had jewelry, he would have sold it, and not gone into stealing as he did. Rich people don't have to steal."

Morales translated, adding, "I believe this taxi driver has a good point, señor. If Papagayo were your son, and if he had the jewelry, he would have sold it long ago. What would prevent him? No one voluntarily lives in poverty or turns to petty crime if they could live like millionaires."

"Maybe. But he's getting the jewelry from somewhere. We have to find the source."

When they finished questioning Manuel Salas, Robin wondered out loud, "What do we do now?"

"Put out an even bigger reward for Papagayo," Alex replied. "I'll pay whatever I have to just to see him, just to be sure. Let the word out that I don't want him arrested. I only want to talk to him and settle my mind. Stress that—no arrest, no pressure, just a talk. He can keep the jewelry if he simply clears up this mystery. Makes it clear what happened to Rickey."

The news of the reward circulated quickly among the lower-class barrios. A thousand sets of eyes went on alert for El Papagayo, each hoping to find a way to collect the reward without letting anyone else in the barrio know who informed. But Papagayo was nowhere to be found.

Only Comanche knew Riki's whereabouts. He and Micaela were hiding in an apartment owned by one of Comanche's cousins who was temporarily working in Campeche. Through Comanche, they learned of developments in the barrio. Their concern grew when they learned the police hadn't stopped looking for them. Curiously, they seemed to be looking for Papagayo more than for Micaela. The huge reward for their capture was even more unsettling.

Comanche came to the apartment to discuss the new reward offer. "The story is that this Barrón guy won't have you arrested, Riki. He is willing to pay a mountain of money just to talk to you. Maybe you should consider —"

"It isn't me he's after. He wants Micaela because he thinks that she stole his dirty jewelry. We refuse to get involved in a trap. That's exactly what this is, a trap."

"Well, you'd better not show your face around until the heat's off," Comanche warned.

"I know. I'm trying to find a housemaid's job for Micaela, and then I might head for some other town. I'm going crazy cooped up here all day."

Comanche needed money, but not badly enough to double cross Riki. He strained his mind trying to find some way to cash in on the reward without turning his best friend in to the clutches of the law. Then, an inspiration fell from out of nowhere. A brilliant inspiration.

He discussed the idea with Angel and a punch-drunk boxer called *Pintado* from Tijuana, who spoke English fairly well. "It will be like taking lemon with tequila," Comanche said.

"Everyone in the barrio knows Angel and I are friends of Papagayo, right? And neither Barrón nor Enrique Morales has ever seen Papagayo."

Pintado blinked his eyes and tried to concentrate on what Comanche was saying. He'd been sniffing paint fumes again that morning—whence his nickname *Pintado*. His reasoning powers weren't in tip-top shape. However, something about this proposition worried him.

"But nobody will believe *I'm* El Papagayo! And besides, won't I get into trouble with the police again? You know, I've already been stung twice. Like, the third time is twenty years, man!"

"Trouble? What trouble? Listen to me once more, and I'll explain. This Barrón guy only wants to *talk* to Riki. He guarantees not to have any police around. Now, Angel will approach Barrón and direct him to the old warehouse by the railroad line. I can watch from across the street and make sure it isn't a trap. Then I signal you to go in. You don't break any laws by walking into an abandoned building, do you?"

Pintado shrugged noncommittally. "But what do I say to this Barrón guy?"

"You tell him you're Papagayo, or Riki, or whatever he wants to hear and talk to him a while. It's that easy, and you get half the reward."

"What can I talk to him about?"

"How should I know? He just wants to talk. Tell him about your last fight. Tell him how much you like to sniff paint. Tell him how beautiful Tijuana is when it rains. Talk to him about anything, I don't give a shit."

"Suppose it's a trap? They'll put me into jail again. I don't need that, man!"

"No, no," Angel said. "You can *prove* you aren't Papagayo. You haven't done a thing wrong. *I'm* the one who made the mistake. After all, you're about the same size as Papagayo. You will be wearing dark glasses. I can make a mistake like anybody else, no?"

Comanche added, "Besides, if any cops show up, I'll give you a warning. You duck out the back way and across the tracks before they can get close."

They produced a tube of airplane cement for Pintado to sniff, and only then did he decide the impersonation would be fun.

The next day, he and Comanche went to the abandoned house across from the warehouse and waited for Angel to bring señor Barrón to the meeting.

With the meeting arranged, Alex and Robin refused to argue further with Morales. "It may be dangerous," Alex said, "but if there's the slightest chance that Papagayo is my son, I'll take whatever chances I have to. I need to know, to put this to rest once and for all."

Morales felt beads of nervous perspiration form on his forehead. "Look, I could have him picked up at the meeting place, and you can talk to him here, where it's safe."

"No. The contact said he wanted no police. He said if we trick them, Papagayo will never show up, and I'll never get to see him."

Enrique Morales shrugged in defeat. "Here, take this gun with you. If anything happens, use it!"

Robin and Alex arrived by taxi; she clung to Alex's arm as they approached the abandoned warehouse. The building stood three stories high, with sides of rusted iron, all windows that hadn't been boarded over were devoid of glass. Other structures along the railway tracks were similarly neglected.

She suppressed a shiver as she said, "This neighborhood gives me the willies!"

Angel was waiting for them. He motioned and they followed him around to the side entrance of the rusting building. He pulled loose a bar on one of the sliding doors and let them in.

The walls echoed with their footsteps; inside was filled with the smell of rats and rotting rubbish. The sound of a freight train laboring in the distance echoed through the shell of a building

"Give me half of the money, as we agreed," Angel demanded, "and then, you wait here. I'll signal Papagayo that it's safe, when I'm sure there are no cops about."

He counted the money, then he scurried through the building and stepped up on a box to pass a signal to Comanche. He also held up a fistful of $20 bills and grinned in triumph. They had agreed that if it were a trap, they could abandon the plan and still walk away with half of the reward. They couldn't lose. Then he made an exit by lifting a metal grate and crawling through a window.

Robin was feeling uneasy in the darkness and stood as close to Alex as she could. "I don't like it here. I hope Morales is wrong about this."

The sound of footsteps rang hollowly as someone walked across the wooden freight dock. Then a silhouetted figure appeared in the door, the sun blazing against his back.

Alex swallowed stiffly and walked toward the figure. "Who are you?" He fingered the pistol's rough grip as he spoke. "What's your name?"

"They call me El Papagayo." The voice was thick with Pachuco accent and glue fumes.

Alex sided around to get a better view of Papagayo's face. "Rickey? Is your name Rickey?"

"Yeah. Sometime dey call me dat name too. Yeah." Alex couldn't move. He felt his knees growing weak. Robin stepped close to Pintado and studied his face closely. "Do you know who your father is?"

Pintado's expression clouded angrily. "What you think? My mother some kinda whore, or somepin'? You bet I know who my father! I ain't no fuckin' bastard!"

"Where is your father? What's his name?"

Pintado scratched the back of his neck as he tried to remember. "Well... last I heard, de old man, he in jail. In Nogales. But everyone dey know his name. His name Armando, but everybody dey call him 'Chiluco'."

Alex stepped closer, close enough to see the dark, scarred face. "Take off your glasses. Let me see your eyes."

"Wait a minute, man! Dey tell me I get money for this. You gonna pay me, or no?"

"Here. Here's the rest of the money. Now take off the dark glasses."

Pintado grabbed the money and counted it before he stuffed it into his pants pocket. Then he took off the glasses. His eyes were clouded with the smoky look of someone who sniffs too many fumes. The brows and lower lids were lumpy with scar tissue from street fights. The eyes were not the startling gray of the Barron family. His eyes were the disgusting bloodshot and feces-brown of the Chiluco family.

Alex had been holding his breath, and now he let go in a deep sigh of disappointment and relief at the same time.

"All right. Tell me about the jewelry. Where did you get it?"

"Jewelry? Hold it, man! Nobody said nothin' 'bout no fuckin' jewelry. I never..."

At that moment, Comanche let out a shrill whistle that echoed across the street and through the warehouse. "*Chota!*" He called out loudly. "It's a trap!"

Pintado stiffened, and his eyes tried to focus. "Gotta get outta here, man," he said with a whimper. "I no wanna get arrested again!"

"Wait! First tell me where you got the jewelry!"

"Oh, *man!* Like, I *told* you. I don' know nuthin' 'bout no fuckin' jewelry! Don' you understand? I'm innocent!"

He disappeared into the darkness of the warehouse with a surprising speed.

Alex and Robin started to chase after him, but the sound of gunfire stopped them. Two guns blazed away, sending loud echoes through the old building. Then from outside came the sound of voices.

"Damn! He got away!"

"We should have brought more men."

The voices were those of Enrique Morales and his friend Hector Saavedra.

Alex was furious with Morales. "How could you have done that? I gave my word it wasn't a trap. I had the thief right there. He was ready to tell me where he got the jewelry, and you and your partner came bursting in on us. No one trusts us now."

Morales looked down at the floor morosely. "This was our one chance of capturing El Papagayo. I was just trying..."

"You were trying to *kill* him, not capture him! How can you learn anything from a dead man?"

Morales shook his head helplessly. "I was hoping to wound him, or maybe... Well, did you get a look at him? Are you convinced that he's not your son?"

"He's not my son."

Morales almost smiled with relief. "Just as I said. I promise to keep looking until I find the source of the jewelry," he added earnestly. "Papagayo will turn up again, his kind always do, and I'll keep him in jail until I know everything."

Alex glared angrily at Morales. "You needn't bother. I've given you a lot of money over the years. You've come up with nothing. Then, just when an amateur like me gets close to solving the question of the jewelry, your stupidity ruins it all."

"But, Mr. Barron, I promise you that..."

"I said don't bother. This whole thing has been a torture for me over the years. I think I've finally convinced myself that Rickey's dead. At this point, I don't want to know what happened anymore. Our business arrangement is terminated as of now."

Robin took Alex's hand, and the two of them left Morales' office. Morales followed after them and shouted as they were entering the elevator:

"I refuse to give up! I'll continue on my own, Mr. Barron. I'll find the jewelry if it's the last thing I do on this earth."

When they were finally settled into the plane home, Robin kissed Alex on the cheek. "I'm sorry you had to go through this again. I wish there were something I could do."

He pulled her close to him and said, "No, everything's all right. For the first time, I think I'm free of all this. Seeing Papagayo, even briefly, convinced me that I've been wrong. For the first time in years, I have inner peace, a final realization that Rickey is gone and has been gone from the very first. God, if I could have felt this way before..."

Chapter Twenty-One

From the street, only the top part of the second story showed above the high stone wall. The house was huge. Soon they were to discover that inside it smelled of expensive leather furniture, subtle perfumes, carpets and books.

All they knew was that the house belonged to someone named Mr. Herbert Tarkington, a commercial attaché with the New Zealand embassy, and that the employment agency had said Micaela would be hired as a maid. The agent accepted the last of Riki's savings and hinted that perhaps another position might open soon, suitable for a young man like Riki. The agent also stressed that the Tarkingtons wanted a *single* woman, with no children.

"Do I look like a child?" Riki had asked.

A small, gnarled gardener answered the door and frowned sternly at the thought of them not going to the back door where servants belonged. Riki and Micaela followed the gardener as he led them toward the kitchen; he was bowlegged and hunched over with age. The drapes on the windows were of a rich tapestry, deep red with shimmers of gold running their length. Micaela's eyes were so large and round they looked as if they might pop out of her head.

They went through the hallway, past several mysterious doors and finally into a huge kitchen with polished marble floors that gleamed like window glass. The kitchen was larger than the entire house at Tezcatlipocas. Whoever the owners were, they had to be fabulously wealthy, of that Riki was certain.

Something uneasy stirred in Riki's mind, some long-forgotten memories, vague images of the time before his real mother sold him to Micaela. The images muddled his thoughts, as if there were something important he had lost and could not recall what it was or where he'd lost it. The gardener closed the kitchen door and then looked at them sternly.

"My name is Alberto. I am the head servant in this house. The maid's room is out this door and up on the roof," he explained in a wheezy voice that reminded Riki of an asthmatic horse. "From now on, remember never to go to the front door again. Your place is in the back of the house unless you're required to be cleaning something in the front."

Micaela nodded respectfully. Riki didn't say anything, because he knew that once Micaela was settled, he would slip away and go to Guadalajara until things cooled down enough for him to return to the excitement of the barrio. This place looked nice, but also boring.

They followed Alberto outside, into a small garden of flowers and trimmed shrubs that flanked a brick walk. The walk led to a steel pole with metal stairs winding about it in a tight spiral all the way to the roof. As Alberto trudged up the steps, each footstep caused the pole to wobble. Micaela looked worried, but bravely followed and motioned for Riki to do the same. About halfway up the stairs, the little man paused and looked down at Riki with a puzzled expression.

"What are you doing here? There is only one job, for a housemaid."

"She is my mother," Riki replied. "I just want to help her get settled."

The old man shrugged in resignation and resumed the spiraled climbing. "Well, you can't stay up on the roof, there is only one bed in the maid's room, and la señora won't stand for it."

The maid's room was one half of the cement structure that sat squarely in the center of the roof; the other half was a laundry room. When Micaela and Riki stepped onto the roof,

Alberto pointed and said, "That's your place. Put your things away, and you can get started on that stack of laundry."

The room was small, with a waist-high partition separating the tiny bath from the rest of the room. In addition to a narrow bed, the room held a dresser and a rather stiff-looking chair. Micaela looked worried when she saw how small her quarters were; no room for a bed for Riki.

"We'll find a *petate* somewhere and we can take turns sleeping on the floor," she whispered hopefully. "That is if the señora allows the two of us to stay."

"I'd like to stay somewhere else."

"No! If you can't stay with me, I'll not take the job!"

"But, Mica, we've spent everything to get this job. I would rather go back to the barrio, anyway."

"I won't have you running the streets, getting thrown into jail again." Her voice took on that stubborn tone that meant no compromise. "If you can't stay, then I can't."

Alberto pushed open the door to the laundry and said, "You had best start working here. The last girl left a pile of clothes to be washed. I hope you aren't too ignorant to run the washing machine?"

Micaela nodded quickly, ashamed to admit that she had no idea of how the contraption might work. The moment the gardener disappeared down the metal stairway, she and Riki began inspecting the mysterious machine. It was of white porcelain and had a round glass window in a door on the front which gave no clue as to its purpose. Riki opened the door and peered inside.

"What's in there?" asked Micaela.

"Nothing. No water faucets or anything. Maybe it's broken."

Against the wall was a cement sink with a drainboard of rough concrete. At least this was something Micaela recognized. On a shelf above the sink was a plastic bag of laundry soap. She turned on the water, and to her surprise, an almost immediate explosion of steamy hot water cascaded into the sink. Soon she was busy washing clothes.

In the country, women knew but one method of washing clothes. They wet the garment in a stream, squeezed soap into it, then pounded it against a flat rock with heavy slaps until the dirt loosened and could be rinsed away in the current. Things here didn't seem much different; Micaela simply used the cement drainboard instead of a rock.

The stream of hot water from the faucet was a vast improvement over a creek of cold running water. The noise of wet wash slap-slapping against cement filled the room and spilled over to the outside as she swung the heavy wash with diligence. She wanted to do a good job on her first day. She wanted clean clothes to present the señora as proof of her worthiness, and then maybe there would be no problem with Riki staying with her.

Riki heard footsteps coming up the spiral stairs. The top of the pole wavered with each shifting of weight. He assumed it was Alberto returning.

He was surprised to see a girl—or perhaps a woman, he couldn't decide which—peer over the edge of the roof. Her honey-blonde hair was gathered into a ponytail, in the style of a child, but she looked as if she might be older—and in fact, she had just turned eighteen years old. Her hair was lighter and prettier than any he'd ever seen, like corn silk in the early morning sun. She wore no makeup, and her complexion was pale, as a person who seldom went outdoors, all of which added to her image of a child. She wore glasses with heavy lenses that emphasized her eyes, making them look permanently wide with surprise.

When she saw what Micaela was doing in the laundry room, a puzzled frown creased her forehead. In heavily accented New Zealand English, she said:

"What's going on up here? It sounds like you are tearing the house down. But I don't suppose either of you speak English, now do you?"

Riki nodded with embarrassment. He understood what she was saying even though her New Zealand accent sounded odd to his ears. The word *are* came out sounding like *ab* instead of the usual *R* sound of American English he was used to.

She stared at Riki, obviously waiting for some kind of an answer. But being in the presence of a girl his age made him nervous, and he couldn't bring himself to speak.

She demanded, "Who are you and what are you doing on our roof?"

Riki swallowed and groped for words.

"My name is Riki Montalvo and this is my mother, Micaela. She is your new housemaid. She's washing clothes."

Her eyes grew wide in horror.

"My God! You're not really doing the washing that way are you? Oh, Mum is going to be angry, for fair! Don't you know how to use the bloody washer?"

"She doesn't understand English," Riki said defensively. "What's wrong with the way she's washing? The clothes get clean, don't they?"

"This happened once before. The girl ruined three of Poppa's dress shirts — made 'em look like a dog's breakfast, she did. And, she got canned in the bargain."

When she saw the confused look on Riki's face, she giggled and said, "You don't really speak much English, now do you?"

He shrugged in embarrassment. "I used to, but that was when I was little. There are lots of words I don't understand. Like *canned*, or *dog's breakfast*." He quit speaking when he realized that she was giggling again.

"You talk funny," she said. "Here, let me show you how the washer works before your Mum gets the hatchet. *Canned* means out of a job, out in the street, fired. Understand?"

The girl opened the door of the washing machine and demonstrated how to put the clothes in, the proper amount of soap to use, and how to turn the power on. Micaela watched every move the girl made, as if trying desperately to remember everything.

Riki swallowed thickly, feeling shamed. Despite the girl's thin, pinched features and sharp nose, she seemed beautiful to Riki. Her skin looked as soft as a silk scarf and when she bent over, her blouse tightened against her breasts in a way that made Riki blush with a mixture of desire and shame for feeling as he did.

"There. Half an hour, it's all done. Then all you have to do is hang 'em on the clothesline outside."

She looked at Riki, smiled and said, "My name is Elaine Tarkington, and I live here. Where do you live?"

When Riki shrugged, she looked astonished, then bit her lower lip. "I hope you don't plan on living in the maid's room? Oh great. Wait 'til Mum hears about that! She won't allow it, you know. She never hires a maid who is married."

"Why?"

"Mostly because one of our servants had a daughter who stole some things, and another one's husband broke in and robbed our house while we were on a holiday. And, well— you'd have to know my Mum to understand. She's rather racist and believes all Mexicans are burglars, thieves or rapists. Doesn't trust anyone."

"But my mother isn't married."

Elaine smothered another giggle. "That's even worse! Having a child out of wedlock? She'll think that's disgustingly sinful. Why doesn't your mother speak English like you? You don't look like her at all."

"She's not really my mother. She took care of me when I was little, raised me as if I were her child."

"And your real mother? What happened to her?"

Riki felt his face burn hot with shame. "I don't know."

"What do you mean, you don't know? Are you an orphan?"

"My mother left me with Micaela when I was about four years old. I think she might have been an American. That's probably why I can understand English."

"She *left* you? Why would a mother do a thing like that?" When he didn't reply, Elaine said, "You don't have to be embarrassed. Are you saying you were abandoned?"

Riki tried to think of a way to stop this conversation, but he couldn't. "No. Not exactly. She... My mother sold me to Micaela." Immediately he wished he hadn't said that. He couldn't understand why he was telling Elaine things he never mentioned to anyone before.

"*Sold* you?"

He nodded miserably.

"What do you mean, she *sold* you? That is horrible! For how much money?"

"No money. For two bottles of rum."

Elaine didn't say anything for an uncomfortably long period of time. For a few moments she thought she was being teased, but the anguished, embarrassed look on Riki's face convinced her the young man was telling the truth. She suddenly realized how very different their lives must have been. For her part, her parents were so over-protective that she felt smothered and imprisoned in the big house, yet here is a boy whose parents care so little that they sold him. For two bottles of rum!

She felt a wave of compassion for the boy, his face red in humiliation, and his obvious devotion to his stepmother so touching. She felt a need to know Riki, to compare their lives, to be close to someone outside of the family. She felt an irrational urge to throw her arms about him, kiss him, comfort him and tell him that he is not alone in the world.

"Where will you go if Mum won't allow you to stay here? Do you have any money?"

Riki shook his head. "I'd like to leave her here, but she says she won't stay unless I stay with her. She's stubborn sometimes."

"I don't think Mum will allow you to stay. She gets upset awfully easy." When she saw the look of disappointment on his face, the wave of compassion became a flood of irrational

286

emotion. Her lips firmed with stubborn resolve. "We just won't tell Mum about you. What she doesn't know can't get her upset, now can it?"

She felt richly rewarded by Riki's smile and the bright look of gratitude on Micaela's face when Riki translated what she said. Elaine felt exhilaration at the possibility of having a friend to talk to, a friend her age living in the same house. She had no friends because her parents would not allow her to go to school, or "play outside" like other children. Elaine was an invalid. A victim of sudden and intense seizures that only strong medicines and quiet living seemed to control. She had heard all her life how weak and sickly she was, and accepted that as a part of her being, much as a person born with a disfiguring birthmark learns to live with it.

But lately, she was feeling rebellious. Now she had a cause. She decided, for the first time in her life, to take a stand against her parents. Or at least try.

"I'll keep this secret at first," she said half aloud, "and figure out how to get around Mum later." She felt a thrill of excitement at the prospect of confrontation, and even more, at having a friend, a kind of *boyfriend* living in the same house with her. She had to cover her mouth with her hand to keep a giggle from slipping out at the thought.

But that afternoon, when the Tarkingtons came home, the gardener met them at the door and let the secret out. Mrs. Tarkington was furious. She threw her packages on the hall table and stalked angrily toward the kitchen. "I bloody well told that agent that I wanted a *single* girl, with no children! The last thing I need in this house is a snotty brat stealing things and…"

Elaine caught up with her mother as she was slamming through the swinging kitchen doors. "Wait, Mum! Talk to them first. They aren't like the others. Her son speaks English. You see, he was abandoned by his real mother and…"

"I will talk to no one! You know perfectly well what I will not put up with in this house."

Elaine compressed her lips stubbornly and summoned the courage to say, "Mum, there have been few times in my life I've ever demanded anything. Now I am going to demand. You must talk to the new maid and her son. You must give them a chance."

Mrs. Tarkington was shocked. "Now, Elaine, calm yourself. You know how excitement can set off an attack. Have you taken your medicine today?"

Mr. Tarkington entered the room. His ruddy complexion became even redder as he listened to his wife and daughter arguing. "Mother is right, Elaine. You must calm down. You know how sick you are, and.."

She stamped her foot angrily. "I don't *want* to sit down! I want mother to talk to these new servants. I want her to keep them on. I like the woman, and I like her son."

The Tarkingtons stared at their daughter in astonishment. Mr. Tarkington cleared his throat uneasily and said, "Look, dear... why don't you go on upstairs, take some medicine and lay down for a while. I'll talk to your mother."

Elaine knew that a continued confrontation would lead nowhere, so she withdrew to the top of the stairs and listened to her mother and father discussing the crisis.

"It will never work out," Mrs. Tarkington said stiffly. "Imagine, a child being abandoned by his mother. What kind of character can he be? Remember the maid we had who stole all of your cashmere sweaters? And you can't forget the time the burglars cleaned out our house?"

"Elaine seems to have her heart set on keeping the boy here. How old did you say he is?"

"She didn't say. A little boy, I should imagine. Doesn't matter, they start as thieves very early here. I absolutely will not permit children in my house."

"Oh, what the devil, let the little tyke stay. Elaine probably wants to play mommy. Rather like playing with dolls, don't you see? After all, we never would allow her to have a dog or a cat,

288

what with all of our allergies, but a little boy, well, I'd rather think we shouldn't be allergic to one of those."

Mrs. Tarkington snorted in derision. "Elaine is eighteen years old—much, much too old to be playing with dolls. Besides..." She stopped in mid-sentence when Elaine appeared in the hallway, followed by Riki and Micaela.

Mrs. Tarkington's mouth dropped open in surprise; her voice came out as a hoarse whisper: "*My God in Heaven.* Herbert, he's not a little boy, he's a *man!* Look at him, would you?" She covered her mouth with her hand in horror.

Mr. Tarkington was too stunned to reply. He slowly rose to his feet and watched Elaine enter the room. His eyes were glazed, as if he couldn't believe what he was seeing.

"Mum and Dad, this is Riki Montalvo and his stepmother, Micaela." She beamed at Riki and then looked defiantly at her mother. "I told them they can stay. I insist on it."

"But, but... How *old* is he? I thought you said a *boy!*'

The hostility was as thick as smoke. Riki looked at the smoldering expressions on the Tarkingtons' faces and regretted listening to Micaela's wish for a job. He said, "I think I'm about twenty or twenty-one."

Mr. Tarkington coughed and glared indignantly. "You *think?* Don't you *know?*"

Riki bowed his head, took Micaela by the arm and they withdrew into the kitchen area, to wait for a decision.

Elaine's mother pinched her mouth into a determined line and shook her head. "This is absolutely impossible, Elaine. Herbert and I have been very patient with you, what with your fighting with your tutors and refusing to cooperate with hem. But this is a bit much. I insist that..."

Elaine interrupted her mother, her eyes flashing in anger. "You insist! You always insist! To the devil with those tutors. I want to go to *school!* Can't you understand that? Other young people are registering at the university, enjoying normal social lives. But you insist on keeping me at home with more of those stupid tutors. I'm nothing but a prisoner in this house."

Mr. Tarkington shook his head in disbelief at her rebellious outbreak. He put his arm around Elaine's shoulder and said gently, "Calmly, calmly! Elaine, you are weak. You'd be destroyed in a university. You just don't realize how difficult life can be. Who would make sure you took your medication regularly? Maybe after a year or so..."

"That has nothing to do with Riki staying here. Why can't he help Alberto around the yard? You know Alberto is getting too old to work so hard."

The argument raged on for a while, but in the end the Tarkingtons reluctantly agreed to give Micaela and Riki a try. They assumed this must be a phase in her life which hopefully would pass.

"We can humor her for a couple of weeks," Mr. Tarkington said later, "and then we'll ease the two of them out of our lives."

"I suppose you're right, Herbert. But in the meantime, let's secure everything valuable and portable under lock and key. I shall instruct Alberto and the cook to inform us at the first suspicion of theft."

Micaela was excited and thrilled at the chance to work in such a fine place. Never in her life had she dreamed of such luxury. The cook, who lived elsewhere and who arrived at eight o'clock each morning, began teaching Micaela the duties about the house. It was like learning a foreign language. Micaela had no idea what the electrical appliances were called, much less how they were used. Anything that plugged into a wall was a complete mystery. Even simple things like operating a water faucet had to be carefully explained. Micaela assumed the running water to be like the water in a stream, inexhaustible, steady — why is it important to shut it off? Because she was so innocent and eager to learn, the cook didn't resent the time spent with Micaela. Soon she had Micaela doing much of her own work. The more work, the happier Micaela seemed to be, the less work the cook had to do.

When delivery men came to the back door, they invariably made eyes and flirted with Micaela. She was now in her late 30's and in the fullest bloom of womanhood. Radiant with happiness, she became more attractive every day. A particularly handsome milkman, with flashing white teeth and a trimmed moustache, enjoyed teasing Micaela.

"Why won't you go with me, my love? Just to Chapultepec Park on Sunday? Oh, I would be so proud to have you by my side. People would say, 'there goes El Lechero, with the most beautiful woman in the world'."

She giggled and covered her mouth with her hand. "Maybe someday. Maybe." She resolved to go with him after she'd saved enough courage. After five weeks, she did.

The salary seemed immense; she saved almost all of it, dreaming of the day she might have enough money to return with Riki to Tezcatlipocas and reopen the store. She sang often as she worked, ancient melodies from the village. The cook helped by doing less and less, while Micaela did more and more. She woke up at five o'clock every morning and eagerly hurried down to the house in order to have the floors properly scrubbed and hot coffee ready before the Tarkingtons arose.

Riki had never seen her smile so much before. *Once she settles in, she'll forget about me and allow me to be my own person,* he told himself. *By that time, things will have cooled down with the police. Then I'll be able to go back to my friends in the barrio.*

He contacted Comanche to let him know of his whereabouts. Only then did he learn of Barron's treachery in setting a trap for Pintado. Riki was thankful he hadn't allowed Comanche to talk him into a meeting with Barron.

"This thing is more serious than you think," said Comanche. "The trouble isn't just blowing away. They are asking for you everywhere. And, that reward still stands. Better stay out of sight for a while."

Riki nodded. "Well, it isn't too bad here. I have a cot in the laundry room for sleeping, and they pay me a little money to work in the yard. So, I'll hang on a little longer."

"The main guy you have to watch out for is Enrique Morales. He's been wandering around the barrio asking questions. The other day, he got drunk at La Porteña and tried to hire someone to kill you. He keeps talking about how you cheated him out of a job and a reward."

"Is he a cop?"

"I think he used to be. He carries a gun, and he looks mean. I don't understand why, but he hates you. Keep a sharp look out for him. He's dangerous."

Alberto grudgingly instructed Riki in the daily chores about the yard: which plants to water, which to trim, where to sweep and how often, how to wash the windows and the autos — things of that nature. Part of the instructions were to remain outdoors at all times.

"The señora insists that you stay away from señorita Elaine," he explained emphatically. "If you want to work here, you will obey."

The old gardener went slower each day. Riki could see it was a matter of time before he couldn't move at all. One day he didn't report to work. Riki never saw him again and without anyone asking, he assumed charge of the Tarkington's yard.

He found the work pleasant, the food strange but good, and each week he received a small salary. A month's wages would be far less than he could have made in a single day working the streets. At times he longed to slip away to the excitement of the barrio. But Comanche's warnings made sense. With a rich, powerful enemy like Barron, one doesn't take chances. After the trap Barron had set for him, he clearly couldn't be trusted. Now, with this gunman Morales after him, he needed to be exceptionally careful. But another motive kept him on this boring job and dulled his desire to leave. He had the chance to see and occasionally speak with Elaine Tarkington.

Mrs. Tarkington watched closely, making certain her daughter and the gardener had little opportunity to be together. Still Elaine managed occasions to slip away and talk to Riki, although briefly. Riki always felt warm and happy seeing Elaine. It also made him somewhat nervous.

"Oh, don't be a twit," Elaine chided him. "What Mum doesn't know won't hurt her. She is a real worry wart."

"I just don't to ruin anything for Micaela."

"Don't worry. Mum is getting to love Mica."

Chapter Twenty-Two

On Mondays and Wednesdays, the regular tutor visited the Tarkington house for two hours. His name was Mr. Clarke—a pear shaped man with a walrus moustache and thinning hair who once taught at an exclusive girls' school in England. Now in retirement, he squeaked out a living by giving private classes. He was short of temper by nature, but in order to retain his pupils, he was forced to repress his anger and pretend to be humble. On Tuesdays and Thursdays another tutor filled Elaine's days, this one a Frenchman named LaRouche, whose job it was to teach French, philosophy and piano to Elaine. She detested both teachers; she longed to be in a regular school.

Every Friday, a lady named Fernandez attempted to teach Spanish. Because Elaine was so recalcitrant, señora Fernandez accepted an unstated truce, leafing through Mrs. Tarkington's ladies' magazines while Elaine read novels. This suited the both of them.

Having to spend time with the tutors weighed heavily on Elaine's nerves. She kept thinking about Riki, wondering what he was doing, wishing she could be with him. He had been working for the Tarkingtons for two months, and she had arranged only a handful of brief encounters.

Then, one day as the tutor was wrapping up a particularly boring session, Elaine had a brilliant idea. She stopped her mother as she was leaving for a bridge party and said in a determined voice, "Mum, I want Riki to sit in Mr. Clarke's classes."

As an answer, Elaine received astonished stare. She

294

continued. "You and Poppa refuse to allow me to enter a regular university, someplace where I'd have other students for companionship. So, from now on, Riki will be my fellow student."

The mother's expression changed to horror. "Oh, my *God!* The gardener? Absolutely not! Most unthinkable."

"It is thinkable. And that's the way it will be."

"Elaine, dear. We're worried about this odd stubborn streak you're developing. You must realize that this Riki, or whatever his name is, is a *gardener*, not a member of the family, not an equal. His place is in the yard. We can't allow him in this house. We simply *can't*."

"Then *you* sit in the parlor and listen to old Mr. Clarke ramble on like a silly twit. If I can't have someone to study with, then send me to a real school."

Mrs. Tarkington frowned and pressed her lips together with indecision. Finally, she said. "Dear Elaine... You know this won't work. The gardener is an ignorant savage, just like all of the people in this Godforsaken country. He'd be bored to death in a tutoring session." When she noticed the look on Elaine's face, Mrs. Tarkington hastily added, "But, if you insist on trying it, I'll grant permission, with the clear understanding that your father doesn't know."

Riki felt mixed emotions when Elaine told him of the arrangement. He was excited by the chance to spend some four hours a week with her, but also embarrassed and angry at Mrs. Tarkington's attitude.

To everyone's surprise, Mr. Clarke didn't explode when he heard a gardener would be added to his class. When he discovered Riki couldn't read English, he shrugged and calmly said, "No matter. Wednesday, I shall bring some children's books. You may start with them."

For the first time since Mr. Clarke had been coming to the Tarkington house, Elaine tried to be attentive and polite. Instead of opening a newspaper to read while he was trying to make a point about English grammar or Shakespeare, Elaine sat forward in her chair and even took notes from time to time.

At the end of the first tutoring session, Mr. Clarke shook Riki's hand, as if he were congratulating an old friend, as he said, "I think this arrangement shall be fine. I'll bring some books on Wednesday."

Elaine was disappointed she didn't have an opportunity to talk to Riki alone. Her mother entered the room the moment Mr. Clarke left. She glared at Riki with suspicious eyes until he self-consciously made an exit.

Elaine stalked to her room and threw herself on the bed midst a herd of stuffed animals. She finished the afternoon daydreaming about Riki. Her favorite fantasy was one in which the two of them went out on a date, to a fancy hotel restaurant where they sipped cocktails and danced the evening away to the sound of a melodious orchestra.

The books Mr. Clarke brought were mostly pictures, with a few lines of printing below each illustration. The pictures were of a boy named Dick and a girl named Jane who played with an ugly spotted dog called Spot. The children had a father who always wore a hat, a suit and tie. They went for frequent rides in a convertible.

Mr. Clarke read through the book and said, "Now go sit over there see how many words you can remember at the end of the day. He seemed delighted, when at the end of the session, Riki could sound out all of the words. "Next week, I shall bring something a bit more difficult," he said with a pleased smile.

Again, Mrs. Tarkington arrived early to supervise Riki's return to the garden. Elaine waved goodbye weakly. This wasn't working out as she had hoped. They were achieving no private time together. She tried to think of something, but her mother was always there, hovering in the background.

They managed to keep the arrangement secret from Mr. Tarkington for three weeks. When he found out, he was furious.

He answered the doorbell when Mr. Clarke arrived the following Monday. Elaine heard everything from her hiding place behind the staircase. Mr. Clarke listened quietly while Mr. Tarkington bellowed and threatened. He ended by saying, "Your job is to tutor my daughter! I'll not pay you a solitary penny for wasting time on an ignorant gardener!"

Mr. Clarke eyed the New Zealander, an amused look of contempt on his face, and paused for a moment before replying. "Permit me to say, sir, that I was at the point of leaving your employ when this boy entered the picture. Until Riki Montalvo appeared, your daughter was impossible — arrogant, insulting. But since Riki has been attending the sessions, she's a different person. Suddenly, she is a delight to work with."

Mr. Tarkington sputtered, saying, "But, but, a *gardener*. An ignorant Mexican gardener!"

"Not entirely ignorant, sir. The boy's progress is amazing. He zipped through all of the lower grade books in my library first week. He seems to have a natural talent for English, almost as if he had a background in the language. The astonishing thing is that he learned most of it from going to the cinema. His vocabulary is excellent, and he acquires new words quite rapidly. I'm enjoying watching his progress. So much, that I've been staying an extra hour every session to work with him. So, you see, you haven't been spending your money on a gardener. But, hire someone else, if that suits you."

Elaine suppressed a giggle when she heard her father clear his throat harshly and say, "No, no. Forget I mentioned it. Carry on."

Once started, Riki began to devour books, starting with very simple ones in the Tarkington library, the ones Elaine read as a child. By the end of October, he had discovered novels, and astounded Mr. Clarke by reading three Steinbeck books and asked for more. Elaine stayed the extra hour, enjoying the book discussions. She particularly enjoyed the extra time with Riki, an hour in which the conversation often strayed from literature.

Mrs. Tarkington, however, kept a close eye on the last hour, always keeping the door ajar so she could listen and watch from the living room. The conversations were quite innocuous, and Elaine felt frustrated. Elaine suddenly developed an intense interest in Spanish lessons. She insisted that Riki sit in Mrs. Fernandez's class with her. She managed to persuade her mother to allow Riki one hour a week being her tutor in Spanish. Mrs. Tarkington relented, but insisted on sitting in on the sessions, even though she detested Spanish and anything connected with it. Before long Elaine was watching soap operas on television and chatting with the servants in a rudimentary, but ever improving Spanish.

Mrs. Tarkington watched these developments with mixed feelings, aware that Elaine seemed to be paying an inordinate amount of attention to the gardener, yet pleased with her sudden interest in education. She was careful to monitor the time Elaine spent with the upstart yard servant. She feared that given Elaine's immaturity, a dangerous situation could arise between her and the devilishly handsome gardener. Mrs. Tarkington felt strong reservations toward Riki, yet she grew immensely fond of Micaela. Micaela's eager approach to work and her contagious smile appealed to Mrs. Tarkington. She personally undertook the job of teaching the rustic country girl the proper way to do things around the house, and how to prepare food acceptable to New Zealand tastes. Micaela was quick to learn and anxious to please.

Riki had never seen Micaela so alive and happy. He hoped nothing happened to ruin it for her. Still, had it not been for Elaine, and for the challenge of Mr. Clarke's classes, he would have been sorely tempted to return to the excitement of the streets. Once, after three more months had passed, he contacted Comanche.

"Don't even *think* about coming back," Comanche said. "This Enrique Morales is like a man with a bone in his throat.

He has been running around like a crazy man, looking for El Papagayo. Just sit tight where you are. I'll let you know when it's safe."

As the days went by, Riki found himself totally absorbed with the classes. They discovered that he had a knack for learning languages, and before long he was conversing with Elaine in a rudimentary French, helping both of them learn the language she had resisted all these years.

From time to time, Elaine managed to create situations where she and Riki could talk privately. Usually, the setting was in the garden, with Elaine standing beside Riki as he worked. At first the conversations were stiff, but gradually, she allowed herself to talk freely, about things that mattered to her, about her emotions.

One day, when Riki was working on a flower bed alongside the house, she sat on the edge of a planter box and watched him work for a while before she spoke.

"I'm so bored with life, Riki. If I thought living would be no more than this... Well, I think I'd do myself in."

"What does 'do yourself in' mean?"

"Kill myself. I've thought about it a lot."

He put down his digging trowel and frowned at her. "I don't understand you. What is wrong with your life? You have everything anyone could want."

"Such as?"

"Such as parents who love you, a fine home, plenty to eat, money to spend..."

She made a sound of disparagement. "That isn't life. Don't you see that I live in a prison here? I can't go anywhere unless Mum or Poppa go with me. Money isn't any fun to spend if you have to buy exactly what you're told to buy, and when your parents stand behind you while you make the purchase. And here I am, nineteen years old, at the age when other girls are dating, going to the university and meeting other people my age, having sex. But no, I'm not permitted these ordinary things. All my parents can say is, 'Elaine dear, you simply can't think about such things. Remember your poor health, dear. Take your Delantrin, dear, we don't want any seizures, now do we?' I haven't had a seizure in years. Sometimes I think I've grown out of them, and that they are just more links in the chains about me. This 'fine house' is nothing but a bloody jail."

Riki shook his head in incredulity. "I've been in jail. If jail looked like this, I wouldn't have been so anxious to leave."

Suddenly he sensed that she was on the verge of tears. He took her hand and squeezed gently.

"I think I can understand in a way, Elaine. When I lived in Tezcatlipocas, Micaela wouldn't allow me to leave the village without her, unless it was to go up the mountain to cut resin. I was never, ever allowed to go down the mountain to the road. I wanted to leave so badly, because I just knew there'd be a lot of exciting things happening out 'there'. But when we did leave, things were so bad I wished we had never left the village. Yet I never thought about killing myself. You must forget those kinds of ideas. You're young. We're both young—there's a lot of life ahead of us."

"But I'm missing so much out of life. And it's going fast, don't you see? If I miss out on life now, as a young adult, there can be no making up for it. You can't understand what it's like to be a prisoner. I feel so desolate."

He thought about his time in jail, but it was too painful to explain. She wouldn't have understood. Instead, he murmured, "You have something I'd give anything to have. You are so lucky and don't even know it."

"What do I have? Nothing!"

"You have parents. I used to dream at night about my mother and my father, especially my father. During the day, I would wonder where they were, and why they deserted me. At night I tried to imagine what terrible thing I'd done for them to be angry with me? Something so terrible that they would sell me? *For two bottles of rum?"*

He shook his head fiercely, and added, "Maybe that really didn't happen. I often think about it and try to convince myself that it was all a mistake, that it couldn't have happened that way. But they never came back for me." He paused when a lump in his throat threatened to close his windpipe. Then he continued, "But your parents would never abandon you. They worry about you. They care."

"Oh hell yes, they care! They love me when it's convenient. When it's not convenient, when Poppa wants to play golf and Mommy wants to play bridge and drink scotch, they're too busy for me. They want me to stay in the house, preferably in my room, like a suitcase in a closet. Then when they're ready to play parents, they want to take me out of the closet and expect me to be a normal human being. Not normal, really, they want an invalid who is too weak to challenge them. They don't love. They possess."

She sighed and twisted a strand of hair about her finger. "You know, Riki, I'd love to live in a little village somewhere. Get my feet muddy if I damned well feel like it. Be able to pet a dog or a cat if I want to without having Mum or Poppa come screaming, 'Don't do that! You know you're allergic to cats!' Maybe even have a dog or cat of my own."

Riki smiled at the thought. "You'd have to carry water from the stream—in a bucket you balance on your head. You'd have to cook over a charcoal fire until you smell like burnt grease. You wouldn't have a maid to do your laundry in a machine, you'd have to..."

"I'd love it! I'd be with people who are capable of love. Simple love, just for the physical knowledge that we all belong together."

"You'd probably marry a man with a pot belly who gets drunk and beats you."

"At least he'd love me."

"Your parents love you," he said stubbornly.

She snorted in derision. "They don't even love each other. Did you know they have separate bedrooms? They just tolerate each other just as they tolerate me. I bet they don't even have sex. Too shriveled up from self-righteousness to do anything sexy."

"That's disrespectful."

"Riki, have you ever been with a girl? You know, I mean sexually?"

He shook his head. He felt himself blushing. He picked up the trowel and began digging in the flower bed, angry at himself for being so transparent. He wished he could bury deep in the earth the memory of that first humiliating experience, at the Gato Negro.

She said, "You don't have to be ashamed. I haven't had sex either. I'm angry about it, not embarrassed."

"That isn't a question you ask people."

"Why not?"

"It's just that... The answer is no. I haven't."

"But I thought there are all kinds of prostitutes — how do you call them, *putas?* — in Mexico City. My mother says..."

"Yes, there are," he interrupted. "I tried once, but... Some of my friends go to them, but, when you've been raised in a small village, and when you hear from early childhood that the Gods punish you for doing, well, doing that with a puta. Besides, it costs a lot of money."

"But, you've had girlfriends, haven't you? Haven't you gone out on dates?"

He shook his head and laughed shallowly. "I've seen that done in the movies. Dating, and things like that. But it's not that way in the barrio. A boy doesn't date a girl unless he's properly introduced. Not until he has the approval of the girl's brothers and her father. It would be an insult to the girl and to her family."

"Can't you just decide to go out, on the spur of the moment? Isn't that done?"

"Not unless you are willing to face an angry brother or a

father with a baseball bat!"

"Oh my, you have a more difficult time having sex than I thought." Elaine's face suddenly lit up as if a brilliant idea had struck. "Riki, I know what! Why don't you and I, you know..."

He blinked his eyes and had to think for a moment, to make certain that he understood what she was driving at. He stiffened and said, "No! I could get fired! So would Micaela!"

"Don't you like me?"

"Of course. I like you a lot. But..."

"Do you love me?"

"Elaine, don't do this to me. I don't have any right to..."

Before any more conversation could add to Riki's mortification, Mrs. Tarkington rounded the corner of the building. She looked at Riki with a suspicious eye. He was grateful that he was digging with the trowel rather than holding Elaine's hand as he had been just a moment or two ago.

Mrs. Tarkington said, "Time for your medicine, dear. And it'll be nap time before you know it. Come along." Before she left, she shot a nasty look at Riki as if to say, *don't let me catch you doing something wrong!* Elaine sighed and followed obediently, steeling herself for a dose of pills and nasty tasting syrup medication.

Riki jabbed viciously into the crusty earth and accidentally cut the roots of a young plant. His mind refused to budge from Elaine's last few words. But it would be too dangerous. She had sounded serious, hadn't she? The idea wouldn't go away — nor would his erection.

Elaine's room occupied the back corner of the house. It was rather large and filled with insipid stuffed animals and toys of her childhood, not her toys, really — these were her parents' idea of what a daughter should have for her room. Whenever Elaine suggested getting rid of the huge purple Dumbo or the lanky stuffed giraffe, her mother would almost break into tears. That would be the end of the argument.

With the taste of medicine bitter in her throat, she angrily swept away enough animals to be able to stretch out on the bed where she could properly feel sorry for herself.

A noise coming from the lightwell outside her bathroom made her sit up and listen. "What could that be?" The bathroom was long and narrow, with the long side opening onto an enclosed sundeck, a sort of well formed by the other rooms of the house. The scraping noise grew louder, so she entered the bathroom and opened the door to the lightwell.

Micaela stood up on the roof. She held a wooden ladder and was letting it down to the cement floor below. When she saw Elaine looking up at her, she laughed in embarrassment and pointed at a pillowcase which lay on the floor of the sundeck. "It blew off the clothesline," she explained.

Elaine picked up the pillowcase and waited until the ladder touched the floor, then she climbed up and handed it to Micaela.

As she climbed back down, a flash of inspiration hit her. She waved at Micaela and said, "It's okay. Leave the ladder here for a while." She gestured, and then tried her Spanish, saying, "*Deja la escalera.*" Micaela understood, but was puzzled at why the girl would want a ladder in the lightwell. She nodded dutifully and returned to her laundry.

"An escape hatch," Elaine said to herself, very pleased with herself. "If I want to get out of the house, I simply climb up the ladder, then down the outside stairs."

She smiled happily and fell into bed again, amazed that she had the nerve to consider defying her parents. She couldn't nap that day; she seldom could anyway. She kept thinking about the exciting possibilities of an escape hatch.

Then another idea sent liquid heat through her loins and churning about in her head. This idea concerned her, Riki, and growing up.

Riki set up his cot in the laundry room that evening and sat down to read. The book was a mystery novel about a newspaper man whose daughter had been murdered, and who was searching for clues pointing to the killer. The story was set in California. For some unknown reason, he wanted to read everything he could find about California, and sometimes felt as if he knew the place, especially San Francisco. He didn't suspect that he had been born in San Francisco. He read until his eyes were too heavy to read any more.

He turned off the light, slipped out of his clothes and lay back in the cot. He pulled a light blanket over his naked body and fell asleep immediately.

Suddenly he was wide awake. Someone was in the room with him. He started to sit up, when a hand pressed against his chest and he knew it was Elaine even before she began to speak in a whisper. "It's only me. Don't make any noise, or they'll catch us."

"How did you get up here?"

"Sh-h-h. Come on, I'll show you."

"I can't. I don't have any clothes on."

"That's all right. I'm going to take you to my room and we're going to have sex. You won't need any clothes." She pulled on his arm and whispered insistently, "Come on! I've made up my mind."

He managed to grab a pair of pants and tugged them on as he hopped across the roof, Elaine pulling relentlessly.

"We'll be caught," he protested. "Micaela and I will lose our jobs." But he knew couldn't have stopped now, even had Elaine loosened her grip on his arm. He didn't want to stop. Yet he was frightened as never before in his entire life. She showed him the ladder. "My escape hatch. Be quiet as you climb down."

"Are you crazy?"

"Shut up and go down the ladder. Don't worry about being caught, because I have my door latched from the inside. Go on down!"

She led him through the bathroom and into her bedroom. He felt his heart thumping and he wondered if it might burst. She took his hand and led him through the darkened room toward the bed.

He almost stumbled over a stuffed poodle, and to his bare feet the furry object was a dangerous animal in the dark. He let out a startled cry.

"Slip into bed," she whispered. "I'll get undressed and join you." He nervously stepped out of his trousers and crawled into bed, pulling the sheet up under his chin. He heard the rustle of a silk nightgown as Elaine pulled it over her head.

A few seconds later he felt the bed jolt as she climbed in and pulled the sheet over herself. He could feel the heat from her body with just a few nervous inches separating their bodies. They both lay stiff and rigid, their hearts pounding furiously.

"I think you're supposed to do something!" she whispered hoarsely.

"What do you want me to do?"

"I'm not really sure, but you're supposed to do *something*, aren't you? I think the man is expected to spark things off. They always do in the cinema. Don't you know *anything* about having sex?"

"Not much. I've heard my friends joke about it, but that's all. The one time I tried it with a puta, I didn't know what to do. When she laughed at me, I ran away."

"I had thought you would be so experienced, being on the street, all that time. Mum seems to think Mexicans are like rabbits in warrens, having sex all the time. Don't your friends do it all the time?"

"Maybe. We never talk about sex unless to make fun of it. None of the girls in the barrio go anywhere without their sisters or brothers with them."

"Don't they date?"

"You mean go out together? Alone? Not unless they are thinking about getting married. Maybe they do *it* then. I don't know." His mouth was getting dryer by the moment. He tried to swallow but couldn't. "What do we do first?"

"I was hoping *you* would know." Elaine thought a while,

and finally said, "Well, I found a copy of *Lady Chatterley's Lover* stuck behind some books in the library. I think it was Mum's and she was hiding it from me. According to what I read there, we should do a lot of touching and things first. I think you're supposed to kiss me down here and things like that." She sounded nervous; her voice quivered. "To tell the truth, Riki, I'm scared. I think I'm changing my mind about all this. Do you mind?"

He felt an involuntary sigh of relief escape from his lungs. "I don't mind at all. I was losing my courage more and more. Anyway, I think that kissing 'down there' is sodomy. Something... something you aren't supposed to do."

"Why not? It sounds like fun to me!"

Riki tried to remember what he had been told as a boy in the village. "I don't remember exactly. I think it causes you to lose your mind or something. Maybe it makes you go blind."

"Not according to the book. Well, anyway, even if we are cowards, I'm awfully glad we're here. At least we can talk without having to look over our shoulders to see if Mum is watching and listening."

They moved closer and Elaine put her hand on Riki's chest and smoothed it lightly over his stomach. "I wish we knew how to do sex. But it's awful scary, isn't it? Maybe someday we'll learn."

When Riki's hand smoothed over her breast, she breathed in sharply, then relaxed and snuggled closer to him. "Maybe someday." Her hand drifted over his stomach and encountered something hard and throbbing, something which made her giggle.

They discovered they didn't need instructions, and that *Lady Chatterley's Lover* wasn't necessarily the definitive textbook on sex. However, Riki was partly right about one thing. When he kissed her "down there," she almost lost her mind. The next evening, when Elaine went to bed early, Riki climbed down the ladder. He did the same every night for the next two weeks.

Each night, after they finished their mysterious explorations into the adult world of sex, they would lay in bed and talk, discussing life and what it might hold in the future.

They grew to know each other very well. Elaine was fascinated by Riki's stories of Tezcatlipocas and his life in the barrio. He told of Comanche, and Angel and the others. They both cried when he told her the story of Pepe.

"Oh, how I wished I could meet your friends," she said. "Your adventures sound so exciting. I'd love to do something like that someday."

"We didn't do those things for excitement. We did them to have something to eat."

"Someday, you must take me to the barrio, and introduce me. I should love to go someplace with you and help you pick some pockets. Anything to leave the dreadful boredom of this place. You just can't understand."

"I understand. When I was a child, I remember I used to lay on this big white rock that sticks out over the black cliff below the village, and I used to look down and watch the autos and trucks and buses roll past. I used to wonder who those people were, who could be so lucky to have autos, and go wherever they wanted. I didn't hate the village, no. But I wanted to see what the rest of the world was like. I would have given anything to live like you are living."

"Oh, would you now? That's sort of like saying you'd give your right arm to be ambidextrous."

"What does *ambidextrous* mean?"

Suddenly, Elaine sat up in bed. "Riki! We can do it!"

"Be ambidextrous?"

"No no. We can use my escape hatch to get out of here. To visit Comanche and Angel!"

"I'd be fired!"

"We won't get caught."

She jumped out of bed and clapped her hands in joy at her new idea. "It's time for me to get out in the world. You must take me to the barrio!"

"You'd hate it there. It's dirty, it's ugly, it's..."

"I would *love* it there, and you are going to take me!"

Chapter Twenty-Three

Elaine grew more and more insistent that Riki take her out of the house. "It will be so easy! I'll just tell them I'm out of sorts and need to take a long afternoon nap. They like that, because it gives them an extra opportunity to go to the club for bridge. Actually, I believe they would be happy if they could keep me asleep in my room every day, take me out for dinner and then put me back, like a book on a shelf."

"If they found out..."

"They won't. I shall climb up the ladder and go down the back way. They'll never spot us. Not as long as I return before dinner is served at seven o'clock. This is our opportunity, with the tutors off for school holiday, nobody will miss us."

"Suppose you get sick? What would we do?"

"I'll take medicine with me. If I start to get sick, I'll just pop a couple of pills. I carry a padded stick and you can stuff it into my mouth so I don't bite my tongue. It'll be easy. Besides, it's been ages since I've had an attack."

She wouldn't give up. Finally, Riki surrendered. "Okay. We'll do it. We'll wait until we're positive your parents are going to be away."

Their chance came on a Friday shortly after Easter. Mr. Tarkington had been called away to Oaxaca on urgent business, and Mrs. Tarkington developed an excruciating toothache and had to go to the hospital for a root canal filling. Before she left the house, she gave instructions to the cook to make sure that Elaine took her medicine and took a nap. "Make sure she stays in her room," she admonished the cook, then she added, "And, don't allow the gardener inside the house, under *any* circumstances!"

As soon as the taxi took Mrs. Tarkington away, Elaine informed the cook that she was tired and was going to nap early.

"Don't bother fixing lunch for me," she called out as she climbed the stairs to her bedroom. She locked the door and hurriedly changed clothes. Her throat felt dry with excitement. *My first day out of prison!*

She loosened her hair from its ponytail and began brushing it into the style she had studied in one of the women's magazines. She had practiced it so often that it fell into place promptly. Then she carefully outlined her lips with the lipstick and surveyed the result in the mirror. *Not bad. But I think one of the first things I shall do, is buy some darker lipstick*, she resolved. *And some eyeliner.*

She put on her glasses and looked in the mirror again. *Damn! If it weren't for these stupid things, I think I'd look almost pretty.* She took them off and went to the window to see how well she could see without them. She couldn't make out the building across the street. She sighed and put them back on and she was ready to go.

Before she climbed the ladder, she made sure Micaela was nowhere in sight. Then she crept to the edge of the roof and signaled to Riki.

He was surprised at the difference a new hairdo and some lipstick could make in Elaine's appearance, and he smiled his approval. He motioned for her to come down and whispered as loudly as he dared, "Mica and the cook are busy in the pantry. Let's go!"

It was easy. Soon they were walking along Avenida Insurgentes, holding hands and laughing. Elaine began seeing Mexico City as if from the eyes of another person, someone happy and free. Everything looked so different walking than it did from the window of their automobile. "This is our day, Riki! I want to meet Comanche and Angel and the rest. I want to see where you used to live and where you used to play."

"There was no playing. It was work or starve." He took her arm and guided her across the street through the traffic to the bus stop. They had to run to avoid a suicidal delivery truck. Elaine was out of breath by the time they reached the curb, but she couldn't help giggling.

"Are you all right?" he asked with concern in his voice.

"I think so. I'm just not used to running or doing anything other than sitting around the house. Don't look so worried. This will be good for me."

Elaine had never ridden a bus before and felt thrills of excitement as the vehicle wended through traffic jams, picking up more and more passengers until they were jammed together like olives in a jar. She could understand how easy it must be for someone to nick a wallet or two. She glanced sideways at Riki and smiled at his bravado, an accomplished thief at such an early age. To her surprise, he was staring out the window with a frown on his face.

"What's the matter, love?"

Riki shrugged and said, "It's nothing. It's just that I hate for you to see how run-down and tawny my barrio is."

"I think you mean *tawdry*. But I don't see it that way at all. I think it's picturesque."

"You aren't used to seeing poor people. This is going to make you feel uncomfortable."

"I'm going to love every part of it. I want to see everything. I want to experience what life in the barrio really is like." She took his hand in hers and squeezed it excitedly.

"It's ugly. Everything and everybody is poor."

"No! I see nothing but charming things. I'd give anything to live free here."

Riki shook his head at her foolishness. He guided her through the streets of the barrio toward Comanche's place, and as he did, he kept an anxious eye out for police or anyone who might recognize him and notify Morales. He hadn't set foot in this barrio since his and Micaela's narrow escape over a year ago. As a disguise, he hadn't worn sunglasses. He hoped his sport shirt and jeans made him look like a tourist.

They paused on the corner across from Comanche's tiny apartment. It looked safe, so Riki motioned for Elaine to cross the street with him. He took her hand and they walked up the three flights of stairs to Comanche's rooms. No one answered Riki's knock.

When they went downstairs and stepped into the street, Riki heard an anxious voice calling out his name. It was Angel. They ran toward each other and embraced in an abrazo. Angel stepped back and grinned at Riki. Then he looked up and down the street with a worried look on his face.

"Hey! Papagayo! You shouldn't be here on the street. Don't you know the *chota* are still looking for you?"

"I was hoping they'd forget Micaela and me by now. Where's Comanche?"

"You won't believe this, but Comanche is an honest man! That's right! He used the money he got from that Barron guy to buy a bicycle repair shop. He's so honest it makes me sick. Also, he's spending a lot of time with his novia—a pretty one, too. Looks like wedding bells, can you imagine that?"

Riki laughed. "Comanche? Married with a herd of little ones? We'll probably have to call him by his real name: Horacio!"

"If he decides to talk to *pachucos* like us." Angel grew serious as he said, "You'd better keep an eagle eye out, Riki. This Morales guy is after you and Micaela for more than just jewelry. He's a crazy man. You've made a fool of him and he won't rest until he has the two of you in prison. That's if you're lucky. He'd rather put a bullet in your head."

"I don't understand. Why are we so important?"

"Part of it is that he thinks you were the one who got the money from Barron that day when Comanche and I dressed Pintado in clean clothes and sunglasses. The word is that Barron got so angry that he cut Morales off his payroll. So, Morales thinks it's all your fault, and..."

Angel stopped talking when he suddenly realized that Elaine was with Papagayo. "*Jijole, manito,* what are you doing with this Gringa?" Elaine smiled and quickly pulled her glasses off and stuck them in her pocket. In her best Spanish, she said, "I am not a Gringa, Angel. I am from New Zealand." She held out her hand in greeting.

Riki laughed at Angel's confusion, and he introduced him to Elaine. Angel shook her hand, grinning as he said, "*¿Quiũbole, chavala?*"

Elaine's Spanish was improving all the time, but she knew little street talk, or caló. Angel began filling Riki in on the latest barrio gossip, but they might have been talking Chinese for all she understood.

After a few minutes, Angel said, "Come on. Let's go to the Palacio restaurant where we can talk without cops looking over our shoulder. Comanche usually stops there during the siesta for coffee."

As they walked to the restaurant, Riki and Angel laughed and talked over the old days. Elaine listened and felt privileged to be a part of this strange new world. These people don't realize how lucky they are, she thought, free to come and go as they wished, free to take a chance on life.

The Palacio restaurant was little more than a long, oblong room with tables in the front and an open kitchen at the end of the room. They took tables in the middle, where they wouldn't be in sight of the street window, yet not near enough to the kitchen to be overheard by the cooks. Steam from a soup pot filled the air with boiling onions and beef brisket smells. Elaine inhaled and sighed with ecstasy of hunger, savoring the cooking odors.

Angel said something to her which she missed. "I'm sorry," she said, "but I didn't understand you. Is my Spanish that bad?"

Riki laughed and put his arm across her shoulder. "Elaine's Spanish comes from a book."

Angel grinned at Riki. "Just like you when you first came to the city. Remember how you had to keep asking us what this word meant, and that word?"

Elaine said, "Would you teach me? I should like to come here often. I could practice my Spanish and learn. Rather like doing homework for school."

The cook had just brought a jar of coffee syrup and a jug of steaming water to the table when Comanche entered the restaurant. He whooped and laughed, and Riki leapt to his feet to grab his friend in a tight *abrazo*. Comanche stepped back and said, "Oh, man, but it's good to see you. But you have to be careful, you know?"

"Morales?"

"Yes. He's keeping this thing going, and he claims you have more of that jewelry. Is that right?"

Riki shook his head and changed the subject by introducing Elaine. "I work for her family," he said. "Very rich."

Comanche took Elaine's hand in his and said, "And very pretty."

Elaine smiled shyly. "I feel as if I've known you for years. Riki told me all about you."

"Lies! Everything he told you are lies, Elaine. I never did any of those things. What did he say? If he told you that I have a *palete* the size of a large banana, well, maybe he was telling the truth about that."

She laughed delightedly. This was the first time in her life she had ever been in the company of people her own age without the watchful eyes of Mr. and Mrs. Tarkington monitoring everything that went on. When the cook brought a plate of tacos to the table, Elaine ordered a rum and Coke. Riki protested, but she said, "First time I ever had a chance to try rum, and I'm going to take full advantage."

At this moment, a photographer entered — one of those who wander about the barrio carrying an ancient Polaroid instant-camera from restaurant to bar to nightclub, hoping to sell someone on the idea of having their picture taken. Elaine smiled in delight when he approached. "Sure! Take a picture of Riki and me, please!"

She pulled her chair close to Riki's and they put their arms around each other and grinned at the camera. Elaine waited for the picture to dry and carefully put it inside her purse. "I'm going to keep this forever, in remembrance of my first date."

It wasn't the last date. At least three afternoons that next week, she climbed the ladder to the roof, crept down the spiral stairway to meet Riki. They would catch buses to the barrio. Comanche had to take care of his business, so he couldn't spend much time with them. But Angel and the boy named Mocho, who also worked at stealing when they were short of money, were free to wander about the city with Riki and Elaine.

"No *movidas* when we're with you," Riki insisted. "I can't risk getting mixed up with the police."

Mocho raised his hand in imitation of a priest giving benediction. "We won't steal so much as an extra breath of air when you are around."

Were it not for a missing ear, which he had lost in a knife fight years ago, Mocho would be a handsome young man. Elaine noted that his crisp, curly hair and *café con leche* skin hinted of something African in his ancestry. She giggled inwardly at the horror her mother would feel if she could see her now, walking in a low-class slum with three Mexicans, one of whom was partly black. To this racist New Zealand matron, even a drop of non-white blood was an unforgivable sin.

They wandered through the barrios, and even walked as far as the Cathedral on one occasion. They walked because Riki refused to ride on a bus with Angel and Mocho. "You two couldn't help stealing wallets any more than you can help blinking your eyes," he claimed.

On the third day, Riki seemed preoccupied. "I can't be taking so much time away from my job," he complained. "Your father noticed that I haven't been watering every day, and that the herb bed is starting to seed."

"Don't pay them any mind, love."

"I have to. We're not going anywhere next week. I have to catch up on the yard work."

He refused all her arguments.

Elaine thought about it at some length before deciding. She would make her own visit to the barrio. Alone. It should be like eating gingersnaps, she told herself. And it was.

She waited until Riki was working on the north side of the house, and she eased down the wavering staircase. She caught a bus on Insurgentes. She found Angel and Mocho sitting on a park bench across from the Del Prado Hotel. They jumped to their feet and shook her hand politely. "We're watching for tourists with fat wallets to get on the bus," they explained.

"Can I go with you? Maybe I could help."

Mocho laughed, but Angel frowned thoughtfully. "Maybe you can," he said.

She followed instructions and approached a group of Americans who came out of the hotel and crossed the street to the bus stop. "Watch out for pickpockets, here," she said. "They tell me they'll steal your underdrawers if you're not careful."

The tourists thanked her and unconsciously patted the places where their valuables were hidden. Angel and Mocho followed the tourists aboard and motioned for Elaine to wait. They returned half an hour later, with broad grins on their faces.

"I haven't done that well since Papagayo quit the gang," Angel said. "Here, this is your share." He held out a fold of pesos. "Go ahead, you earned it."

At first, she tried to refuse the money, but after they insisted, she finally accepted her share of the loot. She loved feeling like one of the crowd. She didn't count the money, but simply tucked it into her jumper pocket.

While she waited for the bus to return home, two small

children came along the street — a little boy and his sister — holding hands as protection against the world and looking hungry. Their noses were runny and neither wore shoes. She stopped them and stuffed the money into the boy's hand. She smiled contentedly when the astonished children stammered thanks and then scampered down the street as if they expected this crazy Gringa to ask for the money back.

That evening, she diligently practiced speaking caló, and the next morning shocked the cook into a wide-eyed stare with some of the new language she was learning.

"Señorita Elaine, I don't think you know what those words mean. You mustn't say those words in public."

"Oh, fuck off, Chona. Mum and dad want me to learn Spanish, and that's what I'm learning."

The cook, scandalized, hid in the pantry until Elaine left the kitchen.

She slipped away the next afternoon, while Riki worked in the yard and her mother napped. This time she didn't go downtown, instead, she strolled along Insurgentes and window-shopped the elegant boutiques. Two blocks from where she had to turn off Insurgentes to return home, she noticed an optical shop with a display of eyeglass frames.

A few paces past the shop, she stopped and returned to examine a sign in the window. It advertised contact lenses, one-day delivery. A sly smile crossed her face. *Why not?* She resolved to bring her eyeglass prescription on her next outing. The following week she placed an order. A few days later she brought the contacts home and put them on to show Riki.

He was stunned at the difference it made in Elaine's appearance. But he worried what her parents would say. They would know she was sneaking out of the house and might blame him.

"Yes, I like the way you look. But you can't keep leaving the house like this. How would you explain this to your parents?"

"Like as not, I'd tell 'em to fuck off." She furtively kissed

Riki on the cheek and whispered, "I'll be waiting for you tonight."

Then she breezed inside the house, leaving Riki Montalvo leaning dejectedly on a shovel in the garden. But his anger dissipated as he remembered her invitation for the evening. As he chopped away at some stubborn thistles that insisted on intruding in the garden, he thought of how much Elaine had changed since he had first met her. From a helpless, sheltered invalid to someone who could tell the whole world to "fuck off." He smiled and decided to simply warn Angel and Mocho rather than punish them.

That Friday, after the weekly Spanish lesson, Mrs. Fernandez met the Tarkingtons on her way out. "I must tell you of your daughter's amazing progress," she said happily. "I used to think she would never learn Spanish, that she didn't want to learn. But in the last six months, she has made unbelievable progress. Why, she has learned words that even I barely know." She shook hands and said goodbye without adding that some of the words weren't permissible outside of a whorehouse. The tutoring sessions had changed from torturously boring hours into a stimulating experience for the both of them. Elaine was teaching the staid Mrs. Fernandez to speak caló

Mr. Tarkington closed the door after Mrs. Fernandez and murmured to his wife, "Six months ago she changed, eh? About the time we allowed the gardener to sit in on the classes, don't you know? I rather thought it would have a beneficial influence. Good idea, I dare say."

"Really. And she spends so much time in her room studying. I hardly have to watch her anymore, to make sure she doesn't attempt to spend time alone with the gardener. You never know what he might try. Mexicans are known to be oversexed, I understand."

"Of course. Where is she now?"

Mrs. Tarkington smiled smugly. "In her room studying.

She said she is going to sleep early. Would you care to go to the club?"

"Yes. I do think a spot of gin and conversation would suit me just fine."

Chapter Twenty-Four

The day Micaela gave Riki the bad news it was raining; it was dark inside the kitchen. Even before she said anything, he knew something was wrong because of the look of despair in her eyes, as though death itself couldn't do harm now. Her voice wavered as she said:

"They're leaving, Riki. Mr. Tarkington is being sent back to New Zealand. We will lose our jobs." She chewed a knuckle and shook her head. "I love it here, so much! We'll never find a place so fine, so clean, or employers so kind. We might have to go back to Tezcatlipocas."

Riki went looking for Elaine and found her in the upstairs study. He wasn't supposed to be in that part of the house, but he felt he couldn't wait. She lay face down on a plush leather sofa, crying into an embroidered pillow. He closed the door behind him and said, "Micaela told me. When do you have to go?"

"The end of the month." She sat up and blotted tears from her face with a damp handkerchief. "But I'm not going with them. That's all there is to it, Riki. I'm staying here with you."

"They won't allow that."

"We'll run away! I'll live with you in the barrio. We'll rent an apartment and live like married people. I think I should like that very much."

He sank to his knees beside the sofa and caressed her hand. "It won't work, Elaine. It just won't work. What would we do for money? I could never earn enough to live the way you're used to. I'd have to go back to stealing."

"No matter. I'll learn to live in the barrio like anyone else. Comanche could give you a job in his bicycle repair shop."

"Morales and his informers watch Comanche's place, hoping for a clue as to where I am. They would kill me in a minute."

"We'll do it some way. There are 17-zillion people living in the barrios and they do all right."

"The 17-zillion people live on tortillas and beans. They don't have to take medication every day as you do. They don't know any other life."

"I don't care what anyone says. I shall *not* go to New Zealand. I have money in my pig bank. We can live on that."

"We can't do it, Elaine. You would be unhappy in the barrio. You wouldn't even know how to wash your clothes without a machine, or how to cook, or clean a house. You've never even made your own bed."

"You told me that barrio people don't use beds. We can sleep on straw mats just like they do, so I won't have to make a bed. I shan't mind sleeping on a straw mat."

He shook his head. "Elaine, the only place in Mexico City that's safe for me is a house like this. It would be a matter of time until the *chota* got their hooks into me and Micaela both."

"Acapulco! That's where we'll go! Last time I was in Acapulco, Mum and Dad saw a sign advertising 'fully furnished apartments.' We went in to look at them, thinking we'd take an apartment for the week rather than a hotel room, and I remember that they had everything we'd need, even silverware and plates, and there's a maid who cleans up every day, who makes beds and..."

Riki interrupted her with a laugh of sarcasm. "Acapulco? If we don't have enough money to live in the barrio, how could we think about Acapulco? How much money do you have in the pig bank? Probably not enough to even get us there, much less rent an apartment with maid service. Besides, where would we get the money to buy your medication?"

She shook her head, her lower lip jutted out defiantly. "No matter. I simply refuse to leave you. I love you Riki. I don't want to live without you."

"I love you too, Elaine. But we must be sensible. I'm not going to discuss this anymore."

She pleaded, argued and cajoled, but he resolutely shook his head and refused to answer. Finally, she said:

"Sneak me out of the house again, Riki. Tonight. And don't protest, because we don't need to care anymore. Let 'em catch us. They're going to fire you anyway, you and Micaela. I heard Mum telling Papa to make arrangements for your severance pay."

When he hesitated, she said, "I have enough money for us to have dinner at someplace elegant. Take me to a nice restaurant so we can plan our future."

Her parents were mildly concerned when Elaine refused to eat anything at dinner that evening. "I just don't feel like eating tonight," she said. She excused herself from the table, saying, "If you don't mind, I think I'll retire early. I have some studying I'd like to do." As soon as it grew dark, Elaine climbed up the ladder. Riki waited on the roof. They eased their way down the spiral stairs as quietly as they could. The pole rattled and swayed some, but the noise didn't rouse suspicions. They walked to Insurgentes, this time somberly, knowing it might be their last time together out of the Tarkington house.

Elaine flagged a cab, saying, "Tonight, no buses. I have enough for a taxi."

Riki told the driver to take them to the Torre Latinamericano. Once an elegant nightclub-restaurant on top of the tallest building in the city, it was now a bit shabby at the edges, but to Elaine and Riki, it was the height of elegance. Riki had peeked inside the restaurant about two years ago, when he and Comanche were looking for tourists to hustle, but they had been chased away by a burly waiter. Tonight, with his best clothes on and a young blonde lady on his arm, the story was different. He couldn't suppress a satisfied grin as he waited to be seated by a waiter in black formal wear.

"Good evening, señores. A table by the window?"

A million or more lights twinkled below, and the two of them stared around them in fascination. Elaine squeezed Riki's hand and said, "Just think, Riki—we could be living down there, somewhere in our own little apartment. One of those lights could be ours. I can hardly wait."

He sighed wearily. "Money? What can we do for money? I can't go back to stealing wallets or making drug deals and end up in jail again. If the police find me, they'll work on me until they get to Micaela. I have to protect her even if I didn't care about myself."

"You worry too much. Something will turn up and things will work out. You know, I just hope we can get an apartment with a large balcony. Someplace where I can lay out and get a good suntan. I've never had one, you know, because Mum thought it was dangerous. It was torture when we went to Acapulco, having to always stay in the shade while everyone else cavorted in the surf and sunshine. I only wish I had found my courage years ago."

She suddenly fell quiet and a fragment of a smile played at her lips. "There's no question about it, Riki, we must go to Acapulco. They'd never think about looking for us there."

Riki shook his head and smiled at her foolishness.

She said, "You'll love it there! The evenings are so warm that you never have to wear a sweater like you do here in Mexico City. The beaches are so soft, and the water so blue it makes your heart glad, and the..."

"Acapulco is a long way, isn't it?"

"No. Papa drives it in less than six hours. And I know there are a thousand buses going there every day, because Papa always complains about how they hog all of the road."

A sly expression came over her face. "You know, we could

324

take a bus to Acapulco tonight! I have enough money." She dumped her purse out on the table and started counting. "Look... there is plenty enough pesos to get us to Acapulco. And, if there isn't, we'll figure something out. Maybe we could steal some wallets or something."

Riki smiled at her and wished they could really go to Acapulco, but after looking at the menu he realized that the money both of them had together would barely cover their dinner tonight. No, there had to be some other way. They spent the rest of the evening arguing. In the end, Riki had convinced her that there had to be some other plan.

"But I am not going to leave you here in Mexico and go back to that dreadful New Zealand. I am most certainly not! I shall tell my parents that in the morning."

While Riki and Elaine sipped at their drinks and argued about their future, an obviously drunk man with a good-looking brunette dressed in body-clinging satin entered the room. With the woman clinging to his arm, the couple made their way across the restaurant to sit at the only empty table, the one next to Riki and Elaine. While he was trying to pull a chair out for his girlfriend, the man stepped back and came down on Riki's foot with his full weight.

Riki flinched and an involuntary cry of pain came from his mouth as he pushed the man away. The woman looked at her date with undisguised disgust.

"You clumsy jackass," she said cuttingly. "You can't even sit at a table without causing a scene."

The man waved his hand at Riki apologetically. His voice was slurred as he said, "Sorry *jefe*. Must be the altitude up here." He grinned and managed to pull his chair close to his girlfriend and sat down. Riki shrugged and went back to his conversation with Elaine. He didn't hear the conversation at the next table.

The man reached over to take the brunette's hand in his, but she pulled away. "Enrique, I am at my rope's end with you," she said testily. "Since you lost your job with that rich Gringo you've not spent a sober day. You aren't earning money, just emptying cash from your bank account. You're throwing pesos like they were cow pies. I think we had better call this thing off."

"Not my fault, *mi amor*. The fault is with that dirty thief who made a fool of me. You will be making a big mistake if you leave me now. I'm getting closer every day to finding my quarry. And, when I do, I will be vindicated. That fat-headed Gringo will beg me to take that job in California. We will have money coming out our asses."

"Keep your voice down if you're going to talk dirty!"

He lowered his voice to a hoarse whisper.

"Sorry, *mi amor*, but it's the truth. Barron will love me when I show him the grave of his long-lost son. I will get the job."

"Don't make me laugh! You don't know where the kid is buried. I know that as well as you do."

Enrique Morales smiled slyly. "But I do know where there is a grave of a little boy, the same age as the little bastard, and buried about the same time. Who's to prove that it isn't the right grave?"

"Who? Well, how about the thief? He has the jewelry and he knows what happened to the kid. When the cops grab him, he will tell everything."

Morales wagged his finger in her face. "Not if I find him first! I find him, get the jewelry, and then," he pointed his finger at his forehead, "Pum!"

The girlfriend shook her head skeptically. "The way you are drinking, I don't think you could find him if he sat in your lap."

Just then a waiter arrived with a tray of drinks. He placed one in front of the brunette and then one in front of Enrique Morales. Morales reached for his, but his knuckles clipped it and sent it spilling across the table and into the woman's dress.

She stood up, a look of outrage on her face. She opened her mouth as if to scream, but she quickly regained her composure. She wadded a napkin and brushed the front of her dress and said, slowly and deliberately, "Let's go Enrique. Let's go right now!"

Morales wiped his hand across his brow in agony and pushed his chair back to get up. When he was almost on his feet, he stumbled backwards. He staggered against Riki, ending up in Riki's lap. With Riki's shove to help him, Enrique Morales regained his feet. He mumbled an apology as he staggered after his girlfriend.

She grabbed Enrique by the coat lapels, stared at him for a second, then she spit in his face and began running for the exit.

Morales looked after her with dismay. Then he reached into his pocket and pulled out what he intended to be a ten-peso note. He motioned to the waiter and said, "Give these kids anything they want to drink." He dropped the money on the table and hurried after his girlfriend.

It was a thousand-peso note.

Elaine giggled at Riki's astonishment as he fingered the money. He straightened his clothes and shrugged, then he laughed, too. The waiter bowed and waited for their drink order. "What will you have?"

Elaine said, "Nothing right now. We need this money to get to Acapulco." She tucked the thousand pesos into her breast pocket.

The showdown came that evening, as they attempted to sneak Elaine back into her room. Riki climbed the stairs first and leaned over to steady the pole while Elaine twisted around the spiral. She had difficulty climbing. The two drinks before dinner, plus sharing a carafe of wine with dinner were having their effect. Turning around and around to climb the stairs kept her head spinning.

She was giggling when she reached the roof. Riki covered her mouth with his hand to keep her quiet. They tip-toed across the roof, being careful not to wake Micaela. Elaine twisted her body about in order to place a foot on the ladder and almost fell sideways to the cement below. Riki caught her, but the ladder went clattering along the roof edge stopping against the corner with a loud clunk.

A light snapped on in Mr. Tarkington's bedroom. Mrs. Tarkington's light followed.

"Herbert! There's a burglar on the roof!"

Riki scrambled to get to the ladder. He grabbed it and pulled it upright. "Hurry! Get inside your room before they get here." He sank to his knees and braced the ladder firmly.

Elaine nodded dutifully and started to get on the ladder once more. When she was standing on the rungs she giggled and leaned over to kiss Riki. "Looks like you will have to sleep up here tonight. A pity. I was hoping you could sleep in my room and we could..."

"Hurry! This is serious!"

She kissed him again and started down the ladder.

The sound of footsteps and Mrs. Tarkington's hysterical voice came from below. "Someone's breaking into Elaine's room. It must be a rapist! Oh, Herbert, I *told* you Mexico would be a terrible place for our little baby."

Elaine tried to hurry, but she missed the next ladder rung and almost fell. She made another try and found her footing. But she was too late. Mr. Tarkington heaved his considerable weight against Elaine's door and the latch gave way with a snapping sound. He stepped into the room. He gripped a blue-steel automatic in his right hand, a flashlight in the other. He reached over to turn on the lamp, bathing the room with soft light.

Mrs. Tarkington huddled behind her husband, her hand covering her mouth in fearful anticipation. "Oh, my God... She's not in her bed, Herbert!"

His reply was a grunt and a firmer grip on the pistol. He nodded toward the open bathroom door. A grim noise came from his throat as fear and anger clutched at his stomach. He moved toward the bathroom. He felt inside for the light switch. Through the patio door, he saw a movement and he brought the pistol up and took aim.

But Mrs. Tarkington grabbed at his arm and screamed, "Don't shoot, it's Elaine!" She clutched the satin bathrobe about her throat and ran toward the door. Her husband looked on in astonishment.

"Elaine! What the devil are you doing on that ladder?"

She was standing on the middle part of the ladder, her foot feeling for the next rung below. Slowly, her head turned around to face her parents. Her voice was meek with guilt. "Nothing. I wasn't doing anything."

Mrs. Tarkington began to whimper. "She was *running away!* Herbert! Our little baby was trying to run away from home!" Her body shook with noisy sobs and she pressed her hands against her cheeks in horror.

"Oh Elaine, baby. Where were you going? Why were you leaving us?"

When Elaine stepped down, she found herself smothered in her mother's arms, the wetness of her mother's tears cold and uncomfortable against her face. Had Mrs. Tarkington not finished off half a bottle of scotch that evening she might have noticed a strong odor of alcohol about her daughter. She said, "Where were you going, sweetheart?"

Elaine took a few moments to summon the courage to speak. Finally, she said, "I'm not going to New Zealand, Mum. I've made up my mind about that, for fair. Not unless you take Micaela and Riki with us."

Mrs. Tarkington stepped away and gave a short squeak of horror, as if she had suddenly come upon a mouse in the pantry. She started to say something. Her mouth opened and closed, but no sound came out.

Mr. Tarkington said, "Now, now, Elaine. Go back to bed, and we'll talk about this in the morning, dear." He slipped the pistol into his dressing jacket and scratched his head while his wife sobbed hysterically and fussed over her daughter. He knew now that something would have to be done about Elaine.

He considered himself fortunate to have apprehended Elaine just in time, before she had actually climbed the ladder and gotten into who knows how much trouble. Where the deuce could she have been going at this time of night? Very puzzling. Without her eyeglasses, too.

Later, after they had tucked Elaine into bed, he and his wife warmed up the coffee and began a long conversation, the most serious they'd had in years.

She said, "Well, Herbert, I've seen this coming on for some time. I get the feeling that we are losing our little girl. Surely, you've noticed the way she wears her hair, that horrid makeup she insists on painting on her face. She has become quite headstrong. We must handle this diplomatically if we don't want to lose her completely."

"Surely you can't be suggesting we give in? That we take that gardener—Riki or whatever the deuce his name is—take him with us to New Zealand? You know as well as I, Elaine is doing this just to annoy us."

"Worse than annoy us, Herbert. She thinks she is in love with him. I can tell about such things. I saw it in her eyes. I told you from the beginning it was a mistake to allow that animal to stay here. Can you imagine the absurdity of it all? A Tarkington, in love with a Mexican gardener?"

"Well, it will wear off once we get her home to New Zealand. What shall we do in the meantime? She just might run off, you know. She almost did tonight. If we hadn't caught her just in time, Lord knows where she might have gone."

"She's never defied us before. Certainly not like that. I'm worried."

Mrs. Tarkington furrowed her brow in thought and didn't answer for a while. They both weighed the alternatives, balancing one against the other, seeking how best to keep Elaine their exclusive property. They wanted her to always remain the sweet little invalid they adored—when they had the time to spare, that is. They both arrived at the solution at the same time, but Mr. Tarkington spoke first.

"Yes, we give in. We agree to take Micaela and her son with us, just as Elaine suggests. Elaine, Micaela and you will fly to New Zealand and get settled in the Wellington house while I wind things down here. The gardener will stay with me and help close up this place. Then..."

His wife interrupted, as she often did, by finishing the thought. "It would be little problem to find cause to fire him, just before your plane was to depart, don't you see? I should rather enjoy taking Micaela with us, though. She is a jewel of a housekeeper."

Mr. Tarkington tugged at his moustache ends and made a noise like a walrus clearing his throat. "Yes, I do believe we've got it, Martha. I believe we've found the solution."

It didn't work out exactly the way they'd planned. Elaine, once she experienced the power of manipulating her parents, decided to press her luck. Actually, she distrusted them. She insisted on staying in Mexico with her father until he was ready to leave. "You go on ahead, Mum, and take Micaela with you," she said firmly. "I'll come along with Papa and Riki."

The Tarkingtons had another long discussion before this new problem was skirted. Mr. Tarkington figured out the solution: "Of course, one doesn't buy first class tickets for a gardener. He must fly tourist class. First class passengers board first. But, instead of an aeroplane ticket, I'll give him some money *not* to go. Money will buy anything in Mexico. Elaine won't know he's not aboard until it's too late."

"But if he won't accept the money?"

"No matter. I'll simply give him an envelope marked 'ticket.' Inside, he will find an explanatory note and some money. I'll tell Elaine once we're aloft."

Mrs. Tarkington nodded approval. "Elaine will be angry for a while, of course. But in the long run, she will get over that. Some day she will be very thankful. Can you imagine Elaine Tarkington as the fiancé of a Mexican gardener? She would be the laughingstock of Wellington society, don't you agree?"

Micaela floated about like a swallow as she darted around her room, making preparations to leave. She was deliriously happy and frightened at the same time.

"They say it takes more than a day to go there," she said breathlessly. "I wonder what an airplane looks like inside. Do you think they're safe, Riki?" Every time she heard a plane flying overhead, she ran outside and looked up, shading her eyes to get a better view. "Will our airplane look like that?"

Mrs. Tarkington insisted that Micaela take only what could be carried in a small valise, "We must be careful about overweighing on the plane. And we must be careful not to bring anything that would slow us down in customs. We'll buy you new things when we arrive."

Micaela placed a few personal belongings into the imitation leather valise that Mrs. Tarkington bought her. She considered taking the leather suitcase that had belonged to Diana Cranston but decided against it. If customs inspected the luggage, they would certainly become suspicious at a maid having so much jewelry.

She worried about this until Riki found the solution.

"When I help Mr. Tarkington pack the household goods, I'll place the jewel box in my suitcase. If anyone in customs finds it, he'll believe it belongs to the Tarkingtons. Valuables wouldn't be unusual. Then when we unpack in New Zealand, we can retrieve the jewel box."

Although outwardly cool, Riki felt almost as excited as Micaela about the new life they were about to enter. And the thought of going with Elaine seemed too good to be true.

During the last days before her mother was scheduled to leave, Elaine satisfied her parents by playing the role of a weak invalid. She did everything her parents asked. She stayed away from Riki and tried not to look at him when her parents were around. This smoothed things over considerably, giving the

Tarkingtons the feeling that all would be well. Still, they kept their eyes on Riki.

Mrs. Tarkington said, "Watch him Herbert. I don't trust him. All of these Mexicans are alike—oversexed, you know. You never know what he might try. My God, but I wish we could have convinced her to go with me."

"Don't worry m'love. The minute you are gone, I shall devote my life to making sure this comes off all right. Not to worry at all." The weight of the blue-steel pistol made his coat sag somewhat. He assured himself that he would not hesitate to use it if necessary.

Finally, the day of departure came. Riki wasn't allowed to go to the airport to see Micaela off; their goodbyes took place in the maid's room on the roof. Micaela hugged him tightly and wept loudly.

"I'm afraid to fly," she confided. "The Saints didn't mean for us to go up into the air like *zopilotes*."

"It's all right. It must be safe, or Mrs. Tarkington wouldn't be flying." The truth was that he was fearful too, but couldn't bring himself to say so. He couldn't understand how an airplane could possibly hold all of those people and still be able to get off the ground.

"Promise me one thing, Riki. If something happens to me, see to it that the jewelry in that suitcase is given to its real owner. Otherwise, don't touch it. Promise me that."

"Where did you get it? Who does it belong to?"

She squeezed him again and didn't reply for a long while. Finally, she said, "I don't know precisely who it belongs to."

"Did you steal it?"

"Not exactly. Well, in a way, I did steal something, but not the jewelry. I should have destroyed the jewelry years ago. But I was afraid that someday the Saints would demand that I return it. I kept it safe for that day, except for that one time when you sold a piece and the three pieces I used to get you out of jail."

"If you didn't steal it, then tell me how you got it."

She shook her head firmly. "I can't tell you that. Not ever. Just promise you will never sell any of the jewelry. That you will try to find the real owner only if I die."

"What's wrong with selling it?"

"The jewelry has a curse on it. The first time we sold a piece, I almost lost you. The second time, even worse. If you sell any more before I am dead, something terrible will happen to me. Promise me you will do as I ask. Don't let the Gods punish us."

He hugged her tightly. "I promise."

Their farewell was abruptly broken by Mrs. Tarkington shouting for Micaela and ordering Riki to load the luggage in the car. He avoided looking at Elaine while he worked. Once he caught a glimpse from the corner of his eye and felt a wave of desire flood through his body like electricity. He wondered if he dared put the ladder back into the patio well. But he knew this would be dangerous. Mr. Tarkington was staring at him and fingering something in his coat pocket. Riki guessed it was a pistol.

Riki was right about the pistol. Mr. Tarkington's suspicions had grown stronger as the day for departure came closer. He saw the sideways glance Riki gave Elaine and the way the boy quickly averted his gaze and tried to pretend nothing was wrong.

That sixth sense that fathers have about a daughter's safety began buzzing through Herbert Tarkington's mind. He was convinced that the boy held nothing but pure lust for Elaine. Raw animal lust. Being innocent and weak, she would not know how to fight off the gardener's advances. He fingered the pistol and felt his trigger finger grow tense.

Mr. Tarkington slept uneasily that evening. Elaine retired early, saying she was feeling weak. He tried to read as he sipped at a drink. He lost interest in the book and made his way to bed before eleven. He got out of bed once to check the doors and windows to make sure neither Riki nor anyone else could creep into the house during the night. When he did drift off to sleep, he dreamed of Elaine being chased by the gardener, screaming for help. In the dream, Mr. Tarkington couldn't move or do anything to help. He forced himself to wake up, only to fall asleep and back into the same dream.

Suddenly a strange noise interrupted his sleep. A real noise. He sat up in bed, more asleep than awake. It sounded like a scraping noise coming from the roof, as if someone were moving about up there. He listened intently but heard nothing further. He decided that it was part of a dream. He lay back in bed and tried to regain his slumber. The image of his daughter being raped kept him restless. After half an hour he gave up trying to sleep.

He threw the covers off the bed and decided to take one more tour around the house and make sure no one could slip in. He remembered latching the garage door and the front door. But how about the kitchen door? Might as well check and maybe catch some sleep.

He slipped the pistol into his pajama pocket, flicked on the flashlight and plodded down the hall. He stopped abruptly when he heard sounds. He stopped and listened keenly. The noise was soft and muffled, coming from the other end of the hall, from the direction of Elaine's room.

His heart jumped a couple of beats. His hand clutched the pistol. Slowly and resolutely, he stalked toward her room, feet trembling with each step. He pulled the pistol from his pocket. It wavered almost uncontrollably as he tried to steady his nerves.

The long hallway seemed dark and eerie. He flashed the light toward Elaine's room, and then he saw the first hint of disaster. From beneath Elaine's door, a light sent a yellow band across the marble floor. She was awake at this hour!

As he drew closer, he clearly heard sounds coming from the

room. He placed his ear against the paneled door. His heartbeat faster and faster when he realized what the sounds were.

There was no question but it was Elaine's voice, but she wasn't talking, she was moaning! A rhythmic moan, half-whine issued from the room. A moan of pain, of agony.

My God in heaven! She's being raped!

He grabbed the doorknob, but the door was tightly latched. Mr. Tarkington dropped to his knees and what he saw through the keyhole was to stay with him for the rest of his life. Elaine lay on the bed, stark naked, the stuffed giraffe under her hips and her legs wide apart. A rapist (from this angle he couldn't be sure, but he knew it was the gardener) was on top of her, his hips thrusting hard as his body slammed against Elaine's.

With each thrust, she quivered in pain and she let forth a small cry of agony. Her hands clawed at the back of her assailant, obviously trying to escape. In her weakened condition, Elaine's struggle was faint, her hands brushing across the rapist's back instead of the kind of fight Mrs. Tarkington would have presented in a similar circumstance.

Seeing his daughter being raped was the worst nightmare Mr. Tarkington could possibly have. He leaped to his feet and twisted at the door handle. "Elaine! I'll save you dear," he shouted. The door held firm against the inside latch. As he had done once before, he threw his body against the door. This time it held, although it did give way some. The new latch that Elaine had installed was much stronger than the previous one.

He backed up for another lunge. He could hear scrambling taking place in the room. He knew he had to break the door this time or the rapist would get away. He rushed at the door with the desperation that only a loving father could have when saving his only child from degradation and torture. This time the door broke loose and slammed back against the wall. There was no mistaking who the rapist was now.

Riki was frantically pulling his pants up as he ran through the bathroom, into the sun patio. He started to scramble up the ladder, clutching his pants in one hand, a ladder rung in the other.

A deafening explosion filled the room, and chips of cement flew dangerously about the patio well, one stinging Riki on the cheek. Riki's pants dropped to his knees. He snatched them up with his left hand and started clambering desperately up the ladder again. The next bullet went wild and crashed through both bathroom windows.

Riki slipped and almost fell to the floor, but quickly resumed his one-handed climb. The third bullet hit the cement beside Riki's head and ricocheted about the lightwell like a swarm of angry hornets.

Elaine screamed and clawed at her father's arm just as he was taking a final, deadly aim at the back of Riki's head. Had she not, it would have been the finish for Riki.

Riki cleared the ladder and managed to hook the top button of his pants as he ran across the roof toward the circular staircase. He knew he had to get to the ground level before Mr. Tarkington could get outside, or he would be like a slow target in a shooting gallery.

As he spun around the spiral staircase, he could hear shouting and screaming coming from inside the house. For an instant, he had an urge to go inside and confront Mr. Tarkington and to take Elaine with him. Then he remembered the sickening sounds of bullets hitting cement, and he had a brief premonition about how bullets might feel chewing through his body, and he chose to spend the night on the streets instead.

Barefoot and shirtless, he headed for the barrio where he had friends to hide him until Mr. Tarkington cooled off. If he ever cooled off.

Chapter Twenty-Five

Herbert Tarkington averted his eyes as he helped his daughter pull a nightgown over her head to cover her naked, ravaged body. He gently patted her head as he'd done often when she was a little girl and needed a strong, brave father. "Don't cry. It's all over now. He'll never come back here, I can assure you. You're safe now."

"But Poppa — You don't understand."

"I do understand. You've been through a lot, my child. I know you'll have a difficult time getting over this nightmare. But believe me, time will heal. Someday you will forget this night as if it never happened."

"But Poppa, I *love* Riki! Don't you see?"

"Yes, of course I see. And that makes it all the worse, doesn't it? His taking advantage of your love. You trusted that animal, thought you actually loved him, and then he turned on you like a mad dog. If only you had listened to Martha and me when we cautioned you. After all is said and done, we grownups do know something about human nature."

"But Poppa..."

"Lay down and rest, dear. I'll call the doctor and have him come here immediately." He locked the door to the sun deck, a futile gesture with its broken window, and as he was leaving the room he said, "Don't worry about him coming back. After our little tete a tete, that depraved monster will think twice about coming near you again. To make sure, you're taking the next plane for New Zealand."

"Please, Poppa, listen to me! He wasn't..." But it was too late. Mr. Tarkington was on the hall telephone anxiously dialing the family doctor. Then he called a security service to have a guard placed on the house. Next, he called New Zealand.

"Martha? Something terrible happened here. I can't tell you over the telephone. But I demand that you send that Mexican woman — Michelina or whatever her name is — send her packing immediately. Do you hear? *Immediately!*"

Elaine kicked the stuffed giraffe from the bed and flopped down angrily. She wiped the tears from her eyes and started making plans.

Riki encountered no friends to take him in, so he slept on a bench in the Alameda park. Even though he covered his naked chest with layers of newspaper, he shivered most of the night. He wished he'd had time to gather up his shoes and socks. The next morning, he searched his pockets and found barely enough pesos to buy coffee and a sugared cinnamon roll at a street stand near Comanche's place.

The morning chill turned his breath into steam as he waited for someone he knew to come along. Anyone. His feet felt as if they were going to freeze. Passersby stared at the half-dressed *pelado* huddled by the food stall.

Finally, Comanche appeared in the doorway of his house. He stretched and yawned as he prepared to head for his bicycle shop. He shook with surprise when he saw Riki. "What's happening, man? What are you dressed like that? No shirt? Where's your shoes?"

"I need a place to stay. And money. Can you help me?"

Comanche motioned for Riki to follow him back into the building. "You need clothes," he said as he took a key from his keyring. "You know the apartment. Help yourself. But money? Well, I don't have a whole lot — I'm getting married soon, you know. But sure, I have a little for my best friend. What happened to your job with those rich guys? And your rich girlfriend?"

When Riki explained what had happened, Comanche whistled through his teeth in dismay. "You know the old man is going to call the law, don't you? He'll never believe you weren't raping her. This is bad business. Even worse, when your name gets on the police list again, Morales will pick up on it immediately and he will figure out where you've been hiding."

"I don't know what to think. I'll try and call Elaine when her father's not there and find out how things stand."

"I wouldn't do that if I were you, Papagayo. She's going back to her country anyway. So, don't give the old buzzard a chance to turn you over to the police. It would be your word against his. And women have a way of claiming rape in order to keep sin off their good name."

"Elaine wouldn't do that. We love each other."

"Maybe and maybe not. They might not believe her even if she tells the truth. Understand, some women fear their fathers so much, they'll say anything to keep from getting the old man angry. That's happened to guys I know. They have a good thing going, but the first time the girl's brother finds out, she denies that she wanted to do it, that it wasn't her idea. Next thing you know the guy's got lumps on his face and he's watching over his shoulder for the next few months."

Before Comanche left for his repair shop, he pressed a fold of pesos into Riki's hand. "Better not hang around too long, Riki. Cops are everywhere."

Riki tried to call Elaine twice, but both times Mr. Tarkington answered; he hung up quickly. The day passed very slowly.

In the afternoon he walked to Tarkington's neighborhood and carefully peered around the corner at the house. He couldn't tell if Mr. Tarkington was home or not and didn't have the courage to come any closer. He would have liked to have at least gotten his things from the maid's room on the roof. The memory of the explosions last night deterred him from going any nearer.

Then he saw a movement on the roof of the Tarkington place. A man in a rumpled khaki uniform walked around the corner of the laundry room. He had the peaked cap of a paid watchman and carried a pistol in a belt holster. Tarkington had hired a guard! Riki pulled back so he couldn't be seen. He hurried away from the neighborhood. He would have to forget about his clothes. At least Micaela's box of jewelry would be safely delivered to her in New Zealand, so Riki only had to lament the loss of his few clothes. They could be replaced, but his skin could not.

For three days after he left the Tarkington household, Riki wandered aimlessly about the barrios. He'd looked half-heartedly for a job but found nothing. He had to be careful not to be recognized, and found it wearying to always be looking over his shoulder for police. Once, he met a petty thief named Marcario Galán, who wanted Riki to help him set up a tourist.

"You can do it better than anybody," Marcario insisted, "with that English you speak, they all trust you."

Riki refused. The memory of jail lingered on like the odor of something dead in the gutter. Marcario slipped him some pesos anyway, for old times sake, so Riki had enough to eat on that day and this next. But the money was gone now, and he was hungry. He wondered how hungry he would have to become before he would risk jail. After three days in the same clothes, and a borrowed pair of shoes, he was beginning to look like a street character. A passing squad car slowed as the uniformed driver cast a suspicious eye in his direction. He moved on.

On the morning of the fourth day, he was sitting on a bus stop bench on the corner of Avenida Uruguay and Isabel la Católica when he suddenly heard Elaine's voice calling to him. At first he thought he might be daydreaming, but then he heard it again.

341

"Riki! I've been looking all over for you. Where have you been?" She called from the window of a bus passing on the other side of the street. "Come help me with my luggage. I'm getting off at the next stop."

He ran after the bus like a dog chasing a car. It finally pulled to a halt two blocks away. He was panting heavily and sweat ran down the inside of his arms. Elaine stood in the door, pulling at two large suitcases. The bus driver shouted at her to hurry.

"Come help," she called. The bus driver cursed her for holding him there.

Riki pushed her aside and grabbed a suitcase in each hand. As soon as he stepped back to the pavement the bus lurched forward. He dropped the luggage and gave the bus driver the finger as well as a few well-selected words reflecting on the sexual habits of the bus driver's mother and grandmother. Elaine grabbed him and held him tightly, placing kisses wherever she could.

"What are you doing here?" he asked, although he didn't have to ask. Obviously, she had run away from home. "How did you find me?"

"I just rode buses around the places you took me. I knew I'd find you in one of the barrios." She kissed him on the nose. "We're going to Acapulco, Riki! Well, aren't you glad to see me? Kiss me." A crowd of passersby stood gawking and snickering at the Gringa girl kissing the grimy street bum.

"Come on. We can't stay here." He picked up the luggage and began walking, to where he had no idea. He wanted to find a place less conspicuous.

"I have money, Riki, so we needn't worry. We'll get a hotel for tonight and we'll go to Acapulco tomorrow." She took his arm and looked at him adoringly. "Oh, but I love you!"

"What about your father? Does he know you're gone?"

"Forget about Poppa. He doesn't listen to me. I might as well talk to a cantaloupe. He's convinced that you raped me, and he's hired a detective to find you. I don't think it's a good idea to stay around Mexico City. If I found you that easy, a good detective can find you even quicker."

"Oh, man—why couldn't we have let things alone? Now your father's going to be looking for the *both* of us. Probably with that gun."

He turned the corner to take a side street to lessen the chance of being seen and then put down the heavy luggage for a rest. "How much money do you have?"

"Here. See for yourself. I took it from Daddy's wallet last night when he was asleep. Also, the thousand-peso banknote from our dinner date."

She handed Riki her purse and urged him to count the fold of banknotes.

He sighed. "There's not enough to live in Acapulco for more than a month or so."

"That's okay. We'll work it out. Poppa wanted to put me on an airplane to New Zealand tomorrow, and I absolutely refuse to go. Not unless you can go with me."

"He'll never take me to New Zealand now. You should realize that."

"That's why we have to go to Acapulco. Oh yes, I forgot to tell you— Mum sent Micaela packing, back to Mexico. She arrived at our house this morning, weeping and looking for you. But Poppa sent her away as if he were chasing away a stray cat."

Riki slapped his hand against his forehead. "Micaela is back? Where did she go?"

"I don't know. I gave her some money, but she was crying so hard I couldn't understand a word she said."

Suddenly he remembered the jewelry. "Did your father ship those crates I packed in the dining room? There's something in one crate that belongs to me. Something valuable."

"The crates go tomorrow morning. What is it?"

"A box, a music box. Oh, never mind. Come on, let's get off the street."

Herbert Tarkington hadn't gone to the police when his daughter had been raped. Instead, he hired Alberto Magaña, a "security specialist" to not only protect Elaine for the rest of her stay, but also to find the rapist and to deal with him harshly.

Señor Magaña posted a guard on the roof of the Tarkington house while he himself undertook the search for the young gardener. The precise method of 'dealing harshly' with the rapist hadn't been discussed, but Magaña assumed this meant anything just short of death.

In this type of punishment, señor Magaña was an expert, a connoisseur in fact. His sexual cravings could only be satisfied by the screams of a victim and the sight of dripping blood. For this, he had already served one short jail term and a longer prison term. Mr. Tarkington didn't know of his new employee's propensity for violence, of course, but had he known he probably would have hired him anyway, given his agitated state of mind. His daughter had been raped and justice must be done. Without undue publicity or police involvement, of course.

But now, things were different. This was *kidnapping!* Mr. Tarkington was almost hysterical when he called at the police station to report his daughter's kidnapping. The police lieutenant who investigated the crime tried to get Mr. Tarkington to slow down and speak clearly, for the lieutenant's English was not of the highest caliber.

"Let us go through these things one more time," the lieutenant said very slowly and precisely, hoping to set an example for the excited New Zealander. "You say burglar, he take money from your wallet, and then he kidnap your daughter. Correct?"

"First he raped her. I saw it with my own eyes."

"You *watch* this thing happen?"

"Yes. Through the keyhole."

"Keyhole? What is keyhole?"

Mr. Tarkington fumed in anger. "A hole in the door,

Goddammit!"

"Why you watch through hole in door? Why you not stop these things from happen?" The lieutenant was beginning to suspect that he was dealing with a sick mind. When Mr. Tarkington slowed down his incomprehensible diatribe, the lieutenant tried again. "Did kidnapper leave note? I think you call it the 'handsome' note?"

"*Ransom* note. No. He doesn't want money. He only wants to use my daughter for his own sexual abuse."

"You know who this burglar-kidnapper is then?"

"*Rapist*-burglar-kidnapper. Yes. His name is Riki something or other."

The lieutenant began writing on his report pad: *Riki Somtingeruder*. He could get the correct spelling later. Gringo names were very difficult for a man who barely passed English in the police Academy. Then he wrote: *no ransom note... Father appears to be a voyeur. Possible parental sexual abuse and probable runaway... Check to see if she took any clothes or personal belongings...*

When he finished writing, he looked at Mr. Tarkington lazily. He really couldn't get excited over this type of case. "Do you know where we find this, uh, Riki Somtingeruder?"

"No. That's why I called you. Here is a picture of the two of them. I found it hidden in the back of her drawer." He handed the policeman the picture that Elaine had taken on that first date.

"You found it where?"

"In her chest of drawers."

The lieutenant held up his hand to keep Tarkington quiet while he looked up the word *drawers* in his dictionary. He found *drawers*, and then gave Tarkington an odd look. He was going to ask why the man would be looking in his daughter's underwear, but decided he'd rather not hear about it. Then he looked up *chest*, and to his horror, found that *chest* means *chichis!* He shook his head gravely.

Tarkington said, "Look, I realize I am upset right now, but I will give anything to get my daughter back safe and sound. I'll pay $10,000 in New Zealand dollars, in cash, if you can just get her back safe and sound. Before my wife finds out what has happened."

The mention of money made the lieutenant's ears come to a point. He knew nothing of New Zealand dollars, but it sure sounded like a pile of money. Suddenly it didn't matter if the man was a pervert and voyeur.

The lieutenant nodded gravely. "I find her, you bet."

After the lieutenant finished his preliminary report, Mr. Tarkington called Alberto Magaña and repeated the reward offer to him. "It's kidnapping now. I want all stops pulled out. I want my daughter returned to me safe and sound. Ten thousand dollars to the one who brings her back safely."

On the other end of the line, señor Magaña smiled as he realized that he had been given a free hand to enjoy himself. A tickle of sexual juices made him shiver in delight.

The restaurant was crowded with people, but Riki still felt that he and Elaine were conspicuous. The newspapers were full of the kidnapping of the New Zealand girl. He kept looking over his shoulder, halfway expecting to see the police or the private detective. Comanche ordered another cup of coffee and nodded thanks to Elaine.

"Thank you for inviting me to dinner," he said as he smiled graciously at Elaine.

"Thank you for allowing us to share your apartment," she replied. "It won't be for long, though. Riki and I'll be leaving for Acapulco soon."

"From what I hear from the kids on the street, *la policía* are sniffing at all the corners looking for El Papagayo. They've figured out the 'Riki' everyone is looking for is El Papagayo and not someone named 'Somtingeruder'. Sooner you get out of the city, the better."

Riki shook his head glumly. Elaine patted his hand gently and smiled confidently. "With the money from Daddy's wallet,

346

we can hide out in Acapulco. And then, maybe we could rob a bank or something."

Comanche laughed and Riki managed a small smile. He couldn't stop worrying about the jewelry box that he'd packed in the suitcase. If he could sell the rest of the jewelry, that would solve everything. Yet how to get it out of the Tarkington house? From in front of the guard?

When he mentioned that it was important to break into the house to get his belongings, Elaine remarked, "What's so difficult about that? You are street criminals, aren't you? Or at least used to be." She opened her purse and took out a plastic pill box. "Oh, oh, I'm almost out of my prescription. I'd better get some more pills. You never know when a seizure could pop up."

Riki looked at her in concern. "Medicine? See what I mean? How do we get medicine for you? Where do we buy it?"

"We don't buy them, silly. I'll just give you the key to the house and you can get them from my bathroom cabinet. Daddy's not going to be there tonight. Walk in and pick up the pills. It'll be duck soup."

"Duck soup? You take duck soup pills?" Comanche looked puzzled.

Riki thought about the key for a moment. "But there's still a guard at your house. Gavilan told me he saw a *guardia* there this morning. I can't take the chance. Elaine, I don't know if you understand, but I am in serious trouble. I've already been in jail once, the *cárcel de primera instancia*, the jail of the first instance. If they arrest me again, for something serious, it means prison. With this rape, kidnapping, and robbery, that could mean twenty years in a cage."

"And for kidnapping," added Comanche, "you go to Lecumberri for twenty years. Think of that, twenty years!"

"But you've done nothing wrong. They can't prove anything on you."

"How can I prove I haven't? The system here is that they

don't prove you are guilty, you must prove you are *innocent*. So, if I break into your house, even though I have the key from you, who knows what else they might accuse me of."

Elaine thought a few moments, and then smiled happily. "I'll go myself. If someone can distract the guard, I'll sneak in the back way and get my pills. But we have to do it tonight, because tomorrow the movers are coming and will clean out the house."

Riki's mind began racing. This was the last chance to get the jewelry. If Elaine could just pick up the suitcase, then if Comanche could find someone to fence the jewelry, then maybe —

They planned for a long time. It seemed simple enough, having Elaine break into her own house. Yes, Comanche knew a fence who would buy jewelry at twenty percent of the value. No reason why it wouldn't work.

They waited until a little after midnight. Then they went into action.

The neighborhood was quiet. They checked to make sure the Tarkington's Cadillac was not in the garage. Comanche looked through the iron-barred garage door and signaled that it was indeed empty. Inside the house, the guard moved from room to room, turning on lamps as he entered, and then off as he moved to the next room.

Comanche and Riki boosted Elaine up to the top of the stone wall after first placing a piece of old carpet to keep her from being injured on the broken glass embedded there. When they heard her feet hit the ground on the other side, Riki went to the side gate and waited for her to unlock it. He swung it open quickly to avoid a squeaking of metal hinges.

"Okay," he whispered, "slip on back to the rear door and give Comanche time to do his part. When you hear the doorbell ring, go in, get the pills, then the blue suitcase. It's next to the smallest carton."

She nodded and suppressed an excited giggle as she tip-toed along the brick walk. Riki moved to a position in the shadows, halfway between the gate and the rear of the house.

Comanche's footsteps were deliberately loud as he walked to the entrance and up the two steps to the door. He coughed loudly and pressed the doorbell.

After a moment, the guard peeked through the narrow door window. "*Quién es?*"

Comanche replied in Spanish, "I have an important message for Mr. Tarkington."

"He's not here."

"Well, I must leave it for him. Open the door."

"I can't open the door. Against orders."

"Then how can I leave the message for him?" Comanche nervously glanced at his watch. He imagined that by this time, Elaine was entering the back door. He needed to stall for another few minutes.

The guard looked Comanche over cautiously, and finally he said, "Just slip the message under the door."

"I can't. It's not written. I'll have to borrow a pen and some paper to write it down. Then I can slip it under the door."

The guard frowned, and after a long hesitation, slipped back the bolt on the door. He handed him a ballpoint pen and a paper pad.

"Don't try anything *chistoso*, my friend, because I have a gun and I know how to use it."

Comanche stalled as long as possible. The guard was becoming agitated, but precious minutes were slipping away. Comanche took his time scribbling a nonsense note in what might look like English. "Hurry up! I got work to do!"

Comanche chewed on the end of the pen and pretended to concentrate. "I'm not very good at spelling, man. You don't want me to give Mr. Tarkington a stupid note, do you?"

The seven minutes were almost up. Comanche folded the note and ceremoniously handed it to the guard. He gained another half minute with apologies and fervent handshaking. The door slammed shut angrily, and he grinned as he went to the gate to meet his companions.

Riki heard Elaine's footsteps along the walk. He ran to meet her. "Did you get everything?" he whispered.

"No. I couldn't get in! The locks must have been changed. What do we do now?"

Riki leaned against the gate, engrossed in thought. Finally, he broke the silence, saying, "It looks as if I'll have to do it after all. I'll climb up on the roof, use the ladder and get into the house that way."

Comanche shrugged and said, "You know the chance you're taking?"

"It's the only way out unless we can talk Elaine into giving up."

"I will not. Not under any circumstances. Besides, you aren't doing anything wrong. I'll vouch for that; after all it's my house, too."

Riki shook his head in resignation. "That's not the way the law works here. But we have no choice."

He said to Comanche, "Give me two minutes, then ring the doorbell again and keep the guard in the front of the house as long as you can. Those spiral steps make noise." Then he was gone.

Climbing the circular stairs was tricky. Riki took each step as close to the center pole as possible to avoid a whipping and rattling of the stair unit. To his surprise, the ladder lay next to the lightwell, as if in invitation for any burglar to enter the house. So far it looked easy.

Gingerly, he eased the ladder into the well. Before he started down, he waited and listened closely for sounds of the guard. The broken windows hadn't been fixed yet, leaving a comfortable space to reach in and twist the doorknob open. The medicine cabinet sat over the sink just as Elaine had described it. He pulled it open slowly to avoid making a sudden noise.

He felt for the medicine bottle as Elaine had described, but to his dismay, the cabinet was empty. He could hear the guard's voice downstairs in angry conversation with Comanche, so he took a chance and flicked on a light. The bathroom was stripped of all of Elaine's things. He glanced into the bedroom and that was empty also. Elaine was going to have to do without her medicine.

He tiptoed down the staircase. The guard was still arguing with Comanche, so he hurried into the dining room where the boxes for shipment were stored. In the dim light he saw the suitcase, still sitting where he had left it. He picked it up and walked into the kitchen, gingerly placing his toes first on the tile floor so his heels couldn't make a telltale sound.

Just as he pulled back the bolt on the kitchen door, he heard Elaine scream.

He frantically twisted the other lock, one that required two hands to open it. Elaine screamed again and someone shouted something Riki didn't understand. A gunshot rang out, shattering the peaceful quiet of the neighborhood. Finally, the door swung open. Riki tightened his grip on the suitcase and began running down the brick path that led to the street.

Just as he reached the gate, a screeching of tires cut through the darkness. Riki stepped into the street to see a black Bentley careening around the corner. When the sound of the fleeing auto died away, he heard the sound of a soft moaning. It sounded very much like Comanche. Lights began sprouting in the windows of the neighborhood.

He put the suitcase in the shadow of the wall and walked softly toward the moaning noise.

Chapter Twenty-Six

Earlier, after Riki disappeared into the dark walkway alongside the house, Comanche kept a close eye on his wristwatch. Riki needed thirty seconds to reach the stairs at the back of the house. Then a full minute to negotiate the winding staircase without making undue noise.

Comanche glanced up at the roof. He could see nothing from this angle, just a wide expanse of tiled cement looming overhead. When the second hand completed the final sweep, he touched Elaine on the shoulder.

"Wait here," he whispered. "If you see a *guardia*, go to the back of the house and warn Riki so he won't come blundering out on the street."

Comanche ambled to the door. Although he walked with a sort of swagger, Elaine could tell he was nervous.

A black automobile, a Bentley, came rolling silently down the street. When she saw the headlights, she stepped back into the shadow of the building. She watched the car drift past the house, its motor idling with a soft purr.

The driver seemed to be a chubby-looking man wearing an old-fashioned homburg. From the way he perched forward in the driver's seat and peered over the steering wheel, he gave the impression of being rather short.

His head swiveled to study the house as the Bentley slipped past. Elaine tensed when she felt the man was looking at her. She realized that her nerves were ragged and she might be imagining things.

She felt a shiver of relief when the car disappeared around

the corner, headed toward Insurgentes. When she was certain the car was gone, she stepped back onto the sidewalk to watch Comanche.

Comanche was laying down a string of nonsense talk, Cantinflas style, while the guard wrinkled his face in an effort to understand. Basically, he was saying that he made a mistake on the note and wanted it back so he could write it correctly.

"I have to write that note over, man. Give it back to me."

"Get out of here!"

Comanche held his foot in the door so it couldn't be closed and kept up the rapid-fire dialogue. The guard's face flushed darkly with anger. When the guard fingered his gun holster, Elaine felt her heart jump a little. Comanche laughed and moved back slightly but managed to keep his foot in the door.

He made another joke which failed to make the guard laugh. When the pistol cleared its holster, Comanche mumbled soothing words. He glanced at his watch. The time was almost up. Obviously, he had gone his limit, so he reluctantly backed away.

The guard glared angrily for a moment before starting to close the door.

Elaine turned to scan the dark passageway, hoping to see Riki, her back to the street.

Suddenly, as if materializing from thin air, two hands grabbed her. One hand clamped over her mouth and nose. The other locked around her waist. She tried to scream. But air could not enter or leave her lungs.

Powerful arms held her body tightly against her attacker's. She wrenched back and forth, trying to pull free, attempting to twist around to see who was holding her. The grip tightened.

Her chest heaved frantically as her lungs fought for oxygen. Fear and anger gave way to panic. She couldn't breathe. A dull buzz started going off in her brain as a prelude to unconsciousness. The hands were strong, those of an expert man who had done this same thing before.

353

Her body thrashed in a violent, final demand for air. The effort loosened the hand over her mouth momentarily. Elaine's teeth managed to grasp a pinch of flesh between her teeth.

The man gasped in pain, then tightened his grip. Elaine summoned strength generated from the panic of being suffocated. She kicked and jerked her head violently and finally managed to pull free long enough to gasp a lungful of air, accompanied by a scream.

As the hand clawed to regain its grip, her teeth sunk into the soft part of the under-thumb. With eyes clenched, she clamped her jaws as tight as she could.

Comanche came running toward her as the attacker grunted in pain. The stranger released the arm circling Elaine's waist. Before she could twist free, he rapped her sharply on the side, just below the kidney. An excruciating flash of pain made her jaw muscles go slack. She felt dizzy, without the strength to scream again.

As Comanche approached, the man dropped Elaine to the ground. He shouted to the guard, "Hey Carlos, it's me, Alberto! Shoot this guy!"

Elaine managed to look up and stare at her attacker. She recognized him as Alberto Magaña, the man her father hired to investigate the "rape."

The shot from the guard's pistol startled Elaine. She saw Comanche dodging to one side and looking back at the guard with amazement. Then a second shot.

Comanche dropped to his knees, his face distorted in a grimace of agony. His hand clasped the back of his leg.

Magaña's man pulled Elaine to her feet and shoved her toward the waiting Bentley. The luxury car had slipped up so silently she hadn't realized it was there. She staggered toward the Bentley's open door.

The guard seized Elaine's arm and twisted it behind her back and shoved her against the car. Deftly, with not a wasted move, Alberto wrapped a band of masking tape around Elaine's wrists. The guard held her legs until tape could secure her ankles. Just as she opened her mouth to scream again, Alberto shoved his palm against her chin, forcing her mouth closed. The guard stripped another length of tape over her mouth.

Elaine felt ridiculously helpless. She couldn't move her hands or arms. She couldn't make any noise. The panic returned as she struggled to draw in enough air through her nostrils.

The guard grabbed her around the shoulder. Magaña lifted beneath her knees. Together, they tossed her into the Bentley's open rear door. She lay with her knees on the floor and her face on the front seat, positioned as if she were praying to some deity for release. Her shoulders ached and her wrists and hands grew numb.

The guard slammed the door closed after Alberto calmly climbed into the driver's seat. He adjusted his homburg tight on his forehead and placed the gearshift into drive. Tires squealed briefly as the Bentley lunged forward.

The guard walked over to where Comanche still lay kneeling on the sidewalk. He pointed the gun at Comanche's forehead.

"What were you trying to pull on me? You knew the girl was there all along, didn't you?"

Comanche looked up and saw Riki stepping from the shadows. To distract the guard, Comanche moaned, motioned to the guard and whispered softly.

"What did you say?" The guard leaned down to hear better. "I couldn't hear you."

Comanche spit with all the force he could muster. A glob of saliva landed on the guard's cheek. "I just said, screwing your mother makes you hard of hearing."

The guard's face turned pale with rage. He grasped his gun by its barrel, turning it into a wicked-looking club, and lifted it above his head. "I'll teach you a thing or two you bastard."

Before he could start the blow, Riki stepped behind him and twisted the gun from his hand.

Astonished, the guard turned around to see a fist flying for his nose. Riki punched him twice more before the man slumped to the ground.

"Where's Elaine? What happened to her?"

Comanche's voice sounded tired. "A man in a black car took her away. This guy shot me before I could do anything."

"Are you hurt bad?"

Despite the pain, Comanche managed to smile. "I was trying so hard to keep out of trouble, and now this."

The guard rolled over and tried to get up, but when he saw Riki's foot poised, he lay back and whimpered, "You hurt me. Why did you hurt me?"

"Who was that in the car?" Comanche demanded through teeth gritted in pain. "He knew you. He said he was 'Alberto'." In the distance came the whooping sound of a police siren.

Alberto Magaña's office was located in his home. A leather sofa occupied one side of the office, and a large desk with a French phone the other.

He dragged Elaine into the room, her feet dragging on the floor. A sharp pain flashed through her back when Magaña dumped her on the sofa. Her hands and feet had lost feeling, numb from lack of circulation.

Magaña dialed a number and as he waited for an answer, he smiled at his prisoner. She felt a wave of fear as the man licked his lips and fondled his crotch.

Then he spoke to the phone, saying, "I've found your daughter..." a pause, "Never mind where she is, when can you bring the money?" another pause, "When I get the money, I'll tell you where she is." He slammed the receiver into its cradle and glared angrily at Elaine. Then he stalked out of the room.

When Magaña returned, Elaine wasn't sure how long she had been laying there; it seemed like hours. Magaña paced about the room rubbing his hand and looking malevolently at Elaine.

"You didn't have to bite me, you bitch. I was only trying to save you from the kidnappers, doing just as your father asked. I ought to work you over but good." He paced the room a couple of times more. Then he turned and asked, "If I take the tape off, will you promise not to bite me?" She nodded. Anything to be able to move and breathe freely again.

He opened a desk drawer and took the pistol from his coat pocket and laid it into the drawer before closing it. Then he leaned over Elaine and jerked at a corner of the tape. The tape made a ripping noise and a searing pain. Elaine squirmed and squealed through her nose.

Alberto grinned as if pleasantly surprised at her reaction. The grin broadened when he jerked the tape a little more and Elaine quivered with pain.

He reached for her nose and pinched with his thumb and forefinger. Elaine panicked. She couldn't draw air in or push it out. Her eyes opened wide in horror and she twisted spasmodically until she broke free from his grasp. Magaña giggled, high-pitched and maniacal.

He reached for her nose again. She tossed her head and bobbed in a desperate attempt to avoid his hand. Eventually he held her nose in one hand and the back of her head with the other.

No matter how hard she shook her head, she couldn't get free. Her lungs heaved in a useless struggle to get air.

He released his grip just as she was losing consciousness. Magaña smiled at her as she labored to take in air through her constricted nose.

Then he shrugged, as if to say he was tired of the game and pulled at the tape again. This time it came half off. Elaine whimpered like a hurt animal. This brought a snickering laugh from Alberto. He grasped the tape firmly and yanked at it with a series of short pulls, each tearing at the skin. Elaine made a squealing noise with each pull. Alberto doubled over in laughter. A dribble of spit came from one corner of his mouth.

Elaine's look of fear further aroused Alberto Magaña. He rubbed a hand over his crotch — as he teasingly pulled at the tape.

When one corner of her mouth was free, she managed to mutter, "Stop that! Set me free and stop hurting me. You're going to be sorry when I tell my father."

Alberto Magaña thought about this for a moment and his face began to look human again. He thought of the $10,000 reward and decided that was far more important than having sex fun with this girl. Still, he had to fight inwardly, for control was very difficult for Alberto. Twice he had been in jail for losing control. The next time would be twenty years. He grabbed the tape again and pulled it free with one strong pull.

"There. I don't know what you're complaining about. It always hurts to take tape off. I'm sure your father will recognize that. And what kind of gratitude is it for you to bite the hand of the man who saves you from your kidnappers?" He pulled the ends of the plastic bindings and instantly her hands and feet were loose.

She rubbed her wrists, as she glared hatefully at Magaña. "I wasn't kidnapped by my friends. I was standing in the gateway of my own yard, and *you* kidnapped me. You tied me up and you hurt me."

"I had to. If I don't get you back, I don't get the $10,000 fee."

"You won't get anything. I'll tell my father how you mistreated me and I'll guarantee you that you won't get a penny."

She stood up and took an experimental step to see if the numbness in her feet would keep her from walking. "Now, take me back to my house. This minute."

Alberto thought this over for a few moments before making the decision. When she turned her back on him and started for the door, he knew he had to do something. He jumped at her and twisted her arm behind her back. She gasped, and he pushed her on the sofa.

"I'll have to tie you up again, you bitch. If I can't get the reward money I've earned, I'll take it out of your skin, and then ask for a ransom for myself. Consider yourself *really* kidnapped."

"You're hurting me!"

His answer was a giggle and a further twist on the arm. "Squeal. I love it when you squeal like a pig being stuck with a dull knife. Squeal! There aren't any neighbors to hear you. Squeal!"

Her arm felt like it was leaving its socket with a searing, fire-like hurt that flooded throughout her body. She heard herself squealing, just as he ordered. Then a wave of nausea. She started to vomit.

Magaña paused when a loud knock sounded at the office door. The pressure on her arm eased. Elaine felt dizzy and disoriented. The room seemed to whirl around like a carousel.

As she sank to the floor, she heard scuffling sounds coming from the office's small anteroom.

She turned to see Magaña came stumbling backwards into the room, with Riki shoving him on the chest. When he saw Elaine, his mouth opened in surprise and relief.

"Are you all right?" he asked.

"I don't know. I think I'm sick. I may be starting a seizure."

Magaña cautiously moved toward his desk.

Elaine said, "Riki, he has a gun in that drawer!"

He moved quickly and slapped Magaña's hand away from the desk.

Magaña threw a punch aimed at Riki's mouth. It deflected harmlessly off Riki's forearm, who repaid the little man with a sharp slap across the mouth, sending a trickle of blood down his chin. Magaña then retreated to the corner of the room, holding his hands up in a plea for mercy.

"How did you find me?" Elaine asked. She moved her arm about gingerly, wincing from the pain.

"The guard at your house. He works for this guy. He didn't want to tell, but we convinced him he wanted to after all."

"How's Comanche?

"He's all right. He caught a bullet in his leg. It was a small caliber. A barrio doctor is going to take it out for him. Are you okay?"

"I don't know. Get me out of here. I feel sick. Daddy's on his way here."

As Riki helped Elaine to her feet, Magaña made a break for the door. Riki started to go after him but decided against it.

"Let him go. We have to find medicine for you."

Elaine clung to Riki with her good arm as they made their way outside. An old taxi, the kind with the checkered band around the doors, waited at the curb. The door opened and Macaco jumped out to open the rear door. He smiled at Elaine.

"Remember me? I'm driving a taxi now. Of course, that's only in the evenings. In the daytime, I still drive the garbage truck."

She thought for a moment and remembered; *macaco* means "callous." Because he drove a garbage truck all day, his friends teased him and claimed he had callouses on his butt. He was one of the many street kids she'd met during their afternoon expeditions to the barrio.

She smiled weakly at him and grimaced when her arm bumped against the door frame when she was climbing into the cab. Riki sat beside her and Macaco smartly saluted and closed the door. Just then, Tarkington's long Cadillac rolled down the street. Tarkington saw that the taxi was getting ready to leave, so he waited patiently for Macaco to drive away so he could take the precious parking space.

When Macaco's cab reached the end of the block, ready to turn, a black Bentley slipped away from the curb, as silent as a whisper, and began following at a discreet distance.

The jeweler lived in a house on the fringe of the Lomas area. It was a smaller house than some in the area, but just as expensive. A tall, wrought-iron gate opened into a brightly lit courtyard where a marble fountain splashed tiny streams of water into a pool. A massive, carved door opened into the house.

"This is the place," Macaco said as he stopped the taxi by the gate. "His name is Carlos Helmich, the best paying fence in all of Mexico. He has a legitimate jewelry store, one of the expensive ones, and he sells this stuff there. He only buys the very best."

"What I have is the best." Riki took the jewelry from the jewel box and stuffed it into his pockets before stepping from the cab. "Keep an eye out for trouble, Macaco. I'll be back as soon as I can." Elaine waited in the cab.

Riki went to the tall gate and pressed a button three times, as he'd been instructed. Soon, a steel panel in the door slid back and two eyes stared out for a moment. Then the door opened and a tall man looked out.

"What do you want? Who are you?"

"Comanche sent me. I have something for you to look at."

The man nodded his head. "Yes. He called about that." A buzzing noise at the gate startled Riki. "The gate's open," the man called out. "You may come in."

Inside the house, Riki looked around with surprise. The outside looked tasteful, but the inside of Carlos Helmich's home was extravagant, with paintings, tapestries, massive furniture, and even suits of armor. Helmich himself looked like something out of a movie, tall and aristocratic, with blonde hair edged with silver. He wore a silk smoking jacket, more suitable to a Prussian count than a Mexican jeweler. Riki half expected him to pull out a monocle and place it in his eye.

"Who is it, Carlos?" A feminine voice called from another room. Her accent was Continental French, and when she glided into the room, she appeared to be the match to Helmich in aristocratic bearing, although she looked to be half his age. Not quite as tall as he, she was slender, with an oval face and gently waving blond hair that curved to her shoulders. When she saw Riki, her eyes lit up as if she were delighted to see an old friend, and she smiled sexily.

"Just a business transaction, René. I understand this gentleman has some trinkets he would like appraised."

Then to Riki, he said, "I detest doing business in my home, and especially at night. But our mutual friend—Horacio, or Comanche, as he is called—insisted that I see you. I hope that what you have to sell is worth our time."

"It is."

Riki walked to a polished table in the center of the room. A mantle of burgundy velvet lay across the table and the light of a chandelier illuminated the velvet as if it were a jeweler's showcase. Riki began laying out the pieces, one by one. As he did so, the light from the chandelier sparkled colorfully from the jewelry and drew gasps of delight from René. She brushed a cascade of blonde hair from her face and reached for a bracelet.

"Oh, Carlos! Look at this one! It's gorgeous!"

He took the bracelet from her hands and turned it over and over. Then he picked up a ring and held it to the light. He reached into the inside pocket of the smoking jacket and drew out a magnifying glass and placed it against his eye as if it were a monocle.

The woman sighed deeply as she picked up a broach of diamonds and rubies. "This one is exquisite, Carlos! I *must* have this for my collection." She fondled the piece and held it to her lips for a gentle kiss. The she looked at Riki and smiled in admiration. "Where is the world did you steal these? They're gorgeous!"

"I didn't steal them. How much can you pay?"

Carlos took the glass away from his eye and dropped into his pocket. "How much? Nothing. Absolutely nothing."

The blonde gasped with surprise. "But Carlos..."

"Nothing," He repeated. "I'm not stupid."

Riki sighed in exasperation. "Don't tell me, let me guess what you are going to say. 'These are worthless, but I just might be willing to pay ten pesos just to take it off your hands.' Señor,

I know these diamonds are genuine. And, that green pendant is emerald. How much cash can you give me tonight? That's all I want to know."

Helmich laughed politely and picked up a sapphire ring, holding it up to the light. "No, my handsome friend. I would never tell you such a thing. Look at this ring. You see? It is the most gorgeous emerald I've ever seen. Surely it came from the only Brazilian mine ever to produce such beauties. Oh, how I wish I had the money this one cost its original purchaser."

René stepped close to Carlos and put her hand around his waist and kissed him on the neck. "Then buy it for me, my love."

"I can't. It's worthless."

Riki felt himself becoming angry. "How can it be valuable, and worthless at the same time?"

"You probably know why, but just in case you don't, I'll take the time to explain it to you." He handed the ring to Riki. "Look inside that ring. Do you see the inscription? You look puzzled? Well, take this glass and look closely and you will be able to read what it says."

Riki had never really inspected the forbidden jewelry closely before. He held the glass close to his eye as he'd seen Helmich do. The inscription read: *from Alex Barron w/love.*

"Well? So, there is writing inside the ring. How does that affect the value?"

"Simply this, my friend, these pieces are not only stolen, but there is a huge reward out for the capture of the thief. It's too bad I am ethical, for I could earn a tidy sum merely by turning you in to the police."

He fingered a bracelet and sighed. "But that would totally ruin my standing in the community. I'd never be able to buy trinkets again. Here, look at this watch. On the back it says, *best performance of the decade — love, Johnny G.*"

René's voice pleaded. "But Carlos, you've bought many pieces of stolen property. This shouldn't make any difference."

"The difference, my dear, is that I cannot sell this jewelry. I couldn't make a peso on it."

"Why not?" Riki demanded angrily.

"Because the description of these pieces is spread all over Mexico. Every police station, every jewelry broker, every pawnshop, every possible source for my sales all have a brochure on these items. The minute I try to move them, they will be confiscated as being stolen property. You see, the victim of this theft is a very powerful man. A Hollywood moviemaker, they say, who will stop at nothing to find the thief. His name is Alexander Barron."

Riki closed his eyes for a moment. A strange feeling of having been in this same place and hearing this same conversation before bothered him. Or was it the name *Barron* that othered him? Everywhere he turned Barron frustrated him. He began to feel ever-increasing hate for this person. What kind of man puts baubles of flashy jewelry on such a high plateau of value?

René fingered the glittering treasure sadly while Helmich patted her shoulder sympathetically. "But, Carlos, you don't need to sell it. You could give it to me. No one would ever know."

"But René, I couldn't afford that."

"Please?"

Helmich looked at Riki in annoyance. "I wish I hadn't listened to Comanche. This is nothing but trouble. Big trouble. But maybe, just maybe, I can help you."

"How much?" Riki's voice carried a note of resignation.

"Do you understand why I can't give you much for all this? I'll have to take the stones to Holland, have them reset, then sell the gold for scrap. I must pay top money for a person who can remake the jewelry and keep his mouth closed. On top of all that..."

"How much?"

"Well, you must consider that I have to..."

"How much?"

Helmich didn't reply for a long time. He looked at the

jewelry and then at René. Then he closed his eyes as if making mental calculations. When he opened his eyes, he shrugged as if in surrender and pulled a painting aside on the wall to reveal a wall safe. Delicately, he dialed the combination and brought out a stack of banknotes. He counted out a stack and carefully closed the safe door and covered it with the painting.

"Here you are. Take it or leave it. And believe me, I am not haggling as to the price. If you refuse this miserable offer, you will be doing me a great favor. Somehow, I feel I am going to get into a lot of trouble over this. Either take the money or do me the favor of taking the jewelry with you."

Riki counted the stack of 5,000-peso bills. He knew this amounted to theft by Helmich, but he was also convinced that this was the final offer. He grimaced and folded the money into his hip pocket.

René squealed in delight and began to pin the broach on her dressing gown. Helmich frowned and said, "Don't think you're doing me any favors. I am not a superstitious man, but somehow, I feel there's a curse on these shiny little things. Please, please don't mention to anyone on the street that you sold me anything. I don't want to attract attention. This business becomes more dangerous each day, what with burglars, hold-up specialists, and..."

Riki closed the door behind him, not wishing to hear any more from Helmich. The money was disappointing, but he had no choice.

When he got into the taxi, Macaco asked, "How did you make out? Did you sell him your things?"

"Yes. But he is a smooth-talking thief. He robbed me."

"Well, maybe I can get even for you. I know some friends who are expert at getting into houses like that one. One little word from me, and we could have your merchandise back in one whole piece."

"No. No, don't bother on my account. Maybe he's right about a curse. Micaela believes that. Bad luck dogged her all her life. Maybe because she kept the jewelry."

"It would be no bother to me, Riki. For old times sakes, I could easily..."

"No. I mean it. Don't do anything for me, because in a couple of days we'll be gone from Mexico City. If you rob him, do it after we leave."

"Where to now?"

"To the doctor's place. I need to see how Comanche is."

Macaco ground the gearshift into low and the old Chevrolet lurched forward. When he started to turn the corner, the shiny black Bentley again pulled from the curb and began following. Macaco's eyes narrowed and he kept his attention on the rear-view mirror as he turned onto a side street.

"We're being followed," he said casually. "Better hold on tight, because I'm going to play some games."

The Chevrolet's worn gearbox groaned as the car began a run for top speed through the narrow streets of the Lomas. After a few quick turns and a detour across the lawn of a large house, Macaco managed to guide the car into Chapultepec Park. Then just to be certain, he made a couple of loops until he was satisfied that he'd lost the Bentley.

Chapter Twenty-Seven

All buses for Acapulco leave from the "South" terminal. To avoid being seen together, Elaine took a taxi and Riki rode the Metro; they were to meet in front of the station.

News of the kidnapping was out now, and the newspapers were having a festival with the story. Tabloids ran chapter heads with type the size of small cement blocks. All front pages carried blowups of the picture of the criminal *El Papagayo* and the kidnapped diplomat's daughter. One newspaper had nothing on the front page but headlines and the photo.

Riki glanced at a newsstand as he hurried by, shuddering to see his and Elaine's picture so clearly. The original print hadn't been too good, and the enlargement exaggerated the blurriness, but to Riki it seemed like looking into a mirror. He ran his hand over his face to feel the growing stubble of beard and wondered how long it would be before it would truly disguise him. So far, it only succeeded in making him look like a *pelado*, like those he'd met in jail.

He waited nervously in front of the station, feeling the imagined scrutiny of each passerby. When Elaine's cab finally arrived, he forced himself to stay back until her luggage was placed on the sidewalk and the cab driver went on his way. Elaine wore dark glasses, and a black wig changed her appearance somewhat. But not enough, Riki decided. Since he looked like a street character, he decided to play the part. He ran up to Elaine and said, "Carry your bags, lady?" Before she had a chance to reply, he grabbed them and started inside the terminal.

She caught up to him and whispered, "Have you seen the bloody newspapers? I can't believe it! They claim you're a 'master criminal' and that you are wanted for everything in the book from murder to illegal parking."

"That can't be true. I don't drive. Did you buy your medicine?"

"I couldn't. The police put out a warning to all *farmacias* to watch for someone buying the medication without a prescription. They know I need it, and they know that eventually we'll have to try to buy some."

He stood back with the luggage while she purchased the tickets. The medication worried him. She had taken the last pill two days ago and had no way of knowing when an attack might come. He could only hope that the druggists in Acapulco hadn't been alerted, but he realized the chances of this were slim.

She returned with the tickets and a worried look on her face.

"What's the matter?"

"Police," she whispered from the corner of her mouth. "Over there, by the ticket counter. There are two plainclothes cops watching who buys tickets."

"How do you know they are cops?"

"Angel and Mocho taught me how to spot them. Don't let them see us together."

Riki followed behind Elaine as she headed for the gate. He tried to look like a pelado hustling a tip from a gringa. When he put the luggage beside the bus, he accepted the ticket from Elaine and pretended it to be a tip and stuck it in his pocket.

"Gracias, señorita." He bowed slightly and turned away quickly. From the corner of his eye, he noticed a man wearing a dark suit—obviously a plainclothes cop—who watched passengers board the bus.

Riki hesitated a moment as he tried to think of a way to get aboard the bus unseen. Then he took the carry-on bag from Elaine and said, "Let me put this aboard for you, señorita."

He waited until she climbed into the bus, then he followed.

The cop turned his attention briefly to the street character with the handbag, probably watching to see if the street character might try to steal it. But he had three other buses to watch and didn't notice that the pelado who carried the tourist's luggage didn't get off the bus.

Their seats turned out to be the very front two, providing Riki and Elaine a panoramic view as they zoomed along the highway toward Acapulco. They held hands, and save for an occasional excited whisper, were quiet for over an hour. Once out of the city, the bus rolled along an excellent superhighway at a smooth, easy clip.

As they climbed out of the city haze, the air became crystal clear and stands of pine trees cast blue shadows across the road. Riki thought of the mountain at Tezcatlipocas and how peaceful it had been there; how uncomplicated life had been then. He reached inside his shirt to take out the envelope with the pesos fattening its sides. Careful to keep the money out of line of sight from the bus driver and other passengers, Riki counted it again.

Elaine squeezed his hand and whispered, "It's an awful lot of money, isn't it? We'll be able to live in Acapulco forever."

"Not forever. Just for a while. I've been cheated. That jewelry was worth at least fifty times what he gave me. And I had to give that doctor almost half of the money to take the bullet out of Comanche's leg and to keep quiet about it. Before long I'll have to look for a job."

"Will Comanche be all right?"

He sighed. "I hope so. But the police are looking for him. They suspect he was involved in the burglary at your house. They're trying to arrest anyone who knows me. Angel told me about the reward your father posted. With that and the reward Barron put on my head, every cop in the country is burning with a fever to trap El Papagayo."

"I don't understand why Barron wants to pay so much to catch you. Tell me the truth — did you steal the jewelry?"

"No. I've told you all I know about the jewelry. It's just that

369

Barron has some kind of hate for whoever has it. Micaela believes there's a curse on the jewelry. She may be correct."

"Why can't you tell me where the jewelry came from?"

"Because I don't know. Micaela kept it in that music box, never wore it, never took it out, not even to admire it. It was as if she were frightened of it. I suppose if Barron claims that it was stolen, it probably was. But Micaela would never steal anything."

He tucked the envelope flap around the money and replaced it inside his shirt. The jewelry was gone now, and it remained to be seen if the curse Micaela believed in would materialize. Intellectually, he dismissed this as village superstition, yet his mind kept returning to the puzzle of where Micaela had obtained such fine jewelry.

"Just who is this Barron person," Elaine asked. "And what is his connection with Micaela?"

"I don't know, other than he is supposed to be a rich gringo from Hollywood. Someday, I hope to meet him and make him pay for all the pain he's caused Micaela and me."

They became quiet, both trying to imagine what Acapulco had in store for them. After a while, Elaine leaned over and kissed him on the neck. "I am so excited, Riki, I feel like dancing in the aisle. We're going to have so much fun! You'll absolutely love the ocean. And we're going to buy you some fancy clothes and you can take me out dancing at one of those little places on the beach."

"I don't know how to dance."

"Neither do I. But it doesn't look difficult. I'm sure we'll learn quickly. We'll buy you a flowered shirt, and some white duck pants that fit real tight about the hips, and a gold chain with a shark's tooth hanging from it."

"The first thing we'll have to buy is some medicine for you. How are you feeling?"

"I feel great."

"How will you know if you're going to have a seizure? It's been more than two days now without any pills. Do you get some sort of warning?"

"I don't know. I don't actually remember much about them. I temporarily black out when they happen, and only know I've had one when I come to, feeling groggy and hurting where I bumped into things. I must have had them a lot when I was little, because I've been taking the medicine for as long as I can recall. Mum always said that if I missed taking even one, that I would have an attack and could bite my tongue off or strangle."

"We'll have to get medicine."

She was quiet for a long while. Finally, she said, "Riki, I've been wondering, ever since I ran out of the medicine... am I *really* sick? My mind seems clearer now, and I feel better these past few days, better than I can remember. Do you suppose Mum and Poppa just *thought* I needed those pills? What if I've been taking them all these years for nothing? Maybe I'm not an invalid anymore. Maybe my illness never was as serious as my parents imagined?"

"What if you have an attack and die? We've got to figure out how to get the medicine."

"I just won't have one. I'll will it away if it starts to come. So, forget about the medicine. I won't take any, even if we find a way to buy it."

They let the subject drop, but it never went very far from Riki's mind. The rest of the trip was quiet, broken only by a few whispers. Neither could sleep as the afternoon wore on and as the sun started to go down.

Acapulco was just a name to Riki at this point; he didn't know what to expect. He'd seen numerous calendar pictures of Acapulco beaches — typically women in bikinis frolicking in the surf — so he imagined that Acapulco would be mostly beach.

But somewhere in the back of his mind was also an image of a beach, and a little boy chasing waves while his father watched over him smiling in approval. The image was so faded and worn at the edges that it didn't qualify as a dream, just an archetypical father-and-son memory.

The sun was half-covered by the ocean horizon by the time the bus climbed the highway's final crest. Then, with one dramatic sweep around a curve, the Pacific Ocean and Acapulco lay spread out below. At this moment, Riki felt a strange emotion inside his chest. Suddenly, he *knew* he'd been here before!

His heart began thumping. He tried to drink in every detail of scenery as the bus began its winding descent toward the city below. Bluer than any sky he'd ever seen and stretching out to touch the red, glowing horizon, the Pacific Ocean dominated the scene, dwarfing the heavily built-up shoreline.

As the bus grew closer, man-made artifacts began taking over, with buildings growing taller the closer they came to the beach. Many hotels stood higher even than those in Mexico City. The four-lane highway turned into a boulevard lined with coconut palms, apartments, and businesses. Traffic increased as the bus penetrated deeper into town, into the tourist district. Lights were coming on in the tall hotels. Animated signs moved and blinked, traffic lights and neon displays flashed and competed for attention.

Riki's impression was one of bewildering color: pastel-colored hotels, restaurants with rich and gaudy facades, flashily dressed tourists, blending and clashing at the same time. The sky, now reflecting red with the glowing sunset, exaggerated the colors with an eerie tint.

He squeezed her hand anxiously. "I know this place, Elaine! I've been here before. I'm sure of it."

"Do you mean in another life?"

"No. When I was a little boy. I remember being in an auto, standing up in the back seat and driving along this very same street! The ocean is just on the other side of those tall buildings there."

"That's right, but..."

He twisted about to see everything, to take in every detail, to search for something familiar. The bus rolled along with traffic and finally turned onto a side street to enter the terminal.

Now nothing looked familiar. For a moment he began to wonder if he had imagined everything. But no, the impression of standing in the car while someone drove along that boulevard was even stronger than before. But it wasn't his father driving. Who? He concentrated, but all he could picture was a man wearing a billed cap driving the car and himself standing in the back seat.

They waited to collect Elaine's two pieces of luggage, then walked along the Malecón toward the hill where the Tarkingtons sometimes stayed on holiday.

"The apartments I told you about are up there," she said, unable to keep the excitement from her voice. "I hope they have one for us."

Riki looked around, trying to remember something else about his past, something to hook his memory to Acapulco.

There was something else, but he couldn't pinpoint it at first. Then it came to him; it was the breeze, soft, balmy and with a touch of ocean moisture as it caressed his face. He had a sudden impression of playing naked in a garden where flowers surrounded a child's swing and the early morning dew made the swing seat wet and slippery. He remembered how the breeze felt on his naked body as someone pushed him back and forth on the swing.

Yes. He knew he'd been in Acapulco before. But where? He felt certain now that if he could ever find the house he remembered as a child, it would be in Acapulco somewhere. In the morning he would begin a search.

The chubby, talkative woman who managed the small apartment hotel seemed dubious about renting to the young couple until Riki produced enough money to pay two months' rent. The apartment consisted of one airy room with a balcony onto which a tiny kitchen was crowded. At the balcony's edge was a table with two chairs. Elaine almost trembled with excitement as she eased the woman out into the hall and closed the door on her in mid-sentence. Then she turned to Riki and smiled and giggled at the same time.

"We did it, Riki. We did it! We have a home all our own." She threw her arms around his neck and said, "In the morning, we'll buy you a swimsuit and proper clothing, and I'll show you the beaches."

He didn't reply. He was standing on the balcony staring out over the bay, his mind far from the apartment. He was in the garden of that house so far distant in the past.

She pulled at his sleeve to get his attention. "What's the matter, Riki? What's wrong?"

"That building over there. See? The pink one that clings to the side of the hill?"

"Way over there? Sure. That's 'Las Brisas' hotel. We stayed there once. Why?"

"I've seen it before, many times. I remember it clearly now. I remember being in a swimming pool and a man was trying to teach me how to float on my back. He was holding me up in the water and I could see that pink building high up on the hill above me."

"Do you think that's where you lived?"

He shrugged. "I don't know. But the swimsuit and the beaches can wait. Tomorrow I'm going to start looking around for something else I remember. The house has to be there somewhere. Below that pink building."

This time Robin got the news. A phone call from Mexico City brought the heavily accented voice of Enrique Morales. "It is urgent that I get in touch with señor Barron. We've found the rest of the stolen jewelry."

It took a moment or so for the import to sink in, then she said excitedly, "Where? Where did you find it?"

"It's a rather complicated story. An ex-convict, a man named Alberto Magaña, and a well-known buyer of stolen jewelry, Carlos Helmich, were making a lot of noise last night, and the neighbors called the police. It seems that this Magaña fellow was torturing the jewel dealer, wanting to know the address of the criminal who brought Mr. Barron's jewelry to his house."

"Where did he get the jewelry?"

"It came from El Papagayo. I've been turning the city upside down searching for him, and suddenly he turns up with the rest of Mr. Barron's jewelry. I think I'll kill him when I find him."

"Do you have him in custody?"

Morales sighed in disgust. "No. He got away again. This time, every cop in the country is after him. He's wanted for kidnapping. Kidnapped the daughter of a wealthy foreigner, and a diplomatic attaché. We have no doubt now that Papagayo's real name is Montalvo—Riki Montalvo." A vision of El Papagayo flashed through Robin's mind—the ugly, scarred-faced tough she and Alex met that day in the warehouse. The name "Riki" bothered her, but she dismissed the sudden, absurd thought that Rickey Barron might be alive.

"When do you think you might find this Papagayo character? I'd like to talk to him before you do anything drastic."

"Don't worry. I wasn't serious when I said I'd kill him, just that I'd like to. With the all-points bulletin the police put out on him, I'm sure we'll have him soon. Probably by the time you and Mr. Barron arrive."

"Mr. Barron and I will be on the next plane for Mexico City. Please arrange for us to speak with the people you mentioned. And with Papagayo, hopefully."

"Fortunately, my connections with the Mexico City police and with the Secret Service are still strong. They cooperate with me fully. They're scouring all of Mexico City for Papagayo. They'll find him and they will notify me immediately. Few criminals are intelligent enough to lose themselves, even in a metropolis as huge as ours."

"Papagayo managed to lose himself, over and over."

"Well yes, but... This time is different. This time Papagayo has money, a lot of money he received for selling the jewelry. And like all Mexican criminals, Papagayo will not resist the temptation to spend. Absurd, but true. The police simply have to watch fancy restaurants, elegant clothing stores, and places like that. Before long, Papagayo will show up throwing money around like it is diseased. We'll find him."

As soon as Robin terminated the call from Morales, she tried to contact Alex. He was on location in a remote area of Arizona. But a flash flood in the mountains had cut off communications with the film crew. She had a friend try to get through via an emergency radio network, but again no success, probably because of the high ranges surrounding the valley where they were filming.

She left instructions with the studio to contact Alex as soon as communications resumed. "Tell him that the rest of the jewelry has surfaced, that I'm on my way to Mexico."

"Where will you be staying?"

"Probably the Mexico City Hilton. If not there, I'll be at our home in Acapulco. Tell Alex I'm taking a set of keys with me.

Rain drenched the ancient Aztec capital as Robin's plane touched down with a screeching of tires on wet pavement. The downpour turned everything gray and cold. She didn't wait for her luggage; she took a taxi directly to meet Morales at the delegación. Morales looked older now, haggard from lack of sleep. His face was the color of old leather, as pockmarked as a peanut shell. He smoked cigarettes one after another. His fingers stained nicotine brown. When he saw Robin, he came to attention briefly and hurried forward to shake her hand.

"Have you found Papagayo?" she demanded without any formalities. "I want to see him, to talk to him."

Morales spread his hands in a gesture of helplessness. "We are doing all we can, madam. We're trying to round up the members of the barrio gang that Montalvo used to run. But they are as slippery as oiled rattlesnakes. One member, a tough named Comanche, was almost in our grasp, but he eluded us at the last moment. He can't run far, though. I understand he has a bullet wound in his leg."

"What about the men who were fighting over the jewelry? What can they tell?"

"Not much. The one called Alberto Magaña isn't saying much. He knows he is facing twenty years as a third offender and doesn't want to be burdened with the label of 'informer' during his time in prison. The jewel buyer, the one called Helmich, is still in the hospital. You may visit him if you wish. He speaks excellent English. By the way, would you like to see the jewelry?"

"Later. First the jewel buyer."

Helmich was propped up and had casts on both arms with splints to keep his broken fingers straight. Bandages covered a place on his cheek and another on his neck to cover a dozen cigarette burns. Magaña had lost all control on this one. A blonde woman, slender and good looking, sat on the edge of the bed, touching her eyes with a lace handkerchief,

"I can't help you much," Helmich said weakly. "Believe me, I am cooperating fully with this investigation. True, I knew the pieces were stolen when I bought them, and I knew there was a reward out for their return. I informed the thief of this. My intentions were to call the police and collect the reward. This would cover my expenses, and, to be perfectly honest, I planned on keeping one small piece for my wife." The blonde touched her hand to his cheek and began weeping again.

"Before I had the opportunity to do more than put the jewelry into the safe, a sadistic animal forced his way into the house. He demanded to know where he could find this Riki Montalvo chap. I couldn't tell him any more than I can tell you now."

"Don't you have an idea? A guess? We need your help, Mr. Helmich."

"Look, if I couldn't tell Magaña under the most excruciating torture any man has undergone, how could I now remember for you?"

René shook her head. "It was horrible. I never want to see anything like that again! I shudder to think what Magaña was going to do to the young man who sold us the jewels. He said he was going to cut off his nose for starters. He would have done it, too. And such a good-looking man, too."

Robin paused before saying in a puzzled voice, "Good looking? Who are you talking about?"

"El Papagayo. A very handsome one—very European-looking."

"But... When I met Riki Montalvo, he looked like a derelict, a horrible-looking tramp."

René smiled condescendingly. "But Madame, I am a connoisseur in that sort of thing. I say he's handsome."

Suddenly Robin felt a weakness in her stomach, as if she were about to collapse. "Handsome? Papagayo? Please—tell me what he looked like? Did he have a broken nose, brown, muddy-colored eyes, a scarred face, and..."

René broke in with a laugh. "But you must be joking! This one had a face like an Italian movie star. His eyes were fascinating, the kind they call 'bedroom eyes'. This one was very different from the usual Mexican crook Carlos deals with. Very different."

"His eyes. What color were they?"

"Ah, those eyes were one of his best features. They were the color of polished silver, or perhaps a smoky diamond. They were the same color of gray that I often see in northern Italy, where I went to school. That's why I say he could be an Italian movie star."

A confusion of thoughts raced through Robin's head as she tried to process this new information. Her heart was pounding in her throat.

She turned to Helmich and demanded, "Give me your

opinion. Is Riki Montalvo a Mexican, or could he possibly be an American?"

Helmich pursed his lips and thought for a moment. "An interesting question. What is a Mexican? and what is an American? I'm pure Mexican, yet my parents came from Austria. Being 'Mexican' is a matter of culture, not of race. This Papagayo person, is darker than me, but so are some Austrians. So, I have to go on his culture, the way he talks, the way he thinks. In that respect, he is thoroughly Mexican. When speaking Spanish, Papagayo has a hint of an accent, yes. But not English. No, more like the way they speak in the eastern mountains, but also with the slick *caló* of the streets of Mexico City. Papagayo is thoroughly Mexican. Culturally, I mean. However, if you ask if he has *mestizo* blood — that kind of Mexican — the answer is no. Not with those gray eyes. He is definitely of European extract, just as I am. If I didn't hear him speak, I would have guessed Italian. Certainly, he could pass for an American."

Robin found it difficult to catch her breath. "I need to talk to him," she gasped. "I have to find him!"

"So do a lot of people," Helmich said wryly.

Then, he looked at Robin intently for a few moments as if testing her for confidence. He glanced furtively to see if any police were nearby, and whispered, "One thing. He needed money in a hurry. He wanted it that night. Obviously, money to travel on. Therefore, don't bother looking for him in Mexico City. Try Cancún or Acapulco."

"Why do you say that?"

"The Mexican criminal mind. For some reason, when they want to hide, they head for Cancún or Acapulco. Stupid really, because the police know that. All they have to do to catch the criminal is search the beaches and sure enough, there will be their fugitive — suntanned, spending money resting up for jail.

Robin put in a call to the L.A. office with an urgent message for

Alex to contact her. While she waited for his return call, she spent an hour wandering about the barrio where Riki once operated his gang of hooligans. Life seemed slow paced, yet grim. Children played listlessly on broken sidewalks, or sat solemnly on curbs watching life pass them by. Robin thought about how noisy American children were when they played contrasted with the seriousness of the Mexican children of the barrios.

Now that she knew the truth, it seemed monstrous and so wide ranging that she had trouble focusing her thoughts. Rickey Barron had somehow survived that wreck! He grew up as a Mexican child, playing the same melancholy games as these little ones. He could have even played on this same street. Had he gone hungry? Shivered in the cold?

She called Hollywood again to see if Alex had been contacted. "I can't wait here any longer. I'm going to our Acapulco place. Tell him it's urgent that he come there immediately! Immediately!"

Chapter Twenty-Eight

Riki and Elaine caught the bus that tediously worked its way along the crowded Costera Alemán, eventually to turn around at distant Puerto Marqués. It rumbled past high rise hotels and fancy restaurants, strung along the waterline like luxurious pearls each with its own patch of tempting beach pleasures. From time to time, they caught glimpses of azure water and thatched beach palapas shading tourists from the sun. Waiters in crisp white shirts and black bow ties balanced trays—high above their heads, on their fingertips—to hurry exotic drinks and garlic shrimp and lobster to tourists lazily waiting service.

Riki felt sad about missing the beach and the thrill of diving under the crashing surf. The surfacing memories of swimming in the ocean surprised him. Somehow, he knew exactly how it feels to have a surging wave pull at his body, twist this way and that, and then an abrupt release and floating to the surface. He couldn't remember it happening. But it must have happened many times.

"Please, Riki. Let's stop? Just for an hour? Let's play on the beach, soak up sunshine, and..."

"Go ahead, if you want to. But I'm not going to stop until I find that house. I can't."

"Okay. We'll find it together."

As the bus groaned its way past the major beaches, Elaine named them and pointed out different hotels where the Tarkingtons had stayed.

What Riki and Elaine couldn't see was the cadre of plain-clothes police and secret service agents combing the beach for

Riki Montalvo, alias 'El Papagayo'. Each carried a copy of the photo Mr. Tarkington had found hidden in Elaine's dresser. Each hoped to be the lucky one to capture Riki Montalvo and collect the reward.

It was a double reward now, one from Barron and one from Tarkington. Each cop studied Riki's picture until he knew his face as well as they knew their own mother's. Maybe even better, for few of their mothers had rewards outstanding. Other police, no less zealous, monitored cabarets and clubs of ill repute, confident that their quarry would eventually show up to squander the booty. They were filled with confidence because although Acapulco is a large city, it's small where tourists and fugitives are concerned.

When the bus crested the final grade to Las Brisas, Riki looked down the mountain slope toward the collection of luxury homes. He asked himself, where? The house has to be down there, but where? Perhaps a hundred, maybe more homes lay terraced on the slope, most with its own swimming pool. Which one?

They jumped off the bus before it stopped completely and started down the picturesque cobblestone streets that wound like jigsaw puzzles around luxury villas and secluded mansions. As they came closer to the houses it became difficult to see the homes themselves. Masonry walls, sometimes a dozen feet high, sealed and protected homes from outside view. Most homes were totally hidden from the world except for an occasional tiled roof.

"See anything you recognize, Riki?"

"It's so difficult. They all look the same with the walls hiding them." He tried to peek through the crack where a heavy wood gate opened into the interior of a home complex. He saw nothing but a couple of automobiles parked on a cement driveway.

"Isn't there something you remember?"

He turned to look at the pink hotel looming overhead. "I

don't think it could be here, because I don't remember the hotel being that close. I have a picture of it being smaller, farther away. Let's keep going down."

The streets twisted about, sometimes stopping at blind ends, sometimes twisting back into a circle and heading upward again. They made very slow progress.

Once a gardener who was trimming bougainvilleas on a wall asked, "Looking for someone?" He looked suspicious as if he were certain that Riki and Elaine were burglars, staking out their next victim.

Riki shook his head and they hurried on. It was late afternoon by the time they figured out the street system. Elaine urged him to give up, at least for that day.

"Tomorrow morning, we're coming back. I know we'll find it," he said. "We're getting closer, because the hotel seems to be about the right size and the right angle from here. The house has to be one of those on this street or maybe the last one down there. Can't be those other places because the cliff blocks the hotel view. On the other side, too many big trees in the way."

Elaine shook her head wearily. "Tomorrow morning you go without me. I plan on kicking back at Playa Caleta. Going to start on a glorious tan." She pulled on his arm. "Let's go home."

The climb back up to the highway was long and tiring. Elaine had to pause to catch her breath from time to time. They stood with their arms about each other's waist, looking over the sweeping panorama. When they were almost to the top, they stopped one last time. The blue of the bay had acquired a copper color from the setting sun, broken by the skyline of Acapulco. Pinpoints of lights began flickering in distant hotel windows. The sky was turning deep red, making the hills behind the town look black in comparison. They watched the view in fascinated silence as they waited for the bus to come rumbling down the hill from Las Brisas.

Riki and Elaine ignored the taxi that turned the corner and prepared for its steep descent down the hill. They had no reason to glance at the taxi's passenger. She didn't notice the young couple either.

Robin stared straight ahead, deep in thought and struggling with her emotions; her speculations were too distant to pay attention to the two lovers standing on the corner, their arms looped about each other's waist. The cab driver put the gearshift into low and started down the steep hill toward the Barron place.

The live-in caretaker swung the wooden gates open to allow the taxi to enter. He seemed agitated as he motioned for the driver to hurry. He opened the car door for Robin and pointed toward the house.

"You have a phone call," he said in Spanish, pantomiming a telephone handset, then pointing urgently toward the house. Then he began helping the taxi driver unload the luggage.

Alex's voice never sounded so good, as he said, "Got your message. What's going on?"

"Get down here right away, Alex. We've found the rest of the jewelry." She hesitated for a moment, not sure that she ought to say more without knowing for sure that Rickey was alive. Another shattered hope would amount to cruelty. She said, "There's been an important development. You must get here right..."

He broke in, saying, "Robin, I'm busy here in Arizona. I don't give a damn about the jewelry any longer. Why can't you handle it for me?"

"Alex, it's important. We're very close to solving the mystery. Please come as soon as possible. Immediately."

He was silent for a while. "I don't know. I could probably get there day after tomorrow. But I'm not sure it's worth it. I finally convinced myself that Rickey is dead. I'm at the point now where I'm better off not knowing details. If the bastard who's kept the truth from me all these years gets punished, that's all I care about."

"Alex, I don't know how to tell you this — but for the first time, I have this strange feeling that Rickey might not have died in the wreck. He's alive. Maybe here in Acapulco."

"Don't do this to me Robin. It took years to face the truth, to stop living with an impossible hope, and now you're..."

"I know, I know. I'm truly sorry. I should have kept this to myself until I can be sure. But Alex, I'm convinced that Rickey is *alive*."

His voice was harsh with resigned anger as he said, "I'll be there; I couldn't stay away now. But I *know* my son is dead. He *has* to remain dead for my sanity. I refuse to spend another night going over the possibility in my mind, over and over and over. Until you find my son and bring him back to life, let's not discuss the idea."

"I'm sorry."

"It's all right. It's forgotten." Then he quickly changed the subject. "The caretaker tells me there's something wrong with the car. Been in the garage too long without anyone starting it, I suppose. He's taking it to get it to the mechanic tomorrow. Better rent a car until it's fixed. Also, be sure not to leave the place unlocked. Caretaker says there've been two burglaries in the neighborhood last week."

"I love you, Alex. And I'm sorry."

"It's forgotten. It has to be that way. Everything is forgotten."

This time Riki knew the way. Within minutes he found the street. Six houses, large and luxurious, rested securely behind a continuous three-meter-high wall. A profusion of flowers — pink, blue, red and yellow — tumbled down from the top of glowing white masonry like a waterfall of color. A narrow strip of manicured lawn faced the street. Six breaks in the walls were filled by steel or wooden doors, each wide enough to admit an automobile. Each wide door was matched by a smaller one for foot traffic. Behind one door, a growling dog, possibly a German shepherd, warned strangers away. Riki paced the street, seeking some way to see behind the walls. One of these houses could be the one. But which one?

He went to the first door. He pressed a button and waited. After a while the door opened a crack. A small, frightened girl, her forehead encircled with a maid's cap, said, "What do you want? The owners aren't here."

Riki didn't know what to say. He fumbled for words, saying, "I need to know what this place looks like... I mean inside. I might have lived here one time. Is there a swimming..."

The door closed with a slam; the lock clicked tightly. The next door had a heavy brass knocker. Riki rapped it several times and waited. The dog across the street became more agitated. Again, he knocked, but no one came to open the door. A trellis clung to the wall between the small and the large door with a thick bougainvillea vine growing up and over the wall. It looked strong enough to hold him.

He glanced around to see if anyone might be watching. Then he scrambled up the trellis until he could peek over the wall. The yard had no swimming pool. Instead, a golf putting green. This couldn't be the one.

He dropped to the ground and looked at the roof lines across the street. No, it couldn't have been any of those because the houses themselves would block out the view of the Las Brisas. It would have to be on this side of the street. One of these three.

He rang the bell of the next house, but again no answer. He stepped back to see if there might be some way to climb the wall. Just then he heard a noise coming from the large doors of the third house. Someone was pulling the latch open. The large doors made a sound like tired crickets as they swung inward.

A lean man wearing the work clothing of a caretaker pulled the doors back and blocked them open with wooden chocks. Then he climbed into a blue Porsche that sat under the tiled carport roof. He had difficulty starting the engine. Riki walked to the opening and peered into the courtyard. He didn't recognize anything. A tiled patio, an open carport and a blue Porsche. The rest of the yard was screened from view by a long wooden divider broken by two swinging doors with panels of frosted glass. The second story of the house loomed overhead.

The Porsche's engine growled sullenly, then sputtered to life, clouds of black smoke spilling irregularly from the exhaust. The caretaker nursed the engine until it smoothed out some and put the gearshift into reverse.

Riki stepped aside as the car lurched drunkenly toward the street. The man was too concerned with keeping the engine running to notice Riki. The car bucked and coughed angrily, as if it resented being taken from its cozy resting place. Preoccupied with his problems, the caretaker failed to close the doors as he normally would.

When the car disappeared around the corner, Riki stepped into the courtyard. He approached the swinging doors, wondering what might be on the other side. He studied the house.

It was a large, two-story building of cut stone, somewhat smaller than the Tarkington's house, but not lacking in elegance. It brought forth no particular memories. He could see no sign of life in the house. He cautiously pushed one of the gates open. A dizzy, swirling feeling crept through his body.

This is it! I've been here before!

The swimming pool. The curving water slide. And—he'd forgotten about it until this moment—a statue of a woman holding a bow, a statue of polished black stone. A huntress, similar to the crystal statue that shattered in his dreams. He allowed the gates to swing shut behind him as he stepped slowly into the yard.

Over there—where the high walls formed a gently rounded corner—was a playground. He remembered now. The swing, the slide, the seesaw. His father used to put him on the seesaw and get on the opposite side to make him bounce and laugh when he hit the bottom.

His throat constricted and tears welled in his eyes, but he didn't know why. He stepped around a small fishpond and touched the swing. The metal in the chains had rusted to a fragile skeleton, as if waiting for a ghost of a boy to grasp them and pull them back to start the swing in motion.

Riki's hand smoothed over the chain and then touched the wooden seat, now a weather-beaten remnant that wouldn't even support the weight of a ghost. The play yard had been left exactly as it had been years ago. He heard an animal-like groan. It came from his own throat. He didn't understand why he was weeping, only that he couldn't help it.

Robin first noticed the stranger as she stood at the upstairs bedroom window watching the caretaker drive the ailing sports car away to the repair shop. She had intended to close the doors after the caretaker left. But now she was afraid to go downstairs.

The stranger wore clean but nondescript clothes, about what one would expect of a gardener or handyman. A black stubble of a beard gave him an unsettling, dangerous look. At first Robin assumed that he worked for one of the neighbors. Somebody's gardener, idly wasting time.

But when the Porsche drove away, the stranger looked furtively about, as if he were thinking about entering the yard. Robin stepped away from the window. She frowned with suspicion and watched for the stranger's next move.

When the man stepped into the courtyard, her heart began beating furiously. She remembered Alex's warning about burglars. Her hand clutched at her throat in a classic gesture of fear. This was serious.

The stranger paused for a moment, again looking around to see if he were being observed. Satisfied that he wasn't, he boldly pushed opened the divider doors and stepped into the garden. Robin swallowed with difficulty as she reached for the telephone. She punched the three digits of the emergency security system. She kept her eye on the stranger and felt fearful impatience as she waited for the security guards to answer. Within seconds the reply came.

"Do you speak English? I need someone to speak English. A man is trying to break into the house." She paced anxiously as she waited for someone to come on the line with whom she could communicate. The intruder was now staring at the statue of the huntress, the one Alex commissioned for Diana after her first screen success. Maybe he would be satisfied with taking that. It was certainly valuable enough, if he could only cart it away.

Then a voice said, "May I help you?"

Robin's voice quivered as she said, "A burglar is in our yard. I'm afraid he's going to break into our house. Send help, quickly!" She stammered the address and added, "Hurry!"

"Our radio car is on the way. I'm also contacting the police patrol for your neighborhood. Keep your doors locked. You'll be safe."

Suddenly she remembered that the door to the garden was open. Not just unlocked, but open! She clutched the dressing gown around her neck and hurried down the winding staircase.

The stranger was standing by the old playground equipment when she reached the open door. His back was turned to her. She eased the door closed. She felt a little better when the bolt was set. She peeked through the curtain to watch. *What's he doing now?*

The intruder's back was to her, so she pulled the curtain aside for a better view. Now he was stroking the chain on the swing. Then he touched the wooden seat and gently pushed it so it swung slowly back and forth. Somehow, he didn't seem as dangerous. There was something about the way he was standing...

Robin felt a vague sense of recognition, as if she'd seen this person before. As she searched her memory for a clue, she realized the man seemed to be quivering. Then it struck her: *He's crying!*

He turned to look at the pool. Enough so that Robin could see his profile. Tears rolled down his cheeks and his shoulders shook with deep sobs. This irrational behavior sent a shiver of fear down Robin's spine. She tried to remember if there was still a gun in her bedroom.

When the intruder wiped his cheeks with both wrists, Robin's mouth fell open in astonishment. His eyes! They were Alex's eyes! The way he stood, the angle he held his head... Her fingers trembled weakly as she reached for the latch. She started to pull it back, but she hesitated. Then, gathering her courage, she unlatched the door.

The door made a slight clicking noise when it opened. Riki turned around quickly, a startled look on his face.

A blonde woman, wearing a dressing gown stared at him, a shocked expression on her face. He hastily wiped the tears from his face with his sleeve, turned to face her. He began stepping back, ready to escape through the doors to the courtyard.

The woman pressed her palms together, as if she were praying. She opened her mouth to say something. But no sound came out. Then she tried again.

"Don't leave. I want to talk to you. Please don't go. *Please!*"

Riki shook his head and backed away. He moved toward the glass-paneled gates, ready to run if necessary. But he froze in his tracks when she spoke again.

"Rickey? Is that you, Rickey?"

He turned his head so he could study the slender blonde for a few moments. Her face was tanned like most rich tourists. Thin lines creased her forehead and face, from too much rich food and cigarettes. A typical tourist woman, not the sort who would know his name. He searched his memory but was positive he'd never seen this woman before. She didn't look dangerous or even angry at his being in her garden, but there was a strange look of anxiety on her face.

Finally, he demanded, "How do you know my name?"

A quivering noise, almost like a moan of pain escaped from Robin's throat. "Rickey? Oh, my God! *Rickey!*" She started toward him, in a halting, half-staggering motion.

Shaking his head in confusion, he retreated until he was pushing the doors open with his back. She ran toward him now.

"Wait! You can't leave! Not now, Rickey. *Please.*"

Riki paused, the gates half open, confident that his escape would be easy. He eyed the woman warily and repeated, "How do you know my name? Who are you?" he demanded.

"I'm your friend, Rickey. Please, don't be afraid. I have something very important to tell you. *Very* important. Come inside." She motioned pleadingly with her hands. When he didn't move, she said, "It's about your father."

He stood still as he stared at the marble statue of Diana the huntress. His breathing halted; his chest paralyzed with tension. The image of a shattered crystal statue flashed through his memories. His eyes closed. He felt drops of tears squeezing from under his tightly held lids.

The woman stood at his side now. She gently put an arm around his waist and pulled him close. He could feel her body shaking; he could hear sobbing. He couldn't move. He felt her lips kissing his cheek and her tears joining his.

"It's okay, Rickey. You're home now. Oh my God. My God." She kissed him again and tugged at his arm to urge him back into the garden. "We need to talk, Rickey. Come with me."

Although reluctant to leave the safety of the courtyard, he allowed the woman to pull him back into the garden.

"In the house Rickey. Can I get you a drink or something?"

He shook his arm loose from her grip. "We can talk here. Who are you and how do you know my name?"

She sighed and said, "You don't remember me, do you? My God, but we have a lot to talk about! I'm Robin. I'm married to your father, and..."

A heavy sob choked off her words. "Do you remember

anything about this house? Do you remember living here when..."

A white iron bench flanked the French door to the house. She guided him to it with a gentle urging. "Sit here, Rickey."

He shook his head, hesitated for a moment, then reluctantly sat down on the cast-iron bench. He still didn't trust the woman. If she went inside the house, it could be to call the police. Much safer here, until the mystery could be solved.

He said, "Yes, I remember something. I'm sure I lived here at one time. A long time ago. Before my mother sold me, and my father abandoned me."

A look of horror blazed across Robin's face. "Your mother did *what*? Your father..."

"Whose house is this? And exactly who are you?"

"My name is Robin Barron. I'm married to Alex Barron. Do you know who Alex Barron is?"

Riki tensed and started to get up. But she pushed her hands against his shoulders and forced him to sit down. His eyes narrowed as he said, "Yes, I know all about this Barron person. He wants to put my mother away in jail for selling some of his jewelry." Bitterness stained his voice. "He's offered a reward for my arrest."

Robin drew her breath in sharply. "No! That's not true, Rickey. Alex Barron is your *father*. Alex has been looking..."

The insistent, jangling command of the telephone interrupted Robin. She looked toward the French doors to the house in annoyance. For a moment it seemed as if she weren't going to answer the phone. Then she got to her feet and said, "That could be Alex calling. I'll be right back, Rickey."

Riki watched her go with suspicious eyes. He glanced toward the doors to the courtyard, to reassure himself that he could escape if necessary. The thought of being in Barron's home was extremely unsettling. One thing he was certain of, Barron could never be his father.

The downstairs telephone was in the library, at the other end of the house. When she answered, she heard a man's voice say, "Security service. Are you okay? A police squadron should be there any minute now. Did our guards arrive yet?"

"*The police!* No! Look, there's been a mistake. Call them back and tell them I was mistaken..."

Her words were broken by the sound of screeching of tires in front of the house. At least two autos had pulled to a stop. The sound of car doors slamming was followed by running footsteps and shouting in Spanish.

She ran through the house. When she entered the kitchen, she looked through the open door and saw Rickey disappearing around the corner of the house. Two uniformed police shouted and ran through the courtyard. They drew pistols as they ran.

A third man, in a sport coat and panama hat, followed closely behind. He carried an automatic pistol, the kind with a folding stock that turns it into a stubby submachine gun. When Robin ran into the court, he was aiming the gun.

"No!" she shouted. "He's not a burglar, he's..."

Her words were cut off by a "*pocka-pocka-pocka*" explosion of gunfire. She screamed and ran past the man to the rear of the garden. The two police were pulling themselves up on the potting shed. The first one stepped up on a box to peer over the wall. He nodded and smiled slightly as he raised his pistol to shoot down into the next-door yard. The echo of the shot made Robin's ears ring.

"Stop! Stop this minute! He's a guest. You can't shoot him!"

The cop hesitated for a moment, looking back at Robin with a puzzled expression on his face. Then the cop remembered his target and turned to aim again. A dark look came over his face. "*Se fué,*" he said in frustration.

The man in the sport coat shrugged and said, "That's all right. He won't get far. I hit him at least once, maybe a couple times. All we have to do is follow the blood trail."

At the top of the wall, a splotch of blood, shaped like a huge insect, dripped three spidery legs down to disappear in the shrubbery at the base of the wall.

"Oh, my God! *No!* You couldn't have..."

"But of course, lady. What do you expect? That's El Papagayo! I have his photo right here. There's a big reward out for him. Every cop in Acapulco is hoping to snare this guy and pocket some of the Barron reward. And I did it!" He smiled proudly. "All I have to do is track him down."

"But he is Mr. Barron's *son*. You can't shoot him!"

"I already did."

Riki's arm swung and flopped as he ran. He had no more control over it than if it were a wet towel. He didn't have to wonder about it; a bullet had shattered the bone in his right arm. At first there was a searing flash of hurt, but quickly the pain subsided into a caustic burning and then to a merciful numbness. When he jumped over the side of the wall, he landed on a net of clotheslines full of laundry.

He grabbed a pillowcase as he got to his feet and wrapped it around the wounded arm. It quickly turned dark red with blood. He tightened it as he limped away. He realized that he'd been nicked in the thigh as well. It was beginning to burn painfully.

He cursed for allowing himself to be tricked by the gringa woman. She had been a good actress, keeping him there until the police came. *Everyone* is after the fucking Barron reward money!

He felt too weak to try for the highway. He guessed that was the way the police would be looking, so he made his way downward, toward the ocean. He held the pillowcase tightly about his arm to keep blood from dripping. It stopped most of it, but the cloth was becoming soaked and heavy as wet leather.

A barbed wire fence ran alongside the asphalt road that separated the beach from the homes. The fence was more for animal control than for security, something to keep dogs off the beach. Riki discovered a section where the strands sagged low. He straddled the wire, then lifted the other leg over. He was surprised to find that his muscles ached to lift the leg. A dark red stain on his blue jeans told him where the second bullet had done its damage.

He looked back in the direction of the house. No one seemed to be coming after him. He began slogging through the soft sand in the direction of a small thatched ramada piled high with folded beach chairs. It was the only shelter in sight. But it also seemed to be far, far away. The beach was semi-private with only a dozen people lounging near the beach's fringe. They were either sunning or swimming. No one noticed the stumbling figure.

If only he could get to the ramada before anyone saw him, maybe he could do something about stopping the blood. He felt dizzy. The beach began to tilt. The last few steps seemed like a kilometer.

When he finally reached the ramada, he was staggering uncontrollably. A sudden jolt brought pain and flashing lights in his head.

He realized that he'd run into a low brace of round wood, rotten, covered with green mildew. The blow broke the bridge of his nose and dug into his eyes. He felt his eyes throbbing and swelling. More blood streamed from his nose, flowing into his half open mouth as he gasped for air.

Suddenly he saw nothing but blackness with red flashes of light streaking past. He dropped weakly to his knees.

He crawled, using his good arm to pull him along and then hobbling on his knees. Finally, he dragged himself into a hollow formed by three piles of decaying beach chairs. When he tried to sit up, he fell face forward onto the sand. Weakly, he managed to roll over on his back. He tried to tighten the blood-soaked pillowcase about the arm. He couldn't tell if this helped much. The blood kept flowing.

Fatigue and lethargy began to take over his body. He

wanted to go to Elaine, but he knew this wouldn't be possible for some time. Maybe never.

He tried to prop his back against the chairs, but he couldn't lift himself from the sand. Black globes suddenly began forming in his vision, black with red and purple edges. He wanted to sleep, to fall into a delicious, non-feeling slumber.

Suddenly, he came back to consciousness with a jolting pain. Someone was kicking his wounded leg. His eyes were swollen so tightly that he had difficulty opening even one of them to see what was happening. A chota stood over him, his brown face grinning obscenely underneath the police cap. A polished boot kicked at him again. A pistol pointed at Riki's head.

"My lucky day," a voice was saying. "I found El Papagayo."

Chapter Twenty-Nine

A tropical downpour drenched Acapulco, turning midday into an indigo colored, semi-night. Lightning slashed angrily at the bay as thunder shook the town with earthquake intensity. Robin worried about Alex's plane landing in this weather as she watched anxiously through the rain-streaked windows at the airport.

She hurried to the arrival gate and waited with clenched fists and trembling lips as the plane taxied to the gate. When Alex finally stepped through the door, she ran to him, threw her arms around his neck, burying her face in his chest.

"Oh, Alex. I'm glad you're here! After all these years, we're coming to the end. We've found him, Alex! We've found Rickey!"

He responded with a peck on her cheek. Robin was surprised at his cool response. "You don't believe me?"

He shrugged apologetically. "It's not that. But I've been through this before. Several times. Go ahead, tell me about it."

As they waited for the luggage to appear on the carousel, Alex listened calmly as Robin filled in the details of her encounter with the stranger in the courtyard. She finished by saying, "I just *know* it's Rickey. You will too, when you see him."

Alex sighed deeply and stared through the window, at the driving rain bouncing off the airport runway.

"I'd like to believe you're right, Robin. Something inside wants desperately to believe. But I can't risk the nightmare of another disappointment. Until you prove to me, beyond the shadow of a doubt, that..."

"This time it's different."

"Every time this happened before, I hoped it was different. Desperately hoped."

He paused for a long moment. Then he said, "Look, you find a burglar wandering around the property. You ask him if he ever lived there. He says yes. Is that all? Do you think there's a single con artist in Mexico who doesn't know of the reward, and every intimate detail of what happened? Why would Rickey wait twenty years to suddenly find his way home?"

"I tell you, it's Rickey. You'll know when you see his eyes."

"If he knew he was home, in his own house, why did he try to escape when the police came? What was he afraid of?"

"Because he's also *Papagayo*. A wanted criminal. He's also your son!"

Alex shook his head, eyes filled with doubt.

"Papagayo, wanted for robbery, rape, and kidnapping. Great kid. Chip off the old block. Besides, I met Papagayo, remember? Trust me, Papagayo isn't my son!"

"There are *two* Papagayos, Alex. Who knows, maybe more. But this one..."

Alex's suitcase popped out of the carousel and slid down the ramp. He picked it up. They started toward the street exit. Robin clung to Alex's arm and led him toward the no-parking space where she left the Mercedes — under the watchful eye of a bribed cop.

"Alex, it's absolutely uncanny. When you meet him, when you see his eyes... You'll know. He moves like you, talks like you. I am so happy!"

"Where is he?"

"We have him in the best hospital in Acapulco."

Alex tossed the suitcase into the Mercedes' rear seat and opened the door for Robin. "While I waited for my flight, I called Morales. He filled me in on this Papagayo character. Robin, this guy is a superb con artist. The best. Can talk you out of your shorts — in English, Spanish, whatever. What do they call him? Papagayo, the *Parrot*, for Christ sakes! He can talk, say *anything* you want to hear. This is just another crude attempt at extortion."

"You'll see." She smiled smugly.

Alex shook his head. "Something I didn't tell you. There's been another development." After a long pause, his voice sounded exhausted as he said, "Morales found Rickey's grave!"

Robin shook her head in disbelief. "He's lying! Where?"

"In the mountains near Tlascala, about three kilometers from the accident site. Morales has two witnesses to the burial." He took several deep breaths before he could continue.

"Rickey was thrown from the truck. An Indian family found him, took him home. Tried to save him. Then, when Rickey died, they were afraid they'd get into trouble. They buried him in a corn field."

"I don't believe it. Morales is a creep. When you see Rickey, you will recognize him immediately."

"He's in the hospital now?"

"Under police guard. They refuse to believe he is anyone but El Papagayo. We have an appointment to see him this afternoon."

They exchanged no more thoughts until they were reaching the neighborhood of the Las Brisas house. As the Mercedes started up the steep hill, Alex said, "What about the jewelry, Robin? According to Morales, Papagayo claims the jewelry belonged to his mother. Claims he doesn't know how she got it."

"His mother! That proves it. He knows the jewelry belonged to Diana!"

"Hold it. There's more. Papagayo also claims that his mother is alive, in New Zealand, or somewhere. According to Morales, her name is Micaela Montalvo. Not Diana Cranston. This guy's a con artist, pure bullshit."

"I can hardly wait to see you change your mind."

As suddenly as the downpour started, it stopped, as if someone had shut off a faucet. When Alex turned into their street, Robin noticed a taxi waiting in front of the house. When Alex stepped out of the car to unlock the gate, a young woman got out of the taxi. She was blonde, rather nice looking, with a sunburned, face, wearing rumpled, slept-in clothes. She appeared to have been crying.

"Are you Mr. Barron?" she asked in a timid voice.

"Why do you ask?"

"I'm looking for Alex Barron."

"You've found him. What do you want?

"I want to talk to you about the boy who was arrested here yesterday. It's quite important."

Alex frowned, and after a moment's hesitation, motioned for her to follow Robin into the house.

She began weeping the moment she stepped inside the door.

"I tried to tell them, but they won't listen. They think he kidnapped me, but that's not true at all. I ran away from home. No kidnapping. That's the truth. Even my father refuses to believe me. He wants Riki put into prison."

Robin touched the girl's shoulder in sympathy and exchanged a look of puzzlement with Alex. "You must be Elaine Tarkington? You're the 'kidnap victim'?"

Elaine nodded. "We ran away together and were going to live here in Acapulco. I have to get this straightened out before Riki gets put in prison and before my father finds me and forces me back to New Zealand. Please help us."

"What do you want from us?" Alex said, with the air of a man expecting to be swindled.

"They won't let him go. They say that even if he didn't kidnap me, they will put him away for twenty years for jewelry theft. You're the only one who can save him from prison, Mr. Barron. You have your jewelry. Why can't you drop the charges and give Riki a break?"

"I don't care about the jewelry. The question is, where did he get the jewelry? Give me a straight story on that, I'll probably drop the charges."

A glimmer of hope in Elaine's eyes turned off the tears. She swallowed and forced herself to speak clearly and earnestly.

"I really don't think he knows much about it himself. Just that his stepmother kept the jewelry in a music box, and she never wore it. And she was afraid to sell it."

Robin leaned forward and urged Elaine to continue. "*Stepmother?* Tell us about that. How did he have a stepmother?"

"Micaela is sort of his stepmother. Riki thinks that his real mother sold him to Micaela when he was a little boy. It's always been a difficult thing for him to talk about."

Alex glanced sharply at Robin, then back at the girl. His voice sounded skeptical as he asked, "Do you know who I am, Elaine?"

"Yes sir. You are Alex Barron. A cinema-maker."

"Do you think I might be wealthy?"

"I should imagine so. Why do you ask that?"

"I'm just looking for the 'hook' in all of this. I'm trying to figure out how Papagayo is planning on taking advantage of this situation."

"I beg your pardon? I don't understand..."

Robin interrupted by saying, "Elaine, if Micaela isn't Rickey's real mother, can you tell me what he remembers about his mother or father?"

"He never talks much about his real parents. He feels they abandoned him. He's never understood exactly why. Look, Riki is a marvelous person. He's never done anything to deserve prison." She sat down next to Alex and touched his hand. "Talk to him. You'll see."

Alex had an anguished look on his face. "When is our appointment?"

Enrique Morales hurried over to shake Alex's hand the moment he entered the hospital.

"When I heard you were in town, I came immediately. I want you to know that I never left this case, even though you cut me off the payroll. It's a matter of pride, you see. Now, in addition to solving the mystery of your son's death, I'm happy to report that I've finally solved the jewel theft. We have one thief in a hospital bed, and the other isolated in New Zealand. A mother and son team, it appears."

"Does he admit to stealing the jewels?"

"I've not had the opportunity to question him personally, Mr. Barron. By the time I arrived, he was already in surgery."

Elaine whispered to Robin, "Micaela isn't in New Zealand. My Mum sent her home when she heard about my 'kidnapping.' Micaela's back in Mexico. Probably back in her village."

"What charges have been filed against him?" Alex asked Morales.

"Robbery, kidnapping, rape, burglary, and lots more, enough to keep him off the streets until he is an old man. That's not even counting the jewelry theft."

As the nurse ushered them into the hospital room she said, "He is a little slow right now. He's on heavy medicine to ease the pain. They had to rebuild the bones in his arm. It will never be the same again—but not to worry, he won't need it where he's going."

Alex hesitated at the door opening. The room was dark. A dim lamp outlined the hospital bed, but not much else. A still figure lay on the bed, head and face bandaged like a mummy in a grade-B Hollywood picture. An ice pack covered his eyes.

Robin pushed Alex gently forward. "I'll stand back while you talk to him. I don't want to influence you. But when you see him, when you hear him talk, when you see those eyes, you will know."

Alex nodded. He felt blood pounding in his temples. He followed Elaine and Enrique Morales into the dimly lit room. Robin and the nurse entered last. Elaine reached the bed first. She touched the figure on the bed lightly and said, "Riki? Are you awake, love? Mr. Barron is here. He wants to talk to you."

When there was no reply, Alex said to Morales, "Turn on the lights. I want to get a look at his eyes."

Alex stepped close to the bed and felt his heart accelerate as Elaine reached over and pulled the ice bag away.

She froze, her eyes wide, a horrified look on her face. Her voice came out in a stifled scream.

"No! No! This cannot..."

Suddenly her throat choked, ending with an animal-like sound of pain. Her body tightened. She began to shake uncontrollably. Robin caught her as she started to pitch forward.

"She's having an attack! Somebody do something!"

Elaine shuddered, her face distorted into a grotesque mask, tongue protruding, saliva thinned with blood flowing over her chin. Twisting and jolting uncontrollably, she began to sink to her knees, hands clawing at the air as if fighting off an invisible enemy.

The nurse rushed forward to grab Elaine around the waist.

Alex stepped back, a look of disgust on his face. "What the hell's wrong with her?"

The nurse helped Robin ease the girl to the floor. "Epilepsy! Gran mal." the nurse said tersely. "Hand me that roll of bandage. She's trying to chew her tongue off!"

When Elaine finally relaxed into semi-consciousness, the nurse said, "She may be okay in a minute. These things don't usually last long."

Alex shivered, then returned to the bed to examine the patient.

His expression quickly changed from hopeful expectation to one of furious indignation.

"It's *him* again! Robin, how could you possibly mistake this animal for Rickey? This is the same creep who pretended to be Rickey the last time."

She hurried to the bed to see what was wrong. A dirty brown face, scarred and pockmarked, stared at her through two glazed eyes—coal-black irises floating surrounded by yellowish brown, the eyes of a drug addict with a diseased liver.

"Who *are* you?" she demanded. "Where's Rickey?"

The figure in the bed gave Robin a vague smile, exposing an uneven row of badly decayed teeth.

She raised her voice and demanded, "Where is Rickey?"

Pintado shrugged weakly. "I don' know, man. He here a lil' while ago. Maybe he go away."

The human wreck struggled to sit up, but was unable to manage, falling back into the bed. His eyes shifted about in confusion as he mumbled, half to himself.

"Hey, Comanche! Where you at, man? How long I gotta stay here?" Then he lapsed into incomprehensible Spanish.

Morales let out a low cry of anguish.

"He got away again! How did he get away?" He grabbed the stranger by the ears and pulled him to a sitting position. "How the hell did *you* get in here? Where's Papagayo?"

Pintado ran his dry tongue over his lips in a futile effort to wet them. "You hurtin' my ears, man. I didn' do nuthin'."

Elaine, beginning to slowly recover, said weakly, "He's a street character they call *Pintado*. A glue fume addict."

Morales shook Pintado's head once more before he let Pintado fall back onto the pillow.

"You scum! How did you get in here?"

Pintado pointed vaguely toward a window which sagged on broken hinges. Outside, a fire escape led down to an alley.

"Through da window. Dey tell me I come here and wait, dey gimme all da drugs I want. All I gotta do is lay here and wait."

"Who told you that?"

"Oh, you know. Like uh... Comanche and Angel, and, maybe somebody else. Maybe it was Mocho. Dey let me sniff a lot of good glue first. Where dey go, anyway?"

Morales beat his fist against his palm furiously. "I told you he was clever, but I never expected this." He hurried from the room and could be heard shouting at the cop who had been guarding the room.

Robin took Elaine by the arm and helped her to her feet.

"Where did he go? We have to find him."

Elaine put her hand over her eyes and massaged them with her thumb and middle finger. Then she looked at Robin with a defiant look on her face:

"I don't know. I really don't. But I'd never tell even if I did. They want to put him in a cage for twenty years, for doing nothing."

Suddenly a doctor, his stethoscope swinging across his chest, entered the room. When he confirmed that his patient had indeed left the bed, his eyes widened in horror.

"I can't believe this! That young man shouldn't have been able to stand, much less escape!"

Robin stared at Elaine and again demanded, "Where did Rickey go? You must know!"

Elaine shook her head. "They're going to put him in prison. Even if Mr. Barron doesn't press charges."

The doctor stabbed a finger toward Elaine's face as he said, "Young lady, if we don't get the proper antibiotics into your friend, he'll be dead within 24 hours. He has a blood infection that should have killed him this morning. It's a miracle he is still alive. And, if that isn't enough, the lacerations on his eyes have an infection that certainly leave him blind."

Robin pleaded, "Where, Elaine? Where would he have gone?"

Alex put his arm around Elaine's shoulder as he said, "I promise that Papagayo will not go to prison. I just want to see him and know the truth. I want to see and talk to a live person, not a corpse. I'm positive that he knows what happened to Rickey."

"I'm telling the truth. I don't know."

They all turned in surprise when Pintado spoke in a dreamy voice. "Dey say he gon' go home. His mama gon' take care him."

Elaine nodded thoughtfully.

"He could be right. Micaela isn't in New Zealand anymore, you know. Mum shipped her back here. The other day, when we were wondering where Micaela might go, Riki said she'd probably return to the village. If that's where she is, then that's where we'll find Riki"

"Where? Where's the village?"

"I don't know precisely. It's called *Tezcat*-something or other. A totally unpronounceable word. I can show you about where it is on a map. He pointed it out to me once."

Within minutes, Morales and Alex had a *Pemex* map of Mexico spread over the bedside table. Elaine traced a finger along a red highway line.

"Right about here. It isn't listed on any map. Apparently never was. Between this town and this crossroad right here."

Morales shook head emphatically. "That can't be. There isn't any village there."

"That's all I can tell you. Riki said it was there."

Morales snorted sarcastically. "Papagayo wouldn't know the truth if it sat on his lap."

"He's a fine person. Honorable and proud!"

"He's a confidence man and a thief."

Robin put her hand on Elaine's shoulder to calm her down. Then she said, "We don't have a choice. Let's find the village."

The doctor said, "I hope so. Otherwise, he'll be dead within three days at the most. Maybe quicker."

Chapter Thirty

Morales borrowed a bulky Cadillac with a siren from a police friend in Tlascala. The siren came in handy for moving traffic aside as they roared along the highway. He seemed delighted to be back on the payroll again, but also concerned about this new development.

Alex held the road map in his lap. Elaine sat next to him, studying highway markings and trying to remember what Riki had said about the village of Tezcatlipocas. Robin and the doctor rode in the back seat.

Alex said, "Johnny Gee and I went back and forth over this highway. Again and again. We drove up every side trail we saw. I can't believe we could have missed finding a village here."

They drove until they reached the intersection with the next paved road. Morales pulled off the road and looked angrily at Elaine. "Nothing. You've been deceiving us, wasting time while your boyfriend gets away."

"He won't get far," observed the doctor. "Not without antibiotics."

Elaine shook her head emphatically. "If Riki says the village is here somewhere, then it's here!"

Morales cut the wheel sharply to make a U-turn. "There's no point in continuing this. I tell you, I've found the grave. Witnesses. There's nothing more we can do."

"No," Elaine insisted. "He told me all about the village. Every detail. I can almost see it... all of the houses of black lava rock, the little zócalo, the church without a roof, and..."

Alex looked at her sharply. "Church without a roof? That's

407

what Lance Rexford said — that he let Diana and Rickey off by a roofless church!"

"It couldn't have been far from the highway, because Riki told how he used to lay on a big white rock and look down at the traffic below, and..."

Alex suddenly grabbed at the map. "A white rock! And an overhanging black lava bluff. I remember that place! Turn around, Morales, I think it's back that way."

"Impossible. There is no road anywhere along here. Not even dirt trails."

"I remember now! We were there once. We rode the jeep part way up a steep trail. I remember seeing a boy and a woman climbing the mountain trail, and..."

Morales shook his head uncertainly. "That wasn't a village. Only a few houses and a little store." The tone of his voice and the expression on his face showed clearly that he was worried.

"Riki's stepmother had a store there," Elaine observed quietly.

They parked the car under the overhanging rock cliff. Elaine found the footpath first and started up without waiting for the others. "This is it. I just know it!"

Morales quickly caught up with her. As he climbed, he loosened the strap that held his pistol in its underarm holster. The doctor carried his medical bag and brought up the rear, his chubby body protesting every step on this high-altitude path.

The path gradually changed from an almost impossible climb to just a steep hill. Then they found the cobbled remains of what had once been the only road across the mountain pass.

"Just as he said," Elaine said between breaths. She was weary of the climb, but she pushed on relentlessly. "The road should curve around that large boulder and then we can see the village."

Alex was aghast. "Johnny and I passed this place over and over. We were so *stupid!* He might have been here waiting for me. And I drove right past it!"

Robin put her hand on the small of his back and rubbed gently. "Don't blame yourself. God knows you did your best."

Morales turned and shook his head, saying, "This doesn't prove a thing. I tell you, I found the grave!"

He looked around for support but found none.

"Look, this El Papagayo is clever, a con man. It wouldn't take much for him to research the history of the jewelry and figure out a scheme to take you in. He probably heard the story from someone in this region and is using us. For all we know, this young lady is part of the scheme."

His voice desperately begged for credibility.

"Don't you understand? I *found* your son's grave! Tomorrow, I'll take you there. You can talk to the witnesses."

Alex didn't reply. He quickened his pace now that the road leveled out.

When the cobblestone trail rounded the huge boulder, things were just as Elaine had predicted. The skeleton of the church loomed ahead. It was outlined in the fading afternoon light like ghostly ruins of an ancient castle. She walked even faster, as fast as her legs would carry her. The oxygen-poor air began to take its toll, robbing her of strength, making her mind fuzzy. She began to pray that she not get an attack.

As they approached the first of the huts, the dominant impression was empty silence. The village seemed to be totally abandoned. Of the first half dozen huts they passed, only one had thatch left on the roof. A cold wind rustled through the rotting leafage.

Elaine's throat was raw from heavy breathing and she sounded hoarse as she said, "Micaela had a store. Riki said it was at the farther end of the village, and that it was the largest house here."

Alex looked around the squalid village, and said softly, "If we had only found this place years ago... Maybe..."

Robin's voice trembled with excitement. "Someone's here!

Look—that house up ahead, where the road turns—there's smoke coming through the roof!"

Morales pulled the gun from its holster, slipped the safety off, then put it back, ready for action. "Stay back," he insisted, "If Papagayo's friends are here, we could face gunfire."

Alex shook his head. "Put the gun away, Morales."

The door to Micaela's store swung open. Two men stepped out and leaned casually against the wall of the building. One handed the other a pack of cigarettes. He lit a *cerillo* to offer his companion a light.

"That's Comanche!" Elaine whispered excitedly. "Riki *must* be here! The other one's Angel, I'll bet anything."

Morales drew his gun and went running toward the store. When Comanche and Angel saw him coming toward them, they threw down their cigarettes and turned to flee. But they stopped in their tracks when Morales shouted:

"Police! Halt right there or die!"

They held their hands away from their bodies to indicate that they were not armed. They turned cautiously to face their captor.

Alex shouted, "I told you to put the gun away Morales!"

Reluctantly, Morales complied, furious and frustrated as he watched the two young men flee down the trail and disappear from sight.

A woman appeared at the door and stepped outside to see what was going on. Elaine could tell by her silhouette that it was Micaela. She shouted out in in her best Spanish.

"Mica! Micaela! It's all right! Everything's going to be fine. We brought a doctor!"

Micaela covered her eyes with her hands and stepped backwards into the building.

The first small room of the house was lined with empty, crumbling shelves, the ghost of Micaela's store. Alex led the way as they stepped through the low doorway and entered what had once been Micaela's living quarters. By the dim light of a kerosene lamp, they saw Rickey lying on a straw petate. He had a poultice of brown herbal material covering his eyes. A rough hospital cast still encased his arm. Micaela followed them into the room, a mixture of terror and sadness filling her eyes. She mumbled incomprehensible prayers in Nahuátl to long-vanquished gods as she knelt in front of a picture of the Virgin of Guadalupe pasted on the wall. Several homemade candles flickered weakly on the floor, casting a wavering orange glow on the religious image.

Morales looked down at Riki with a smile of disgust. In Spanish he said, "Well, well, at last we meet. Can you hear me, Papagayo? This is Enrique Morales speaking. I've been looking for you for a long, long time. Can you hear me?"

"I hear a pig."

Robin stepped closer and knelt down by the petate's edge. "Rickey, this is Robin Barron. Do you remember me?"

"You bet I do. You tricked me." His voice was weak, but it burned with bitterness. "You called the police. Kept me there, talking lies until they came. I remember you."

"I called the police, that's true. But that was before I knew who you were."

"Get away from me. I don't feel like talking. I feel like dying."

Alex said, "Can we take that stuff off his face? I want to see his eyes."

Elaine touched him on the cheek and said, "Riki, it's me, Elaine. Please help Robin. Answer her questions as best you can. She can help us."

"She already did."

"Listen, Mr. Barron is here. He promised if you tell him everything you know about the jewelry, how Micaela got it, he'll not press charges. You won't have to go to jail."

He was quiet for a moment. Then he said, "It's a trick Elaine. Just like that woman tricked me into waiting for the police."

Robin's voice was soft and soothing. "It's not a trick Rickey.

Tell us everything. Tell us about how you came to this village."

"I told the Acapulco police all I know about the jewelry. Micaela kept it hidden in an old suitcase. That's all I know. There's nothing more to say. I sold the watch in Córdoba because we needed money for food. Later, Micaela gave a few pieces to a lawyer and one to a judge to get me out of jail. That's all I know."

Alex whispered to Elaine, "His eyes. Please uncover his eyes so I can know for sure."

The doctor looked disgusted as he moved Elaine aside and lifted the herbal mess from Rickey's eyes. He stared at the wet brown fibers and tossed it toward the corner with revulsion.

"Witchcraft! These ignorant Indios, with their so-called remedies. They kill more people than the illnesses do."

When the doctor began rummaging in his medical bag, Alex leaned over the patient and looked closely at the eyes.

He could tell nothing. The face was swollen and red with infection. The flesh around his eyes bulged like overripe mangoes, angry purple and black. Pus ran from the slits in the eyelids. His lips appeared to be turning blue. The doctor busied himself preparing an antibiotic syringe.

Alex knelt beside the straw petate and said, "Look, Rickey or whatever your name is... just tell me one thing. How did you happen to live in this village? Did you come here as a little boy?"

Morales moved next to Alex and whispered, "Don't forget, this is Papagayo. A confidence man."

Alex nodded as he nudged Morales aside.

Rickey grunted in pain in response to a hypodermic syringe sinking into a vein.

"I think I remember coming here with someone who said she was my mother. But I don't think she really was my mother. She couldn't have been."

"Why not?"

"Because..." after a long hesitation he continued, "Because she sold me to Micaela. After that, she left and never returned."

Alex exchanged glances of astonishment with Robin. She shook her head in disbelief.

"What do you mean, your mother sold you?"

Rickey lay quiet for a long moment, and when he replied, his voice sounded hollow and distant.

"My real parents abandoned me in this village. I don't know if it's true, but everyone claims that my mother traded me to Micaela for two bottles of aguardiente. They say they saw it with their own eyes."

Alex swallowed thickly and asked, "What makes you believe your father abandoned you here?

"I don't know. He never came to take me home. I waited for him, but he never came."

"Where did you live before you came here?"

After another long pause, Rickey said, "I'm not sure. Probably in the United States somewhere. Certainly, at that house in Acapulco, at least for a while. I remember swimming there, the swing and the slide. I remember somebody teaching me to swim in the pool."

Alex nodded. He swallowed tightly before urging, "What else?"

Morales said nervously, "I know what you're thinking, señor Barron. But that's El Papagayo talking. He knows what you want to hear, and he'll say anything to save his skin."

Alex forced himself to relax. He sat back on his heels and listened as Robin began questioning.

"How old were you when you came here? When did you start living with your stepmother?"

"I don't know. Very young."

"What was the name of the woman who brought your here?"

His voice sounded hurt and angry at the same time. "Why are you asking me these questions? What does this have to do with the jewelry?"

Elaine said, "Tell her, Riki. She can help us. Tell her everything."

Alex tensed as he waited for the answer. He felt blood pounding in his temples. Morales touched him on the shoulder and whispered, "Easy, easy. A con artist, remember..."

"I don't remember her name."

"Could it have been Diana?"

A slow frown distorted Rickey's face, causing obvious pain. He nodded. "That sounds right. Maybe it was Diana. I remember that she..."

Morales snorted in derision. "Every newspaper in the country carried that story with your wife's name."

"Suppose you were to see your father again, would you recognize him?"

"I can't see anything. I couldn't recognize my own hand."

Robin put her hand on Alex's head and smoothed her hand through his hair. She said, "Rickey do you know who this man is? Alexander Barron? Have you ever heard that name before?"

"Sure. He's the one who kept after Micaela until she almost lost her mind." His voice trembled with anger. "His money paid to have me hunted and shot down like an animal. Yes, I know who he is."

Elaine interjected, "Riki! Don't say that. Mr. Barron is the only one who can help you now. If he drops the charges..."

"But when your eyes are all right, could you recognize him?"

"My father didn't want me then, why would I want to recognize him now?"

Robin beckoned to Alex. He shook his head and motioned for her to continue questioning.

"Rickey, why do you think your mother sold you for two bottles of rum."

He held his breath for a while, then gave a long, drawn-out sigh. "I don't know why she sold me. I didn't like her, and she probably didn't like me. I remember she hit me sometimes."

"And what about your father?"

"Who knows? Maybe he was mad at me. I remember breaking something that he liked. He was very angry."

Alex moved nearer to Robin's side. He swallowed and stared down at the figure laying in the bed. His voice was a hoarse whisper.

"What do you remember breaking? What?"

After a pause while the doctor did something uncomfortable to his leg, Rickey shrugged. He thought deeply before replying.

"A glass statue. A woman holding a bow and arrow. It shattered into tiny crystals."

Alex touched Rickey's unbandaged arm. His mouth gaped open, and then he closed it to swallow with difficulty.

"It really *is* you! *Rickey!*"

A choking sound in his throat cut off the words. He laid his head on the edge of the bed. His body shook convulsively.

"After all this time, I..."

Robin touched Rickey's shoulder and eased his head back against the pillow. "Rickey, this is your father. There've been some terrible mistakes made. Some tragic misunderstandings. But things are going to be okay from now on."

Morales grunted in disgust. "Can't you see what he's pulling on you? He's a professional, and you're falling for his merchandise. Why don't we put this off until morning? You'll have time to think about this and see things more clearly."

Alex shook his head sadly. "Get out of here Morales. I never want to see or hear from you again."

Morales started to protest, but the look in Alex Barron's eyes warned him. He shrugged his shoulders helplessly, and slowly walked toward the door.

When Alex's hand squeezed on his shoulder, Rickey turned and tried to force his eyes open. He failed. "What kind of mistakes? What kind of misunderstandings?"

The doctors were ready to take the bandages off before the week was up. Robin and Alex held one of Rickey's hands while Elaine the other.

Rickey grinned. "Don't worry, I won't try to escape."

Alex said, "I'm nervous. What if you don't recognize me?"

"I recognize you. I used to dream about you a lot. I saw your face almost every night. I used to wonder why you never came to get me. If only I had known. If only..."

Elaine kissed him on the cheek. "It's okay now, love. Everything's going to be all right."

The doctor pushed her away and started in with his scissors. Elaine held his hand tightly. Riki smiled contentedly.

"What about your father? Does he know where you are? Will he make you go back to New Zealand?"

Alex said, "Don't worry about that, son. Mr. Tarkington and I had a long talk. He wants to see you later on today. I think he's going to apologize and welcome you into his family if that's your goal."

Rickey squeezed his father's hand. "Thanks... what do I call you? Father? Papa?"

"How about *Dad?*" Alex tried to make it light, and tried to say something else, but the words caught in his throat.

Just then, the doctor cut the final bandage tape and paused dramatically. He smiled mischievously as he pulled the bandage away.

"And now for my unveiling of my art. Notice the fine stitching? There will be very few scars."

Rickey struggled to sit up. Robin put her hand under his back and helped him. He looked at the gray eyes of the man standing there. The two of them registered shock, for each it was as if he were looking at his own eyes.

Alex held out a hand. "Hello, son." The corners of his mouth twitched uncontrollably. "It's been a long trail. But we finally found our way."

Rickey grabbed for the hand, then pulled his father close enough to throw his good arm around him in an abrazo. They both began sobbing as the others tactfully edged out of the room. Elaine was the last to leave. She looked at father and son and smiled through the tears that streamed down her face.

Rickey's stay in the Mexico City clinic involved another week. Specialists flew in from New York City, San Francisco and Europe. Except for some permanent damage to Rickey's arm, he began to heal nicely. Later, he barely recalled his time in the clinic, except that his father, Robin and Elaine seemed to be there constantly.

After a week, they decided to move Rickey to the Acapulco home for further treatment and therapy on the damaged arm. Alex insisted that both Elaine and Micaela join them. The return to the Acapulco house was yet another emotional trauma on top of so many others, that Rickey felt numb. With his father's arm over his shoulder, they walked from room to room and talked, getting to know one another. Robin followed, listening and sharing the euphoria of it all. She held Elaine's hand and the two of them struggled unsuccessfully to keep from crying.

They hadn't been home more than twenty minutes when they heard an insistent ringing of the doorbell. The maid hurried to answer. In a couple of minutes she returned, a look of distaste on her face.

"There are two *pelados* at the gate. Shameless vagabonds who claim they know señor Rickey. Shall I send them away?"

"Who are they?" Rickey asked.

"They say their names are 'Angel' and 'Comanche'."

Rickey smiled at the maid.

"Send my business partners in."

About the Author

Besides the novel *Gift of the Black Goddess*, John Mack Howells is the author of ten books on travel and retirement, one book on the breakup of the Soviet Union, and one book on the history of printing.

Other Books by John Mack Howells

Choose Mexico
Choose Costa Rica
Choose Spain
Choose Latin America
Choose Southwestern Retirement
Choose Pacific Northwest Retirement
Where to Retire
Retirement Choices
Retirement on a Shoestring
RV Travel in Mexico
Russians and Others
Tramp Printers